THE PURPLE SHROUD

THE PURPLE SHROUD

STELLA DUFFY

virago

VIRAGO

First published in Great Britain in 2012 by Virago Press

Copyright © Stella Duffy 2012

The moral right of the author has been asserted.

A CIP catalogue record for this book
is available from the British Library.

Hardback ISBN 978-1-84408-777-8
C format ISBN 978-1-84408-813-3

Typeset in Bembo by M Rules
Printed and bound in Great Britain by
Clays Ltd, St Ives plc

Papers used by Virago are from well-managed forests
and other responsible sources.

MIX
Paper from
responsible sources
FSC® C104740

In memory of my sister-in-law Leah Silas
1957–2011

BRITAIN

Atlantic Ocean

GALLIA

KINGDOM OF THE FRANKS

BURGUNDLANS

A L P S

R. *Rhine*

R. *Danube*

Milan

ISTRIA

DA...

R. *Po*

LIGURIA

Ravenna

Rimini

Urbino

TUSCIA

R. *Tiber*

Adria...

PYRENEES

CORSICA

Rome

Ostia

Cuina

Naples

LUC...

Pompeii

KINGDOM OF THE VISIGOTHS

SARDINIA

Cordoba

Mediterranean Sea

Cartegena

Carthage

SICILY

Gibraltar

Hippo

NUMIDIA

Justiniana

Septem

CARTHAGO

MAURETANIA

BYZACENA

TRIPOLITANIA

- - - - - - - Roman Empire before Justinian

LOMBARDS   Peoples

0   500 miles

0   500 km

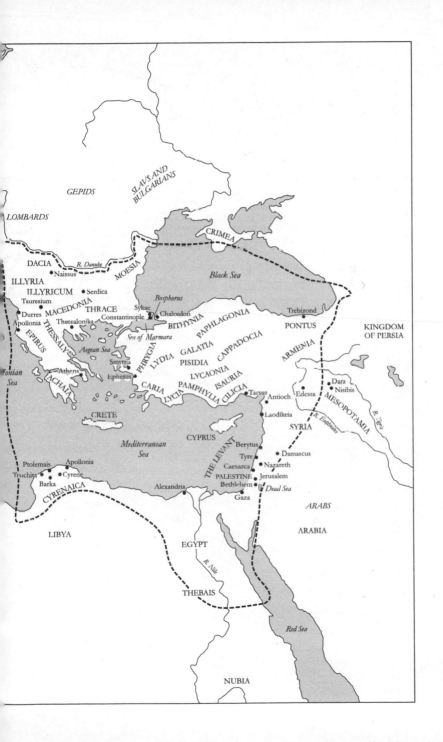

Theodora's Constantinople

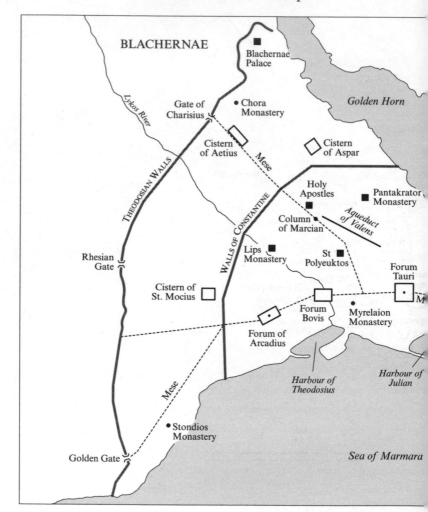

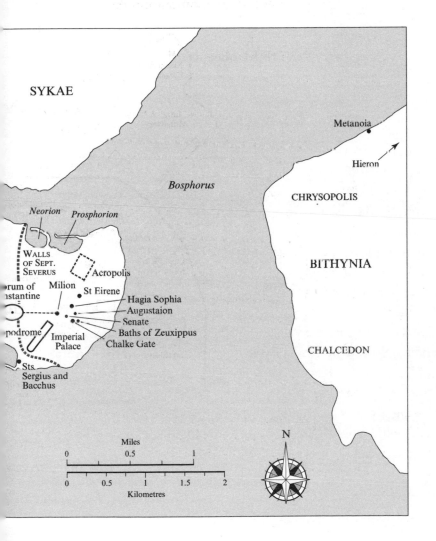

SYKAE

Metanoia

Bosphorus

Hieron

CHRYSOPOLIS

Neorion   *Prosphorion*

BITHYNIA

WALLS
OF SEPT.
SEVERUS   Acropolis

rum of   Milion   St Eirene
nstantine   Hagia Sophia
                                    Augustaion
                                    Senate
podrome   Baths of Zeuxippus
          Imperial   Chalke Gate
          Palace

CHALCEDON

Sts.
Sergius and
Bacchus

Miles
0   0.5   1

0   0.5   1   1.5   2
        Kilometres

N

Acknowledgements

As ever, thanks are due to my agents Stephanie Cabot and Lucinda Prain, and to the triumvirate of editors – Antonia Hodgson, Emily Murdock Baker and Stephen Morrison, all of whom were enormously generous in their work on this book. Zoe Gullen, Zoe Hood, Rebecca Lang and many others at Virago, Little, Brown, and Penguin (US) have been hugely enthusiastic about these two novels and have made the work of creating and selling them much less like work. I am indebted to the Ravennese of the Giallo Luna Nero Notte who first showed me the mosaics in the Church of San Vitale, Ravenna. Gratitude, as always, to my wife Shelley Silas and to the Board who understand precisely what 'being a writer' is like. Finally, I'm grateful to Theodora herself, with whom I have worked, dreamed and played for the past six years.

Before the Purple ...

Born in AD 500, Theodora began life in Constantinople as a dancer, an acrobat, and – as with many who earned their living on stage and off – a sometime courtesan. By the time she was eighteen this daughter of a bear keeper was the star of the Hippodrome stage, and horrified her loved ones when she deserted her fame to become mistress of the Governor of the Pentapolis, in North Africa. Following the painful breakdown of that relationship, she underwent a religious conversion in the desert outside Alexandria, later making a new life in Antioch.

When she was twenty-one, her mentor Timothy, Patriarch of Alexandria, sent Theodora back to Constantinople to meet the new Consul, the studious and serious Justinian, nephew of the Emperor Justin. The ex-whore ordered by a leader of the Church to make herself amenable to a potential Emperor. No one working behind the scenes to bring Theodora to prominence – including the eunuch Narses, already a vital figure in Justinian's political life – expected their relationship to be anything more than a useful alliance. Everyone, including Theodora and Justinian, was surprised when the strategic coalition became a marriage of love. On the death of his uncle, Justinian was named Emperor and Theodora was anointed Empress beside him, ruling together from the seat of government in Constantinople.

The men surrounding the Emperor Justinian have their counterparts in Theodora's entourage – Narses is Justinian's chief of staff; Armeneus, Narses' lover, is Theodora's adviser and assistant. Theodora's sister Comito is married to Sittas, one of Justinian's highest-ranking soldiers. Theodora deplores the ambition of her husband's favoured general Belisarius, Justinian despises Theodora's close friend Antonina – Belisarius' wife. Both households keep a wary eye on Justinian's cousin, the general Germanus, married to the aristocratic and ambitious Pasara. Where Justinian surrounds himself with scholars and soldiers, Theodora keeps her family and friends close. The Empress's entourage is made up of ladies and eunuchs, including her daughter Ana, Comito's daughter Indaro, Theodora's oldest friend Sophia, and Mariam, the silent and damaged girl she rescued from sex-slavery – making sure that the slaver was damaged in turn.

For many years the Emperor, whoever has assumed the purple, has also inherited an Empire divided between two opposing factions, the Greens and the Blues, run along lines of family history, workplace loyalty and political allegiance. The Emperor has ruled a state regularly at war with Goths in the west and Persians in the east; he has held together a complex of nations and states riven by religious discord and a growing desire for self-determination. It is into this Empire – factionalised, warring, waning – that Theodora is welcomed by the people; the people's Empress.

One

First, a silk robe, quiet and gentle against her skin. The robe is soft, warm, it needs to be for these long walks underground, through tunnels carved deep into the earth and rock beneath the Imperial Palace. The tunnels are cool, even in summer, and Theodora knows they are at their coolest now, in autumn. Here, surrounded on three sides by water, the intense heat of summer creates a moisture that sits in the still underground air and, when the world above turns cold, that moisture turns with it until the tunnel walls become dank and chill. Torches are left to burn at all times in winter, giving heat as well as light, bright pathways beneath the Palace, but at this time of year the tunnels are lit only when necessary, leaving the air purely cold, a heaviness that seeps in through the finest weave. The Empress's clothes are always of the finest weave, but even the perfect silk cannot hold back a creeping damp that edges into her bones, her knee and ankle joints, her lower back; bones that were hard-worked and twisted and fractured in childhood, and now remind her with a constant throbbing ache of every glorious tumbling leap she ever made. All of it part of the cold that sinks and settles and pains her for weeks at a time. Pain she shares with no one, not even the

Palace physicians; if the walls have ears, the courtiers and attendants have all too open mouths. The girl fastens the under-robe at the Empress's waist and breast and Theodora is glad of the silk. She makes a note to herself that she should remind her husband's men to dress him for the season. If she notices the drop in temperature, then he, eighteen years her senior, certainly feels it. The staff can be stupid, waiting for orders, and it's not the kind of thing the Emperor would pay attention to, his own comfort.

Next, a fuller gown, reaching to her feet, three-quarter-length sleeves added, fitted and then fastened just below the elbow. Then her outer robe, the purple itself, heavy with embroidery in gold thread, her signature pearls sewn in around the bodice and again at the hemline, pulling the already weighty cloth down flat from the breast. She knows the shape suits her figure, worked with her seamstresses to create this image, as comfortable as can be managed in a cere-monial robe, and flattering too. She is small, and needs the height given by a plain line. More pearls; pearls for purity, for the Christ, for wisdom. Several strands in different lengths are lifted over her neck and laid so they rest evenly across the bodice, falling from her just-covered collarbone. The longest strand drops between her breasts to create an arrow, pointing to her tiny waist. Again, the illusion of height. The arrow motif is picked up by earrings in red gold, threaded with pearls and emeralds. The girl stabs her lobe with the second earring, missing the piercing, and gasps as she does so, realis-ing she has hurt her new mistress. The Empress gives no sign that anything is amiss other than a short intake of breath, quickly checked. The girl tries again, and this time succeeds. The earring sits, not without discomfort, but now it is merely the pain of heavy gold hanging from flesh and gristle, an everyday pain.

4

Finally the Imperial chlamys is carefully unfolded, spread out and then gathered back into the proper form, servants' hands taking extra care with this cloak that marks their mistress as Empress. It is draped over her shoulders and pinned into place, from where it falls to her feet. She feels her collar and shoulders droop with the weight, despite her preparation; her desire the new dresser does not see that the chlamys is a burden to the Augusta. The piece is, of course, weighty: these particular ceremonial versions are excessively decorated, have been so heavily embroidered that the fabric has grown to two or three times its original density with intricate layers of gold and silver thread, and with still more jewels – her preferred emeralds this time, a pale green to offset the deeper purple. As well as the encumbrance of the encrusted fabric, there is the extra burden of the purple, as heavy in import as weight. And she is still the only woman to wear it. She stands inside the purple and the jewels and she becomes what they represent. It is all Theodora can do not to sway under the burden, carrying the Empire on her back.

She does not sink, will never sink. These attendants, this new girl dressing her so carefully, so nervously that she risks marring the silk with sweaty fingers, these people she sees constantly, in her rooms, going about their tasks at all hours of the day or night, have no idea how much it costs her, in physical pain, in boredom, and in the constant nagging hunger for solitude and quiet, to stand here and be dressed, to waste the time it takes in preparation. First the bath, and then the massage and the oiling of her skin, next the makeup – she applies her own, she has at least insisted on that, time to herself for the task – and then the chore of dressing. On a ceremonial day it can take half the morning from waking to fully dressed. She would rather pull on an old robe and be out in the world. Much of the time she would simply rather be out in the world, but she is Augusta and has no choice, and so she stands still, and steady, in that lack.

Finally she steps into the brocaded slippers, built up a little in the heel to give her a touch more height, as well as an elegant shape to the ankle. If her husband notices, so be it, and if others choose to look, she does not mind. A moment to let the costume settle, to let her spirit rise to the demands it imposes, and Theodora is ready.

A call is given and answered a moment later, answered again, and again, the corridors and tunnels, raised walkways and colonnaded paths echoing. There is a tangible shiver throughout the Palace, staff and servants and slaves stand to attention in readiness, even those hidden from regal view in distant offices, or in the kitchens far below. Those who believe themselves unnoticed in their menial tasks, opening gates or lighting corridors, take up a slightly more respectful stance nonetheless. The shiver spreads to the Hippodrome. They are coming. Slaves stand alert at the Kathisma doors. Thirty thousand pairs of eyes focus on the empty space that will be filled. Justinian and Theodora are on their way.

Justinian held out a hand to stop the slave opening the door before him. 'Theou doron,' he greeted his wife for the first time that day, as every day, calling her his 'gift of God', the play on her name obvious even to the nine-year-old Nubian slave hiding in a dark corner of the hallway, hoping to see the Imperial couple without being seen, 'How are you?'

And Theodora greeted him as she always had since his elevation to the purple, with a deep formal bow, her eyes low, voice quiet, 'How are you, sir?'

Justinian smiled, masking a yawn and pulled her closer with one hand, rubbing the other over his face.

6

She saw the bags under his eyes, darker than usual, and asked, 'No sleep? Again?'

'There were things to do. Figures we needed to work on . . .'

Theodora hissed, soft enough for only Justinian to hear, 'You are August.'

Justinian nodded. 'The purple would confirm it.'

'The Treasurer works for you, not you for him.'

'And we need the funds his reforms will bring. The Goths and the Persians won't wait while we arrange our finances for war . . .'

'So your Cappadocian drunk dismantles our postal service, knowing it's the poor who are hardest hit?'

'Perhaps you'll be pleased to know he also has plans for increasing the taxes on our wealthier citizens?'

'I'd be happier if I trusted him to do his work without you overseeing every step. It astonishes me that Narses allows it, I'd have his balls if he wasn't already a eunuch.'

Justinian smiled, there was no point explaining again that his treasurer's reforms of the Empire's postal service were a welcome distraction from the weightier matters he also dealt with on a daily basis. Theodora was, he knew, concerned only for his welfare, and he liked that she was.

'Good. Now you've finished re-castrating my Chief of Staff as well as decrying my treasurer, shall we go? The people are keen to get on with today's races . . .'

Theodora bent her head, acknowledging the subject was closed, for now. 'We're still dining together?' she asked.

'Yes, Belisarius will be joining us.'

'And his wife?'

'If you must,' Justinian answered, biting his lip as he always did when agitated, 'but keep her away from me.'

'Antonina's my friend.'

7

'Then sit her beside you.'

'She's no less ambitious than her husband.'

'I trust Belisarius,' Justinian replied.

'And I like Antonina.'

'So we are balanced?'

'In all things,' Theodora answered him, lightly touching her husband's hand.

They both understood her touch was a cue to let the matter drop, with the full Hippodrome waiting on their arrival, there were more pressing matters than wondering which of their circle was least trustworthy. Justinian had been brought up in the court, Theodora in the bowels of the Hippodrome; they knew there were few they could fully trust.

Theodora took a step back, nodded towards the rising clamour behind the closed doors. 'Shall we?'

The Emperor of the New Rome gestured for the slaves to open the doors.

As the light flooded in, along with the sound, sight and smell of a packed arena waiting for their ruling couple, Theodora whispered, 'Head up, shoulders back, look straight ahead, north to the horse statues, back to the obelisk, then south.'

Justinian nodded. 'Acknowledging the highest benches as well as the senators and the wealthy in the front, yes I know.'

'It's the people we need on our side, as much as the rich.'

'I agree, but perhaps you don't need to remind me every time?'

'It's my job, to remind you of the people.'

'It's your job to be my wife.'

Theodora gave a little curtsy. 'That too.'

Then they walked out into the light, and a full Hippodrome crowd saw the Empress arrive a half-step behind her husband, her head bowed as Justinian acknowledged his people – he the country boy made good, she the infamous ex-dancer, ex-actress, ex-whore, now loyal, royal Augusta.

Thirty thousand spectators, and almost as many opinions about the August and his wife. Over two years since they came to the throne, almost four years since the law had been changed permitting Theodora-from-the-Brothel to marry Justinian and become Empress of Rome, the citizens of Constantinople and beyond were still divided as to whether their double act was a good thing or not. For now the division was in the new leaders' favour, but there was no guarantee it would stay that way. The Imperial couple worked daily at making their presence felt, and harder at making that presence welcome.

The Empress stood beside her husband in the Kathisma, the strength of two as one, the many as one, a symbol of the new Rome. The people cheered and Theodora waved back, feeling the rush of their approval, enjoying it as much as she ever had as an actress. Enjoying it more now because, in her plans for the City and for those closest to her, she finally had some measure of control. Her sister Comito was well married to Sittas, one of Justinian's favourite generals, and the sisters would soon begin considering husbands for their daughters Ana and Indaro. There were staff to command, her entourage to organise, extended family on both sides to care for, and always, primarily, Justinian to counsel and support.

Back in her rooms, the Empress's staff helped her remove the ceremonial robes. She'd quickly learned that while her preference was to wrench off the chlamys the moment the Kathisma doors were closed on the Hippodrome crowd, disregard for the symbols of state did not go down well in the

Palace. Many of the staff had been raised in the court, most knew far more about protocol than she did, and they all had an immense respect for the purple, if not always for the person wearing it. Emperors might come and go, and with them their political and religious appointees, but those who actually kept the Palace running, turning the cogs of state, usually remained in place. Theodora needed them on her side. The gossip that linked one set of Palace rooms to another also spread well into the City and beyond. Now that she could not charm her audience with a sly smile or a quick wink, the ex-actress had to win her applause by proxy, letting the rumour of her brilliance within the Palace bring the people to her, not as theatrical star, but as worthy Augusta. She had been subject to the whims of the powerful all too often in her youth; now she preferred her staff to enjoy working for her because they liked and respected her, not because it was their job to do so. If she must pretend to love the heavy Imperial chlamys and vener-ate the purple in order to gain that affection, then Theodora would do so.

Free of the cumbersome symbols of state, she began the rest of her day's work, accepting the civil and Palace petitions brought to her by Armeneus, the eunuch who was lover to Narses, her husband's Chief of Staff. Armeneus had worked for Theodora years before when she had lived in the Pentapolis in North Africa, had known her both destitute and riding the waves of success: now he was her assistant in all the business associated with her role, just as Narses worked at Justinian's right hand. Eventually she called a halt to the requests laid before her, from the never-ending stream of needy and demanding who came to her state rooms request-ing aid, to stand at the wide windows and look out, past the Palace grounds, down to the old wall, to the lighthouse and the water beyond. Theodora was used to hard work – as both a performer and later as a religious devotee, she had become skilled in mastering her body and her will – but even as a girl she had always craved solitude. Despite the power and privilege of office, solitude was the one thing in very short supply. She took a deep breath, turned back into the room, looked at the dozens waiting on her, waiting for her judgement, waiting for her approval, waiting on the Empress, and gave up the hope of a brief walk away from her rooms today. Her only role was Augusta, and nowhere was offstage.

Two

Theodora and Justinian knelt before the massive figure of the monk. He wore a short robe made of the matted fur of a dozen unidentifiable animals in an uneven, undulating mosaic, and the smell of the imperfectly cured skins was strong. The monk's body was also a patchwork, his heavily muscled back and chest, arms and legs were cross-hatched with tattoos and scars. Mar the Solitary was called the athlete of God by those who worshipped with him, and God's brute by those who disliked his showman tactics. A star of the preaching circuit, he was not above beating religious sense into his followers, scoring with a knife, branding with fire; he encouraged his disciples to wear their prayer as he did, badges of belief cut into the skin. For twenty years, since his conversion from Zoroastrianism, Mar had travelled the Christian world, from the seminary near Nisibis on the Persian border in the east, to the old city of Rome in the west – he was not one for self-doubt.

When Justinian heard the preacher was passing through the City he requested an audience. Mar replied that if the August wanted his teaching, he could hear it with his staff. According to Armeneus, the giant had spoken rather less politely, but no one was prepared to carry the full insolence of his actual message back to the August. The preacher's beliefs on the nature of the Christ were antithetical to those of both the Emperor and the official belief of the state, and Mar the Solitary was one of the few from his side of the schism – Theodora's side of the schism – still allowed to speak without censure. Some said the Emperor was playing a wise game; allowing Mar to preach made Justinian and the Patriarch of Constantinople appear more even-handed than their current attack on Pagans and Jews might suggest. Others thought the preacher a useful safety valve; with so many angry about John the Cappadocian's new tax increases from the Treasury, with Blue and Green factions fomenting their rivalry even more than usual, and the droughts of the previous year affecting crop sales, mutterings in the street were at fever pitch.

As Theodora remarked to her husband, 'Your antecedents in the purple knew the value of a fool at court. I'm sure this one can be of use to us too.'

Mar the Solitary rarely preached in the presence of the establishment, so his appearance inside the Palace and before the full staff – at his request – was of rare interest. As was the way he launched into Justinian and Theodora.

'You forget your origins at your peril. Theatre tart. Peasant boy.'

An audible intake of breath spread through the crowd, Mar ignored the tremor of scandal and continued, picking on others who were shocked that the preacher knew of them at all; more shocked when he pointed out their truths.

'Eunuch. Farmer. Baker's son. Bishop's bastard. Tax evader. Tax collector.'

The latter two glared at each other, though the tax evader was more scared of John the Cappadocian's interest in him than the treasurer was of being named a tax collector. It might have been a term of abuse when St Paul was still Saul of Tarsus, but Justinian's treasurer believed the Empire was God's kingdom on earth. He noted the name of his neighbour, and many others thanked a combination of the Christ and their ancient household gods that they hadn't been singled out instead.

Mar approached Pasara. Married to Justinian's cousin Germanus, her pride in her illustrious Anicii antecedents meant Pasara believed that she, not Theodora, should be wearing the purple. The preacher looked her up and down, and she shrank back in embarrassment when he poked a heavy finger against her breastbone.

'Arrogance. Pride is a sin, lady. With your breeding, you should know that – unless breeding is all you have to be proud of?'

Theodora kept her eyes downcast, her hands clasped, and bit the insides of her cheeks to keep her smile from showing.

Mar left Pasara, her face red with shock and anger, and moved on to Armeneus, Theodora's own household chief.

'The August says he will restore the glory of the Empire. But on what will he build it? The likes of you, eunuch?' Mar held the younger man's whole face in his huge hand and quietly added, 'Head of the Augusta's staff is a title of merit, and following your mistress to Constantinople has been good for you. But don't forget your home. Here they ignore all but the City. You, African, know better – one day, you will live it.'

Mar swept away, his voice booming as he rolled around the courtyard. Where other preachers might praise infants as an example of Christian purity, Mar simply picked up any who tumbled into his path and handed the child to the closest adult, continuing his oration. Palace parents were furious that their little ones received no more attention than a chair left in his way. Furious, and silent. No one wanted to test the preacher's temper when Justinian and Theodora were dealing with it so well. So far.

Theodora was worried about her husband. As a dancer she had been drilled in precision and stillness by her master Menander's voice and the brutal application of his cane. Justinian was not used to this kind of physical stress. The strains he imposed on his own body were to do with the long hours he worked, sleeping little, eating only when it didn't get in the way of the business of Empire. Theodora saw him sway and knew she needed to take charge. She couldn't allow Justinian to collapse in public; that would be more dangerous to his reputation than this attack from Mar.

The priest turned back. Arms raised, fists clenched, he ran at the couple, pulling up short just as his right fist turned into an open, blessing palm, half a step from the Emperor. Narses raised a warning finger, holding back two guards who were on the balls of their feet ready to strike, and everyone leaned in to listen as Mar finally knelt with the August and Augusta.

'So, Emperor – Master, as you would now be called – on what will you rebuild this Empire? The backs of the soldiers, the workers, the farmers? The people who call for freedom from your endless taxes and demands. The backs of the Goths and the Persians you must fight off? Or the Slavs and those wild Herules and the other Barbarians you bring into our community in your quest to make all one? It is only for the Christ you should raise the Empire – none other. Take care; if you forget your debt of charity to the people, they will turn on you and all your Palace.'

Theodora was about to demand that the preacher shut up and let her husband sit, when the Emperor himself stood up, using the huge man as a prop, and turned to Narses.

'I need a stool, and one for the Empress. Benches, too – many here are tired, and it's getting cold. I won't have my people become ill for the desires of an itinerant preacher.' He turned and smiled at the horrified Mar. 'No matter how celebrated. Those of you with children, take them inside, keep them warm. They are the Empire's future, after all.'

Mar glared at the Emperor, a silent gasp spiralled around the courtyard, all eyes wide. Eventually the priest found his voice again. 'August?' he said.

'Teacher,' Justinian replied, draining the glass of watered wine a nervous servant brought him. He held out the glass for a refill, and drained that too before continuing, 'We appreciate your visit, such an audience is rare and valuable. We agree that all too often we fail the Christ, and also that the new Rome will be restored with the strength of all our people. You are right, the people are at their greatest strength when they are comfortable, yes? Our Empire reaches wide, but here in the City we are also civilised, I would not have the Augusta bruise her knees merely for a show of piety. You and I both know that show is not the same as truth.'

Justinian emphasised the word show, raising his arms a little, his fists lightly clenched, and the quiet imitation of Mar's signature action was not lost on any of their attentive audience, many of whom held their hands to their mouths to stifle shocked laughter.

He went on, 'I would not have my slaves overworked because you prefer a large audience for your preaching and they will now be hours behind in the tasks they must do. As you say, preacher, we must care for the people or risk their rejection. I am also of the people, as is our Empress. And so, we ask your blessing. There's much to be done.'

Theodora couldn't keep the grin from her face and even

Narses' eyebrows were raised. The Imperial couple knelt again, were formally blessed and, together, they walked away.

Much later that night, after Justinian had worked through a dozen arcane laws with his legal adviser Tribonian, editing them down to three simple concepts for the great Codex where he meant to bring all Roman law into one, several hours after Theodora had actually gone to sleep, Justinian came to her rooms. She woke from a dream of her favourite bird, an owl, with dead and bloody carcasses in its beak, and was glad to welcome Justinian to her bed.

Their bodies had become well tuned to each other in the ten years since Narses and the Patriarch Timothy contrived to bring them together. In Justinian, Theodora had finally found a lover with whom she was comfortable in love as well as in the physicality of sex, while Justinian himself found that when their bodies were paramount, even he could shut off his mind, just a little, and allow that he was as much flesh as thought. But not on this occasion.

Theodora was sliding back into sleep when she felt her husband carefully move away from her. 'Stay,' she said.

Justinian didn't answer, he leaned across the pillows to push her dark hair from her face, kissing her eyes.

Theodora groaned, reaching for her husband's hand. 'You're not going to your bed, are you?'

'I can't. I can't sleep tonight.'

Fully awake now, she sat up and pulled a woollen wrap around her shoulders. 'Don't go yet. I ache myself, so you must be in pain from all that giant put us through today. You need to rest.'

'No. There's too much I need to do. The people—'

'The people love to see a priest silenced,' she interrupted, 'they'll adore you for standing up to Mar.'

'I really did need to get on with our work.'

'Of course, but you wanted to shut him up too – yes?'

Justinian laughed, and even in the low-lit room, Theodora was delighted to see the bags under his eyes deepening as the heavy lines on his normally solemn face shifted, showing his pleasure. Her husband rarely laughed aloud.

He agreed. 'I'd had enough of kneeling. And he was boring. I far prefer a persuasive whisper to a declamatory sermon.'

He crossed the floor to pull back a hanging from the big window. Theodora insisted on a sea view wherever possible, and had chosen a room with an expansive outlook for her bedchamber, not caring that the windows meant her room was always a little chilly, colder still when the heavy curtains were pulled back to let in the sea air and a broad view of the Bosphorus opening into the Sea of Marmara. Small ships already headed out in the pre-dawn, making for the best fishing spots, their tiny lamplights bouncing across the choppy waters of the strait. Closer to home Justinian could hear market traders setting out their stalls in the City, their calls caught on the high winds, bouncing off the Palace walls.

'I've had nearly five years of power, but all the people see is reform with none of the benefits. And now we have to deal with the Persians breaking the promised peace . . .'

'Their new king Khusro would say we do the same.'

'And he might be right, but after six years of warring on and off, I'd hoped his coming to power would make a difference. Perhaps with support from Belisarius and Sittas . . .'

Theodora frowned. 'Your generals become dangerous when they are too friendly with each other.'

'They're good soldiers, they respect each other, of course they're close.'

'Yes,' Theodora agreed, 'but wouldn't it be better to send

them on separate campaigns? It's bad enough that the people think of Belisarius as their golden warrior, we don't need Sittas showing he thinks so too.'

'I believe we have more to worry about from the people than from my own men. I trust my generals.'

'Then we'll both pray they keep that trust,' said Theodora.

'The problem isn't inside the Palace, it's out there. The people are disappointed with our slow progress, even though I'm sure they want to rebuild Rome as much as I do.' He turned to her. 'You do want it too, don't you?'

'I want things to be better, yes. I despise the Cappadocian, and I think Belisarius is too keen for the glory of battle, but I trust you. I know how hard you work.'

'How else to show the people I have their best interests at heart?'

Justinian kissed his wife and left her, happy to be heading back to his office, back to his papers. Happy too that she understood his dreams for Rome.

Three

Theodora was not allowed to sleep for long. Soon after Justinian had left her, Armeneus brought a message from Narses that she would be required in the Petitioners' Hall, fully robed, in time for the morning hearings.

'And why?'

Theodora's tone was light, but Mariam's shoulders stiffened anyway. The girl had followed the Empress slavishly, and almost silently, since the day Theodora had her rescued from a sex trafficker; there was little about her adopted mistress she did not know, and less that she did not anticipate. Quietly she waited for the next words, be they explosion or acquiescence.

'Today's petitioners, Mistress.'

'I thought Narses was hearing them?'

'He was, Mistress, but messengers arrived in the night from our spies in northern Syria—'

'Meaning they'll now spend the day poring over Persian maps and border lines in preference to listening to a bunch of patricians complaining about taxes.'

Theodora turned to the window. Larger ships were making their way out now, to the Holy Land, south to Africa, or all the way round to Italy and even Mauretania. She unclenched her hands, calmed her breathing, each action an intention. She belonged to the Palace routine as much as she had ever belonged to her theatre's company master – she would not sneak away for a walk along the shore today, or even grab a short moment alone in the colonnaded courtyards.

'So, we must do as Narses commands.'

Armeneus headed for the outer door to let the appeals staff know the Augusta was on her way.

'Armeneus?' whispered Theodora.

'Yes, Mistress?' Armeneus leaned in.

'Tell Narses he owes me.'

'Of course, Mistress.'

The Empress and her entourage of ladies and maids made the long walk through to the Petitioners' Hall and Theodora made a decision as she walked.

'I would like a Petitioners' Room in our own part of the Palace,' she said to Armeneus.

'In the women's quarters, Mistress?'

'Why not?'

'It's not usual to invite strangers – and some of the petitioners will always be men – to the women's quarters.'

'It's not usual for an Empress to hear the petitioners instead of the Emperor. It's not usual for the Empress to be attended by an acrobat dwarf who still has a sideline as a madam . . .'

Sophia interrupted her, 'If you're referring to me, you might at least use my name.'

Theodora nodded at her old friend. A vital part of her entourage since she had moved to the Palace, Sophia was one of the few people who knew Theodora from her former life who still had the courage to speak up to the Empress.

'Sophia,' Theodora said.

'Mistress.' The dwarf grinned from her place a few paces

behind Theodora and added, 'And I need that sideline, as you call it – you think the pittance you pay me keeps me in comfort?'

Theodora smiled coolly. 'You understand it's believed to be an honour to work for the Augusta?'

'Apparently so. And you'll understand you're not meant to know about my sideline.'

'Regardless,' said Theodora, turning back to Armeneus, 'if the Emperor's staff are happy for me to take on my husband's work when it suits them, we can at least see that it suits me too.'

'I'll speak to Narses, Mistress.'

'No, I'll speak to Narses, you'd end up agreeing some halfway idea with him that neither solves my problem nor creates a new solution.'

'As you wish.'

They swept on through Theodora's favourite courtyard, where the old Empress Euphemia's intricate mosaic fountains poured cool water against gold and blue. Theodora's pleasure in their beauty dimmed as she remembered the malice of the old woman who had baited her for so long. Lovely though they were, she was planning to have these fountains made over, hoping to remove the pain of the old woman's disdain as she did so.

'As I wish, yes,' she answered Armeneus, 'but when it comes to getting funds for my own projects, it's hardly as I wish, is it? The Cappadocian keeps the purse tight shut when it's to do with anything I want.'

Armeneus stopped himself saying there had already been an enormous list of changes, in particular the elevation of her position to enable the Empress to make any demands at all. He knew his mistress and he also knew that despite her hatred of her husband's new treasurer, and she wasn't alone in that feeling, much of her complaint was for show. Like many who worked in the Palace, Theodora was proud of the petitioners' system. Those who came to court to plead their case might have a long wait, or need to come back several times before they were seen, but most were seen eventually, and their concerns given attention. Not that they always received an impartial hearing.

Among that day's claimants were the usual round of widows asking for support, refugees begging asylum, and several divorced women trying to reclaim dowries from ex-husbands. All were delighted to find Theodora was hearing them, given her reputation for clemency towards women in distress.

Then a much more assertive petitioner pushed forward to state his case.

The patrician asking for financial aid was fat, sweating, and furious at having to wait on a long line of women before he was required to bow and kiss the Empress's foot. Theodora had learned the old form of obeisance from Menander when she was a child in his classes, and had instituted it as Palace protocol as soon as she and Justinian came to power. She also insisted they were called Master and Mistress; the new term of address had caused concern in the Senate, and was obviously something this patrician was not comfortable with either.

He barely touched her proffered foot with his lips and then heaved his bulk to stand unsteadily in front of Theodora. 'Augusta . . .' he began.

Theodora frowned and, not hearing the correct term, turned to Antonina, ignoring the man. 'Would your husband prefer meat to fish this evening, do you think?'

Antonina smiled and played along, 'Belisarius is fond of both fish and meat, though our fishermen have been landing abundant catches recently. Big, big catches.'

The petitioner tried again, 'Lady . . .'

At this Sophia whistled softly and Theodora said, to no one in particular, 'Yes, the last time we had lamb it seemed particularly lardy.'

'Mistress.' The patrician eventually forced himself to use the correct term and Theodora, looking at him properly for the first time, felt she recognised him.

'Have we met?'

'No, Mistress. If I could just explain my problem to you – I have come to a difficult . . . a problem, there is . . .'

The man stopped as Theodora leaned forward, the chlamys dragging on her shoulders and neck as she moved.

'I think we have met.'

Theodora remembered a night, a lifetime earlier. Part of Menander's company of girls, dancing for a group of wealthy men, a sumptuous dinner in a private house, her sister Anastasia grabbed by a man in the front row and pulled on to his lap. Theodora felt again her little sister's fear, saw herself coming to Anastasia's rescue, fighting off the man and then turning that fight into a joke, a comedy routine, saving the evening from ruin and earning a beating from Menander for her pains. Anastasia had died young and in childbirth, her memory was precious to Theodora, and if this fat man before her was not the patrician who had lunged at her sister, then he looked very like him. Which was enough.

The patrician was still explaining his petition: 'I have a hole, Mistress, in my finances. I made a loan, to a member of your own staff and I hope that the Palace might reimburse me? For a patrician to be in need reflects badly on Rome. I am not one of those,' he waved at the group of widows standing to one side, 'used to begging for my living. This hole . . . it is not right . . .'

Theodora raised her hand and the man stopped, believing his case heard. She stood and Sophia leaned forward to enjoy what was coming. Antonina darted a look at Armeneus, who moved closer, his job always to tread the fine line between acknowledging his mistress's status and reining her in when the famous temper looked as if it might get the better of her.

Theodora stood a few paces from the patrician, a good head and a half shorter than him, impressive in her held anger. Small and fine, the wiry strength that had stood her in good stead when she had trained daily as an acrobat and a dancer was present now in her poise, her bearing.

She smiled round at her women, at the staff attending them, the petitioners still waiting, and then, speaking quite deliberately, and slowly, she asked him, 'A hole, you said?'

The patrician was confused. 'Yes, Mistress, a hole in my—'

'You have come to the Imperial Palace to tell us you have a hole?'

'Perhaps not exactly a hole . . .'

He tried again, and was again silenced by Theodora simply lifting her forefinger.

'We have seen widows begging for their children's stomachs, refugees petitioning the generosity of Rome, and you mock these cases of genuine need by declaring your hole?'

Her voice was still quiet, still low, but perfectly pitched so that everyone in the deep chamber heard each carefully articulated word.

'I don't . . . I'm not . . .' he blustered.

Now Theodora responded with a chant, repeating herself and gesturing for the ladies to accompany her, 'Showing your hole in the Palace? Showing your hole?'

It took no time for Antonina and Sophia to join in, half a moment more for Comito's daughter Indaro, always a bright point in the Empress's entourage, to take up the chant and turn it into a song. Even Theodora's daughter, the shy Ana, quietly sang along. Armeneus sighed, well aware this story would be all over the City before nightfall and that the higher-ranking members of society needed no encouragement to shake their heads at Theodora's behaviour.

The chant grew louder and the fat man realised it was an impossible situation. Careful to bow first, he kissed the Empress's foot, although she skipped every time his lips came near her toe, and then he backed out of the chamber, sweating, mumbling, hurrying from the Palace. The ladies and their attendant eunuchs laughed, many of the remaining petitioners applauded, and Theodora went back to her seat on the raised dais, the ceremonial robes a little less heavy.

'Good. Who's next?'

Two more refugees were granted leave to stay in the City, and then a young man came forward, not much older than Theodora; his face weather-beaten, he looked like a sailor or a pilgrim. He bowed and kissed Theodora's foot with no fuss. When he stood up he was smiling.

'I'm pleased to see you looking so well, Mistress.'

'Really?'

Theodora was wary. Since her elevation in status many claimed to have seen her naked on stage or cavorting in a private house. Most had embellished or completely invented their tales – certainly she had not been quite so busy or as wild as many of the storytellers suggested.

Armeneus stepped forward. 'Your petition? The Augusta is busy.'

'I'll tell it,' the man answered, the Italian accent clearer now in his stilted Greek.

'Would you prefer to speak Latin?' Theodora asked in Latin.

The man shook his head. 'No, Mistress. My Greek is ugly, I hear it especially in this court, but it offers more choice for conversation, more room for thought. As an artist I find it elegant.'

'I've always found Greek useful, especially when discussing faith ... or love.' She smiled and the young man smiled back. 'But as you can see, my staff become nervous when I chat, they're worried I'll enjoy myself too much – yes, Armeneus?'

Armeneus said nothing. If Theodora was in a good mood having attacked a patrician, and chose to spend the rest of the day charming Italian peasants, he was not going to complain. The more they got through here, the happier Narses would be.

'You may remember me, Mistress, if I tell you my name is Stephen and I am a mosaic artist.'

Theodora stood up, and again her entourage stood to attention with her.

'Come closer.'

The man approached, and Theodora stared at him.

After a long while she spoke again, 'Alexandria?'

'Yes, Mistress.'

'You were there when I met the Patriarch Timothy, before I went into the desert. You told me I should not give up.'

The man agreed. 'I'd seen plenty of lost souls in my own pilgrimage.'

'You thought I was lost?'

'It was no special knowing. You were tired, another traveller waiting on the religious; I'd seen the same in the Holy Land, the Church dealing with us in its own time. I wanted to cheer you up. And I had once seen you on stage, I could see the difference from the girl you had been ...' he stopped himself. 'Is it all right to say that here?'

'Very many have, and much more,' Theodora sighed and Sophia grinned. 'So, you knew nothing, but encouraged me to stay anyway, to wait for Timothy, who became my mentor.'

'You looked like you needed encouragement.'

'I did. And are you here because you think I owe you?'

'No, Mistress, I'm here because I want a job.'

'I have a household chief who's irritating me today, any interest in taking over from him?' she asked, looking at Armeneus, who glanced up from his notes and nodded, the image of passive courtly protocol.

'Thank you, no. I want to create the mosaics for the new church in Ravenna.'

Theodora frowned. 'We've only just agreed the building work there, it'll be years before the foundations are laid; with all this fuss from the Goths, it's bound to be a slow build. You'll wait a decade or more before the internal decoration begins.'

'And I'll be a better artist by then.'

'You think highly of yourself.'

The artist shook his head. 'I think highly of my aims for myself.'

'Good answer. And what will you mosaic?'

'You, Mistress, and the August.'

Theodora laughed. 'You don't even try flattery? Shouldn't you tell me I'm so beautiful I must be immortalised? That it's vital I'm seen across the Empire; a symbol of womanly obedience for the fiery wives of Ravenna?'

All her entourage laughed at that, as she intended them to, and the artist continued, 'Mistress, I am highly skilled now. By the time the church is ready for the mosaic work, I mean to be great. And so will you.'

'You're brave – am I not great already?' Theodora was enjoying this.

'As young as we are, Mistress, you and I still have much to accomplish, to build on. I with my talent, you with your . . .'

'Gold?'

'And power,' he agreed. 'I need the Imperial seal to prove my workshop has the commission for the completed church. Many things may happen between now and then. I need to know I'm promised the work.'

'Where I can command, I hardly need pay as well.'

Stephen evenly returned her look and said, 'Where you can pay, the work will be better.'

Antonina burst out laughing at this and Sophia applauded. The artist was too rugged for Antonina's tastes and probably too earnest for Sophia, but Theodora knew her friends enjoyed having new men about the place, especially men as interesting as this one.

'Eat with us tonight,' said Theodora. 'You may begin your sketches if you like, or I could ask one of my friends to show you the Palace, you can study the mosaics we have here. Sophia probably has something to show that will inspire you?' She was pleased to see the artist suddenly lose his bravado. 'What? You're scared of my friend's hunger? It's true her appetites are larger than her half-size frame.'

Stephen held up his hands and spoke more quietly now, 'Mistress, I have no clothes for an evening in the Palace.'

Theodora nodded. 'I travelled like that, it is freeing – and frightening. Armeneus, find the artist a room and clothing, enough for a few days, he'll need time to make his sketches. Sophia can give him a tour later. We'll see you this evening.'

With that the Empress marched from the room, calling after her that Armeneus should also set up the contract for the artist, make sure the architects in Ravenna knew her wishes, arrange for the seal to be given, then grant whatever the last three petitioners were there for, she didn't care what it was, she was tired of this now and she assumed everyone else was too. Her women followed in her wake, Armeneus was left to follow her commands.

Theodora walked quickly through the corridors, hurrying away from a memory of herself at eighteen, betrayed by the friend who had replaced her in her lover's bed, exhausted, alone, seeking solace in the Church in Alexandria, the last place she would have expected to find comfort, the only place left to her. She charged down corridors and pathways and walked back into herself as Augusta, Empress, as one who might not have all the freedom she wished, but who certainly did have the power – and the right – to make another's livelihood, possibly his life.

Four

The meal was a success. Antonina happily commandeered the visitor, leaving the Emperor entirely to his conversation with Belisarius. Justinian, no soldier himself and painfully aware that his precursor in the purple had been a favourite with the troops, was always keen to have the best advice on military matters. And Belisarius had plenty of ideas, too many for Theodora's comfort.

Theodora did not doubt the young general's courage or his military wisdom or his honed, toned good looks; what she didn't like was the way everyone else treated him as some kind of demigod. Sittas believed Belisarius one of the best strategic minds of the age, an opinion echoed by Germanus. As Justinian's cousin, Germanus had been annoyed but accepting when the Emperor Justin chose the scholar nephew Justinian as his successor, rather than himself, the military man. Germanus knew his greatest skills lay in soldiering, not diplomacy or the back-room discussions that were so much a part of government and bored him senseless. His wife Pasara however, had made no secret of her disgust when Theodora was raised to patrician, and subsequently made Empress. And yet, even with these old hurts rankling, both Sittas and

Germanus, and all the disapproving women, roundly applauded Justinian's admiration for Belisarius.

Theodora knew from her stage career that the public could be fickle. Today they were pleased with their studious Emperor, enthusiastic about his many building projects. On another day however, there would be incursions from the Persian border, or stories of Vandals and Goths attacking in the west, or the Green faction might again whip up rumours that Justinian, from the opposing Blues, was showing favouritism; on that day the people might prefer the idea of a soldier Emperor again, someone to maintain order at home and abroad. Justinian did not see the young and successful Belisarius as a rival. Theodora thought it fortunate for both of them that she did.

The meal was ending and Antonina and Belisarius were keen to take Stephen home for more wine and stories of Italy. Belisarius because he believed the Ravennese's experience of living so close to Goth rule would be more useful than the information he had at second hand from their spies; Antonina simply because the much-praised young general she already had as husband was never quite enough for her. Not that Belisarius noticed; on the rare occasions he tore himself away from military matters he was as besotted with his wife as everyone else was with him. Or perhaps, as Theodora once remarked, he was simply too damn in love with his own image to notice that Antonina didn't gaze after him as often as everyone else did.

One by one the guests left, each careful to bow before the August and Augusta as they did so. Theodora took special delight in Pasara's evident dislike of the gesture, keeping her low in the bow as she spoke to her.

'Pasara, I hope you enjoyed your meal?'

'Yes, thank you . . . Mistress.'

There was the slightest hesitation before she spoke the demanded title, and Theodora noted it, as Pasara no doubt meant her to. Germanus caught his wife's hand and the exalted, but not Imperial, couple left together. Pasara might be an aristocrat, comfortable with the intrigue and double-speak of court, but her husband understood that Theodora had been raised in the Hippodrome; even without the purple on her back the Empress would always win in a war of words.

Theodora was impressed to hear Stephen turn down the invitation to spend a few more days in the City in Antonina's care. He pleaded the need to make as many sketches of Theodora as possible before he took his place on board a ship leaving in two days' time, and while Antonina was obviously disappointed, she didn't press her case. She had the golden warrior at her side after all; a last late drink would suffice. The artist's own goodnight was full of gratitude. Theodora knew the exhaustion of poverty, and understood exactly why Stephen was so moved. He had journeyed to Constantinople purely on hope: he could now go home and get on with his life, marry, start a studio, take on an apprentice or two, secure in the knowledge that one day his name would be made. Most of the Palace staff wouldn't have noticed, but Theodora had changed his life this afternoon. It occurred to her that she had probably changed the fat patrician's life as well, and she was quite pleased about that too.

Theodora waited until Narses was busy farewelling Belisarius before she turned to Justinian. 'Are you working tonight?'

'Tribonian has some papers for me to look over,' Justinian said.

Theodora smiled.

'What is it?'

'You,' she said, 'your leniency, just because he's a good lawyer.'

'A brilliant lawyer.'

'Yes, but any other Pagan would have lost their job. Most of them have. Yet he's allowed to keep on with his gods and goddesses ...'

'I thought you liked Tribonian?'

'Like hardly comes into it where your staff are concerned. Unlike the Cappadocian drunkard, he is polite to me. Unlike Belisarius, I trust he's truly on your side. Unlike Germanus he has no thought that your title might have been his.'

'And unlike Sittas?'

'Unlike my brother-in-law, he's not a bore.'

'Because he likes to talk strategy? It's his job, you were once devoted to your work.'

'Not quite, I loved my work, but I've always had a deeper devotion to living my life. I wanted to do it all, experience it all.'

'Most people think you did.'

'Most people would – mostly – be right,' she smiled.

'Maybe that's why Tribonian annoys you less than the rest of them: his paganism reminds you of your old world?'

'I think it's more that I know he has no designs on your position. And even if he did, the people would never allow one scholar to take over from another.'

'So it's only military men I need worry about?'

'Yes.'

'Wise of me to keep them close, then.'

'Perhaps. But you don't often work late with Tribonian, what else is there?'

Justinian shook his head. 'I don't want to bother you.'

Theodora looked squarely at her husband. Justinian talked to her about everything, used her as his voice of the people, and not without reason. Now forty-six, the Emperor's life had been centred on the Palace since he was eleven years old, Theodora, still two years off thirty, had lived, worked, struggled and survived in the Empire they now ruled over, had travelled from Constantinople to Cyrenaica on the northern shore of Africa, through Alexandria and Antioch, all the way back to the slums of their city.

'What is it?' she pressed him.

Justinian darted a glance at Narses, but Theodora saw the look and raised herself on her toes to stand more squarely in his eyeline. 'The eunuch's busy. I'm here, and yet you don't want to talk to me about it, so I can only presume it's the Church?'

Justinian sighed, rubbed his heavy-shaded eyes, a gesture that always made her wince as he rubbed them redder still. 'Isn't it always and ever the Church?'

Theodora nodded. 'Our curse to be born in a time of such faithful confusion.'

If the August couple's building programme had created consternation among those who worried it was costing the state too much, there was even more interest in Justinian's swiftly enacted religious laws. Within months of taking office, the Emperor banned Jews, Pagans and Arians from holding many official positions. It was hardly unusual to attack the Jews, or the small but defiantly separate Christian sect of Arians, the Pagan bans were more problematic. While the City was nominally Christian, there were many still praying to the old gods as Tribonian did. But Justinian was adamant: if he was to achieve his dream of a revitalised Rome, then all must be one – one Empire, one Church. More recently he had, to a muted outcry from some academics, and loud applause from his chief priests and theologians, closed down the Academy in

Athens. He felt it both a grand and a depressing gesture at the time, but it was also important in uniting Christians under his rule, uniting believers still profoundly divided over the most basic of questions; five hundred years since the death of the Christ, the Church was still trying to specify the nature of His divinity. The Emperor believed in the Council of Chalcedon's ruling, that the Christ was both divine and human, a union, but not a mingling, of divinity and humanity. A smaller number, including Theodora, disagreed, and were equally sure that while the Christ possessed both states, His divinity and His humanity were entirely and inextricably mingled.

The distinction echoed across the Empire. Those in the West leaned towards Chalcedon, many of those in the East against. What really worried Justinian was that the anti-Chalcedonians in Syria, the Levant and Egypt – including Theodora's mentors Severus and Timothy, Patriarch of Alexandria – were more interested in self-determination than in one Empire with one Church. As Timothy's acolyte, living in the desert under Severus' rule, Theodora had converted to the anti-Chalcedonian belief and its more esoteric rites, not least because the rituals and gesture of the practice appealed to her sense of theatre. The politicians and churchmen who, through Narses, had brought Justinian and Theodora together had hoped to effect a union between both sides. They trusted that leaking the truth of the Augusta's faith would convince the anti-Chalcedonians they had someone on their side within the ruling elite. New-nation preachers in the East, Goth-puppet Patriarchs in the West, and the Palace in the middle, trying to hold it all together.

Justinian took Theodora's hand and led her to the back of the room, away from their departing guests. An ornately inlaid door was opened by a slave who had been waiting in the corner all evening, positioned purely on the off-chance that the Emperor or Empress might want to use this door. Justinian walked through, Theodora nodded her thanks to the slave and followed her husband. Just two years into the job, and still young compared to the last two Empresses, she knew that the ratio of smiles to rants needed to be heavily weighted in favour of kindness. Given that the story of her morning's meeting with the patrician must be all over the City by now, it did her no harm to smile at the slave, acknowledging him in gesture if not in word.

Like many of the Palace's public rooms, the informal dining room where they had eaten also had a small antechamber. Originally conceived as a way to observe the main room, there was a raised dais running the length of the wall it shared with the dining room, and small spy-holes drilled into the panelling, through which it was possible to watch the diners without being seen. Although there were no windows in this room, several grilles high up stopped the antechamber becoming too stuffy – Justinian's forebears had not wanted to suffocate while they spied on each other – and a little of the dining room's warm candlelight filtered through after Justinian closed the door. Alone for the first time all day, Theodora and her husband kissed, pulling each other closer, reaching for skin beneath fine silk, looking fully into the other's face. Theodora had too often had to close her eyes to shut out the person who paid for her body; now she preferred to see her husband, to watch his pleasure in her, to show him hers.

Hand to mouth, mouth to mouth, mouth to flesh, skin to skin, inside and outside purple silk, soft robes and heavy jewels, full from the meal and the business and the gossip of court and heads stuffed with plans and possibility, the Emperor and Empress were acutely hungry for each other. Their sex was quickly over, neither fully disrobed, neither fully satisfied, but good enough, close enough. There were times when Theodora wanted to shout her pleasure in her husband's body, shout especially because she knew that so many dismissed him as stolid and scholarly. He lived up to the studiousness of his reputation at work, in his office, in his library; he was thoughtful and measured in all matters of state. But when they came together with the mutual desire that had surprised both of them at the start of their relationship, Justinian was as skilled and seductive as any of her previous lovers, and he could be surprisingly frivolous too. Theodora tried to tempt him now.

'What are you doing tomorrow?'

'Preparing for the Persian delegation. Narses thinks the ambassador will want to meet you too.'

'All the foreigners want to get a look at the Emperor's whore-wife. Fine, then I'll meet you in the morning, before work.'

'Before prayer?' Justinian asked.

'Certainly, before prayer. I'll give you something to think about instead of worrying about Tribonian's soul.'

'Please do.'

They straightened their robes, and she tidied her hair, replacing the earring that Justinian had knocked to the floor in his eagerness to reach her. Just before he opened the door, the Emperor picked up his small wife, lifted her with out-stretched arms and laughed aloud as he pulled her tight to him again, kissing her and setting her down carefully. He then went back into the near-empty dining room, walking ahead of Theodora as was right for his position, the look on his face daring Narses to say a word.

In the middle of the night, Theodora woke suddenly. She wasn't sure if the scream of the owl was in her dream or real-ity. She went to the window, careful not to disturb Mariam who slept in the small room next door. The moon was high and Theodora looked out, beyond the wall to the sea and Bithynia in the distance. A bird or a bat, too far away to tell, flew low across her field of vision, swooping down to the furthest reach of the wall where the old bricks had finally crumbled and fallen in recent days. She shook her head, reminding herself of her role even as she sneaked into Mariam's room, reminding herself of her exalted position as she pulled on Mariam's plain robe and sandals, and then carefully let herself out of her own room. The simple cloak close around her shoulders covered her hair and face, granting her the anonymity she craved as she walked the corridors of her own Palace, past guards who didn't even glance up, and out to the open air.

Theodora walked as quickly as she dared away from the main buildings, following the slope down to the wall above the rocky shoreline, the broken section she knew offered an opening to the water, the City, her old world. She hitched up the skirt of Mariam's robe and vaulted the last of the low walls that separated the formal courtyards from the empty land just before the outer wall, whooping aloud as she did so, her pleasure in the physicality, in the freedom, in the moon and the strong scent of the sea too much to contain any longer. And then she came to a sudden halt as she realised she was not alone. Years of dance training had given her a sure sense of physical proximity, and she felt, rather than heard, that someone was close.

She took a slow breath to calm her breathing and therefore her voice, then turned and spoke quietly into the deep shadows cast by the moonlight hitting the wall, 'Yes?'

'Mistress, I thought it might be you.'

Before she could reply, John the Cappadocian walked out

of the dark, prostrated himself and leaned in to kiss her foot, lifting the foot slightly and almost knocking her off balance.

Almost. Not quite.

'Sir,' Theodora spoke sharply and stepped back, leaving him fumbling on the ground, 'that is not necessary out here.'

The older man lifted his tall, wiry frame from the ground. 'Perhaps not.'

Theodora was trying to think how much he could have seen or heard; whether he had been down here since she ran out of the main building or had followed her.

The Cappadocian came closer, and now she could see the heavy lines on either side of his mouth, dragging his smile into a leer. 'You're not sleeping well, Mistress? Perhaps you still find it hard to use your excess energy inside the Palace?'

Theodora waited to answer until she could trust herself not to snap at the man. The Cappadocian treasurer always seemed to be insinuating a great deal more than just her onstage career. He made her skin crawl, and he knew it.

'I sleep perfectly. Not that it has anything to do with you, Treasurer.'

'Yet you walk in the middle of the night? So far from the women's quarters?'

He smiled then, and Theodora knew he'd happily restrict the women of court as tightly as he famously restricted his own daughter, keeping her confined to the house.

'Or perhaps, you come – as I do – to inspect the grounds? I've made a note of the problems with the old wall, we don't want people sneaking in. You'd agree, Mistress?'

'Our builders are busy with other projects for me.'

'Surely Palace security is more important?'

'Than my wishes?'

'I work for the August, Mistress.' Theodora's tone had been quiet, and hard, and the Cappadocian's was just as strong, most especially when he added, coming close enough for her to smell the mint leaves he habitually chewed, 'As do we all.'

She turned then and walked away, back up the slope to her sumptuous prison, furious to hear the man chuckling behind her, free to walk all night if he wished, free to do exactly as he wanted.

Five

A week later, Theodora stood at a gate to the inner grounds and watched as a group of builders carried materials down to the outer wall. Narses, on his way to a meeting with the Persian delegation, stopped beside her.

'You approved the Cappadocian's request, Narses?'

'I did, Mistress, for material and workers to rebuild a crumbling wall.'

'When you knew I wanted them to continue remaking the old Empress's courtyard?'

'This will take a half a day.'

'And last a lifetime.'

Narses sighed, started to speak, stopped himself, and then spoke anyway: 'It's important we ensure the Palace's security.'

'To make it impossible for those who might cause problems to enter the Palace grounds?'

'Yes. Or to keep safe those who might wish to leave through exits other than the Chalke Gate.'

'You think I'd sneak out?'

The Chief of Staff looked at the woman he had been instrumental in bringing to the Palace, the woman he had plotted might become his mistress. 'I know you find this place confining, Augusta,' he said.

'And that I have a deep concern for the people affected by that damn Cappadocian's plans.'

'Mistress,' Narses said, 'the Cappadocian treasurer is as rude to the eunuchs as he is to the women at court, I'm no fonder of him than you are, but the Emperor approves of his work. You and the August are very keen on the new Empire, rebuilding in Antioch, in Ephesus, naming new cities after the Emperor. It all costs, and those costs invariably create problems. We have our spies in the streets, you don't need to worry about the people.'

Theodora turned, annoyed. 'I thought my understanding of the people was one of the reasons you brought me to the Palace?'

Narses stepped back, ignored the chimes from the water clock and looked plainly at Theodora. 'There was a time when you would have told me your concerns.'

'Or you would have demanded them from me,' she said.

'Possibly.'

'Our roles have changed.'

'I can still listen, respectfully,' he said.

'Eunuch, you have often acted as if you're listening respectfully, and then found a way to use what I tell you to your own advantage, or even against me.'

Narses laughed then. 'Against you? You're planning to overthrow the state so soon? You've barely had time to become accustomed to the purple.'

'That's just it,' Theodora said. 'The purple restricts me, which I resent, and yet I feel myself becoming used to it. I never wanted to be one of those women, the whore-wives who marry into wealth and power, doing nothing to earn it themselves.'

'They would say providing an heir was part of that deal.'

'They would, and we all know I haven't done so. I may never do so.' Theodora did not say that she believed the illness she'd suffered many years ago in the desert meant she would never conceive again. 'But even if I did, it wouldn't be enough. I've worked all my life. I've worked hard to become the Augusta ...'

'It's a role, Mistress. You play it well.'

'Some days it feels more than that, it feels like fate.'

The eunuch frowned. 'You think it was ordained?'

'I know you believe you made all this happen,' she said, 'you and Timothy, bringing me to Justinian. But I could have refused you, gone back to my old life.'

'And why didn't you?'

'I fell in love. I didn't expect it, you certainly didn't, but my rise to this place was so unlikely I used to hope there was something fated in our coming together, greater than all your plotting.'

'And now?'

Theodora shook her head. 'I don't know. Out there I had a purpose, I was one of Menander's girls, working backstage, working on my back, what could be harder? Later, in the main theatre company, and again with Macedonia in Antioch, I played roles in order to survive. Now the real struggle is to live the role. I must be Augusta all the time.'

'And the purple is too heavy a burden?'

'I was raised in the Hippodrome, Narses, I understand as well as you that our ceremonies are theatre. What feels real is my marriage. So I have to put my hope in the possibility that our coming together, as August and Augusta, is meant. If I can find the reason for being beside him, I might feel that it's not just fate pushing me around. Meanwhile, I waste time being cruel to bastards like that fat patrician last week, simply because I can.'

Narses raised an eyebrow and Theodora smiled, brought back from the edge of frustrated tears by how well the older man understood her. 'Yes,' she added, 'and because it makes me laugh.'

He bowed then. 'In that case, perhaps now is the time to tell you Ana is pregnant.'

'My Ana?'

Narses nodded.

'Dear God,' Theodora shook her head, 'I had no idea she had guts enough to talk to a man, let alone screw one. Do we have any idea who's the lucky boy?'

'It seems we've all been underestimating your daughter,' he grinned, 'she's been sleeping with Probus' son.'

Theodora laughed aloud then at the idea that her bastard daughter should have been secretly sleeping with not only a member of the Palace elite, but the great-nephew of Anastasius, who had ruled for twenty-seven years before Justinian's uncle Justin was Emperor. Given her own lack of illustrious antecedents, it couldn't have been a better match.

'Let's get them married, and quickly. With any luck it'll silence that bitch Pasara, she's been making sure we hear about her own new pregnancy night and day. You know she's planning to call the child Justin if it's a boy?'

Narses' reply was noncommittal, 'I believe the Emperor approves of the name?'

'He's more trusting than I am, sees it as a mark of respect for his uncle. And you know as well as I do that my lack of children in the purple has always delighted Pasara. So, Ana's pregnancy is doubly pleasing: not only will we have a child in our own household, but Probus is bound to be related to the Anicii somehow. I'm sure Pasara will love to hear that my flesh and blood is polluting her own pure breed.'

*

Theodora's show of joy in her daughter's pregnancy and Pasara's certain discomfort evaporated as soon as Narses left her. She and Pasara were almost the same age, relatively old to bear children, but certainly capable of doing so if only years mattered. Comito had announced her own pregnancy in the spring, and Antonina, older still, was also talking about her hopes for a child – Belisarius was young for one so successful, he wanted a son to follow him.

Justinian came to her rooms in the evening, as he often did, wanting a chance to talk together without courtiers and staff listening in. He knew about the scar, low across her belly, from when she had been so ill in the desert, he was the only one she never needed to pretend with.

'They're everywhere, damn pregnant women.'

'The sages would say it's a sign of a healthy court.'

'The sages would point out that I am barren.'

'Your daughter's making you a grandmother. That's hardly barren.'

'But the baby won't be ours.'

'It will be born in the purple and so will the child Comito's expecting.'

'It's not the same.'

Justinian took Theodora's hand. 'Leave the plotting to Pasara and the gossips she gathers around her; we'll be remembered long after her child's children have turned to dust.'

Theodora shook her head. 'And those gossips think I'm the ambitious one.'

'You are. Ambitious for me. It's a fine combination, don't you think?'

In the morning Theodora prepared to speak to her daughter. Despite her good intentions she and Ana had never become any closer than they were when Ana was a baby and handed over to Theodora's mother Hypatia, the cost of a wet nurse far less than the sum Theodora could earn back at work on stage. Theodora had tried to mother her daughter since her return from Antioch, had tried even harder since Hypatia's death two years ago, but it was not a great success. Both women had been relieved when Sophia stepped in, telling Theodora to stop feeling guilty, the best she could do now was change the future. The Empress might never be a real mother to Ana, but Sophia believed there was a chance they might yet find friendship.

'Do you love Paulus?' Theodora asked, having summoned Ana to her rooms.

'He says he loves me,' Ana answered quietly.

'That's not what I asked.'

'I apologise, Mistress.'

Theodora sighed, tried again to explain herself to her daughter. 'I'm asking if you love him, if he will make you happy.'

Ana shrugged. She had few words ever, even fewer to converse with Theodora about something so personal. 'I expect so. I hope so.'

'I don't want you to be unhappy. I know we've never really talked about these things.'

'I talk to Sophia.'

'Yes, you do,' Theodora replied lightly, trying not to show her hurt. 'You'll have to keep the baby of course, it's too late to get rid of it, but in many ways it's easier to keep a bastard here than in poverty outside. All the same, you don't have to marry him if you don't want to.'

'But we're a useful union, surely, Paulus and I? The baby will bring together the families of the last three Emperors.'

'I am aware of that. As is Narses.'

47

'I'm glad to be of service.'

'Ana, I want you to be happy.'

'And you want this as my mother or as the Empress?'

Theodora stared at her daughter, impressed. The reply sounded like a retort, no matter that Ana's head was still lowered, her eyes slightly downcast.

'Clearly, pregnancy suits you.'

'I'm pleased to be having a child, I'm happy to be useful to you, I'm glad Paulus wants me. It will do.'

Theodora shook her head. 'You don't have to put up with what will do, Ana, you're the daughter of the Empress. We can wait, find a nurse for your baby, find a man you truly want.'

'But whoever you choose for me will need to be useful, won't he? A link to some important family or other? I can't do as I want,' Ana said, 'as you did.'

'And look how well that worked out for me, deserted and homeless in Africa. Few of us can do as we wish, Ana – not always, not often. Even Justinian constantly weighs his own desires against the needs of his role.'

'I know how it works. Paulus says he loves me. It will do.'

'When did you become so detached?'

'When did you ever care?'

Theodora sucked in her breath and Ana waited for her mother's attack. She knew she was pushing it and was surprised at herself, more surprised when no retaliation came.

'I've always cared, even if I've not always acted on that care, or shown it. And I'm sorry, as you well know. I only . . .'

'Want me to be happy. Yes. Then you can relax, I am, very happy.' Ana looked up now, nodding. 'I'm pleased to be pregnant, pleased that Paulus is someone you approve of. And I'm thrilled to be forming my own new bonds, even if I have to stay within the Palace. You can't save me as you saved Mariam, you don't know how to talk to me, and I don't know how to talk to you. Perhaps we'll find a common bond in this baby. Sophia thinks it might help both of us.'

'I'm delighted the dwarf tart approves.'

Theodora stopped herself remarking further, acknowledging what Ana had just made plain: that Sophia had known about the pregnancy, as had Narses, as had any number of others, long before Theodora did herself.

'May I go now?' Ana asked, 'I'm tired.'

'Of course.'

Ana bowed as protocol demanded and then, raising herself before her mother, leaned in close. Her whispered voice and pose reminded Theodora pitifully of the small girl who had always been too scared to speak when Theodora saw her late after a show or running out to rehearsal, but her words were a gift.

'Just between us,' Ana said, 'and please, never mention this again, and certainly not to Sophia, you'll be glad to hear that Paulus is a good – a very good – lover.'

Then Ana left the room, a broad smile on her usually composed face, delighted to have, for once, silenced her mother.

Six

The marriage was arranged with appropriate discretion. No one was surprised when Armeneus informed the household that Ana wanted a quiet blessing, and within a fortnight the Augusta's bastard daughter was married, dressed in a simple and elegant gown quickly made by the Jewish family of weavers and seamstresses who had housed Theodora when she first returned to Constantinople after her years away in North Africa and Egypt. Pasara looked on the ceremony in horror, and Theodora was pleased to note her discomfort.

That evening, kissing her daughter, blessing the union both as mother and as Empress, Theodora was astonished to find herself on the verge of tears. She left the banqueting room as quickly as she could without causing too much gossip among the staff. Given the increasingly unhappy state of current negotiations with the Persians over their incursions into both Mesopotamia and Syria, there was no surprise that the Empress appeared to have better things to do. With Justinian exhausting himself trying to find resources for an already under-funded army, while his translators looked for nuance in every missive from their spies behind enemy lines, Theodora had a ready-made excuse to attend to her husband rather than her daughter.

Sophia found Theodora in her receiving room.

'You called for me?'

'I called for you some time ago.'

'I was working.'

'I'm Augusta.'

'So I hear. But the purple on your back doesn't make it any easier for me to cross the City. The long stretch of the Mese doesn't empty of drunken soldiers just because you send a servant to find me, nor does it mean Blue louts stop harassing Green brats and allow me a clear path to you.'

'How disappointing.'

'What is it? Has Ana left her husband already?'

'No. In fact, I doubt there's a happier couple in the City.'

'The August must be pleased. It's a good union, and fertile already.'

'He is. We are.'

'But?'

'I am pleased. And I felt ...' Theodora shook her head, rubbed her face, 'I felt everything.'

'Ah. Maternal emotion? That's new.'

'I have had those feelings before, Sophia, I just ... I was never there when Ana was small, I had to work, you know that. And she didn't ...'

'Interest you?'

'Mother of the Christ forgive me, yes, she didn't interest me.' Theodora shook her head. 'I'm shocked and delighted to feel the emotions I thought life had wrung from me.'

Sophia nodded to a silent slave, motioning for the wine he held. She took the full jug and sent him out of the room, then poured generous glasses for herself and Theodora.

'So you finally feel something normal for your daughter. Something approaching love. Why are you upset?'

'It was the relief. For the first time I fully realised that neither Ana nor her child will have to experience what we had to. Better yet if she gives birth to a boy.'

'Any child born in the Palace would never have to go through what we did.'

'A girl would still need to be married off. We give ourselves up for work or we do it for marriage. Either way, it's still our work.'

Sophia went to sit beside her old friend. 'Theodora, not all women who marry hate to fuck. Not all women who fuck for coin hate to fuck. You didn't. I know for a fact you enjoyed our work sometimes.'

'Sometimes. Other times I hated it.'

'And you love being Empress all the time?' Theodora didn't answer and Sophia continued, 'I know you had your glorious conversion in the desert, but you can't tell me you've entirely forgotten that you did like it, our work, sometimes. And you've told me, much as I've asked you not to,' Sophia mocked, screwing up her face, 'how utterly you enjoy it with the Emperor.'

Theodora laughed and shook her head at her friend. 'No,' she sighed, 'you know I'm not talking about sex anyway, not really; it's about how it is for girls, our girls.'

Sophia helped herself to a glass of wine from Theodora's table. 'You still want to save them all? Mariam wasn't enough for you?'

'Nowhere near enough.'

'Then what's your plan? You're Augusta, remember? You can do anything you like.'

'I wish . . .'

'You can do a damn sight more than wish,' Sophia talked

over her mistress, 'if you want to save them all, then save them all. You've been going on about setting up this convent or house or whatever it is you want to make for the old whores . . .'

'I will.'

'When? Last winter was dreadful, signs are we have a worse one coming. Do it, make it happen. Only don't kid yourself they're all going to want it.'

'What do you mean?'

'You find being cooped up here hard enough, and this is a palace – the Palace. Don't imagine every whore you scoop off the street will thank you. Some will, the older ones probably. The punters have been demanding cuts in the whores' fees too, there's always a knock-on when things are tight, but there are still those who prefer life on the street.'

'And old whores are the hardest to change.'

'Very true – look at me!'

They laughed and Sophia poured more wine.

'Start with the young girls first, they're not so used to the life. There's half a dozen brothel keepers' names I could give you right now.'

'I can't just close them down,' Theodora replied. 'Most of those keepers paid for the girls, they have contracts with them, they pay their taxes.'

'If you buy their girls back they'll be out of business by the morning.'

'You think my household has so much?' Theodora asked.

'It's got a damn sight more than mine.'

'And if I do, where will the girls go?'

'Wherever they want. Back to their vile peasant villages and even worse peasant boys no doubt, but they'll be free of their brothel contracts and that's a start.'

Theodora poured herself the last of the wine, calmer now,

enthused by the idea and interested in her friend's enthusiasm. 'And putting those half-dozen brothel keepers out of business wouldn't do your own business any harm either.'

Sophia finished her glass and looked at her old friend. 'Every one of my girls has already bled at least once; none of them are children. Every one of my girls goes to a clean man, only one at a time, and gets a good share of the fee he pays. None of them is beaten, coerced, or thrown out when they get too old or find themselves pregnant. I'm proud of how I run my business.' She paused and then nodded. 'But yes, that Cappadocian bastard in the Treasury is making things hard for all of us. I could do with a little less competition.'

Theodora called in eight brothel owners the next day. She knew there was no point closing down their businesses completely: the City would always want its whores and the women would still need work. Instead she put up the funds to buy twenty-five girls out of their contracts, young girls who had either come to the City with their refugee families and been lured away by the promise of pretty sandals or a warm bed, or, worse, who had been sold by their own parents. In hard times a good-looking child could fetch a nice fee for a farmer suffering under the burden of a bad harvest and high taxes.

The girls themselves were less easy to deal with. For the first two weeks Theodora housed them in the women's wing of the Palace, but it quickly became obvious they needed a permanent home, not least because her household food budget increased threefold, while the amount allocated to her managers remained the same.

'Twenty-five girls?' Narses frowned. 'You don't think I have enough going on right now?'

'I thought this might be a pleasant distraction.'

'Twenty-five girls trained only to be whores? I'm too old for this.' Narses sat at his desk, head in hands. Sighing, he looked up at Theodora. 'Menander always said you would either rule the world or be hanged by it.'

'Menander said many things, let's hope he was only half right. Come on, Narses, I'm trying to do the right thing.'

Narses sighed, turned to a map on his wall pinned all over with notes and diagrams, lists and letters.

'Let's see . . . we could send them off to attack the Persians? Little girls can be devils with knives. Things are uncertain in the west again too, soldiers complaining about not being paid their full fees – maybe we could throw a girl into each regiment? That'll keep them quiet for a week or so.'

The scribe kneeling beside him on the floor started to write down his master's thoughts and Narses kicked him, not lightly. 'Don't be stupid, boy.'

'Not quite what I had in mind,' said Theodora.

'I imagine you very likely had nothing in mind at all. You made a grand gesture and now I have to deal with your mess.'

Theodora had been playing along with Narses; now she had had enough. 'Leave us,' she said to the scribe, who scrabbled up and ran from the room.

Slowly, Narses rose from his chair, 'Mistress?'

'You're right. I did make a gesture. I know you're busy – the Persian negotiations are difficult, the peace impossible to agree. There are problems with the Treasury, the religious arguments rage on. You have far more important things to concern you than twenty-five girl whores. But you were sold to be a eunuch, yes?' Narses nodded and Theodora continued, 'Your parents gave you to this life, you had no choice, and yet you've done well. We both have. Yes, we've both worked – and planned and schemed – to have the lives we now lead—'

'And we continue to plan and scheme,' Narses interrupted.

'True, we can never relax. And I agree with the August that the Empire, his vision of one people, one land, will be good for all of us. But you made me study history and strategy when I first came to the Palace, encouraged me to care about more than just my position, whether or not people bow correctly, remember to call me Mistress ...'

'Unless it suits you to use that as a stick to beat them with?'

'Yes, unless it suits me. The point is, I want to make things better in my City.'

'Because you think you were fated to wear the purple?'

Theodora shook her head. 'Because I'm sick of the idea of fate, of feeling like it's being done to me. If I choose to take what feels like my destiny and turn it into my ...' Theodora stopped, groping for the word.

'Mission?' Narses offered.

'That'll do, my mission – to be Justinian's partner, to use that power – then at least it makes some sense of why I'm here. We need small improvements as well as huge change. I see no point otherwise.'

Two days later Narses told Theodora that he had found an old palace, on the eastern side of the Bosphorus, large enough to accommodate five hundred girls, or women, or whatever his mistress wanted to save next. Builders were engaged to renovate the house, then the first group of girls and a number of women, also ex-whores, were sent over several weeks later. Theodora named the old building Metanoia – Redemption. She was particularly pleased Narses had found a house across the water, Bithynia had always been a favourite area of hers as a working girl, dancing in Menander's company for the pleasure of rich men.

'Good, I love the journey there,' she said to Armeneus

when the girls were safely settled in the house, with religious in attendance. 'Now I have a reason to visit.'

'You're free to travel across the water any time you like, Mistress.'

'Yes, Armeneus,' she answered, 'I'm Augusta, but now that I can travel and do good at the same time, it looks better, don't you think?'

The next day, Theodora and an entourage of over a thousand crossed the Bosphorus in a shining flotilla of glittering boats and, as promised, the scene was truly impressive. The Persian delegation, seated on the raised patios of the Palace overlooking the water, also took note, as they were meant to. The same evening they sent home a messenger to say that perhaps the Empire's finances were not suffering quite as badly as they had been led to believe.

Seven

The day after her return from Bithynia, Theodora rose early and called for Armeneus. By the time he arrived, his robe quickly pulled on, his face still creased from sleep, she was fully dressed, Mariam by her side.

'Mistress?'

'Surely I didn't disturb you? I assume my husband had already called Narses from your bed?'

It suited Theodora that Narses knew she could condemn him at any time for keeping Armeneus as his lover. Given Narses' power in the Palace, anything that gave her a little sway was welcome.

Armeneus sighed but answered his Mistress, taking care to keep his tone light. 'Narses did not sleep, he's been working all night on a letter to Khusro suggesting peace terms.'

'Good idea, I should send one myself.'

'A letter to the Persian king?'

'Why not? They have wives in Persia, don't they?'

'I believe so.'

'Good. We'll do it tomorrow, we're going out today.'

'We?'

'Apparently it's too dangerous for the Empress to go into

the City alone, so I'll take you and Mariam with me. A happy family. I'll look less obvious with the pair of you alongside. You'll need a warmer robe, and stronger sandals I think, not Palace clothes, nothing too fine. And get a move on, the markets will open soon. I always hated it when it was too crowded.'

Now Armeneus noticed the simplicity of Theodora's shift and saw she had the oldest of her cloaks over her arm.

His heart sank and he shook his head. 'It's not safe, even in disguise. The factions ... there've been fights, flashpoints all over the City for the past few nights.'

'So I heard in Bithynia. And it's exactly what I want to see for myself. If you know where they are, even better. The people rarely speak truth to the Palace: once inside these walls, everyone exaggerates their problems or, worse, they pretend nothing is wrong, obsequious before majesty. My women can tell people I'm bathing or sleeping or something, we can be in the City all day and no one need know.'

'Mistress, I'm sorry, no.'

Theodora moved closer to her friend and servant, emphasising her small stature. Knowing he felt uncomfortable leaning over her, she said, 'And how will you stop me, Armeneus? Tie me up?' She held out her hands, turning her wrists upward the better to suggest submission. He did not move. 'No? Then will you physically hold back the Augusta? I know some say I've all sorts of tricks, from poisoning to witchcraft. What do you think?'

'I think that a girl from the Hippodrome didn't have much power of her own, so any she could conjure up through rumour was probably quite useful. And I think you like the rumours now because they make you seem more powerful. It's occurred to me that you might even have started those rumours yourself.'

'Nice theory. Are you prepared to test it?'

Armeneus sighed and shook his head. 'You know I'm not.'

'Good. Then come on, I'll take Mariam and go out alone if you won't accompany us.'

'It's for your own safety.'

Theodora stared at the young man in front of her. 'You think Theodora-from-the-Brothel doesn't remember what the people can be like? I know things are "difficult", as you so coyly put it. The girls in Metanoia say there's talk of replacing the Emperor. I can just picture Hypatius or Pompeius as puppet-master, and if I can, I'm sure the people can too. It's simple, Armeneus: to whom do you owe your allegiance?'

'We all answer to the Emperor. Who I serve on a day to day basis is not the point.'

'Oh, I think it is,' she replied. 'Didn't Mar say you'll go back to Africa some day? Did he mean you to go this soon? I'm sure it could be arranged.'

Armeneus shook his head. The threat of exile was too great a risk. He went to fetch his cloak.

They followed the paths under the Palace into the deepest level beneath the Hippodrome, walking alongside the Imperial vaults. The City's records were stored here, between old costumes and animal skins, alongside theatre props, ancient armour and weapons, as were Theodora's memories of watching her father train his bears, watching her father killed by the bear he'd loved best. Now she walked swiftly, escorted by Armeneus acting the role of angry Palace official – hurrying the intruding refugee and her child through corridors where they should not have found their way.

Armeneus had no problem working up the semblance of

anger and took great delight in pushing her hard, poking her in the back, until Theodora finally turned on him.

'That's enough fun, eunuch,' she hissed.

After that, he was more gentle in his prodding, but no less aggressive in his tone of voice. Theodora led Armeneus and Mariam up through the corridors beneath the Hippodrome until they came out at the northern entrance, where the four great Greek horses rose up, shining in the morning sun.

'You see these horses?' Theodora said.

'Yes, Mistress,' answered Mariam.

'I don't think I ever passed them in my youth without wanting to climb up and ride them through the city, pulling the whole Hippodrome behind. Now, when no one could stop me doing so if I chose, I have to stop myself.'

Armeneus looked sideways at his mistress, surprised again at the things she missed from her past and those she didn't. He said nothing and they walked on, into the Mese, now choked with traders and salesmen, stallholders and shoppers. Armeneus slipped into the role of quietly solicitous husband shepherding his wife away from any impertinent gaze. Theodora pulled her cloak tighter to hide her face, and they walked out into the Forum of Constantine, Mariam between them, just like any other family new to the City, trying to work out where they were and what came next.

One youth from the Blues called to another; soon there were several standing together. The lads were close to the old triumphal arch, grouped around an elderly man. The first of the Blue youths bent down and whispered something, the old man, grateful, smiling, handed over his basket to the whisperer and took the arm of the second youth. They walked with him for a few paces and then, having exchanged a look over the man's head, the first youth let out a call, the second answered

61

it, and the man was pushed over, his basket emptied in his face, bread and eggs and wine smashing around him on the cobbles. The wine jug cracked into five pieces, one of the shards cut the old man's cheek, and three apples rolled, bruised, into the gutter. From the other side of the Mese, several members of the Greens saw the fuss, took it as a signal to fight and then the old man was forgotten. Knives were pulled, one boy cut another, a second intervened, a third yelped as the blade found his young skin, and the colour then was neither Blue nor Green, but red. It was quickly over, the local police marched several young men off to face charges, while others slipped into the winding side streets that churned away from the Mese, keen to fight another day.

Theodora shivered, watching them go. Her own childhood had spun from rejection by Greens after her father's death, to the welcome embrace of the Blues. She knew the factions to be both fickle and volatile, but when she was a child the partisan fights were over racers or athletes, whose singers and performers were the best, surging chants from one side of the Hippodrome to the other. There had been street battles then too, but there was something about the scene they had just witnessed that felt different, sharper. One young man with a knife beneath his cloak was not new; several young men, each one openly carrying a blade certainly was.

On another street they saw three young soldiers outside a bar, arguing with the owner.

'Boys, go home, you've only just got back from duty, your mothers must be missing you. And be honest, you know you can't afford it.'

'Then run up a tab for us.'

The second, nodding at his friend added, 'We're out there in those fucking mountains, the army can't get us enough armour or weapons, let alone feed us properly, and when we come home you won't even give us a drink.'

'Son,' the bar owner answered, 'I did my time, I was in Sicily, Carthage, and on the Persian border too. At least in the west you could be sure you were winning or losing, but out there in the east?' He shook his head and spat on the ground, 'That war's been going on for ever, there's nothing you lot will do to change it.'

'Damn right, those Persians will never give up,' the third soldier responded, kicking the wall with a dusty foot.

'Nor will Rome, mate,' said the first soldier, his tone cautioning his friend.

If the bar owner had been a military man there was no telling who his friends might be, the young soldiers didn't want to be accused of demoralising troops if this innkeeper happened to tell one of their superior officers.

'Yeah,' the third continued, too impassioned to care what he said or who heard him, 'but at least these old men were paid. Or their families were, when they didn't come back. They treat us like dogs when we're over there and worse when we come home, as if it's our fault the war costs so much, our fault taxes are put up to pay for it.'

The bar owner looked at the three young men before him, frustrated, dirty and angry. Any one of them could easily take him in a fight, but they weren't in fighting mood, they were too tired, too hurt for that.

'All right. But you're only getting the cheap stuff – watered. And leave my barmaid alone, she's lazy enough without you lot distracting her.'

Theodora heard the same everywhere they went, all morning and well into the afternoon. Through the main markets, along the full length of the Mese, in the elegant porticoed shops, in the bar where they finally decided to eat, against the advice of Armeneus, who was worried they'd be noticed if they stopped for any length of time.

'You should have let me buy something for Mariam from the street stalls,' he said, ignoring Mariam's small sound of protest; she was not keen to be used in Armeneus' argument with her mistress.

Theodora waved away his concern, 'Street food would turn a Palace-fed stomach in no time. We'll sit. The customers are drinking, we're eating, you know who'll be doing the talking.'

Theodora winked at Mariam and headed to the back of the room, taking a seat before Armeneus could stop her.

All around they eavesdropped on anger. Even among the drunk old men at the bar, the usual apathy was tempered with bitterness, irritation worming its way into each interaction. They heard housewives complain about the bread distribution and firemen denounce their ward managers, street preachers breaking their usual diatribes against the world to eat a few mouthfuls before beginning again with even more dire warnings of apocalypse to come.

When the plates of mutton stew were brought to their table, Theodora inhaled the aromas of her childhood. Nothing like the expensively spiced food of the Palace, this was solid, warming, workman's food served with fat chunks of day-old bread, all the better for dipping. Nevertheless, Theodora pushed her bowl aside after a few mouthfuls, claiming a headache.

'I'll go outside for some fresh air.'

'Mistress . . .'

'Not so loud, Armeneus. I won't be long.'

'You shouldn't go alone.'

'So you all keep saying,' she answered, 'but I am going out, and you will stay. We can't leave Mariam alone with all these strangers, she's just a girl after all.'

Theodora walked out as Mariam quietly reached for another chunk of bread.

Theodora walked along the harbour-front of the Golden Horn, revelling in the freedom. Even though the sun was close to setting, the City was still hard at work. At one dock, men unloaded a cargo of wine and garum fish sauce from Sicily, goods expected six days ago, the ship delayed by the fierce Mediterranean storms that were predictable only in their unpredictability. The captain stood on deck, the late delivery fee causing him to curse and bribe in equal measure. All along the docks Theodora watched ships unloading grain or spices, cattle or furs, taking on board the traders and merchants heading out again to do new deals.

At the point where the main waterside road turned uphill, winding back towards the centre of the City, to the Hippodrome where she had spent so much of her childhood, Theodora stopped to watch a group of whores. They stood around a brazier counting out their last night's takings. One share for the taxman, another for their landlord, a third share for the young ex-soldier they used as guard and lookout, with not quite enough left for each woman. They stood close to the fire, the eldest of them plainly shivering even though the chill night winds that crossed the Black Sea from the north had only just begun. Theodora knew about the havoc of disease; the girls who worked backstage as actress-whores were protected from the worst illnesses, but most moved on to street work once they were older, and sailors and traders were as likely to leave disease as coin. Most of these women were never fully well, fully warm.

One of them saw Theodora watching and called, 'No work

tonight. The storms last week mean all the ships have been delayed or their goods disturbed. The bosses are keeping their men hard at it.'

Theodora shook her head, wanting to say she wasn't looking for work, but she kept her mouth shut, aware there was no other good reason for being out alone in the City at this time of day.

Another of the women, mistaking Theodora's head-shake for incomprehension, added, 'If the bosses keep them hard at it, there's no time for them to go hard at us – yes?'

The women laughed then, a combination of resignation and tiredness, yet with friendship in their shared, forced jollity. A camaraderie that made Theodora catch her breath.

The eldest nodded. 'You hurry home, girl, and tell your mother to find you a nice husband. Send him to work for you instead, there's too many whores down here as it is.'

Theodora needed to come closer to their group to move past, and as she did so her cloak fell back a little, slipping away from her face.

A young woman took a long look at her, then reached out. Grabbing Theodora's arm, she said, 'I don't know about a husband, but doesn't she look like the Augusta?'

She pulled back Theodora's cloak, fully revealing her face. Theodora jumped, began to wrench her arm away, her mouth already open to call guards, let out a command – but she stopped herself just in time.

The young woman held her more gently now, laughing. 'It's all right love, we're not going to bite. You do look like her though, honest.'

'Taller, isn't she, the Empress?' another woman interrupted, coming closer to peer into Theodora's face.

A third disagreed, leaning a beefy arm across Theodora's shoulder so the Empress caught the smell of the woman's unwashed body and the garlic she had been chewing all day to ward off the pox.

She pulled Theodora closer, ruffling her hair. 'No, it's all that ceremonial stuff they wear gives her height. The Empress was always short, strong, that's why she was such a good acrobat.'

'And everything else acrobatics is useful for,' the second laughed again. 'Can you act?' she asked Theodora. 'There'd be cash in the comedy for a Empress-impressionist! No answer? Scared of us are you, darling?'

Theodora shook her head. Her famous voice would betray her, so she simply stood there with no choice but to allow them to stare, to look at her more fully than anyone outside the Palace had done for years. Any reaction might confirm she was indeed the Empress, and the gossip would be all over the City before midnight. She could just imagine Pasara's glee at the Augusta being found on the dockside, back among her own kind.

The oldest woman pushed the others aside now to get a better look herself. Theodora could taste the fumes from the heavy rose oil she wore on her thinning, wrinkled skin. She smiled broadly at Theodora, revealing a wide mouth with her four front teeth missing.

'You're not pretty but you're young enough –' she put out a hand and grabbed at Theodora's left breast – 'and there's been no baby hanging off this, I can tell.'

Now her smile left her face and she moved in closer, her hand pinching Theodora's breast, fingernails digging in. 'The thing is, girl, there's not enough work as it is.' She removed her hand to pluck at Theodora's cloak with her strong fingers. 'And this tat you've borrowed from your maid's fooling no one. We don't need some fancy bitch down here trying to upset Mummy and Daddy, scare them so they'll let you off marrying whoever they've lined up for you. Take whatever they're offering – he probably is beneath you, but at the moment you should be glad of any man. Now fuck off.'

The woman pushed her, spinning her out of their circle and Theodora stumbled away, their laughter ringing behind her.

As she went the younger woman called out, 'Or there's still a job for you in the theatre – you're a dead match for the Augusta, honest. Unemployed whore plays Palace whore played by ex-whore. Nice.'

The women turned back to the far more pressing reality of their coin count.

Theodora pulled her cloak tighter. The loneliness of her position could not have been made more clear, and the laughing women had exposed a fear she could never shake: the fear that she wasn't in her position as Justinian's love, but as a symbol of so much the Palace needed to placate. Constantinople had always been busy, overcrowded with refugees, with people coming into the City to escape an old life as often as to make a new one. There were the angry religious, keen to set fire to what they saw as the world's domination. Hungry and disaffected troops marching to and from the ghastliness of the Persian border were not new, Blues and Greens would always fight each other. The state knew this as well as anyone, the state benefited from it, had established the factions precisely for this purpose, if the Blues and Greens were fighting each other, they were not fighting their rulers. The City was at the centre of the world, and Theodora could feel the change, she knew it was on the boil.

She led Armeneus and Mariam back to the Palace across the Forum of Constantine and right to the Chalke Gate. No need to hide herself now. As they approached, she threw back her cloak, lifted her head and, in the simple act of changing her bearing, altered her status so utterly it was obvious she was Augusta. It was a trick Armeneus had seen before and one he never grew tired of. She walked through the gate and walked into her position. Back in her office she called for Narses. Theodora understood the friction between the Palace and the people better than most; she had gone out to find reasons for her own unease, and had seen plenty. Justinian, and she as his wife, were in power because the old Emperor Justin had granted them the succession; they stayed in the purple because the people allowed it.

Eight

There was, inevitably, an argument. Narses, furious at being dragged from yet another urgent meeting with his Persian spies, was angrier still when he discovered where Theodora had been while her ladies were repeatedly assuring him she was sleeping, bathing, resting the whole day. The more Narses patronised, the sulkier Theodora became; the angrier she was, the more he lectured. Armeneus watched, aware that he hadn't heard the last of Narses' fury himself, and wishing his lover and his mistress would pay better attention to the matter in hand; while they were busy scoring points off one another, no one was dealing with the unhappiness beyond the Palace walls. Eventually Narses left, their debate at an impasse, and Theodora waited, knowing she would have to face her husband before she was allowed to sleep.

Justinian walked into Theodora's rooms with no announcement and stood in the centre of the Empress's main reception chamber. Servants scattered on the floor around him, no one certain if they were meant to ignore what was going on or scuttle away as quietly as possible.

Theodora knelt immediately.

'You had no right to go out into the City alone,' he said.

'I was not alone.'

'I'm not interested in sophistry, wife.'

'And I am not interested in being treated like a disobedient child, husband.' Theodora looked up. Unable to stand without his permission, she stayed on her knees. 'You need to know what's going on out there, I can tell you ...'

Justinian shook his head. 'I have people to tell me what's going on, I hardly need the Empress to risk her own life and the honour of the purple ...'

'Keep me on my knees if you must, but don't imagine that your Palace-bred lackeys have any idea how it is out there. This lot, for example, who even now don't know if they should get up and leave us, or stay lying on the ground like so many dead ants. Get out! Now!' she shouted, and the half-dozen maids and eunuchs struggled up, heads still bowed, and shuffled from the room on their knees, not wanting to raise themselves higher than their mistress, yet anxious to do her bidding.

Only once the doors were closed did Theodora continue, her voice quieter, but no less determined.

'Your Palace staff are too scared to go anywhere other than the main streets – they think they'll be stabbed if they walk fifty paces either side of the Mese. We used to laugh at them when we were girls, watching them spying on our conversations, as if the chatter of a bunch of Hippodrome tarts might be of use to the Emperor's people.'

'You've always told me that you saw the real world in your nights with those rich men, those private dinners.'

'We did,' Theodora agreed, 'but we weren't stupid enough to talk about the secrets we heard from whore-screwing senators in front of a couple of Palace bores who wouldn't know the difference between backstage gossip and divine truth.'

'So I should fire those young men working for me inside the Persian military? Does everyone know they are spies too?'

'That's different.'

'How so?'

Theodora looked up at Justinian, 'May I sit? I've been trained to stay on my knees for hours, for any number of reasons, but I am Empress now, and no longer as keen to prove my physical supremacy.'

Justinian pointed to a narrow stool and gestured for Mariam to bring it.

'How kind. How comfortable.' Theodora said, sitting down.

'Don't push me, Theodora.'

Justinian's voice was cold and Theodora paused. Her husband usually found it funny, charming even, when she'd overstepped the mark, but clearly he didn't find her charming today. Theodora took time to arrange herself on the stool, layer her robe over her legs, thinking fast. Defiance wasn't working and he'd never believe abject apology; she'd just have to try harder with the truth.

'There's a deep anger on the streets,' she said.

'I'm sure you're right,' Justinian answered, 'which makes it more worrying that you'd put your own safety at risk.'

'What risk? A wife, with her husband and child? They had no idea who I was because they didn't look at me. They saw the image of mother and child and ignored me as they do all mothers.'

'Plenty saw you come back into the Palace.'

'Because I chose them to. I know the people, Justinian, it's one of the reasons Narses and Timothy pushed us together. And sometimes it's good to be with them as people, as ourselves, not as August.'

Her husband laughed then, quietly. 'This from the woman

who insisted on the titles Master and Mistress, that people bow and kiss your foot?'

'I needed to establish my status quickly when we were elevated.'

'You certainly did that.'

'And it's out of respect for the purple I ask them to bow. Not for me.'

Justinian nodded. 'Yes, I believe that is why you do it.'

'It's also from respect for you that I went out today.'

'In respect you broke my rule and in respect you defied my order?'

'That's right.'

Justinian stared at her, shook his head and, standing, turned once, twice, walked away to the far wall, his fists clenched, and then walked right up to Theodora. Leaning over her, raising both his arms, he let out a roar.

For a moment, Justinian shouting, fists clenched, arms raised, Theodora saw all the men who had ever hit her, from her stepfather to Menander, from Hecebolus who had deserted her after she followed him to the Pentapolis in North Africa, to the many men she had whored for and the few men she had loved, all the men except her father and – until now – except Justinian. Theodora sat utterly still, waiting, ready to take whatever was coming. Then, his anger released, Justinian ran his hands through his hair and burst out laughing and Theodora knew she had him back, the husband who trusted her, who cared about her in a way that no one else ever had.

Justinian took her hand, led her to a couch by the window, their view of the water, with gulls crying and distant sailors' calls, caught on the wind, flung back at the City hills.

'Explain,' said Justinian, sitting beside her.

'We could have been any family of travellers. Armeneus is

black-skinned, so they didn't worry about what they said in front of him, and they never care what they say in front of a wife or a girl, we don't matter. A child and a man beside you is the best disguise a woman can have – unnoticed because she's just like all the others.'

'I'd have thought you hated that.'

'I often want to be left alone.'

'Yes, but you wouldn't want to be ignored for long.'

'True,' she agreed, 'not for long.'

They talked on, Theodora sharing what she'd felt in the City, in particular the volatility between Blues and Greens.

'I can't stop the progress now,' Justinian said. 'If we want to restore the Empire, if we want to stop the war with Persia, regain Italy from the Goths, bring the Christ to our neighbours, then I have to allow the Cappadocian to keep on with both tax rises and cost-cutting, I have to make both factions understand I won't tolerate misbehaviour from either side. But you're right, I need to find a way to explain better. I will. Perhaps you should coach me.'

'Teach you to speak from the Kathisma, overlooking the Hippodrome where every Emperor has stood, saying expressly what the people don't want to hear?'

Justinian shook his head, unsure. He kissed Theodora and as he stood up, she pulled him closer to her, whispering, 'I thought you were going to hit me.'

Justinian stared down at his wife, frowning, biting on his full lip. 'I thought I was, too,' he admitted.

Then he turned to go and the two door slaves who had stood silently throughout, studiously not watching the couple, sprang into action for their Emperor.

Theodora could not rest easily that night. Waking after several hours of interrupted sleep, sweating and uncomfortable despite the winter chill of her cool room, heart pounding and head aching, she had no clear memory of the dream that disturbed her, but she knew it had not been good. She called Mariam from her room next door, asking for light. When the shadows finally stopped leaping in the lamplight, Theodora pulled herself from the bed, and reached for the statue of the emerald Virgin that had been her talisman for more than a dozen years. She stayed on her knees for an hour, in the prayer-trance she had learned in the desert outside Alexandria. She prayed to avert trouble, to save lives, to blunt knives and keep sharp tongues still. She prayed against worry and uncertainty and the rising tension outside the Palace walls, and even in the deepest part of her trance she found no ease, just a growing certainty that trouble was coming.

Eventually she went back to bed, allowing Mariam to stroke her forehead with a camomile-soaked cloth while humming the lullaby Theodora had taught the girl when she first came to live in the Palace, the lullaby that was a shared gift between them, soft notes and quiet words. Mariam doused the light and went back to her own bed. Theodora's eyes were closed, and her breathing regular, but she was not sleeping; she acted sleep to allow Mariam to rest. She lay awake until the late winter dawn began to rise beyond the hills of Bithynia hoping – and failing – to hear the owl, her owl, in the dark. She rose unhappy and exhausted. Outside it was raining, the City was dark and cold.

Nine

Constantinople was in Theodora's bones, and although she could not read its mind, she was right to be worried for its body. During the night a small fight had broken out near the Forum Bovis. Quelled by the local street police, apologies were made almost as quickly as offence was given, the handful of young men put away their knives, went home late to their beds and slept better than their Empress. All might have been well if two of them, one Blue, one Green, had not found themselves on the same side of the Mese the following day.

One smiled. 'Sleep well?'

The other bowed. 'Better than your mother, I'm sure.'

'What do you mean?'

'Only that she's offering a good price this morning – a cheaper whore won't be found this side of the Theodosian Walls.'

The first bared his teeth and then his knife. The second's knife was already unsheathed. One lunged, the other was ready, as were friends from both sides. Flesh was bruised, skin was broken, then skin was cut, blood spilled. The postponed fight began again in earnest.

Three hours later, one man was dead, another mortally

injured from a knife wound to his gut, and several more flaunted jagged cuts and bone breaks that would take months to heal and leave lifelong scars. The Blues blamed the Greens; the Greens insisted that not only had the Blues started it, but also that Justinian's favouring of the Blues had finally gone too far. Lawyers and police hurried to meetings in the Palace, the Emperor consulted his advisers. Narses had a quiet word with the City Prefect, Eudaemon.

The next day Eudaemon ordered the release of two dozen young men from both sides, keeping six in custody, three Greens, three Blues. All six were questioned, their actions investigated, two were finally released, and the remaining four – two from each faction – were sentenced to death.

'Death? He can't do that – for fighting?'

A horrified Theodora stormed into Justinian's rooms where he sat with Narses and Belisarius.

The Emperor rubbed his eyes. 'We asked Eudaemon to show that he is dealing evenly with the factions.'

'And this is his answer? A death sentence?'

Belisarius raised an eyebrow, but kept his eyes firmly on the papers before him.

'Mistress,' Narses spoke up, 'Eudaemon is appointed to investigate and rule on these cases. If the Emperor intervenes it will look as if he's trying to save members of his own faction – and yours, I might add. It will appear that he's overriding the Prefect.'

'He should override the Prefect. Blinding, banishment – either or both are perfectly common for murder. This was a street fight, these things happen. No one set out to kill.'

'They were carrying knives,' Narses said.

'And how many men do that on our streets? Women too, sometimes. It doesn't mean they intended to kill.'

'Yet they did,' said Justinian, 'so they must be punished.'

'But hanging? It'll bring the people out on the streets again, they'll come to watch and stay to complain.' Belisarius grinned and Theodora rounded on him. 'You have something to say, soldier?'

Belisarius smiled his charming smile and stood, bowing to his Empress, speaking in his careful, beautifully modulated tone. 'Only that I initially assumed you were concerned for the young men's lives, but of course, Mistress, you're more worried about how it will play out in the City.'

'I'd have thought you'd understand that concern only too well, Belisarius.'

'I hope my master is seen in the best light at all times,' he answered. 'It's one of the reasons I'm careful about my own conduct. I'd never want to bring any hint of shame into the Palace.'

Belisarius spoke lightly, but even so, Theodora heard the accusation in his words.

Narses intervened before she could attack: 'Augusta, I've spoken with Eudaemon. He believes a strong hand now to show he's in control will stop any further passion on the streets. The Prefect is sure this will work. Green and Blue, both on the scaffold, a clear indication of our impartiality.'

Theodora shook her head. 'I suspect it will be a clearer indication of his power. And it's power itself that's angering the people right now.'

Theodora left the men to get back to the Persian peace treaty, heading for her own rooms, and what comfort she could find there. She wanted to go out to her church, the Hagia Sophia she had always run to as a child, creeping in to find quiet; ease in the century-old building, comfort for her aching bones from cool marble and the caress of warm stone steeped in decades of prayer. Instead she dismissed Mariam and knelt at her own small altar, doing her best to ignore the noise and undercurrent of tension in the Palace, shutting out the screaming gulls beyond her window, holding the emerald Virgin to her breast, praying for her city long into the night.

The morning dawned cold and damp and Theodora rose early to pray. Across town in his small apartment right out by the Golden Gate, the City hangman was also up early, sharing his breakfast of honey bread and fried fish with his wife and their three-year-old twins. The man enjoyed the complicated craft of his work, combined with the simplicity of its purpose. Not a full-time executioner – even the ever-swelling population of the City did not warrant a full-time position – he had the family business to deal with in the morning.

'I'll get the deliveries done first.'

'Your brother can't do that?' his wife asked, wary that her husband was too generous for his own good.

'His cough's still bad, a day at home going over the accounts will do him no harm.'

'Even now?' she asked, wiping one boy's face and settling the other more carefully on his stool.

The hangman smiled. 'The Emperor's building boom's been good to us, but that doesn't mean I'm any keener to add up our profits. If the roads aren't too busy, I'll check in at the docks, see if the hemp due in yesterday can't be offloaded today.'

He didn't say, in front of the boys, that he would also go across to Sykae with his most trusted carpenter to check the scaffold and make sure all was well, testing the rope for weight and strength. A quick break for prayer in the monastery next to the scaffold, and then down to business. He would not eat again until the prisoners were cut down and pronounced dead, that was the fast he had instituted for himself, and so he reached now for another piece of bread, an extra fat dollop of mackerel roe for flavour. Even so, he left the bulk of the loaf. He knew his wife would be hungry again soon, she was a little woman with an enormous appetite and their third child was just beginning to show. He kissed her and picked up both of his boys. Holding one under each arm, he squashed them to his chest with a roar and a laugh. Then he pulled on the warmest robe he possessed, inherited from his father who had walked the shore every day, summer and winter. The hangman went out to do a good day's work.

Theodora knelt at her small altar all morning. She accepted the cup Mariam offered, drank two mouthfuls of water; no wine, no bread. She continued to pray.

Justinian and Narses had worked through the night. They took the breakfast brought to them and ate while looking through their plans. All that was needed now was for this tremor of unrest to be settled. Hopefully, Eudaemon's hangings would do just that, and then the forward momentum could begin again.

Belisarius came to their meeting a little late. He'd spent much of the night with Mundus, the two generals strategising potential scenarios, discussing lieutenants and troops, each variable dependent on the adversary. Both soldiers well understood that true wisdom, the kind that allowed a man to trust his own split-second judgement even when it was weighted with the fate of thousands of soldiers, came only from experience, but their training encouraged them also to plan for possibilities, and Belisarius knew no man so skilled at making up outlandish, yet not impossible, situations as his friend Mundus. Nor did he know anyone with such skill in imagining solutions to violence closer to home. Antonina hid her scorn when her young husband came to bed exhausted after a night of war games, and instituted a regime of her own games first thing in the morning. Belisarius was late to his professional duties, but smiling.

At midday Mariam brought Theodora food and drink and the Empress refused both. She prayed on.

By mid-afternoon the hangman's errands were done, his stomach rumbling as he waited by the scaffold for the prisoners. A crowd of onlookers had already gathered, Greens and Blues, some begging for mercy even now, others there to ensure justice was done – no Green to be condemned if a Blue was let off, no Blue to hang where a Green did not.

Ten years ago the present hangman had crossed the Golden Horn to deliver a new rope to the old hangman and, as it was a hot day, he stayed for a cup of wine. The old man had talked about the skill involved in getting everything just right, double-checking the weight of each condemned man to make sure the neck snapped cleanly, ensuring the prisoner died fast and neat. His art was the precision of death, untainted by opinion. The young rope-maker liked the idea of being untainted by opinion. A few months later, taking receipt of another delivery, the older man mentioned he was looking for an apprentice, and the rope-maker jumped at the chance. Working part-time for the hangman was an opportunity to move away, even a little, from a world where the only smell was hemp in his hair, on his skin, in his clothes. The rope-maker-turned-hangman found his vocation on the scaffold in Sykae. There he could smell fear and death, and the life and love he had at home tasted even sweeter. When the old hangman died, the young rope-maker took his place.

Now he stood in front of the prisoners, ready to weigh them up, measure their necks, get the job done, but his stomach was rumbling, then griping, then churning. He left the four condemned young men standing in line, two having wet themselves in terror, one in shock and the last still defiant, still screaming true Blue abuse at the Greens. Leaving the Prefect's guards to keep watch, the hangman ran out to the courtyard and threw up his breakfast, all of last night's meal, and everything else until all that was left was bile and that still coming in a thin, bitter stream. He vomited until he was giddy and then, cursing his appetite and the mackerel and its roe, he went back to the prisoners' holding cell.

The crowd outside were louder now. The hangman began again, measuring the men whose last moments were in his care and he did so with shaking hands, eyes unfocused from the sweat dripping down his brow.

One of the Greens looked at his executioner and laughed, 'Brother, you don't need to do the job if it's making you sick. My friends and I will happily give you the day off.'

He turned to his fellow prisoners for confirmation, getting a weak smile from one, a whimper from another, stoic silence from the last.

The hangman shook his head, 'I do my job, friend. The how and why are not part of it. Sorry.'

'Fair enough,' answered the Green. 'Can't blame a man for trying.'

The hangman smiled gently, used to both the sullenly frightened and the terrified talkers. 'I never do,' he said.

The rope was heavy around the neck, resting on the shoulders. The hangman asked for forgiveness, the prisoner gave it, or not, was crying too much to give it, or spat in his eye in rage, or stood deaf and mute in the silence of shock. The eyes were covered. The rope was tightened, a thick coil of it, forcing the prisoner's chin up, the better to snap the neck more cleanly – that part of the process to be quick, painless if possible, if the interminable build-up, endless anticipation could ever be called painless. For each prisoner every second was as long as his life – and as short. The sentence was read aloud again, as it had been by the Prefect, but now in the hangman's stumbling mutter. Then the prisoner's name was called, a wail wrenched from his wife in the crowd as she fainted, the scuffle as family picked her up, a yell of bitter fury from the prisoner's brother, the sentence progressing anyway, as it always did. The rope tightened, the trapdoor dropped, a neck stretched, the prisoner jerked, his eyes bulging, body straining, one final ejaculation of life, and then the neck bones snapped apart. Done.

Once the first Green was cut down, tension began to rise. Back across the water of the Golden Horn the Palace shone in a cold afternoon sun which would soon set. The whispers began before the hangman raised the second length of rope – the Emperor is Blue, as is his wife, she who was once Green, who the Greens famously denied. Is this a trick? Do the powers-that-be mean to hang only Greens and save the Blues from the noose? A chant formed in the throats of those waiting, ready to break into full voice. Then the second prisoner was brought forward and a moan went up from the Blue side of the crowd. He was theirs. The Greens were briefly satisfied, the Blues downcast. The muttering continued: it had come to this, their own Emperor allowing such brutality, merely to make a show of his impartiality, the state's impartiality. The people were not impartial, they were furious.

The rope was placed around the man's neck, the spectators became more agitated, more uneasy, their cries were louder, loud enough to be heard over in the Palace. The faction leaders shook their heads, reminding each other that the Emperor was more interested in the Empire than the City, in the

Persian border than the lads fighting for it. Hanged for a street fight. Hanged where, often enough, the same crime might have been punished with blinding or exile or loss of land, loss of citizenship. Hanged to shut them up.

The second neck was broken, second wasted seed given up, second man taken down. It was darker now, the winter sun almost set. The crowd were restless, the hangman was sweating, shaking. The hangman's assistant, worried his boss would collapse and leave him to deal with the crowd, suggested they could speed matters through, dispatch both men at once. With one Green and one Blue still to hang, whichever man they dealt with first, an extra few moments of life granted to one and not the other would set off a ruckus. This crowd were difficult enough as it was, the Prefect's men were having a hard time keeping them back from the scaffold. Could they not hang both men at once and be done with it?

The hangman agreed. He preferred to give each man his due, it had been a mark of his career that a condemned man's crimes were given their allotted time, that the victim's family would see the full effect of their reparation, an individual life for an individual life. But his guts were churning, his body streaming sweat, he'd had to run off the scaffold once, he couldn't risk it again; this was the best way, two at once.

Two ropes were raised and the crowd groaned. Two men brought out, made to stand closer than they wanted, than their people wanted: even this near to death the lifelong enmity raged on. The assistant checked the nooses, the hangman made his calculations as to the correct counterweights to use now that there were two waiting to die. The ropes went round the necks, the crowd were screaming, the sun fully set and the square lit by torches. The hangman asked forgiveness, one gave it, the other did not. The men's faces were covered. The hangman and his assistant stepped back, the lever was pulled. And nothing happened. The trapdoor did not fall, the men did not drop, no necks were broken, no lives ended. The hangman adjusted the knot, pulled the nooses tighter around both necks, heavy hemp weighing down condemned shoulders. Hangman and assistant stepped back again, the lever was pulled again, with more force this time, and then the trapdoor fell partially but not completely. Now both men were hanging but still standing on the tips of their toes: they were alive, their necks stretched and burned by the rope, but not broken.

The crowd had had enough. They swarmed up on to the scaffold from the ground, Blues and Greens together. The hangman was sensible enough to leap back down into the scuffle, becoming one of the crowd, and watched his assistant beaten aside by the mass of people. Ropes were cut, hoods removed, condemned men whisked away to asylum in the Church of St Lawrence. No chance to rub their bloody and bruised necks, throats hoarse from near-asphyxiation, they were hurried into small boats and ferried over the water. As factions worked together with monks to cover their tracks, hiding from the Prefect's police, confusing those following them, the rescued men were rushed away. The faction leaders said it was a sign from God, their men had been saved. Natural justice in the form of the hangman's shaking hands had pardoned the remaining men – one from each side, so it could not be considered anything but fair. They should be freed. They would plead their case at the games in three days' time, the Emperor would hear their cause, justice would prevail.

Justinian and Narses held emergency meetings, Tribonian and his advisers studied precedent, John the Cappadocian and Eudaemon the Prefect drank late into the night debating the possibilities. Belisarius and Mundus drilled their troops: always better to be prepared. The hangman went home to his wife, as ashamed as his roiling guts and sweating brow would let him be, stopping every hundred paces to throw up. He crossed the City frightened too – worried that if the men weren't freed the incensed mob might come after him. Right now they praised his accidental pardoning, in another three days they might condemn him for the two dead. He packed up his wife and children and headed out to her family's farm, two days' journey closer to Thrace, just in case.

In the Palace, talks went on late into the night. At their final meeting, both Eudaemon and Tribonian insisted it was not possible to recant now: the condemned men had been tried and sentenced, the law on this was clear. Had there been some sign of intervention, a thunderbolt, a comet perhaps, then maybe they could all agree – as the Green and Blue leaders claimed – that God had intervened; there were times when it was expedient to accommodate the people's fondness for signs and symbols. Unfortunately there were no signs. The hang-man had simply made a mistake in calculating weight, haste had created its usual chaos, and to pretend otherwise would give the faction leaders the upper hand. Public feeling was already running too high, the Palace had to take control, and quickly. The majority of Justinian's counsellors were adamant: the Emperor wanted a return to the glories of old and now was the time to show the strength of old.

'It's the only way, sir,' said the Prefect Eudaemon.

'It's the Roman way, sir,' said the Pagan lawyer Tribonian.

With the volume increasing in the council chamber and the calls for aggression louder, Narses stood up. 'Gentlemen, please, I'd like to suggest another possibility: that we consider clemency at this time.'

'Clemency?' Mundus frowned. 'Not like you. Getting soft in your old age?'

'Finally realising he's a eunuch,' Belisarius muttered, not quite under his breath, but not openly either.

Narses nodded to the generals, both ready to get their men out on the streets at a moment's notice, and went on, 'I understand your enthusiasm for the fight. You've both done so well for us in distant lands, it's only natural you'd want to show your prowess on our own streets, but yes, I believe clemency will help. It will encourage the people to see the August as less removed, more interested in their concerns.'

'They know he's interested in their concerns,' interrupted Sittas.

'They have done,' Narses replied smoothly; 'but just now, they seem to think he cares only for the greater Empire, and it's not Italians or Syrians or Egyptians we have rioting on our streets, it's the people of the City fighting out there. So, if the Emperor chooses to show kindness to his citizens, those closest to his heart, it won't do him any harm.'

Justinian nodded. He took Narses' views seriously and had no appetite for bringing war closer to home. The younger generals weren't so easily persuaded.

'August,' Belisarius said, 'Narses may call it clemency, but there's every chance the people will see it as spineless.'

Mundus stepped in. 'We believe it's a simple matter to stamp out any hint of riot before it even begins. If the monks can't be persuaded to hand over the condemned men, we would choose to storm the Church of St Lawrence, capture the prisoners, carry out the execution there and then, and be done with it.'

'The longer this drags on, the more chance there is for greater disruption.' Belisarius spoke quietly, seriously, for once not flashing his lovely smile, and it was clear most of the soldiers around the table agreed with him.

Theodora whispered to her husband, 'Even if your generals are right, this isn't the time to allow Belisarius to head a show of Rome's strength. You want him to be your emblem ...'

'Not stand for myself?' Justinian interrupted her, his hand over hers, speaking more quietly still in this room full of advisers and counsellors and trusted friends.

'Not your August self, sir.'

Justinian nodded, thinking that while his wife might be too keen to judge the younger man, she also had a point. Things were bad enough, he didn't need to send the golden boy out there in his place. He spoke to the room: 'I'll go to the games tomorrow as planned. I will not speak publicly about this matter, or any other. It's better I don't add my voice to the clamour.'

Belisarius agreed. 'It's certainly wise to be present at the races, show the power of the August.'

Narses added his own thoughts, wanting to soften Belisarius' emphasis on power: 'Further, Master, it's up to your ministers to carry out their tasks using their own best judgement and they've done that. There's no obligation for the August to speak, and doing so when our spies report that the Green and Blue leaders plan to call again for clemency would most likely provoke further debate.'

Narses did not add that although the Emperor spoke well on matters of law and the future, he was a less skilled speaker on more passionate matters, and it was in all their interests for him to remain silent as their figurehead.

Justinian acknowledged his Chief of Staff's tact with a rare smile and Narses went on, 'Above all, it's important to show you are Emperor of Rome in both title and action. If you disallow the Prefect's judgement it might be interpreted as suggesting the Emperor is higher than the law.'

'We'll send out an edict stating the August will ensure Roman justice is done, for the sake of those killed in the riot,' said Tribonian, making notes as he spoke.

'And for their victims' families,' Theodora spoke up.

'Yes,' Justinian replied, 'for their families and, not least, for Christian law.'

'Nicely put,' Narses sighed, not reassured, but pleased a decision had been made.

'Good, then we'll enjoy the games tomorrow,' Justinian said. Ending the meeting, he sent his advisers to get what little sleep they could, while he returned to his rooms to read. Theodora prayed through the night once more.

Ten

The cold day meant thicker cloaks, deeper purple. The August couple walked the distance from the Emperor's rooms to the Kathisma in silence. Theodora had never yet walked this corridor beside Justinian without wondering if this would be the day when the public rose up and, instead of adoring the girl who had risen so high, brought her crashing down. She knew better than most how fickle the people could be. This morning, for the first time in ten years by his side, her fear was for her husband.

The heavy doors were opened and they emerged to the contained force of thirty thousand bodies gathered in one space. Justinian held his wife's hand and gave his greetings to the crowd, who responded more quietly than either had expected, politely showing due deference. Perhaps all would be well.

The Emperor and Empress took their seats. The Kathisma was draped simply in purple, Theodora had advised there should be no added gold for glory, no greenery for celebration. The Emperor's envoys had spoken with the faction chiefs, making it clear that the Prefect's justice would be carried out as soon as possible, and the Imperial couple knew this news would already be all round the Hippodrome, the crowd talking of little else. As agreed the night before, Justinian would not speak about what was going on at the Church of St Lawrence, the frightened and damaged men inside, the Prefect's guards outside. The people had chosen to make the two men the focus of their complaint. Justinian's silence would confirm the impending execution, but the Palace hoped it would do so without implying he was in favour of the execution and aggravating the situation. The Imperial couple were silent and solemn. Theodora thought they no doubt suited the dull sky above.

Before the first races began, the Blue and Green leaders came forward out of the tense hush of the waiting crowd. They spoke together, requesting politely, and in formal language, that the Emperor rescind Eudaemon's ruling. The Mandator looked to the Emperor: his role was to speak for the August when the August chose not to speak for himself. The crowd were silent. Theodora felt their waiting in the air, on her skin, and knew Justinian felt it too. After a very brief pause, Justinian turned from the faction leaders to the Mandator and gave the signal for the games to begin. The Mandator made his usual cry, the racers readied themselves. The public, crammed in even tighter than usual, made no secret of their displeasure, and the games began.

The same process continued throughout the day. At regular intervals the faction leaders came forward and offered their respectful plea to the Emperor; at regular intervals, each time with the same pause, Justinian behaved as if he had not heard them.

The races went on, Blues and Greens chanting for their own men, their own racers. Their call of 'Nika', of victory, for a Blue winner or a Green winner no less vociferous than any other day, but Theodora heard another tone in the cries, a warning in the way the word swirled around the Hippodrome, as if the resounding 'Nika – Green!' or 'Nika – Blue!' was to do with more than the race just won. As the twentieth race approached she finally began to feel her heart slow a little, stretched her fingers to loosen the tension that had been building for hours. Their day in the Kathisma was nearly done. All might be well.

At the twenty-second race, just two contests from the end of the day, the cry changed. For the first time in her life, a life in and of the Hippodrome, Theodora heard the cry of Nika given, not to one side or the other, but to both. The Blues called Nika to their eternal opponents the Greens. The Greens called Nika to the Blues. The warring factions were one, chanting Nika in unison.

'Long life to the Blues!' the Greens shouted.

'Victory to the Greens!' answered the Blues.

Nika to and for the benevolent, humane, victorious Greens and the Blues. Together.

Justinian looked shocked, but Theodora interpreted their call only too well, hissing at her husband, 'Stand up, we're leaving. Now.'

He turned to her, almost a smile on his lips, bemused and astonished. Theodora had seen this look all too often on the faces of her audience: now was not the time for the Emperor of Rome to explode in wild cathartic laughter, and she stood, then knelt as quickly as possible, so she didn't seem to be lead-ing her husband. The action brought him to his senses. Justinian rose with her, turned away from his people and left the Kathisma. Theodora followed a step behind, pushing him from beneath her robe.

A roar rose from the crowd at their backs, a jeering, hys-terical, thrilled, 'Nika! Nika! Nika!'

The final races were cancelled and the crowd streamed out of the Hippodrome into the streets of the City, a wild, excited, unified people.

Narses, already waiting in the chill of the Kathisma corridor, led the Imperial couple away. No one spoke until they were safely in Justinian's private office. Theodora dismissed the waiting servants, poured her husband's wine, passed it to him, noted his shaking hands and forced him to swallow half the glass before she let him speak.

'What was that?' asked Justinian.

Theodora shook her head, impossible to answer without saying this was exactly what she had feared.

'Do we free the prisoners? Give in to the crowd?'

Narses answered, 'Sir, we can't.'

This time Theodora couldn't keep silent, 'We could have.'

'Yes, Mistress,' Narses retorted, impatiently, 'we could have, but we didn't.'

'And now it's too late?' Justinian asked, though even as he did, he knew it was a statement not a question.

'If we give them what they ask now, we'll seem weak,' said Narses. 'If you countermand Eudaemon's order, they'll say you're taking the law into your own hands.'

'I am August.'

'Yes sir, and this is Green and Blue together, looking for excuses to riot. They'd as soon turn on the August for going against the agreed form of decision-making, as attack Eudaemon for refusing them.'

Theodora looked up, impressed and a little horrified by Narses' reasoning. 'And it's safer for us if they take their fury to the Prefect?' she said.

'It is. They'll take their anger out on the Prefect's Palace – no doubt they'll free a few prisoners, or many more. It's not the first time we've had a riot in the City, it won't be the last. This is what the people do: they shout, they fight, then they get drunk, screw each other and go home to sleep it off. There are more games tomorrow, by which time their hangovers will have them back to flinging insults at each other.'

Justinian looked at his two most trusted advisers. 'Is Narses right?' he asked Theodora.

Theodora frowned. 'I'm not even sure he knows if he's right, for once. None of us have seen the factions like this before. But yes, I agree it's too late for you to rescind the Prefect's order. With the people in this mood, it's vital the August appears to be upholding the rule of law, I just don't ...'

Her speech faltered. All three stood, listening. The sound of running anger was clear from beyond the Palace wall.

'What?' Justinian prompted her.

Theodora shook her head, her skin chilled. The frustration that her opinion had been dismissed until now threatened tears that pricked at the back of her eyes. 'I don't think they'll burn themselves out tonight.'

Theodora was right. The rioters, without each other to attack, turned on the City itself. The amorphous mob, mottled blue and green, went first to find Eudaemon. They broke into the Praetorium, killing the half-dozen officers who offered resistance, welcoming those who agreed to join with them – a one-sided agreement given in return for their lives – and freeing ecstatic prisoners. The Prefect himself was nowhere to be found, having fled the building the moment news of the conjoined cry of Nika reached him. His absence did nothing to calm the crowd and within another hour the Praetorium was on fire. Next, wheeling around towards the seat of Empire itself, moving as one and at speed, the rioters attacked the Chalke, the famous, inviolable, almost sacred gate to the Imperial Palace. The Chalke guards were no more than ceremonial figures, chosen these days for their good bodies and good looks, posted at the grand entrance to look splendid in their uniforms and make the finest impression on new arrivals to the City, princes and refugees alike. Faced with a flame-hungry mob, these boys who were not yet men simply melted away; those who did not live in the Palace ditched the most distinctive parts of their uniform and joined the crowd, preferring to be swallowed up than spat out. The Chalke and its massive bronze doors were burned down. The mob, and the wind now guiding it, then rounded on the Senate House. Easy here to demand justice and find no answer – the senators were long gone. The people offered fire to their absent leaders and were richly rewarded. The cold January darkness turned hot and yellow-bright.

Theodora stayed on her knees in vigil all night before her private altar, with Mariam and Ana sitting beside her. Theodora prayed for the rioters' safety as much as she prayed for those inside the Palace walls, and prayed most fiercely for her City. She knew only too well that for all its stone and marble and golden glory, the City was easily broken. To maintain its place as the jewel of the Empire, it was necessary that the people wanted it to shine: tonight they wanted it in flames. In the early hours of the morning Antonina joined them. She prayed for the baby only she knew she was carrying and for her husband's safety. The command had not yet been given, but surely would, and then Belisarius would go out into the streets, determined to bring order to chaos, and she knew he'd be glad to do so. Antonina had given her body up to this child for her husband's sake; she hoped he was not about to give his up for the state.

As Theodora prayed she heard the constant drum of feet

running through corridors and echoing in passageways, urgent messages brought in from beyond the walls. Every now and then she turned from the emerald Virgin in her hand so that a servant could whisper the latest development. Just before dawn she was told the flames had taken hold in the Senate and then the Mese; what must burn next was inevitable – child of the City, she knew the geography of her home only too well and had to see it for herself. She left the women and went alone outside. The night air was thick with smoke and the screaming laughter of the rioters.

Theodora walked through courtyards of the Palace that were now deep orange with reflected flame. Close to the north wall there was an old pear tree; she hadn't known she was heading for it as she walked, but some part of her realised she needed to climb, to be up high, to see better, just as she had as a child, as an acrobat, climbing trees, walls and aqueducts, craving the best vantage point. Now she climbed the tree that must have been here since Emperor Anastasius' time or longer, knowing it would show her what she did not want to see.

Theodora did not cry as the Church of Hagia Sophia burned. She did not cry as she heard the crowd yelling and whooping in joy when the heavy wooden doors began to scorch and warp. She did not cry when the flame-heated alabaster windows finally cracked and then shattered. She cried only when she heard, above the roaring flame, a breaking and then a falling, when she heard – or imagined she heard – the women's gallery crash down to the centre of the church below. She shed her tears then, not for the church that was falling, not for the building itself, or even for the souls of those who had set the fire, damned as they certainly were, but for the only place of safety she had known as a child, for the only place, other than centre-stage, she had ever felt able to be truly herself. She cried for the child Theodora and the girl Theodora and the young woman Theodora. High up in this tree which she had climbed like a fearless child, she sobbed for the City she loved and the people she now hated. Shocking herself, having never imagined she could be anything but one of them, with them, Theodora despised the people who laid low her City. That hate confirmed her home was now inside the Palace walls, and then she cried even harder.

Eleven

Early on Wednesday morning, after a night of fear and fury, Justinian again met with Theodora and his advisers. This time there was no disagreement about what to do; there was no other option – they would follow form. They would go to the games, again, as usual. The races would be held. Theodora suggested that more entertainments between events might be useful. She would speak to Sophia, ask the performers for their suggestions. If the crowd were in the mood for some crown-mocking, then perhaps a short and sweet piece in praise of misrule would be useful. It wasn't certain that this would assuage the mob, but they must be exhausted, and, perhaps, regretful of last night's actions now they could see the state of the central City in the cold, smoky daylight. Narses was about to detail the night's losses when he saw Theodora's face and put away his list. There would be time to deal with this later: for now they had to present a united front to the people. The Emperor and Empress must show themselves with all their staff and the strength of the Palace backing them. Narses did not add, or need to, that many of those staff would be fully armed and all would be constantly watchful.

*

Justinian and Theodora walked to the Kathisma, both shaky from worry and lack of sleep. Theodora had sent out a messenger to find Sophia and he returned saying she was neither in her apartment nor in the rehearsal rooms beneath the Hippodrome. Theodora knew Sophia had many friends who could hide her if her public friendship with the Empress caused any trouble, as well as plenty of rich old men with huge estates outside the City if things became too dangerous on the street.

Justinian leaned towards his wife and said, 'Sophia will send word from Bithynia or Chalcedon tomorrow, I'm sure. She's probably been over the water since last night, watching the flames and just as concerned for you.'

Theodora kissed her husband's hand. They both knew he might be right, or not. Just as they both knew that when she assured him the crowd would be quieter today, tired after last night, she was voicing a hope rather than a truth. The doors were opened again and they walked out to discover exactly what the day would bring.

More of the same, and worse. The races were abandoned before they'd even begun: the performers Theodora had directed when Sophia was not to be found were booed off before they started. This time the Green and Blue leaders stood together, speaking in formal Latin; both were native Greek speakers and had clearly worked hard on their speech. They called for the release of the two men who had survived hanging, and then added to their demands: Eudaemon must go, and Tribonian, and the Cappadocian. A massive cheer rose up from the crowd at the last demand. Throughout it all, even the crowd's insistence that John the Cappadocian be sacked, Theodora stood monumentally still and patient beside her husband, who was himself stoic and silent. Mannequins in purple, they remained impassive until the first of the wooden seats were set on fire. The crowd cheered the August's retreat and then surged back into the streets, setting fire to the Baths of Zeuxippus as they went. No senators were inside; any still keen on discussing the City's business were doing so in hillside homes far from the action. The mob weren't in the mood for murder yet. This was just an attack on the City's structure, its form. Exactly what the Palace was afraid of.

Narses joined them and Theodora led the way back into the Palace, pleading with Justinian, her voice a furious whisper. 'This can't go on, they'll bring the City down – their City.'

'You think I should give in?'

'On this occasion, yes,' she replied. 'It's gone too far, God knows where those prisoners are now anyway.'

'We have information . . .' Narses spoke up.

Theodora dismissed his offer with a wave of her hand as she turned down the last corridor to the council chamber, practically running to get there. 'It doesn't matter, they don't matter. The City is burning. Freeing the prisoners – assuming they are still in the church . . .'

'They aren't,' Narses interrupted.

'Even if,' Theodora continued, one arm out to stop the slave already opening the doors for her, the other hand raised to silence Narses as she hissed out the rest of her warning, 'even if they were raised high in the Hippodrome so all could see they were safe and free, it's too late. This is not about those men any more, it's about us, about the Palace. It has always been about the Palace.'

'I'm sure you're right.' Justinian spoke quietly now.

'Good. So do what they ask, get rid of Eudaemon, Tribonian and the Cappadocian.' Theodora was angry and upset, still in shock from the response of the crowd a few moments earlier, and keen to get into the chamber to begin making the changes demanded. Even so, a sly smile began at the corners of her mouth, her eyes glinting in the corridor's half-light. 'I'll tell the Cappadocian myself, if you like?'

'Thank you, no. I'll do my job, you do yours.'

Theodora smiled more openly now, and answered, 'With pleasure.'

Then Narses leaned over her shoulder to add, 'Mistress? That means getting out of the August's way so he can enter the room first.'

The slaves opened the doors. Justinian led the way, his wife a pace behind, befitting her rank. Not that anyone waiting for them noticed. As soon as Justinian entered the room, the shouting began. After a very peremptory falling to the ground, the feet-kissing was dispensed with in a single gesture by Belisarius, which Theodora saw as ostentatious and Justinian considered quite thoughtful given the current state of affairs.

This choice August. Sack the Cappadocian. Don't fire Tribonian. Fire Tribonian, but keep the Cappadocian. Use Eudaemon as your speaker, let the people regain their faith in the Prefect. Get rid of the Prefect, keep the others. Keep them all. Fire them all.

'Fire them all.'

This last from Theodora, when the counsellors had finally stopped shouting, seemingly realising, as one, that it was inappropriate to yell their demands at the August. She waited until Narses had given up trying to take notes. She waited until Belisarius had retired to the back of the room, furious and trying not to show his anger when Justinian dismissed his suggestion that he and Mundus take their troops out to pick off the ringleaders, make an example of them, summary and bloody justice being Belisarius' preferred option for stopping the riot in its tracks. She waited until the room was silent.

'Dismiss them. All three,' Theodora repeated, adding the number to make sure everyone knew what she meant.

Tribonian and the Cappadocian were in the room. The former looked up at the Empress, horrified. He knew she could be irritated when he took her husband from her, but he'd thought she agreed with their work, not least because she had personally benefited from legal changes, many of which he'd had a hand in drafting.

He put his hand to his mouth almost immediately, but his surprise found its way into the silent room anyway. 'Mistress?'

'The people want scapegoats, Tribonian. You and the Prefect are ideal for the job, the Cappadocian too.'

Theodora did not look at the treasurer, who was glaring at her from the other end of the room.

'Of course the Empress must say as she believes,' John the Cappadocian said, 'and she knows the people better than most of us here, but I urge—'

Theodora stopped him with a look. 'Shut up, Cappadocian, I may well be saving your life.' She turned to Justinian as several of the advisers found a way to cough or stutter away their laughter: 'Sack all three, make a public announcement, from the Kathisma. They're exhausted out there, they'll want to stop this, I'm sure. Many will be as heartbroken as we are over the loss of the church and the Baths. The seats from the stands, generations of boys who've taken knives to carve their names on the underside, all burned away – it's their history they're destroying and they know it. They've been awake for three days and nights. Give them what they want. It will give you time to take back what you need – the City as well as the people.'

Justinian watched his wife, considering. Belisarius was already with her, as was Narses.

'And then?' Justinian asked.

'If we're lucky ...' Theodora shrugged and said no more, her palms open, silently begging her husband.

'They'll go home.' Belisarius finished for his mistress, just a little irritated that her plan meant he had no reason to call out the full force of his men.

'And August,' Narses added, 'once things are calm again, you can quietly reinstate your servants. The Cappadocian, Tribonian—'

'Not the Prefect, they won't allow that,' Theodora interrupted.

'No, Mistress, they won't. But in time, with a peaceful City, they will allow the Emperor's most trusted and experienced advisers to re-take their places. That is what you meant, I believe, Augusta?'

Narses looked at Theodora. She knew he had her best interests at heart, had warned her often enough of the danger of opening her mouth in front of those she didn't trust, men exactly like the Cappadocian.

She nodded. 'That's right, Narses. The Emperor fires them, and then he hires them. After a time.'

Belisarius and Mundus counselled caution. They were happier to put their faith in action than in words, but agreed this plan would work for the moment — they could charge out with their men later if needed. Tribonian accepted the judgement calmly; he would continue with his work on the Emperor's legal reforms, and would simply do so from a smaller and unofficial office. A message was sent to Eudaemon, hiding in Bithynia, that he should consider heading even further east. And the Cappadocian eventually knelt before the Emperor and agreed to do as he was asked. It was noted he did not kneel directly to Theodora.

Two other men added their agreement: the brothers Hypatius and Pompeius, grand-nephews of the old Emperor Anastasius, the August of Theodora's childhood. It was likely the people would soon start calling more forcefully for a new Emperor. Ana's father-in-law Probus, concerned about this himself, had left the City two days earlier; if he wasn't around to be chosen by the people, he couldn't be condemned for treason either. Hypatius and Pompeius had stayed on, they had roles in government and any absence would be easily noted. Justinian had taken care of Hypatius and Pompeius, given them good jobs as he had done with all those who might threaten his claim to the purple, and both men understood that safety lay in supporting whoever was in charge. Right now Justinian was law, barely. They gave their full backing to the plan.

With everyone agreed, a messenger was sent to the Blue and Green leaders, telling them Justinian would again appear before the people, this time to grant their wish; he would sack all three of the ministers the people blamed for their unhappiness. It was not necessary to spell out that everyone in the council chamber hoped it would stop the people blaming the Emperor.

Twelve

Justinian returned to the Kathisma late that evening. Blues and Greens stood together as if they had never done anything else, and greeted his declaration with cheers and catcalls. The jeers that rang out from the back of the crowd weren't for the Emperor, though Justinian didn't stay in the Kathisma long enough to make sure, they were for the faction leaders, and they came from those who saw this as their chance to demand still more, take more than had been offered.

After the announcement, people streamed out of the arena, through streets of upturned carts and burnt-out shops, picking their way between ancient statues that had toppled into the Mese. Some of the more stringent of Constantinople's Christians had used the cover of riot to pull down the old statues to the ancient gods, and while there were plenty still standing, enough had fallen to make a point. Theodora was right: most people were tired and, pleased with Justinian's announcement, they headed away, either home to wash and sleep, or down to the bars along the harbour where they knew they could eat and drink for many hours yet. No one quite felt it was all over, but a concession had been made, there was time to take a breath; the faction chiefs would go to the Palace in the morning and begin more formal discussions with Justinian's councillors. Change was on its way, if not quite fast enough for some. Chiefs from both factions went into another meeting; some possibilities had been mentioned, there were new demands, new names, to be considered. Nothing was settled yet.

Among those jeering the Emperor's announcement was a group of five youths, a mix of Blues and Greens. Like their leaders, they came from the outlying suburbs of the City, and had enjoyed running free through streets usually patrolled by the Prefect's men or by police forces of their own factions. Not yet ready to go home, they watched the old men move off to discuss the newly whispered idea that a figurehead should be put up, someone to depose Justinian himself, but the business of bargaining meant nothing to them. They were out for a laugh, and it was too early for bed.

Rufus and Nikolaos led the others out of the Hippodrome, through the Nekra Gate. All five were on edge from three days on the streets, returning to their homes only to take a little food and then run away from scolding fathers and worried mothers. The youths would never have been together in normal circumstances. Rufus, Otto and Lucan were Blues, two brothers and an old friend, Nikolaos and Titus were Green cousins; they had come together when they found themselves part of the mob attacking the Chalke. Shouting and pushing among mostly older men, the boys had stepped back from the main group when hammering against the stone of the building turned to actually setting fire to the doors. The majority of those attacking were current or ex-soldiers: they knew what they were doing and they worked as a band, even though they were strangers. The boys were only there for the excitement, to be part of something bigger than themselves; they were still scared of the authorities, worried they might be seen and noted from the sentry boxes, their names given up to Palace officials – or worse, in Rufus' case, his fist-happy fireman father.

It was true that Otto, Rufus' little brother, had sometimes shown too much enjoyment on their occasional excursions into the City's grain silos, where they would catch feral cats and then roll them down the Fourth Hill in barrels. And Nikolaos' cousin Titus certainly seemed to have left a secret behind in Dacia, something shared only between the two boys' mothers. Rufus was sure there was a girl back home carrying Titus' bastard, but Nikolaos liked to tease that it was more likely to be a Dacian lad he'd left behind. These were the kind of boys to skip lessons, tease sisters; boys who might, perhaps, have visited a whore or two, though only the eldest would have been brave enough to follow her into a bed. They were not bad boys.

With most of the shops and bars closed in the Forum of Constantine, they went further afield, to a place Lucan knew from his sailor uncle, just off the Forum Bovis, but were quickly sent packing by a trio of whores who'd had enough of youths invading their usually quiet local and wanted a night off, definitely no men. Doubly rejected, they made their way through a narrow alley up towards a dingy little bar near the Church of St Polyeuktos. They failed here too, the Blue owner – and his Blue clientele – had decided not to drop their grudge against the Greens. The owner came out from behind his bar and looked them up and down.

'Varus' boys? Blue, yes?'

Rufus nodded, his arm around his brother. Lucan edged closer to Nikolaos and Titus, suddenly aware of the hush in the dark, low-ceilinged room, and the number of silent men around the tables.

'But those two,' the bar owner spat on the floor by the cousins, still staring at Rufus, 'have the haircut of Green men, am I right?'

Rufus nodded again, slower this time.

The barman shook his head and several of the men at tables stood up. 'What the fuck's it coming to? Our old church burned down, and our lads – our own Blue lads – wandering around with these Green cunts like they belong together.' He came closer to Rufus now, and leaned right into the boy's face, whispering, 'You do not belong together. Rome has always run on factions and it wants to stay that way.' Rufus could smell the rough wine on the man's breath, saw up close the fat scar down his left cheek, felt a heavy and calloused finger jabbing his collarbone with every word as the man repeated, 'You – do – not – belong – together. Got it?'

Rufus nodded, pulled Otto closer, took a quick step back and then all five of them were off down the street, terrified boys, not men, scared and shaking and angrier than they'd ever been. Angrier still at the sound of laughter and cheers that followed them, stumbling as they ran over stones and vicious shards of marble, alabaster, stumbling over the broken City.

It was fear that set the boys running, but it was anger that led them to set the fire. Anger at the old men and the middle-aged men, at the rich men running the City and the poor men who, for no reason but age, believed they had the right to tell five boys what to do. There were others who would have approved of them as they ran; visionaries who hoped that all Roman youth might work together for the wider Empire, who believed it possible to overcome the factional desires the

108

state had both promoted and decried, religious who wished that the divide was between the faithful and the unbelieving, not the Blue and the Green.

The boys came to a halt, panting, eyes streaming with tears from running against the cold night wind and, possibly in Nikolaos' case and definitely in Titus', spilling out in very real fear.

'Fuck them,' Titus declared now, quickly running a hand over his face so that sweat and tears mingled. 'Fuck those old men. We can do what we like. The whole City can do what the fuck it likes.'

'Yes,' Rufus shouted, an arm around each of the Green cousins. 'We don't have to buy any of their lies, we can make a new City, burn this one down and start again.'

'Mate,' Lucan interrupted, 'the burning's already started.'

'It has,' Rufus agreed, 'but it's not been started by us, not yet.'

The other four looked at him. He was smiling and it was a smile they had not seen before. It was a smile that was exciting and frightening and very tempting. Then, after a look that passed simultaneously between all five of them, Lucan let out a piercing scream and Rufus joined him. Nikolaos and Titus began to whoop, to jeer, and Otto, silent until now, and perhaps angrier than the others because of his greater fear, opened his mouth and shouted a call to action:

'Let's burn the fucking walls down!'

They tried to. Otto had meant the Palace walls and all four of the other boys understood this was his intention. In a city of walls, old, new, Constantine, Theodosian, it was only the Palace enclosure that still seemed a challenge. There were plenty of smouldering beams close enough. There was the cordoned-off mess of Hagia Sophia, dangerously hot, despite the water poured by the combined force of Green and Blue firemen. There were the soggy, steaming ruins of the Baths of Zeuxippus, the waters of the Baths no challenge to the flaming torches thrown by the rioters. They ran around for over an hour, dodging cordons, skipping under them in Otto's case, but every cinder they tried was knocked from their hands by their seniors, no fonder of the Palace than the boys, but not keen on further loss either. Riot might breed riot, anger give birth to hot fury, but a razed city would be no good to anyone, whoever stood in the Kathisma. The faction leaders had been very clear in their instructions to their subordinates – no more fire.

At last the boys gave up their attempt on the Palace itself and moved on, tiring, but not sated. And so, when they rounded the corner from the burnt-out hollow that had once been Hagia Sophia, when they saw the Church of St Eirene, still standing, unguarded, open, alone, it took a moment before one of them – Otto again – saw it as a target rather than simply a dark church in a darker night.

The boys were too young to worry about attacking a symbol of the faith, too angry to care that this was the oldest church in the city. They were also too angry to notice how close it was to the old hospital, or that the wind had changed. What had been a cold wind coming directly over the Black Sea from the north, was now a milder sea breeze from the east. A breeze that would turn a fire, set against the church walls, from a quick flare to fast flame, then whip that fire around and throw it at the hospital walls.

Four hours later, the first church of Constantinople had been razed – and the Hospital of Samson was destroyed too: patients burned in their beds, the nuns and monks who worked there horrifically injured as they tried to carry the sick from the collapsing building, or burned to death alongside patients they would not leave.

'Fuck,' Otto said, tears in his voice and then on his cheeks.

'Yeah,' the four friends echoed, heads and hands shaking, 'fuck.'

Thirteen

The deaths of the innocent sick, as well as the loss of the City's first church, pushed even the peacemakers inside the Palace beyond breaking point. At the same moment as the Green and Blue leaders were gathering outside Probus' empty home to ask him to accept the title of August in Justinian's place, Belisarius and Mundus were riding out with their own troops against the rioters. Belisarius' men were Goths, Mundus' troops were Herules. Neither Goth nor Herule had any great love for the City or its people. Despite the success of their kings in the west, the Goth soldiers were accustomed to arrogance from the Constantinopolitans, and the Herules were considered uncouth savages; fierce warriors yes, but not Romans, not citizens. The two generals led teams of men who had fought for the Empire but had never felt accepted or appreciated by its citizens, and their readiness was as cold as the iron they prepared to wield.

Unfortunately the first opposition they met was neither a group of angry young men, nor a passionate and political mingling of Blues and Greens, but five monks from the ruined Hagia Sophia, processing down a crowded street, carrying the few relics they had scavenged from the burning church: three saints' skulls, a holy femur, a scrap of cloth miraculously untouched by flame. The monks swayed as they walked, exhausted and grieving over the desecration of their churches and blessed relics. They did not mean to walk straight into the soldiers, and the soldiers tried to give them a wide berth, but the road was narrower than usual, and as debris left by rioters in the preceding nights cut off access routes there was nowhere for either group to go but forward into each other. Armed soldiers headed straight into a small group of monks, followed not by rioters but by the praying faithful as the monks held the sacred relics aloft. Heads cooled for a moment, hearts stopped, priest looked into soldier's eye, priest blinked. There was a second when all might have been well. And then that second passed.

Blood in the Mese, screams echoing from the remains of the Chalke Gate, armed troops and rock-wielding youths clashed in the Forum of Constantine. A girl, pushed out of the way into a Mese shopfront, watched as a Goth soldier reached down from his horse and kicked her brother in the head, one, two, three kicks before he was down on the ground and cold. An old man, rammed up against the Palace wall, was searched for weapons, and smacked in the face anyway when his pockets revealed nothing but a thin leather bag of feathers he had collected from the ground on the day his wife died and carried with him for fifteen years. The old man watched now as those feathers were scattered into the cold morning air, and he crumpled down the stone wall, losing his beloved all over again. A child screamed as she was separated from a foolish mother who'd thought perhaps the markets might be trading today, and had ventured out to try to fill a pan that had remained empty for two days. A young boy was trampled. A man stabbed. A soldier battered to death by an angry mob in one dark corner of the City, and in retaliation a girl was pulled from her home in the next street and raped by four soldiers chanting the name of their dead comrade as they broke her, teaching her to hate them.

By midday, Constantinople was boiling, and by mid-afternoon the women of the City were out on the street, pulled from kitchens and back rooms by the screams of their daughters and the blood of their sons. Fighting off the Goth and Herule mercenaries, they were almost angry enough to spit at Belisarius too. Almost, not quite, and the golden soldier understood that retreat was the better part of that day's valour — fighting the City's women could only end in disgrace. Belisarius sent a messenger to Mundus just five narrow streets away, the messenger returned with agreement; the two generals and their men bled back into the Palace.

Theodora slammed into Justinian's main office, ignoring the advisers with their books and folios open, clamouring that their master consider one plan over another, this solution instead of that.

'Women are out in the streets now. Fighting. You have to do something, say something.'

Justinian nodded. 'I know. We're doing our best.'

He indicated Belisarius and Mundus, both of them still half-armed, covered in the grime and gore of the morning's battle, Narses taking notes as they caught their breath and threw down the first food and drink they'd had all day. Belisarius broke off from explaining the paths they had taken to look over at the Empress. A grin broke out on his tired face.

'There's nothing to smile about, General,' Theodora said.

'Of course not, Mistress. It's just, you're so worried the women are fighting, when you are yourself ... well ...'

'Angry?'

Now Belisarius stood up straight, shoved his glass into the hands of a startled servant, pushed Narses out of the way and, bowing to Theodora, spoke quietly. 'We are all angry, Mistress. Things have not gone well today, not at all, so if you have a solution for the August, then I suggest you make it, and quickly.'

With that he walked from the room, with no bow to his Emperor, no permission to be dismissed.

The room was silent, waiting for Theodora's reaction. She stared at the door he had left swinging with his exit; slowly she exhaled, and turned back to her husband.

A look passed between them and then Justinian said quietly, 'Belisarius is tired, Augusta.'

'Apparently so.'

For two long days the Palace waited. Narses' spies kept him informed about what was going on within the individual factions and what their leaders were planning together. A delegation from both Green and Blue had gone to Pompeius suggesting that either he, or his brother Hypatius, take the August's place and rule with the factions' support. Pompeius, the better speaker, had managed to fob off the faction leaders while promising nothing, and as soon as they had gone he reported the conversation to the Palace. Hypatius was a less skilled politician than his brother; when asked if he would take the rioters' side he fumbled his reply to the leaders, unable to refuse their request outright. He wanted to stay on their good side, but on the other hand, he was loyal to Justinian and the very thought of leading the Palace, trying to bring order to the current chaos, filled him with dread. Both great-nephews of Anastasius turned down the offer, but only Pompeius reported his meetings to Narses. Hypatius was embarrassed even to mention he had been approached. His silence was noted.

Narses sat quietly with the Emperor and Empress late on the Saturday night. After the street fighting and brutality of Thursday things had stayed quiet. At Theodora's suggestion, Justinian was preparing to appear in the Kathisma on Sunday morning: he would carry the Gospel and stand before his people, a penitent. All three listened carefully as Narses' spy recounted the rebel leaders' discussions with Hypatius and Pompeius.

When the spy left the room, Narses asked, 'What do you think about Hypatius, August?'

'He would never accept their offer,' said Justinian, 'he knows he couldn't lead, doesn't want to.'

Theodora agreed. 'Even so, it might be useful for us to have someone to cast as a rebel leader?'

'How so?' Justinian asked.

'We have the superior power; the generals are with us, the army is too, for now. In the long run, if we hold, the rioters will be overcome. The people are unhappy – this is the tantrum that comes every dozen years or so. But it will pass, and when they are sober, when they are themselves, they will remember they love the City.'

Narses picked up from her: 'And when that calm comes we'll need to make a reckoning.'

'Apportion blame?' Justinian asked.

'Yes,' Narses answered.

'The Palace cannot condemn the majority of the City,' said Justinian.

'No,' Theodora said, 'but it could condemn a rebel leader, however reluctant.'

Justinian looked from his wife to his chief adviser, glad for their support, their faith in him and in his rule. And he felt a little sorry for Hypatius.

Sunday morning. It was cold, colder than it had been all week. Justinian and Theodora again walked along the corridor to the Kathisma. The Emperor was plainly dressed, a simple purple wool, no gold embroidery to pick out his status, and the warmth of the torches lighting the dark corridor made little difference to the chill in his body, down his spine; the ice that had settled on his chest seemed to have bled into his feet and his hands.

Theodora waited as her husband went out to face the people alone, to show them the Gospel he held, to offer an amnesty to the rioters in return for peace in the City, to call on all good men to do the right thing. And through the heavy doors she listened as the crowd responded, mocking his attempts at piety, at peace.

'Why trust you now?'

'We know you and your uncle conspired against Vitalian.'

'How do we know this is not another plot?'

Justinian was given no chance to refute the old rumour before another call came. And another, and another.

The shouting became jeering, and the jeering became braying. The bar-room joke where the Greek version of Justinian's name sounded a little like the word for donkey had been a good laugh for years now. The August himself had used the joke to his own advantage when he'd publicly called himself a stubborn Slav while explaining how forcefully he would protect the Empire. At the time, with his wife by his side, on a warm spring day, he had been applauded for doing so. Now there was no applause and the force of the cheers greeting Justinian's exit was as ferocious a sound as any Theodora had heard in the Hippodrome.

*

Justinian walked silently back into the Palace. Once he was in the main body of the building he was all quiet urgency, dictating commands as he went.

'Hypatius and Pompeius are to leave the Palace immediately. Send them back to their own homes. Any senators still within the walls, whether working for us or waiting out the riots, are also to leave. Send Narses to my office and call Belisarius. Now.'

The messages were delivered, counsellors gathered.

Hypatius begged to stay. He too had heard the crowd, knew there were calls for him to take the August's purple; he neither wanted it, nor wanted to be an Imperial scapegoat. But the servant carrying the message and the guards accompanying him were clear: Hypatius must leave. Having been so publicly rejected by the people, Justinian needed only the most trustworthy around him. He limited himself to slaves, servants, and his closest allies – Theodora, Narses, Belisarius, Mundus, and a handful of less publicly recognised advisers. He kept Germanus close too.

'Germanus has only ever shown himself loyal to me, to Rome,' he said, in response to Theodora's uncertain look. 'He doesn't want to be August, he likes being a soldier.'

'He might have persuaded you of that, but Pasara still has high hopes for him – he hasn't managed to convince his wife.'

'No. Sometimes wives take too much convincing.'

Justinian left her and went to speak with his men.

The Emperor and his advisers talked urgently, considering both attack and exit strategies. Occasional short bursts of argument over one strategy or another were followed by quieter, more formal discussions, interrupted just once by a burst of laughter from the men, with much back-slapping and head-shaking, and then a return to street maps and charts, discussion, planning.

Theodora sat with her women in an adjoining room, chosen for their waiting because it was comfortable, and because the windows faced the outer courtyards and the Bosphorus, not the Palace walls and the rioting beyond. And because, if the worst came to the worst, there was a pathway from the patio leading directly to the small, private Palace harbour. Ana and Mariam sewed silently side by side, neither young woman interested in what she was sewing but both happier to do something with their hands than nothing. Comito sat with her daughter Indaro. In the last season of her pregnancy, Comito's concern for Sittas, away on the Danube frontier, had lessened as each passing day suggested there was more to fear here at home. Antonina, newly pregnant but no less concerned for her future, placed herself with a clear view of the men through the folded-back doors, trying to judge from her husband's stance and attitude what he might be thinking – whether he really was as supportive of the Emperor as he said, or whether they'd both be better off somewhere else right now.

Of Theodora's close circle, only Sophia was not with them and the Empress missed her friend. Sophia would have made things feel more easy, she would have been joking at the men's expense, mocking their inability to stamp down a bunch of Green and Blue idiots, and Theodora knew the anger she'd have provoked in the men would have been a welcome distraction. But no one had seen Sophia for three days, not since the fire that brought down the hospital. Theodora hoped her friend was long gone, entertaining other exiles who were also waiting it out, ready to return when someone finally stood in the Kathisma with the people's blessing, whoever he might be. Theodora, who would have been happy to be with her old friend, shook her head again at the turns of fortune that had brought her so high and now threatened to take it all away, in violence and fire. And then, with the others, she sat down to wait.

Fourteen

The crowd were in the mood for a new Emperor. After the Kathisma doors had closed on Justinian, the Gospel in his white-knuckled hands, the bulk of the crowd laughed and relaxed for a while in the mess that was now the Hippodrome; they had made their point. Finally, the calm after the morning's Emperor-baiting turned again to agitation, and a carefully orchestrated cry went up from one end of the arena and was echoed at the other. The call was for a new August. The faction leaders congratulated themselves on the authentic tones of the actors they had employed: but the words only needed to be heard once before they were the crowd's new call and the sole cause of the day. As one, they streamed through the gates and out into the City, massing first at the Forum of Constantine, and then charging on through the chaos in the streets. The Green leader's men led them to Pompeius, whose villa with its famous three-directional sea view was closest of all the likely candidates' homes. When they found the house empty, the mob ransacked it anyway, and then, taking their cue from the Blue leader this time, ran on to find Hypatius.

Knowing what the people wanted, but without his

brother's stronger sense of foreboding, Hypatius came to his own door. He told the leaders politely and quietly he could not accept their commission, he did not want to usurp Justinian, he was not the man for them. The crowd were not persuaded, the faction leaders accepted no refusal, and two hours later Hypatius was hoisted up from the body of the Hippodrome and into the Kathisma, a laurel on his head, his robes in disarray, terrified of the Palace guards just two heavy doors behind him, and just as frightened of the mob proclaiming him August.

Even as he was lifted to the Kathisma, Hypatius grabbed hold of a Palace servant and whispered urgently to the boy, ordering him to run to Justinian and tell his master, their master, that Hypatius was still loyal to the August.

'Explain that I will stand here only to placate the people. I do not want the purple. Tell the Emperor I said so.'

The servant nodded, but as he made his way round to the staff passageway he noted that Hypatius placed the laurel more securely on his own head, that he waved back almost in time with the crowd chanting his name, that he seemed to smile as the people applauded him, shouting Nika again. Nika – their own victory, Nika – Hypatius's new crown, Nika – Justinian's downfall.

The men and women at either end of the adjoining rooms heard the stillness and then the cheers. A look passed from Antonina to Belisarius, another between Justinian and his wife. A loud cry from the Hippodrome, a second, a third, and then, in the silence of the room, it was easy to reckon the speed of news. Running feet were heard in a distant hallway, then on the stone floor of a corridor, then the polished wood of the passage outside. There was the sound of a guard questioning a messenger, a muffled answer, and finally the doors were carefully opened. The guards holding the doors stood aloof and still; they were not worried, whatever happened, their jobs were secure. No matter who held the title of August, their concern was for Palace protocol.

Narses nodded, the doors were closed. Two people, a messenger and a young servant, approached. The servant headed for Narses, the other made for Theodora who, alone of everyone present, was not surprised he wanted to speak to her. The messenger wore the colours of the City theatre company. Theodora and Comito felt bile rise in their throats.

The young man dropped to his knees and kissed the foot Theodora offered. Both acted out protocol, politeness, both without thinking and then, trained in conveying all news in the same measured tone, the same careful speech of state, he began.

'Mistress, I am charged with informing you—'

'Sophia is dead?'

Comito spoke and Theodora was grateful she had not been forced to say the words herself, the news the sisters had been dreading, even as they half expected it. All Theodora's imagining of Sophia safe from harm, Sophia across the water, had been to protect herself from what she already felt to be truth. Sophia was dead and had been for some days: it did not take a theatre messenger to tell her what she knew in her gut, had known in the dreams she avoided by refusing to sleep. The Empress let the young man speak anyway, she knew he must have been rehearsing the whole time he'd run through the bloody and broken city. He deserved the chance to deliver his big speech.

'We heard she was in the Church of St Eirene. Or near it, perhaps.'

Theodora nodded, there was a quiet bar around the back of the Eirene, they'd often been there in the old days, members only, drinks given half price to old theatre stars this boy could never have known, a membership made up solely of actresses and soldiers.

'She must have left the church. Two people reported seeing her near the hospital. She had a young man with her, a soldier or a rioter, we're not sure. He was wounded, she was taking him to the hospital.'

Theodora whispered under her breath to Comito who was now standing at her side, 'Stupid bitch had probably sent him into shock, she always liked to fuck in a storm.'

'She was trampled, Mistress,' the messenger continued, 'in front of the hospital steps. She was bringing the soldier in, when too many others were trying to get out. And the fire . . . there were carts, horses bringing water.'

Theodora suddenly knew what he was trying to tell her: 'There is no body?'

'There is a body,' he replied, not looking up, 'but it is . . . she is . . .' and here he lapsed into a messier, less formal Greek as he explained that the woman he knew the Empress loved, the woman he and all his fellow theatre apprentices adored both as mentor and star, had not only been broken, but dismembered when she was run over by a chariot, racing to or from the fire and the chaos, no one knew which. They had brought her broken body back to the Palace.

While Theodora took in the news about Sophia, the servant who had brought Hypatius' message was trying to speak to Narses, but Narses was busy watching his mistress and pushed the nervous servant away, told him to wait. Then, when Theodora fell to her knees, all her women falling at the same time – whether to comfort her or simply because they were not permitted to stand while the Empress knelt – Narses was too busy trying to read Justinian's reaction to his wife's collapse to listen to the servant muttering about Hypatius. The riot had entered the room, leaked into the one place they'd felt safe.

The Empress was sobbing silently, her body rocking, her face contorted as she tried, and failed, to hold in her grief, to maintain the composure of her rank. Her pregnant sister raged against City, state, and people alike. Ana and Indaro fell wailing to the floor, Mariam holding them both, and then, in the middle of it all, as the women wept and the men rushed to hold them, the rumble that had been growing outside became louder still, seemed to bounce off the walls and into the Palace itself. It was the sound of the people calling Nika, calling Hypatius for Emperor, acclaiming their own victory.

Justinian looked at his wife, his rock, heartbroken. He saw his men bewildered; Belisarius all for action, Germanus still against. He turned, at last, to Narses for an answer and when, for once, he was offered none, the old eunuch as uncertain as the Emperor, Justinian made his decision.

'Call a boat, for the Empress and myself. For all of us. We'll go to the Augusta's estate in Bithynia. The people do not want us dead, they want change. We'll give them change. We will leave.'

He looked around at the shocked advisers, some relieved the August had finally made a choice, others horrified it was the choice to run, still others delighted, glad to finally get away. The Emperor clapped his hands and people sprang into action.

Action that stopped almost immediately. The Empress, speaking from the floor, from the mess of purple silk she twisted in her hands, lifted her head just high enough to say:

'We are going nowhere.'

Theodora pulled herself up, her women stumbling to their

feet with her. Slowly she walked to Justinian, becoming steadier with every step. She pulled him close, far closer than they usually stood in public, and spoke quietly to him.

'I apologise, sir. Do you remember, after the coronation, when we wept together? I promised you I would never show my distress so openly again. You told me we were August, that we must give the role its due respect, we agreed we would keep any fear, any upset, only for each other, you remember?'

Justinian nodded.

'You said then, Master, that the purple was bigger than either of us.'

'I did,' he agreed. 'It is.'

'Then we cannot run from it.'

Turning to the whole room, the Palace guards awaiting orders, the generals ready to fight or to flee, their only job to do the August's command, to Narses and Armeneus pushing the fearful servant from the room, and turning also to her women, who were still crying but more quietly now, Theodora spoke, specifically to Justinian, and through him to them all.

'I am your Empress, sir. I stand in the purple beside you, here with your men, your advisers, your generals. I know it has been said that too often I speak where a woman should remain silent. It may be inappropriate, but this crisis does not call for what is appropriate, it calls for what is right.'

Her voice was quiet and calm, and while they could plainly hear the growing chant of Nika outside, everyone in the room was drawn to Theodora's words. They moved closer and she went on.

'I will give you my opinion –' there were several raised eyebrows at this, but not a word to stop her, and she continued: 'this is not the time to flee. Even if perfect safety were to welcome us with open arms on the other shore, we should not run. We know it is impossible for anyone living to escape death in the end. And we know it is impossible for an Emperor to become an exile.'

She turned as she spoke, so that now she stood beside her husband, facing the generals and the guards who had come together, around their women, and she switched from Latin to a more impassioned Greek to add, 'You've all listened to me before now, and trusted me – sometimes. I've helped you understand the people, and have been useful in that, I hope. But I am more than the young woman who came to the Palace eleven years ago. I am married, anointed, crowned. I wear the purple. And I will not be separated from it. I will never be called anything but Mistress.'

She took her husband's hand, speaking quietly again, as if only to him, but turning out to the room, ensuring everyone could hear: 'Master, if you truly mean to leave, go to our harbour. We have gold, coin, there is a world that will receive you. But who will you be, if you go? There is an old saying – purple makes the perfect burial shroud.' Then Theodora turned back to stand before Justinian, whispering so that only he could hear her, 'I intend to wear it until I die.'

Fifteen

The day turned on Theodora's speech.

Justinian agreed. His wife's words, flowing from Greek to Latin and back again convinced him. This was the way she spoke to him privately, the way they spoke to each other, using the language, the words, that best conveyed the deepest, clearest meaning. She rarely spoke this way in public: for years Theodora had schooled herself to show disagreement with her husband only when it was in both their interests to do so, when it was useful for the people to assume that one or other of the Imperial couple were on their side. If they could not have both, then most would be satisfied with August or Augusta speaking for them.

Theodora had missed the stage, but she had not missed its intrusions. Showing her private self here, in the very centre of government, was a huge risk. Justinian knew this, was grateful to her for it, and heard her words as the challenge they were. He stood beside her and now seemed to fill his purple robe where a moment before he had appeared diminished by it. Those men present who had, like their master, contemplated running away, were shamed into action. Those who had been aching to fight all day,

Belisarius in particular, were grateful for the spur to begin final preparations.

Narses' assistants were sent out to judge the current state of affairs and quickly returned to report that Pompeius had now joined Hypatius in the Imperial Gallery, they were protected by a group of Palace guards who had turned against Justinian. The two brothers were waiting to be welcomed by the crowds massing in the Hippodrome. Narses heard this, grimly pleased he hadn't taken Hypatius' earlier reassurances seriously, all too aware that had they paid attention to that communiqué, rather than to the messenger who'd brought the news of Sophia's death, they might be preparing for exile instead of readying themselves for a decisive battle with the rebels. There were one or two in the chamber who queried if there might not be clemency yet. Narses dismissed their concerns with a fist smacked against his open palm and a quick retort.

'The people demanded the dismissal of senior government figures, and even when we met their demands they kept on with their aggression, firing our churches and burning the sick in their hospital beds. The Augusta has reminded us of our strength. Mercy is not an option.'

Narses sent out a group of eunuchs to go among the people in the Hippodrome and the many still swarming around the gates and remind them of centuries-old factional divisions. To Greens they would acknowledge the long-standing Green affiliations of Hypatius' family, undermining Blue confidence in Hypatius as August; to Blues they were to offer bribes, generous sums that would recall the continued support Justinian's regime had given the Blues. They would point out that the Emperor's family had always been Blue, and that the child Theodora, along with her newly widowed mother and sisters, had been cruelly rejected by the Greens when they most needed help. Would the Blues do the same now that she was their Empress, begging support?

The eunuchs, given an hour among the people, did their best work, starting with a whisper here, a mutter there, then a faked fight.

'My master Hypatius' wrath will be bitter if we cannot persuade the people to back the Emperor,' said one of the eunuchs.

'Your master is a fraud,' the other answered. 'Everyone knows Hypatius is with the people and only pretending to back the Emperor to fool the court.'

It was an old tactic, acting out the wider issues between just two protagonists, forcing the people closest to think more clearly about why they were there – and then in came the rest of the eunuchs with coin and promises, pulling fine threads of dissent and confusion among the crowd. Though the majority still clamoured for Hypatius, and while the rumbling chant of Nika continued, sparking from one section of the Hippodrome to another, the eunuchs returned to the Palace to report a real sense of frustration among the people, alongside a growing irritation that Hypatius had not been made ruler more quickly.

While the eunuchs worked the crowd, Narses directed two very different operations. First he ensured that the Palace guards loyal to Justinian – and there were many more since the Emperor had reasserted his strength – took over from those who had sided with Hypatius. It was a simple matter of sending in men who could act a little, well enough to convince their over-excited friends that since most of the guards were now prepared to stand with Hypatius and Pompeius, they could take the waiting in shifts. Soon enough it would be time to follow the new leader through to the Kathisma, bringing him out to the people, where he would be lauded and welcomed. As the earlier shift happily left the Imperial Gallery, each guard was silently slaughtered, his throat skilfully cut within a dozen steps of the door. In no time a pile of bodies lay at one end of the long corridor to the gallery, while every man inside the room – with the exception of Hypatius and Pompeius – was true to Justinian.

With Hypatius and Pompeius unaware they were now under guard, and the first stirrings of dissent and mistrust among the rebels gathered in the Hippodrome, it was time for the second phase. Belisarius and Mundus led their men out from the Palace and around the Hippodrome. They entered through two different gates – Belisarius and his Goths used the gate usually reserved for chariots, Mundus and the Herules came through the Nekra Gate. Most of the people inside were readying to crown their new Emperor, congratulating themselves on the task achieved. Many were sitting back; days of rioting had brought them here, and now they waited among the broken seats and burnt stages of the damaged arena. Not one had any idea what was coming.

It took a few moments for those in the centre of the vast space to realise something was wrong, a little longer to understand they were in danger. Full awareness of their terrible predicament came only when other bodies smashed into them. It took screams and full-throated, quickly-throttled cries. It took the smell of fresh blood, the sound of snapping bones, the stink of men losing control of bladder and bowel. There was a human stampede to the gates – but the gates were blocked by Belisarius and Mundus and their soldiers. They were currently in use for entry only.

In the Imperial Gallery, Hypatius and Pompeius heard the screaming outside and rushed to the doors to find themselves locked in with men who no longer behaved like guards, men who were suddenly, and quite obviously, gaolers.

Justinian and Narses waited. Their work would come when the bloodletting was done.

In one of the small Palace chapels, Theodora and Comito carefully washed Sophia's shattered body, while Ana cried for the woman who had been more mother to her than Theodora, and Mariam and Indaro kept up a prayer chant on their knees. When the fierce north wind whipped the screams from the Hippodrome in through the chapel windows, the women shivered in the candlelight.

Theodora spoke as she stroked her old friend's bruised and broken face: 'Comito, if the baby you're carrying is a girl, you will call her Sophia.'

And her sister, washing the cold, bloodied feet, said, 'Yes.'

Just three hours later, Theodora stood beside Justinian, looking down into the Hippodrome from the Kathisma. They were not wearing the purple, neither stood there to be presented to the people, there were no torch lights to pick them out, illuminate their status. They stood back a little, in the shadows, wanting to see and wanting not to see. Mundus estimated twenty thousand dead, Belisarius believed the total would rise higher through the night as the piled-up bodies were moved to reveal more beneath.

'A capacity crowd.' Theodora's voice was less than a whisper.

'What?' Justinian was finding it hard to take in what he saw.

'Thirty thousand. When the arena is full to capacity, for the big races, the big festivals, there's not really room for a proper show. The most we can offer them is a few speeches, a poem. They used to go down well with a full house, the old poems.'

She sighed, rubbed her eyes with her hands and her palms came away wet.

Justinian was looking at her, waiting for her to help him make sense of what had happened.

'I dreamed this, years ago,' she said, 'I dreamed the Hippodrome full of blood.'

'What came next?'

Theodora shook her head. 'I woke up, woke myself up. It was too awful.'

'It is too awful,' her husband agreed.

'And it's done.'

'But not finished.'

'Hypatius and Pompeius?'

Justinian nodded, frowning. 'I would let them leave, if I could. They could go into exile. I believe Hypatius, the message he sent. I believe he meant to hold the purple for us.'

'Yes, he probably did, but it's too late now. We took our stand, Justinian. We stood up to the rioters, we had to, they wouldn't stop. Until this . . .' she gestured out to the arena where exhausted soldiers were already moving among the bodies, ordering slaves, beginning the work of clearing the ground. 'They burned down half the City, the Baths, the Senate, Hagia Sophia . . . Sophia . . .'

Theodora started to cry again.

Justinian reached for his wife, pulled her close to him, turning her face from the carnage below. 'We'll build it again. And better. We'll bring them with us, they'll want to rebuild, it'll be our City, theirs and ours, the people and the purple.'

Even in her distress, Theodora smiled, shaking her head. 'Nice phrasing.'

Justinian frowned, chewing on his bottom lip. 'Sorry. But it would be the right thing to do, yes?'

Theodora shrugged. 'I suppose so.' Her energy was too low, her grief too powerful for any other response.

'And I'll rebuild Hagia Sophia, for you, I promise. It will be a monument and a symbol into the future. It will be astonishing.'

'Will it bring back my friend?'

Justinian kissed the top of her head. 'No.'

'No,' Theodora said. She shook herself, stood straight again. 'Then we should get on with it.' She looked down into the arena, then out across the still-smouldering City. 'But there's clearing to be done first, we'll need to lay the foundations well. Hypatius and Pompeius must go.'

All through the night, mothers, wives and lovers searched among the bodies for their husbands, their brothers and sons. The tens of thousands dead were Blue and Green, Church and state, Roman and Barbarian. There were even women, corpses of those who had decided to join their rioting brothers, women who had trespassed on the Hippodrome's arena and had paid for that trespass with their lives. It was said that neither Belisarius nor Mundus would have allowed their troops to kill a woman, even in battle – not in the City itself, not Roman women – but the men they commanded were not Roman, and locals did not expect such niceties from Goths and Herules. The soldiers themselves said the women were more likely to have been crushed in the stampede when the fighting broke out, and it was clear when dawn finally came that if many of the rioters had been killed by the sword, just as many had been broken underfoot; whether by soldiers under Imperial command or by the flailing terror of others trying to escape, it was impossible to say. The riots that burned and scoured the City found their end in the crucible of the sand-covered, blood-covered arena.

*

As citizens and slaves picked their way through a cold morning of reclamation and burial, the brothers Hypatius and Pompeius were condemned to death. Neither Justinian nor Theodora usually favoured execution; Theodora had spoken eloquently for the alternative of banishment in the past, but this was not an ordinary time. Anastasius' great-nephews did not fight their case, there was no point. They were led silently from the great chamber and hanged with the minimum of fuss and no spectators, their bodies thrown into the sea, the better to stop their graves becoming places of attraction for any remaining dissent. Their land and goods were, of course, confiscated, though Justinian let it be known their families could expect the return of the properties – most of them, at least – in a year or so.

Narses laid out the plans for the future. 'Everything will be done with the best attention to form, and to order. No corners cut, no jubilation shown in victory. I want no glorying on our part, nothing to give them any reason to rise again. This is not a Triumph. There will be services in whichever of the churches are unharmed, and the Emperor and Empress will attend as many as possible – we want them out among the people. They'll dispense alms to the hardest-hit areas, we already have temporary shelter going up for the newly homeless. As for the Senate, they'll meet wherever they can, we'll resume normal City and State business immediately. The delegates will be back to negotiating peace with Persia before spring. There was a moment of wavering. It's over: now we move on. I have no intention of losing this momentum.'

He did not say it was Justinian's wavering, his fear, they had all shared in, or that Theodora had pulled them back from terror and flight. He did not need to.

*

For the next two months Narses worked Justinian and Theodora tirelessly, sending them out on an endless round of local pilgrimages, visits to the sick and injured. Justinian attended public discussions about the best way to rebuild, Theodora was seen more often than ever, praying with her reformed women, praying with her sister, or with Mariam and Ana, praying at the newly cleared site of the old Hagia Sophia. The people did not need to know she prayed in bitterness and hate as often as she found charity or compassion, nor did they need to know that she and Justinian were already commissioning architects to rebuild the old church, not just as a monument to God, but as a monument to their reign – something that would stand for ever for the two of them, no matter the inconsistencies of the people.

Theodora said to Narses, 'The people are the same whether viewed from the Kathisma or the stage: they say they prefer to love the generous prince, but everyone most enjoys jeering the wicked king. They've had their say. Now we'll get on with the job.'

'The Emperor is still angry, Mistress.'

'Yes, but he knows an angry ruler looks ugly on our coins, and there are better ways to show our power. He's fallen out of love with the people, which makes the purple more attractive to him. But we need the people to like the look of it as well, and so we smile.'

'And you, Mistress? What about your love for the people?'

Theodora looked at Narses and shook her head; she would not put words to the sting of betrayal she felt.

In his role as Chief of Staff, Narses cloaked the Imperial couple's sharpened energy in even greater ritual and an elaborate playing out of the prescribed court and Church calendar. The ceremonial looked good, and gave the people confidence in the rulers they believed they had allowed to stay in charge. It was only behind closed doors that Theodora permitted herself to weep for her lost friend, to despise those who had taken Sophia from her. When Comito gave birth, Theodora was by her side, holding her sister's hand throughout. And when she held the tiny Sophia for the first time, still bloody, not yet bawling, and pulled the caul from her face to allow the child her first breath, she promised herself she would be a real mother to this baby.

Sixteen

Three days before the Easter festival Justinian stood in the Kathisma. Again he held the Gospel, this time with Theodora by his side, and now they were cheered by the crowd. It was a small crowd, admittedly: the building work in the Hippodrome meant that most of the bench seats had to be replaced, and even those delighted to see the Imperial couple back in place were well aware of the blood that had soaked into the ground in winter. By the time of the City's own festival in mid-spring many of the worst-hit areas had been cleared for rebuilding, and work had started on the Baths and the Senate. Several new statues had been erected where those of the old gods had been torn down. Also in piety, the religious advisers in Justinian's office began a campaign hoping to bring both sides of the Chalcedonian split together, united against the Arian heretics.

Hurrying in opposite directions, Narses and Armeneus met in a corridor. The procession of a saint's holy thigh-bone down in the courtyard below was a reason to stop by a window and stand together for a moment.

'If we're lucky this anger against the Arians will narrow the Chalcedonian division a little,' said Narses.

'The Arians are rebelling?'

'They are not. But the people will think a war waged merely to return Carthage to the map of Rome is too costly. If we tell them we're fighting Gelimer and his Arian Vandals, or the Arian Goths in Italy, and if they worry that those Arian heretics would force us to believe as they do ...'

'Then they're happier to pay.'

'Much happier,' Narses agreed.

The men touched hands then, carefully, and parted. The work of rebuilding the City and the Emperor's reputation was too demanding to allow them any longer together.

Throughout the long hot summer that followed, Justinian and Narses continued their negotiations with the various Persian delegations, consulting their own spies, both among the Persian military and from deep inside Khusro's court. They had no doubt Khusro was doing exactly the same, though since Hypatius' body had finally washed ashore, there was a sense that those who might previously have been tempted to sell information to the Persians should be more worried about their own future than anything they could earn from the enemy. Justinian also picked up his work on The Digest again, to bring all Roman laws together. Tribonian continued assisting him. He did so with no title and no official payment, but given that the alternative was exile, the Pagan lawyer was happy enough.

After the rebellion Theodora had more influence in the Palace than ever before. Justinian and many others were clear that the Empress had not only saved their skins when she persuaded her husband to stay with the purple, but she might have saved the Empire as well. Had they caved in and allowed Hypatius to become August, the Sassanid rulers of Persia would have seen it as their opportunity to try those borders even more fiercely, just as the Vandals now threatened in Carthage. There were many who now saw Theodora as the ruler to watch. So when she called for Sophia, her sister handed the baby over. It was not much of a hardship, Comito had raised Indaro and cared for Ana, she had done so while maintaining a successful singing career, supporting their mother and stepfather and the five step-brats until their mother's death. If Theodora now wanted to play mama, she was welcome to it. In her mid-thirties, with no work but to attend her sister first, and her husband second, Comito was happy to put herself in third place – not her new child.

One late summer morning, seeing the now heavily pregnant Pasara struggle to rise from her deep bow, in a room full of people sticky with heat and bad-tempered already, well before noon, Theodora was surprised to find herself feeling compassion for the woman. She supposed the grief she felt for Sophia or the tenderness for her namesake baby must explain it, and leaned down to help. The younger woman shook off her hand.

'You seemed uncomfortable, cousin,' Theodora said quietly.

'Oh no, Empress,' Pasara answered, both hands holding her belly now, her eyes locked on Theodora's, 'it's Justin here who was uncomfortable.'

'You're naming the child Justin?'

'Why not? He'll be related to the old Emperor after all, Germanus was Justin's nephew, just as, through my own family line, we are related to the Emperor Anastasius.'

'I know who your relatives are, Pasara.'

'Then you know how fully noble my son will be.'

'Assuming it is a boy.'

Pasara shrugged. 'Even if I give birth to a daughter, at least she'll be of the purple from the inside out.'

Theodora leaned in closer, her voice quieter still. 'As opposed to?'

'From the outside in, of course, Mistress. The purple will not be a cloak used to cover and to hide. But still,' she said, smiling lightly, 'I'm sure it is a boy. Now, if you'll excuse me, I should rest.'

Theodora nodded permission for her to leave, aware that reports of the Empress physically attacking a pregnant woman might not sound very promising to the newly placated people, but when she heard Pasara's final, half-whispered remark as she left the room, she wished she had slapped her, and publicly.

'After all, exhaustion might cause any kind of deformity. Just imagine if my child was born a dwarf!'

Pasara's ladies giggled and shushed her as they swept from the room, and Theodora whispered to Comito who stood closest, 'Do you think the people would understand if I smacked the arrogant cow in the face? They loved Sophia almost as much as I did.'

Comito nodded. 'I'm sure it'd be fine as long as you avoid kicking her in the belly. It's not the baby's fault its mother is a bitch.'

Theodora shook her head and with gentle concern in her voice, spoke up to the room of interested women: 'Pasara's concerned about her child's health. Given the heat this year, I'm sure she does need rest, it will be better for them both if she goes nowhere at all.'

Mariam leaned forward to whisper, 'Mistress, there are Germanus' birthday celebrations next week, a procession's been arranged to his house in Bithynia, it's far more pleasant over there, less building work, less dust . . .'

'Yes, it is.' Theodora cut her off. 'Still, I'll have to insist Pasara doesn't leave her room for at least the rest of the summer. If she's worried about deformity, then it's better she runs no risk of exposing the child to dirt and dust. I'm sure we can find someone to entertain Germanus in Bithynia – the soldier's nowhere near as fussy as his wife.'

A brief ripple of laughter went round the room and Theodora got on with the rest of her day's business, petitions to hear, alms to grant, young working girls to free from sex slavery to the marginally less restrictive confines of the Metanoia convent. Pasara was horrified to find the Empress's household guards blocking her doors later that afternoon, and more furious still when Germanus said it was her own fault for baiting the Empress and stayed away three full days celebrating his birthday.

The baby boy was duly born, after Pasara had spent the last five weeks of her pregnancy in the heat of her inner rooms and, while she smiled from the women's gallery as the baby Justin was baptised, she made sure to say nothing the Empress might overhear.

Two months later when Ana's son was born, Theodora insisted he was named Anastasius, both after her own dead sister for whom Ana was named, and after the old Emperor Anastasius. Later still, when Justinian's sister gave birth to a son, he was also named Justin. Theodora said the name both honoured the current Emperor and recalled the child's great-uncle; the baby was, therefore, twice-purple. And she made sure to say so, very clearly, the next time Pasara was in court.

Theodora was also insistent about another matter.

'Armeneus, I want you to do something and I don't want you to tell Narses about it.'

Armeneus raised an eyebrow and continued his totalling of his mistress's accounts. 'Yes, Augusta?'

'I'm serious. Narses is not to know.'

Armeneus put aside the papers he was working on, motioned the door slaves to stand outside, and then turned back to Theodora. 'Always best to make sure we're private, in that case.'

Theodora shrugged. 'I don't mean Narses is never to know, I'm not stupid enough to think that I can ask you to bring something into the Palace without it getting back to him eventually.'

'But?'

'He'll say no. So I want you to at least make the arrangement without his knowledge.'

'I'm sure I can do that. What is it you want me to fetch?'

'It's more of a who.'

'Oh.'

She stretched and rubbed her face. 'I want you to bring Macedonia here.'

'The woman from Antioch?'

'The spy, yes. The woman Narses and Timothy employed to bring me to Justinian, to bring Church and state happily together.'

Armeneus shook his head. 'Narses doesn't keep a list of his spies hanging up in his office, and I'm sure, since you came to power and she was known to be associated with you, she'll have long since left Antioch.'

'No doubt. There's nothing to blow a spy's cover like her lover becoming Empress.'

Armeneus stared at Theodora, taking in what she'd just said.

Theodora smiled. 'Did Narses not tell you?'

'Ah . . .' Armeneus shook his head, 'I'm not sure he knew.'

Theodora laughed, 'There's nothing he doesn't know. And it was a very long time ago. I am Augusta, devoted to my Master, my faith, and the purple. I'm not asking you to fetch me a lover, Armeneus. After everything we've just been through, I need a spy.'

Seventeen

The task Theodora had given Armeneus was not an easy one. Even more difficult without consulting Narses, that oracle of all things to do with the Palace and state, from protocol to policy, and especially of matters so well hidden that even Justinian didn't know of them. Or claimed not to. Armeneus sent out his own people and, many weeks later, word came back that Macedonia had been living in a convent near Damascus. As ordered by her Empress, she was now on her way to Constantinople. She would travel quietly so as not to draw attention to herself, they were neither to expect her nor look for her, she would send a message when she arrived in the City. There was no equivocation, no suggestion that what was being asked was an imposition. It was almost as if she had been waiting for the summons.

When the excessive heat of that long summer finally broke, another relief came with the cooler days and easier nights; the protracted negotiations with the Persians were done and the Endless Peace was announced. Khusro and Justinian's men met in the grand ceremonial chamber to put their signatures to the document that had taken years to agree and now pledged peace between their nations. Later that evening, the public areas of the Palace were filled with celebration. The best singers and dancers from the City's companies were hurriedly brought in to entertain the dozens of civil servants and military personnel involved in drafting the many phases of the agreement. There were also celebrations in the City. Almost nine months since the uprising, the vast cleared spaces that had been the Hagia Sophia, the Chalke Gate and the Baths were a daily reminder of the riots and the dead. For the people, weary of their sons dying on the Persian border or coming home maimed, tired of paying for wars they did not understand, this was a chance to turn their back on destruction and celebrate. Anyone looking at the history of such treaties would have known that peace on the eastern border inevitably meant escalated fighting in western and African territories, but the people were keener to party than to analyse and, at least for the moment, it suited the Palace to provide for everyone's pleasure.

Theodora stood in a raised walkway running close to the Palace wall; on either side were windows with shutters thrown wide. To her left were the celebrations of the City, to her right those of the Palace, behind were her own rooms, ahead her husband's. She watched Justinian in the courtyard below, making his way among the military men of both sides, accepting their congratulations and generously passing them on to his less conspicuous aides. She saw Comito and Antonina sitting with the other military wives. Protocol forbade them to sit with the men, but neither was prepared to forgo being seen as the wife of a great general on a night like this, and so, with the other wives, they edged as close to the centre of the event as possible. Theodora watched Antonina vainly waving at Belisarius, indicating he should bring the Persian ambassador to meet her. She smiled at her friend's naked ambition, and frowned at those circling Belisarius, keen to speak to him, to see him, to be seen by him. Theodora wished she could have Sophia with her now, mocking the politicking below. Instead she stood alone and missed her friend. Seeing Belisarius with his arm around Germanus' shoulder one time too many, she shook herself and called for her ladies; it was no good standing here feeling lonely. She made her way down to the main entrance to the central courtyard, telling Mariam and the other women to wait on her command, wait until her entrance was announced.

Theodora knew that this evening, as much as the levelled space where the Church of Hagia Sophia had stood, as much as Sophia's death, was a direct effect of the rebellion. Such lavish hospitality for the Persians, so constantly, so recently, their enemy, could never have happened a decade or even a year earlier. The whole Imperial compound shimmered with hope and excitement: no expense had been spared to accentuate the idea that, although the peace deal exchanged border security for a large sum of Roman gold, the Empire had plenty more where that came from. Both sides knew this wasn't strictly true, but they also understood the peace was as much a mask as those the actors wore, and the clauses assuring Persian peace on the borders were more a hope than a promise. Tonight was about celebration, calculated to show the August fully in control, easy with his newly confirmed power, and happy to share the bounty that power granted him.

Local priests chanted in one corner of the central courtyard, a backdrop of fountains splashing on the glittering mosaic tiles of gold and lapis, the water an obvious symbol of new life in the Christ. In the opposite corner, granted permission just this once, Zoroastrian acolytes addressed their prayer song to the flames of their god. Torches were lit all along the walls and in every alcove. On a raised patio in one of the outer courtyards adult acrobats juggled child acrobats and Theodora grimaced watching them, she had performed the same routine as a girl. That child currently being thrown in the air with apparent joy would no doubt be counting every bruise tomorrow. Theodora lived with constant pain from many of the routines of her childhood. Daily she was forced to remember the time she'd been thrown too high to land properly and had finished the performance with an audible crunch as her kneecap met the jawbone of the man meant to catch her. Closer by there was a group of dancers, singers backing them, a dozen girls in all, and none of them too young to be taken as a whore by a drunken member of their illustrious audience, several of whom were watching a little too intently for her liking. She would arrange for Armeneus to send a couple of eunuchs with the party when they returned to the City; the girls might not plan on earning more before the night was out, but she wasn't sure she could trust their teachers not to sell them.

Standing in the shadow of the doors to the Great Hall, Theodora looked out, confirming her route. Carefully she loosened the heavy purple silk around her neck, not quite revealing her shoulders, showing a collarbone still as sharply defined as when it was praised on the stage, skin made up to seem equally youthful and smooth, the barest of shading on her eyelids to highlight the green of the eyes her husband loved so well. She cleared her throat, straightened her back, the full headdress of precious stones interspersed with the glistening eyes of peacock feathers gave her a good hand's width more height than usual – well worth the pain of wearing it. Then she walked out into the people.

The Empress did not turn to any who called her name as she cut a slow and determined swathe through the crowd, she did not acknowledge those who bowed as she walked, or the foreigners who, finally glimpsing the famed Theodora, stared with undisguised interest. She walked on from the outer courtyard to the central patio, leaving behind in her wake prostrate Romans and curious Persians. When one woman, tall, fair, paused for a moment before her bow, waiting to catch her eye, Theodora almost lost her poise, almost reached out. Then Macedonia bowed low before her Empress, Theodora took a deep breath, and walked on, forcing her face and hands to a still calm. She swept past the woman she had not seen for eleven years, grateful that she had come as promised, grateful that no one else was paying any attention to her ally in the crowd. Armeneus had not mentioned Macedonia's arrival, perhaps he didn't know. All to the good.

Theodora brought her attention to the task in hand. The assembled Persian scribes and merchants, civil servants and traders, had less training in the protocols of this new Rome and now they half-stood, half-knelt as the Empress passed by. None of them wanted to appear rude to these Romans who already believed them barbarians, but nor were they keen to bow too low to one who had officially been their enemy just three days ago. Theodora kept her pace constant, her gaze directly ahead, and walked carefully on to where she knew Justinian was seated with his advisers, surrounded by Khusro's chiefs, all of them men, all of them proud – and most of them men who preferred not to deal with women.

She rounded the corner to the seating area and prostrated herself, the precious gems of the headdress and heavy necklaces of pearls fell into the wide pool of her gowns, several shades of purple silk laid low before the Emperor. The men surrounding Justinian gasped. Some of the Persians stood uneasily, several Romans exchanged uncertain looks, not sure what their Empress was doing – and then, as first Sittas, then

Belisarius, Germanus and all the others close by sank to the ground and prostrated themselves in order to be lower than the Augusta, her intention became obvious. Theodora remained prostrate until every one of the men, high-ranking Persians included, men far too schooled in courtly protocol to contemplate snubbing the Empress, were also flat on the ground. Only then did she accept Justinian's hand to raise herself.

'Sir,' she greeted him with a smile.

'Theou doron,' Justinian replied, bowing deeply himself.

By the time their guests looked up, August and Augusta were seated together, the finest generals of Rome, and the most senior negotiators of all Persia, on the intricately paved ground before them.

Narses, neither bowing nor kneeling, watched from across the courtyard. He caught Theodora's eye and nodded, bringing his hands together to silently applaud his mistress. She had, as always, played her part well; only she knew how well. Although the Endless Peace proposed just that, and returned a good deal of borderland to Rome, it had cost Rome an enormous sum of gold, and Narses needed to ensure the negotiators understood exactly what was expected for the price tag. There were new routes across Persia still to be confirmed, as well as dozens of spice, gold, and silk dealers who had requested meetings. That was the easy part of his evening's work, they could always rely on the traders to find a way to communicate. Other introductions would be far trickier. Just months ago the generals who now stood together in apparent amity had been fighting each other in the bloody mountains outside Dara. Rome had paid for peace, and Narses had to ensure that the military men on both sides kept to the bargain when the Persians went home and his own people turned their attention to Africa and the west. He noted who was fully prostrate and who merely knelt into a low bow. He watched those who rose first, and especially the Persians who did so smiling, acknowledging and approving Theodora's status-play. Narses respected a good tactician, and it was these men he now moved to, to make sure they understood him as well as he understood them. He did not see Macedonia move quietly from the courtyard, leaving the Palace as unobtrusively as she had arrived.

Soon after, Justinian stood at the centre of a group of local silk traders, each pleading with the Emperor, each man louder than the last.

'Master, the peace is all very well, but silk is still more costly than gold.'

'Far more,' another agreed, 'and our trade routes through Persian territories are not yet fully protected.'

'Yes gentlemen, we understand your plight,' the Emperor answered, preparing to leave them. 'You know the Empress has often noted that your difficulties will not be solved until the Empire manufactures its own silk.'

The wealthy traders nodded and loudly blessed the Empress's wisdom.

'All the same,' the Emperor continued, 'there is nothing we can achieve tonight in the matter of the silk routes. Peace will have to do for now.'

He left the bowing businessmen to their carping and went to find his wife.

Theodora stood with Narses, watching Belisarius hold court at a table of military men. Narses had gathered the most senior officers from both sides, ordered plenty of wine served by pretty boys and girls, and now had them all telling stories about Vandal military tactics. Not only did this keep them from recalling their triumphs over each other, it also offered useful information to which Rome paid particular attention. Watching Belisarius in action, noting his sharper and more probing questions about training and tactics as the older men became more drunk and less guarded, Theodora grudgingly admitted the golden general's strategic prowess.

'Surely you're not smiling on our general?' Justinian asked Theodora, pleased and surprised.

'If Belisarius can complete this African campaign you're so keen on, if he can do well for us, then it will be the better for Rome.'

'Of course,' Justinian agreed.

'I just hope he really is thinking of Rome and not of himself.'

Narses smiled and moved away to order more wine for the soldiers. 'As do we all, Mistress.'

Justinian looked at his wife. 'Thank you,' he said.

'What for?'

'Your little power play back there.'

Theodora had a moment of shock, thinking he meant Macedonia and then realised he couldn't possibly have seen her. Even if he had, he had never known what she looked like.

'Good. I like to be useful.'

'You are. I'm sure this is dull for you, you've seen acrobats a thousand times, attended more parties than most of us could count . . .'

'Not usually in ceremonial purple.'

'No, and I don't imagine your neck can take that headdress for much longer.'

'This is an important celebration, you've worked hard for it.'

'Yes. And now the peace is settled, we'll look to the west. We're doing well.'

'We can do better.'

'And we'll do better still with this gentleman's help.'

Justinian reached out a hand to a young man who had arrived to bow before them, elegantly kissing Theodora's foot. Standing tall and smiling proudly, he showed no sign of the nerves that often affected those new to the Palace, though Theodora knew she hadn't seen him before – she would definitely have remembered him if she had.

Justinian introduced him. 'Anthemius of Tralles. He has plans for a new church and, if we like what he builds there, perhaps for a new Hagia Sophia,' the Emperor leaned in to his wife and said, more quietly, 'rebuilding your church.'

Theodora smiled politely and nodded to the young man. 'I apologise, I was about to go inside. Will you meet with me tomorrow? The old church was a favourite of mine, and I would very much like to know your plans.'

Anthemius agreed to come to her rooms, Justinian wished his wife a good night, and Theodora walked back into the Palace, her entourage reluctantly following.

Much later that night, when the guests had either left the grounds or returned to the Palace rooms where they were staying, when the heavy scullery doors were closed so the noise of the massive clear-up operation disturbed no one but the servants, Narses lay in his bed, Armeneus by his side.

'You can't blame her for liking the look of him,' the younger eunuch said.

'I don't,' Narses said. 'Architects are all too often effete artists, this one looks like he knows how to dig foundations and lay the stone himself. Which is just as well, if Justinian gives him the Hagia Sophia commission he'll need to create something astonishing and in record time. The Emperor wants a church to stun the world and he doesn't want to wait.'

'What about the partner?' asked Armeneus.

'Isodore is bright as well, perhaps too arrogant to be truly good-looking.' Narses smiled, kissing the shoulder of the tall, dark-skinned man by his side. 'But it's not misplaced, they have wonderful ideas, that's why I brought them to Justinian's attention.'

'But not Theodora's?'

'I'd rather she hadn't met him quite so soon.'

'She could have taken a lover before now and she hasn't.'

'There's no guarantee she'll want the architect either,' Narses said, 'but I watched her tonight. Theodora usually loves or hates on first sight and rarely bothers to hide her feelings. It was a studied indifference she showed Anthemius.'

'And that's a problem?'

'I don't know, but it's certainly new.'

In her own room Theodora lay wide awake, thinking of Macedonia, wondering when she would contact her, and how. She was consciously not thinking about the young architect. She was consciously not comparing how both Macedonia and Anthemius made her feel, how awake both made her feel.

Eighteen

'You look well.'

'I look more than a decade older, Mistress,' Macedonia said, smiling up at Theodora from her bow.

'We all look that,' Theodora said, gesturing for Macedonia to rise and follow her.

They were at Metanoia, having arranged, through messages passed to unknowing servants, to meet in the grounds, the better to speak privately.

'No, you don't, your skin is as fine as it was when we were last together.'

Theodora nodded. 'Perhaps. I do have certain comforts in the Palace – a protection from the elements that was never available in the desert. I've become a cosseted wife, Macedonia.'

Macedonia laughed, shaking her head. 'I can't believe that.' She paused, then said, 'nor do I believe you would have called me here if you didn't have a task for me.'

'I might have just wanted to see you.'

Macedonia looked at the ex-lover who was now her Empress. 'I think, in many ways, I am one of the last people you'd want to see here, in your new life, reminding you of the freedoms of the old.'

'You know me well.'

'I did once. I imagine, Mistress, that you have called me to work for you.'

'I have.'

Theodora explained her dilemma, the need to be out among the people, the need to truly know what they were thinking, and the impossibility of getting close to them again, both as Empress who could never again be a commoner, and also since Nika.

'I find I have lost some of my love for the people since Sophia's death, since the riots. I'm not sure I want to be of them any more, even if they do appear to want us. So yes, it is to do with people, how distant I now feel, but it's also . . .'

'The faithful?' Macedonia asked and continued, when Theodora nodded her agreement; 'You know my faith is as yours, with the Patriarch Timothy, and with Severus.'

'And the state is formally Chalcedonian in belief, and Justinian would have the state and the Church be one. I am the Emperor's support in all his work, but it suits the Palace sometimes to allow us to speak against each other.'

'And sometimes your stance has very little to do with actual belief?'

'Yes,' Theodora said. 'We can argue about the nature of the Christ's divinity until we exhaust ourselves, but the Egyptians and the Syrians, those in the Levant, will continue to share the belief you and I hold in His single nature, the belief Rome rejects. They will continue to press for prayer in their own languages and, no matter how much they – or we in the Palace – claim it is to do with faith, it has always been as much about their relationship with Rome as anything else.'

'And what is it exactly you want me to do?'

Theodora shook her head, 'There is no "exactly". I have my position in this Palace, I am Augusta, can influence a little, either through my own pressure or by encouraging the Emperor to hear my views, but in the Church . . .'

'You are still a woman.'

'A prominent woman.'

'Where I am not,' said Macedonia.

Theodora agreed. 'And those men, despite their faith, have the appetites of men, not saints.'

'Ah. You would like me to whore myself to the priests in the City and discover their plans?'

'No, I know what the priests here plan. It's the priests in Rome, in Italy, I'd like you to whore yourself to.'

'That's asking a lot, Mistress,' Macedonia said.

Theodora looked squarely at her ex-lover. 'No more than you once asked of me.'

'True.'

'And it may not come to that. We will send you to Rome. Justinian has spies there, of course, but sometimes there is information he does not share with me. And there is also information I want for myself I would rather not discuss with him.'

'Such as?' Macedonia asked.

'I hear the Goth Regent Queen is very beautiful.'

'I see. And there may be those who think Amalasuntha would be a politic partner for your husband?'

Theodora shrugged. 'I would not be the first wife divorced to make way for a new marriage that is also a peace treaty.'

They had come to the end of the long walk away from the main house. Before them was a low wall, and the rocky shore-line, the Palace and the City far distant across the water. It was time to turn back.

Macedonia stretched her arms high above her head and then brought her hands together in a loud clap. 'Good. Good. Thank you, my friend. Mistress,' she corrected herself, 'I thought I had resigned myself to convent life, but now I feel it, here, a real joy –' she brought a fist to her breastbone. 'I'm excited to travel, work, do what I'm good at.'

'Then you'll go?' Theodora asked.

'I have a choice?'

'No.'

Both women laughed and Theodora linked her arm with Macedonia's. They walked back to Metanoia together, Theodora's boat took her immediately back down the Bosphorus, back to the Palace, and the following morning another boat picked Macedonia up before dawn and carried her south, where she transferred to a larger ship bound for Rome, away from the interested stares of the busy Constantinople docks. In the tiny cabin Macedonia was to share with five other women, all travelling alone, all religious acolytes among whom she could hide herself, she unpacked the trunk that had been left for her. It contained maps, letters of introduction to fellow believers in Rome, and a brief list of the few spies and messengers she should trust to bring messages back directly to Theodora. There was nothing to indicate the trunk had been sent by the Empress, until Macedonia opened the coin purse tucked into a small pile of plain, warm clothes. As well as a collection of very useful gold, she pulled out a long string of fine pearls. Macedonia put them around her neck and thought she could smell Theodora's perfume on them.

With Macedonia safely dispatched to be her spy in Rome, Theodora went back to another pressing matter, one she had been trying to ignore – the young architect. Narses had been right in his observation to Armeneus, Theodora's apparent indifference was studied and she worked to keep it that way. She maintained her distance when Anthemius began attending the Palace weekly with plans for the rebuilding of Hagia Sophia, even as every new draft delighted her more. Justinian would take a quick look, listen to one or two of the more technical explanations about the shape, the façade, or the huge excitement that was the proposed dome – vast and impossible and very real – and then leave the finer points to Theodora. Preoccupied with his attempt to close the gap between the disagreeing factions in the Church, and with the pressing plans for war against Gelimer's Vandals in Carthage, Justinian had simply asked Anthemius and the engineer Isodore to praise the Christ in the design and to astound him in the ambition of the project. He left the finer points of artistry, budget and workforce to his wife. Theodora knew how to lead a company, understood better than most what would please the people, and had always been good with budgeting, albeit on a much smaller scale. Justinian hadn't seen her as interested in anything since Sophia's death; with this project, and with Comito's baby in the Palace, he was pleased to see his wife active and engaged again. As time passed, first into deep winter and then the hope of spring, Theodora could have wished for a less thoughtful husband.

Still, she kept herself at a slight remove, even when, after Isodore had left their meetings, Anthemius would stay on and tell her about the practical jokes he played on his friends.

'Your jokes are beautifully cruel, Anthemius.' Theodora laughed as he spoke of the wizened old Zeno running naked from his house in the middle of the night, an arrangement of lamps and mirrors persuading him that midday had come at midnight, the Apocalypse was now.

'The best comedy always has some peril, you'd agree, Mistress?'

The Empress nodded but chose not to follow him into a

conversation about the attraction of danger. She also turned down his offer of site visits to their two building projects for the August. Anthemius and Isodore were given the commissions once Justinian and Theodora saw their plans for the little church of Sts Sergius and Bacchus, and then for the new Hagia Sophia itself.

The night came when Anthemius burst in on them at the evening meal, ignoring protocol to speak without bowing and share the news of the astonishing find at the great church site.

'The coffins have been found. The apostles' coffins.'

'The coffins laid by Constantine?'

'Yes, Master,' Anthemius answered, offering up a clumsy half-bow as the Emperor's voice reminded him where he was and whose meal he had just interrupted.

Justinian rushed out of the room with Anthemius to inspect the site, and Theodora watched them go, conflicting emotions dulling her appetite for the tart of pears and eggs before her. She ate on anyway – their chef knew she enjoyed the dish, any change in routine would be noted – but somehow both the pepper and the cumin lacked flavour and the soufflé of risen eggs might as well have sunk to a flatbread for all the attention she paid it.

Two days later the coffins were moved using Isodore's elaborate arrangement of cranes which meant the old bones in the crumbling coffins did not even tremble as they were lifted from the earth. Justinian, full of praise for the architects, gave the dead saints their full religious ceremony and an honour guard of his own men.

If Theodora had not found Anthemius attractive already, her husband's enthusiasm for the young man and all his works would have forced her to applaud him.

And Theodora did find him attractive. As she came to

know the architect better, his mind appealed as much as his face, his humour, his workman's body. Her union with Justinian had been arranged to suit many parties, and the younger Theodora had not expected to find sexual satisfaction in the liaison. At that stage in her life, broken by rejection, pacified through her conversion, and simply wanting to do Timothy's bidding, she agreed to be introduced to the Emperor and also agreed to find any way she could to make him like her. She had been delighted to discover that Justinian was clever, perceptive and hugely ambitious. Later she was even more pleased to find that despite his scholarly reputation, he was also a good lover, passionate, considerate and skilled.

Anthemius too was clever, perceptive and ambitious – and he had a very fine face. Fine arms, legs, back, chest, head, feet, body. It was only his hands that were not quite so lovely. The architect had the hands of a man who spent as little time as possible at a desk, too engaged in his own work to direct from an office, too interested in what he was creating to delegate the dirty work. Anthemius had bitten fingernails, ingrained, at all times, with a layer of marble dust or City earth or stone dirt. More often than not they were also cut or bruised from his hunger to pick up his men's tools, to show an apprentice a cleaner line to cut, or learn from a master craftsman how to lay a deeper foundation, build up a smoother surface. The architect did not mind if he was learning or teaching: all he wanted was perfect workmanship.

Theodora was glad of his workman's hands, because Justinian's hands were lovely. Anthemius' less than perfect hands kept him from Theodora's bed for quite some time. But not for all time.

Nineteen

The anniversary of the Nika riots was marked by the constant ring, crack and thud of hammer and chisel resounding from every wall. Spring came early and then it was Easter again, with its public ritual and processions, the court keeping time with the Church. In the throes of the massive rebuild, the City was either all mud or all dust, nothing between, men working day and torchlit night, chipping away at marble and stone, building upon deep foundations, adding finishing touches to the projects deemed most urgent. The Hippodrome seats and broken boards were replaced, damaged statues exchanged for new, any sign of the dead obliterated. The new Baths were completed, as was the Senate. The unfinished Chalke was already in use while a team of artists worked on designs for its completed decoration, a golden mosaic depicting the Empire's defeat of both Gelimer's Vandals and the Goths in Italy. No matter that Belisarius' troops had not yet left the City. The general was sure of his coming success in Carthage, and Justinian was keen to immortalise it – in his own favour. Adjoining the Chalke was the Augustaion, the open square where tens of thousands of rebels had gathered just a year ago and where their dead bodies were piled not long after. The square was smaller now, its size diminished by the layout of the new Baths and the foundations for the rebuilt Church of Hagia Sophia. The City planners had not set out to lessen the space, but when the various architects came together and compared their drafts for the work, no one in power thought it a problem that there would be less room for public assembly, public anger.

For three months Theodora met with Anthemius at least twice a week. She heard the stories of his successful family and entertained his brothers – the doctor, the lawyer, the lecturer, the linguist. She put up with the engineer Isodore's polite but obvious dismissal of her interest when she asked him to explain more about the great dome they were planning for the huge church, how exactly it would work, how it could possibly be held in place. Then she enjoyed a glass of wine and Anthemius' company as he mocked his brilliant partner, his inability to talk to women, his incoherence in the face of power. Anthemius suffered from neither fault.

As the dusty summer of building continued into the longest days, warmest nights, Theodora knew she was becoming too fond of the younger man and asked Justinian to assign someone else for these meetings.

'The paper I'm working on, "On Pimps and Prostitutes", needs more attention. I think the builders can manage without my overseeing them for a while?'

Justinian barely took in her request. Overwhelmed with both theological and military problems, he simply praised her discernment and insisted there was no one else he trusted to make sure the works followed his own desires so clearly.

'Only you know what I care about. If I can't supervise the

work as closely as we would both like, I trust you to do so in my stead.'

At her husband's insistence, Theodora continued seeing Anthemius twice a week.

The architect bowed before his Empress, lowered himself further to kiss her proffered foot, stood up to smile and said, 'Mistress, I have a treat for you.'

'You do?'

Theodora was surrounded by her ladies. Mariam stood close by with the baby Sophia, Ana played with Anastasius, Comito and Indaro were rehearsing for a private Palace recital in the rooms beyond, Comito's voice both stronger and more colourful with age. Armeneus sat at a desk against the wall, where he was checking the Empress's accounts and shaking his head at the expense of the silks Theodora insisted the children were dressed in; after a youth of cold and hard work herself, she had no intention of letting the young ones feel the bite of a northern wind. The penitents at Metanoia were not so lucky: the fabric allocated for their dress cost a great deal less, despite their numbers being many more.

Theodora brushed away Armeneus' query over the disparity. 'Metanoia is a place of redemption, it's only right we offer our penitents the same opportunities for physical and moral redemption I experienced myself. They have a roof over their heads, that's more than we had in the desert.'

She nodded to Anthemius. 'Now, what's this treat?' she asked.

Anthemius called one of his apprentices to him. The nervous boy held up a wooden box and the architect lifted off the lid. Carefully, he pulled out a thin, palm-sized piece of cold, heavy marble. It was dark green. The green of the Sea of Marmara in her dreams when Theodora had been in the desert all that time, the green of the statue she prayed to daily, the green of her own eyes, she knew, Justinian had compared them to their sea often enough.

'It's for the women's gallery, Mistress.'

Theodora nodded, understanding immediately. 'Where is it from?'

'You mentioned your love of the water,' Anthemius answered, gesturing to the view. 'I've been looking for the perfect match. This piece comes via a spice dealer, a Gujjar from Bhinmal, his cousin knows a man . . .' he shrugged, the intricacies of trading and deals irrelevant now. 'We will order more if you like it. When the women's gallery is complete, it will be laid to mark your place − where the Empress will stand for now, and in the future.'

It was a room full of busy, noisy people. Theodora sat in the centre, using all her theatrical training to stay calm, to maintain her distance from the architect, the man who had just handed her a tangible piece of her own dreams. The man who was promising, with no prompting from her, to recreate a scene from the dream she'd had fourteen years ago in North Africa. Rejected by Hecebolus, travelling alone to Alexandria and hiding in a deserted church, she had slept alone, cold and lost. That night she had dreamed this new Hagia Sophia, dreamed the light that Isodore promised would flow from the dome, dreamed its grand scale and its excess, dreamed the impossible beauty. Now Anthemius offered to mark her place in stone, to mark the green marble spot she had also dreamed, before her conversion, before her hope, back when all she had was her own will not to give in, and little enough faith in that. Theodora took the piece of marble Anthemius offered her and saw that perhaps his hands might be beautiful after all.

That afternoon, Anthemius of Tralles, the architect, the

brightest son of a family of fine young men, became Theodora's lover.

Her hand in his, calluses and stone cuts rubbing against oiled and smoothed skin. Her mouth on his, lips different to Justinian's, less full. One muscled arm twisted around her back, a broad hand on her bare stomach. His skin, browner, stronger from days outside, supervising his sites. Her fingers in his hair, hair finer, paler than her husband's. Her legs stretched against his, her back against his belly, now her breasts to his chest. Her lips, mouth exploring a new torso, a new body. She traced a small scar on his right calf, a serpent tattooed on his lower back, coiled into her hand's width, following its spiral with her tongue. When Anthemius looked into her eyes, Theodora remembered again that he had found the green marble for her, remembered too that she was Augusta and he the architect of her church and there was danger, real danger, in their touch, and that danger was as potent an aphrodisiac as any herbal concoction the old whores ever knew. Her pleasure rising, as he faltered, hesitated, as he became aware of the risk and she watched him push it away, intent on her mouth, her skin, her body. Intent on her flesh, not the Empress Theodora or his commission or this room in this Palace, just her body and his. They were not skilled at each other, she was new to him as he was to her, they had no pattern for this, no template. Theodora, fourteen years fully faithful to Justinian, gave herself over to enjoying the new, thrilling to the new.

Afterwards she fell asleep in his arms, new arms, a new hold, for a few moments. When she began, slowly, to come to her senses, swimming to the surface of a post-sex stupor, she did so reluctantly, unwilling to acknowledge the risk they had just let into their lives, unwilling to let the moment go at all. Eventually all sleep was gone and she was only Augusta.

'I don't need to tell you ...'

'No, Mistress, you don't,' he stopped her, and they were themselves again, Empress and architect.

Theodora gave him directions and left him to it.

Anthemius left the private room within the private rooms, leaving by a back door hidden behind a woven hanging. He walked through one dark passage after another and then into an underground tunnel.

Theodora hoped a long walk through the bowels of the Palace might persuade him that those rumours of her dungeons and torture chambers were not entirely exaggerated. She knew the whispers of poisoned and tortured political enemies, she knew that sometimes court officials disappeared at short notice, and she knew too that Narses could be utterly ruthless in his determination to protect the August. She had employed that pitiless strength for her own ends on occasion and was ever wary of seeing it turned against herself.

She didn't need to worry. Heading through the underground passages, Anthemius walked past corridors with stark dead ends, and others that seemed to wind on and down, leading into further, darker rooms. He walked carefully and silently, making his way with a strong sense of direction, a lit torch, and a builder's eye for detail – this stone must be from the original Greek occupiers on this spot, that from a later Roman palace, this just since Constantine. Anthemius had no desire to bring down his rising star as court architect, or to risk his working relationship with the Empress. If this happened again, the gloriously pleasurable delight and terror of fucking the Empress, then good, as long as they maintained secrecy. If not, he was happy being her favourite. In bed, or as an architect, either was good for him, though it was true there was more future in the latter option. Anthemius had a mind of pure design and elegant lines, housed in a body well suited to pleasure, but he was also a businessman. It would need all his care to ensure that when the affair, if it became an affair, ended – as it surely would – Theodora still wanted him around.

The final corridor, slanting upwards, led him out into a tree-lined avenue close to the wall, not far from the Hagia Sophia site. He reached into his bag, pulled out a measure and began calculating distances. Anyone watching would have thought the architect was simply hard at work as he also calculated how long to wait before calling on the Empress again, how to behave in her presence, how this new development might help his career. Anyone watching would also have seen him smiling a little more than might be expected from the study of an old stone wall.

Theodora was less easy. After two days with the unspoken secret burning at the back of her throat, she called Antonina to her rooms, sent Mariam and her other girls away, and told her friend what had happened.

'About time. You're Empress, not the Mother of God . . .'

'No, Antonina.'

Theodora might joke about Antonina's lack of faith, she was not prepared to have her own belief mocked.

'Don't glare, you'll get wrinkles. It's absurd how faithful you've been to Justinian.'

'He's been faithful to me. Belisarius is to you.'

'So they say, and we like to believe. Who knows? Anyway, that's not my point, Justinian was no whore before you met him.'

'And I was?'

'You were more experienced.'

'In number, of course, but Justinian's very . . .'

Antonina covered her ears, 'Please, he's August, there are some things I don't need to know. The point is, you've been really good, impeccable. It's perfectly normal to lapse.'

'The Church doesn't think so.'

'The Church is confused about its very nature – you think whether or not a woman commits adultery is truly that important?'

'It is to me. And yet . . .'

'Yes?'

'I feel awake, alive.' She grinned, whispering, 'Before everything that happened last year, the riots and the damage and losing Sophia, I'd just assumed this was my destiny – the purple, the Augusta – simply because I couldn't understand why else I should be here.'

'But now?'

'Since then I've started to think it's not quite that. It might be fate, that I am Augusta, Justinian's partner, that may be what I'm meant to be. Certainly when I was in the desert I learned to give myself over to that understanding, trusting my teachers knew best.'

'What's changed?'

Theodora shook her head, then smiled. 'I'm older. And giving in to fate was easier in the desert, listening to Severus' teachings, than it is here, in the world.'

'You want some control.'

'If Augusta is my destiny, so be it, but I need to find a way to make it my mission as well.'

Antonina nodded slowly, and said, 'Then you can say you chose this life, instead of feeling it was chosen for you?'

'Yes.'

'We all rationalise how we live, and in a life as scrutinised as yours, there's even more reason to do so. But how does taking a lover have anything to do with seeing your position as choice rather than fate?'

'Anthemius is different.'

Antonina laughed, 'Oh, they're all different, Theodora, that's why we make them our lovers.'

'But I'd forgotten the pleasure of difference.' Theodora was speaking more urgently now. 'I've schooled myself to turn away whenever I've looked at another man.'

'Other men? Plural?'

Theodora ignored her friend's smirk. 'I have to be Justinian's constant. I want to be that for him.'

'But you want the new as well?'

'I do. And I want it because I choose it, not because it's forced on me by circumstance or someone else's idea of what will be good for state or City. I want it for me.'

'You know, Belisarius thinks he takes me on campaigns with him so he can keep an eye on me ...'

'But actually it's so you can keep an eye on his men?'

'My golden general and his lovely men,' Antonina smiled, stretching her elegant arms above her head then bringing her hands together in her lap, the picture of a passive wife. 'I know he's faithful to me, but that doesn't stop every tart from here to Carthage trying it on. Besides, when the men are in training, away from their families and ties at home, there are so many more of them to choose from, all crammed into those tents together. Not all our soldiers want to fuck each other. I'm doing the Empire a service by keeping up the men's morale.'

'And I'm sure my husband is grateful.'

'I'm sure he's not.'

Twenty

Theodora was not able to dismiss her adultery with the composure Antonina brought to her own affairs, but nor could she ignore her desire for Anthemius. The knowledge that the danger she welcomed into her life might bring her downfall at any moment was a powerful attraction. The next time they met, a long-booked arrangement to discuss the artists commissioned to decorate the small Church of Sts Sergius and Bacchus, she used Comito's daughter Sophia as a prop to keep him at arm's length. Anyone in the room would happily have taken the child from her, at least two maids were employed to do nothing but attend to the baby, but Theodora was Augusta and if she chose to fuss over little Sophia rather than talk with the architect – the maids knew which option they'd have taken – no one was going to argue with her.

When Anthemius came to the Palace a few days later, with new plans for the Church of Hagia Sophia and asking the Augusta's preference for stonemasons, Theodora's response was the same, and the time after. At last Antonina took her friend aside and told her to stop being so stupid.

'You're being too obvious.'

'I'm doing nothing at all.'

'Theodora, people gossip whether there's something to gossip about or not. A month ago you were all over the plans for the great church and all over the architect as well.'

'I was not.'

'You were, but most people thought it harmless fun. Now you practically ignore him, and when there's nothing to prompt speculation – truly nothing – that's when gossip becomes most rife.'

The Empress pulled her friend a little closer, and walked to a corner with her. 'I've been in this Palace too long. If I'm not careful I'll end up like that damn Pasara, so concerned about my image that it's all I am.'

Both women looked across the room then, aware Pasara was watching them as she so often did.

They nodded to the aristocrat and Theodora continued, 'I'll take more care.'

'You should take less care.'

'Thank you, Antonina.'

'Augusta.'

Antonina left with an exaggeratedly low bow and a broad smile accompanied by a sly wink and Theodora couldn't help thinking her old friend could do with some of Pasara's attention to form.

The following days were spent trying to pace herself around Anthemius, to find a place between holding him at a distance and holding him too close. For several nights he held her closer than anyone but Justinian ever had, safely trusting that the Emperor was days away, meeting with the Bishops in Thrace. Yet also unsafe in the awareness that if Macedonia could send Theodora messages from the house of the Pope in Rome, then the chances of this affair remaining hidden, so much closer to home, decreased with every delicious night.

The third time that Theodora yawned her way through the morning service in the Palace chapel, Comito took her aside, grabbing her arm very much as an elder sister, not as subject to Empress.

'Pasara is speaking openly about the architect as your lover. Is it true?'

'What?' Theodora answered, ignoring her sister's question. 'Has she said so to you?'

'Not to me, but to Germanus, who told Sittas.'

'Who told you,' Theodora breathed out and removed her sister's clawing hand from her wrist, 'and you believed third-hand gossip?'

Comito looked hard at Theodora, at the rings under her eyes, at the yawn she was even now trying to stifle, and thought of the smile she'd seen on her sister's lips only moments earlier.

'I don't usually watch you grinning thorough the long chant of the liturgy.'

'You wouldn't be watching me at all if you were attending to your own prayer.'

Comito shook her head. 'Someone needs to take care of you, little sister, and I'm better placed to warn you than Pasara, no?'

The first thing Theodora did was call for Narses. The Chief of Staff stood before Theodora, waiting for her to speak. When she did not, he hissed and scratched at his shaved head with both hands, hands Theodora could see were itching to turn into fists.

'Speak, Narses.'

'I'm waiting for you to say it, Mistress.'

'Say what?'

Narses stared straight at her. 'If the Anicii's story is true or not?'

Theodora shook her head, saying nothing.

'Given your haste in calling me to you,' said Narses, 'I'll assume Pasara speaks the truth.'

'I didn't say.'

'You don't need to, it seems your years of training have deserted you.'

'What do you mean?'

Narses stared at her. 'You are blushing, Mistress.'

Theodora could feel the heat in her face, knew Narses was right and knew it was still safer to say nothing, no matter that her cheeks were giving her away.

'Do I need to dismiss the architect?' Narses asked.

'You can't, his plans for the church are perfect, and no one else could work with Isodore,' Theodora said quickly. Sending Anthemius away would only confirm the rumour as true and besides, while she craved the architect's presence, she craved the completion of his work almost as much.

'Then you must go away.'

'I can't do that either. If I go anywhere those who dislike me will step in and push Justinian to leave me for the Goth's Regent Queen.'

'Amalasuntha?' Narses asked, genuinely confused, 'What's she got to do with this?'

Theodora shook her head, not speaking.

'Mistress,' Narses continued, more surprised now than angry, 'you're jealous of the August's support for the Goth child and his Regent mother?'

'I am not concerned about the child. I'm concerned that my husband and his court have taken it upon themselves to promote the needs of the Goth queen.'

'It's politic to support her regency, that's all.'

'Many would think it wise for Justinian to marry her, a useful alliance,' Theodora said. 'I hear she's very beautiful.'

'They say that about any queen.'

Narses glared at Theodora, wanting to undercut her fear, to understand what he saw as her absurd jealousy, and instead he saw, briefly, a hint of the damaged and uncertain young woman she'd been when she came to the palace.

He ran his hands over his shaved head and tried again, using her name for the first time in a long while: 'Theodora, we need Goth rulers in Italy holding firm for us. Supporting Amalasuntha's regency is sensible, that's all.'

'Before our marriage there were those who suggested she would be the perfect match for him, bringing East and West together.'

'Amalasuntha herself was married then.'

'And she's been a widow for seven years. My people tell me there are suggestions she's holding out for my husband.'

'Your people might also suggest that you're going the right way to push him into her arms. You need to get away from this gossip about the architect, prove there's no foundation to it.'

'I'd rather get rid of Pasara. Can't we marry Germanus to Amalasuntha? He'd like that, he's always been a social climber.'

'And in line for your husband's throne,' Narses answered quickly. 'I hardly think giving Germanus rule over half of Italy is taking care of the August's interests. I have another plan.'

Theodora sighed; she should have known better than to think Narses would have come unprepared. 'Of course you do.'

'I think it's time you visited some of your people.'

Theodora listened.

'Go to Bithynia. Not just a visit to Metanoia but a full procession, a real event. Take your staff, the whole entourage. We'll make a show of it – gold for power, combined with penitence to exhibit your piety.'

'I don't know. Justinian needs me here, he's hoping to bring the bishops together after their work in Thrace.'

'Yes, and he doesn't need your actions to undermine his confidence before he's even started with them.'

'There's no sign he's heard the rumour?'

'I don't think so. Assuming it is only a rumour?' Theodora didn't respond and Narses went on, 'And the Emperor keeps his own counsel more often than not.'

'You know his thoughts as well as anyone.'

'No, Mistress, not where his feelings for you are concerned,' Narses admitted. 'But perhaps we can make this work for the August. We'll send John of Tella with you, he's always been the mouthiest of your anti-Chalcedonian priests. With him out of the way the bishops may well come to an agreement here.'

'I wouldn't bet on it.'

'Neither would I,' Narses said and shook his head. 'In truth, I can't imagine anyone making sense of this mess the Church has made for itself, but the Emperor is doing more than betting on it, and we're bound to support him. Besides, Bithynia will be lovely in spring, and you can show penitence by visiting some of the monasteries. You can leave an endowment, the monks always welcome gold.'

'From whose purse?'

Narses moved closer and spoke more quietly, but the vehemence of his tone left Theodora in no doubt about his feelings: 'Yours, Mistress.'

'From my household budget?'

'No, from your private purse. The Emperor has given you estates that earn plenty, even if they're not always mentioned at tax-collecting time. I'm sure your accounts could endow a few religious houses. You should know by now that every action results in some payment or other.'

'Don't judge me, eunuch.'

Narses looked down at his Mistress, more than a head shorter and many years his junior. 'Then don't place yourself in a position to be judged, Mistress.'

The conversation finished, Narses left to continue preparations for a journey Theodora knew he had already decided on long before she had called him to her rooms. She sat alone, furious with the eunuch and more furious with herself, for minding his censure, for being found out, for betraying Justinian whom she did love, and for still wanting Anthemius. Wanting him very much.

Late that night Anthemius came to Theodora's room as usual, quietly entering through the side door from a hidden corridor. He waited in the dark antechamber while she ordered her servants to leave, waited while she made up an excuse for Mariam to go too, and then, unusually, he waited while Theodora ranted at him, stood quietly while his mistress, the Empress, the Augusta, furiously blamed him for her predicament.

'I'll go back to Tralles.'

'Don't be stupid,' Theodora hissed, 'you have the church to finish. You work for the Emperor, you can't just leave.'

'I'd rather risk his anger at leaving a project unfinished than Narses' censure over . . . this.'

Theodora glared at him. 'This? This what? Why so coy all of a sudden? Why not name it for the fucking it is?'

'Mistress . . .' Anthemius crossed to her, his voice gentle, but the hand he held to her mouth strong and fast, 'you've taught me well about the gossip in this place. Be quiet.'

Theodora shook her head, biting at his fingers to push him away. 'I hardly think gagging your Empress will look good as you sneak from the City.'

Anthemius stepped back. 'I apologise.'

'No,' Theodora said, 'I do. Of course you're worried, I am too. Narses is sending me away. Perhaps it's a good idea. You can look around for a young woman in my absence, someone safe and easy.'

'I don't want safe and easy.'

'What do you want?'

'You.'

He smiled, and she smiled, and then she laughed, holding her own hand, and his, over her mouth again, holding in the hysteria and the shiver of danger and the pleasure that was fear and wanting and waiting for gratification. The doors were quickly locked, shutters closed, Anthemius' body slammed into Theodora's, her hands locked with his, mouths closed fast on each other, eyes open to peril and indulgence and the yawning gap between the two that made their joy in each other still more fierce.

For the next three weeks Theodora saw Anthemius only with her women in attendance, visited the building sites on public excursions, and otherwise stayed away from the works. She threw herself into supporting Justinian's business with the bishops, urging those of her own belief to lean towards his plan, just as he did from his side of the divide. Anthemius smiled as fondly at the Empress while surrounded by her ladies as he ever had when meeting with her alone, accepted the baby Sophia's presence in the room when he explained his drawings and designs, and did not look back when he walked away. Theodora, seated, could not stop herself watching him go.

At the end of the month Theodora, Comito, the younger women and babies, the priest John of Tella, along with an entourage of ladies-in-waiting and assistants and all the staff needed to care for them, prepared to travel. Pasara and her family had expressly not been invited, and she was left behind, feeding her anger. Mariam too stayed behind, her absence not a punishment but to save her from travelling; during her two years as a child sex slave she had been dragged from place to place and Theodora wanted her to be spared the memory of those days. Enormous quantities of food, wine, gold, silks, jewels, clothes, carpets, drapes and hangings were hoisted on to the five ships that formed the Empress's grand procession to Bithynia. The two days of loading were supervised by Armeneus, who was not at all happy that his mistress's affair meant he was forced to leave Narses behind for the next month. At last all was ready and Theodora was called. She had spent the previous night with Justinian, as she had done every night since Narses decided the trip was necessary, making love to Justinian, sleeping with Justinian, taking care of Justinian – playing the traditional wife as opposed to her preferred role of equal consort, and doing her best to ensure that no matter what poison Pasara might have passed on, her husband would think of her fondly while she was away, desire her more keenly from the moment she left.

The Emperor and Empress walked together down to the dock.

'You look tired,' she said.

'I am,' he agreed, 'but the work on the edict is going well, I'll have a break soon.'

'And then begin plans for sending Belisarius' troops to Carthage.'

'Yes.'

'Antonina will travel with them?'

'She will.' Justinian started to say more and then stopped. Leaning closer to his wife he said quietly, smiling still, 'I used to think Belisarius was a fool, frightened to leave Antonina behind in the City.' Justinian had been holding her hand lightly, guiding her down the path, a touch just to show they were together, so the people would view the August as one, and now he grabbed Theodora's fingers so tightly that they were crushed into each other. 'Now I understand,' he whispered, 'that Belisarius would rather put up with her infidelity than lose her altogether.'

Theodora nodded, not trusting herself to speak.

Justinian went on, 'I will not lose you, Theodora.'

It was a question and a statement at the same time. They were closer now to the councillors and staff who were waiting to wave them off, Theodora had no time to explain or defend herself, which was no doubt what Justinian had intended.

She whispered, 'No.'

'Nor,' he added, loosening his grip just a little, stroking his thumb along her fingers, 'do I want to lose you to Narses' idea of what a good wife should be.'

'The eunuch likes his ladies to be quiet.'

'It was the eunuch who brought me a grown woman in the first place. We had no call for a malleable girl. Perhaps he has forgotten that. The dutiful Theodora is too placid for our Palace and, I admit, less useful. I miss my adversary, my cohort. I need your mind and your energy more than I need your wifely obedience.'

Theodora smiled then. 'But you do require wifely obedience?'

Justinian was not smiling when he answered, 'Yes. A little.'

Then the Emperor stepped back on to the dock, and the Empress stepped aboard the first grand vessel, all five ships were untied from their moorings, and Theodora gave a deep bow that brought everyone else down to the deck to honour the August, including a furious ship's captain who had better things to do right now than bob up and down at the theatre whore's will.

The boats pulled away and Theodora stood, eyes locked with her husband's, astonished again at how well he understood her.

That night Theodora lay in a thick-walled and dark room in the Metanoia convent, close to the Bithynia shore. Her room was no more than a slightly enlarged cell, with a mattress as lumpy, and blanket as thin, as any used by the women in the convent. She thought about how well her husband understood her. Anthemius held her in the small and dark room, lifting her on to his body and pulling her to him so fiercely with his tanned arms, his dust-ingrained fingers, that he left bruises on her back and thighs that would last for weeks. Their teeth smashed together in furious kisses and as they bucked and fought to breathe, each trying to find the other, as they sucked in the scent, taste, the richness and the full, hungry flesh of the other, there was a moment when Theodora saw Justinian quite clearly. His dark eyes, his beautiful hands, his faith in her, and his trust in their shared vision. And then Anthemius was all she thought of, and then they slept.

Twenty-One

Anthemius left Theodora's bed before dawn, returned silently to the boat that had brought him across the Bosphorus, paid the mute ferryman who was used to carrying tired men back from Metanoia to the City, and was at the Hagia Sophia site by the time his workmen arrived. He would not see Theodora again until her return from Bithynia.

The Empress's first appointment was with Domnica, the woman in charge of Metanoia. Starkly religious, wearing robes pulled so tightly that her bones were sharp beneath her all-encompassing gown, Domnica was thin to the point of emaciation. She prostrated herself fully in a bow that Theodora thought more ostentatious than observant. She had cold, dry hands she clasped together in either reverence or fervour, the Empress wasn't sure which. Theodora outlined her first thoughts about the establishment.

'I'm concerned to hear it's not unusual for men to find their way into the building late at night.'

'I have tried to deal with it, Mistress, but without the power to fully punish these sluts satisfying their lust, it has been hard to put a stop to it.'

Theodora heard the anger in her tone and probed further, 'You have tried?'

'Oh yes' – and now Domnica's cold hands were clenched so tightly her knuckles were stark white – 'I have tried refusing food, even refusing water to those caught meeting with men.'

'Denying them water?'

'And still they sin,' Domnica answered, disgust colouring her simple words.

Theodora nodded. 'Yes, some appetites are hard to subdue. Still, we want no more men ferried across the water by the obliging sailor out there.'

'Of course, Mistress,' Domnica said eagerly.

'The women are either penitent and welcome to stay in the house, free from the pressure of poverty and pimps, or they're not, in which case they're welcome to leave. I want nothing in between.'

Domnica could not have agreed with Theodora more, and saw the Empress's statement as an opportunity to list the penalties and punishments she wanted to implement. Theodora noted that all of them involved some form of denial, from food to water to sleep to conversation. In her time in the desert Theodora had known men and women who devoted their entire lives to penitence and some who found a perverse pleasure in exploring and punishing the sins of those less pious.

Domnica finished her speech, telling herself as much as the Empress, 'We will beat their sin from them, if need be, or starve it out. Or both.'

Domnica wiped the spittle of invective from the corner of her mouth as she brought her rant against the sins of the flesh to a close, and Theodora knew the woman was a danger to those she supervised, as well as herself.

*

Later that day Theodora met with Jacob Baradeus. The teacher travelled the length and breadth of Asian Rome, preaching in Syriac, Aramaic and Coptic as well as Greek, and was a constant barb to the Roman authorities. Occasionally he enraged local leaders enough for a call to be made for his arrest and then he would slip away, disguised in his beggar's rags, leaving only silence in his wake. Months later he would turn up again, speaking for the anti-Chalcedonian Christ that the Western Church condemned, as well as self-determination for the smaller nations under Rome, but always so gently that his passion was rarely noticed until it was too late to stop the whispers and sugges-tions of rebellion. Baradaeus was also known for his healing abilities; Theodora's religious mentor Timothy, who'd known the preacher in their youth, attributed it to his education in the Levant. Severus, who had taught Theodora in the desert and for whom miracles were a more everyday affair, believed the ragged priest possessed a healing gift. Both men trusted him implicitly and Theodora turned to him in relief. After a long afternoon in discussion, from which Armeneus noted that Theodora returned particularly thoughtful, Domnica was deposed as the ruler of Metanoia and an older, kinder woman took her place.

Theodora and her own priest John of Tella met with Jacob every day that week. A week that was six days too long for most of her ladies, who gazed across the shimmering water, imagining the towers and scaffolding of the City and wished for even the building-site comforts of home. Theodora talked with each of the women and girls in Metanoia; she listened to their stories and sent those who were unwell or especially unhappy to Jacob when she thought it necessary. Where she heard penitence and an eagerness to remain, the women were welcome to stay. Where she heard resentment of the rule but a greater fear of the world – girls who railed against the close confines of a convent but were too scared of pimps to return to their old lives – she suggested they remain until they had learned a trade, sewing or weaving. Although the law had changed and marriage was no longer impossible as it had been when Theodora was a girl, not all men had changed with the law, finding husbands for these damaged young women was still difficult. The younger girls found it easier to agree with her, the older women had further to bend, and not all of them welcomed the Empress's interest. Several agreed to leave after these conversations, some were asked to leave, and one made a show of her exit.

Domnica raged at any who came near her, furious at her loss of status, 'How dare that stage whore, living in luxury and ease, question my integrity?'

Her rants were loud and prolonged, but they bounced from the stone walls of her small cell and fell into silence when none of the women she had bullied chose to respond.

Determined to make her point, Domnica waited until the Empress and her people were assembled in the convent court-yard, loaded up and ready to leave for the healing springs at Pythium. The Empress was kneeling for blessing from both Jacob and John, as were the women and girls, who had lined up at the entrance, when Domnica called down from the tower on the western corner of the wide building, where the view across to Sykae was clearest, the afternoon light bright-est. Leaning out into the courtyard, her now-loosened robe flying behind her in the wind off the water, with a curse against Theodora on her breath, she threw herself to the ground below.

Children's eyes were covered by adults' hands, half a dozen

women ran inside pulling crying girls behind them as the rest looked on in shock.

Theodora remained on her knees and spoke quietly to the priests: 'You have not finished your blessing.'

They completed the prayer and only then did the Empress rise. Bowing to the house, nodding to the woman she had left in charge in Domnica's place, she joined those waiting for her.

As their caravan rode away Theodora took Sophia from Comito and kissed the hand that reached for her mouth, whispering to her niece, 'See, Little One? I knew she wasn't fit to lead. Far too extreme.'

The rest of their time in Bithynia was more relaxed. There was a week at the hot springs in Pythium where the women were pampered, the children played in warm sun all day and ran through fields with a freedom they rarely experienced in the Palace. Theodora sat beside her sister.

'You remember when we were like those two?' she asked, watching the toddlers Anastasius and Sophia tumbling and crawling over Ana and Indaro, all four squealing and giggling.

'Not quite,' Comito answered. 'We tended to squeal in glee when we'd stolen pastries and sweets from market stalls.'

'And squeal in pain from Menander's cane.'

The sisters smiled in remembrance of their brutal, beloved master.

'I sometimes think we were more free than these little ones, though,' Theodora said. 'I hear you and the girls shushing them all the time.'

'Our babies have more than we could have dreamed of. Yes, they have to be quiet at times: they do live in the heart of government, it's not much to ask.'

'I don't know, these Palace children will never have the freedoms we did.'

Comito turned back to her sister. 'Surely you're not pining for the days when you weren't mistress of the world? I know you crave solitude sometimes, but you love the machinations of the Palace as much as any of the men, maybe even as much as Narses.'

She was teasing, but Theodora agreed. 'I do, mostly. I don't love some of the problems that come with it, the endless negotiations and persuasions.'

'Hmm.' Comito closed her eyes against the sun and, settling herself more comfortably on the thick cushions laid out for their ease, said, 'You don't have to always negotiate, do you? You could just make some things happen.'

'Like what?'

'You did with Metanoia.'

'Yes.'

'And you have plans for my daughter already, no?'

Comito's eyes were still closed, her tone light, but this was the first time either had mentioned Sophia's future, and both knew it was a delicate subject.

'I think I do,' Theodora said, 'she's very young yet, it will depend . . .'

'On how she turns out?'

'Among other things.'

'Like Pasara's brat?'

Theodora sighed. 'You'd think over here I could forget about her.'

'But you hear her barbs anyway?'

'All the time.'

'It's because we weren't brought up to think ourselves worthy of all this.'

'It's because she's a bitch.'

'Yes, that too,' Comito agreed, sitting up, eyes wide at the sound of the toddlers smacking heads. In the split second of silence between the crack and the wail that would come when they realised they were hurt, she stood, turned to her sister and repeated herself, very clearly, 'You could just make some things happen.'

Comito hurried off to soothe her howling daughter and Theodora realised her sister was as ambitious for Sophia as she was.

From the springs they journeyed on to three different monasteries where the Empress, as she had promised Narses, handed over large endowments. A new roof at one, a rebuilt wall for another, a gilt mosaic for the third. The artist commissioned to create the gilt and lapis mosaic was keen to flatter the Augusta and offered to add her to his picture: perhaps he could depict her helping the local women, blessing the children of the small town?

'That won't be necessary,' Theodora began, aware that paying to enshrine herself was hardly what Narses had in mind when he'd demanded this fiscal penance.

John of Tella spoke up: 'Your household is funding these mosaics, Mistress?'

'Yes, but there's no need to make my image simply because I'm paying.'

The priest nodded in agreement. 'True, yet the roads on this side of the Bosphorus, travelled long enough, would take us to Antioch, to Syria, to those who worship and believe as we do. Men like the holy Severus.'

'Who brought me to my conversion.'

'And who even now is spoken of as anathema by the Chalcedonians.'

John lowered his voice and the mosaic artist moved away, aware that if the priest persuaded the Empress he stood to increase his commission fee considerably.

'Mistress, if you give endowments to your people, and if they want to create your image with that gold, then I don't see it as arrogance.'

'No?'

'It could be seen as a sign that our faithful are welcome in this Eastern stretch of Rome, where local languages flourish, and our worship puts its emphasis on form, on gesture, rather than the texts.'

'My image in this mosaic would do all that?' Theodora asked, smiling.

'Your image in this monastery would confirm that the Emperor is working towards the reconciliation of both sides, it would say his Empress is engaging with the people in the way she knows best.'

'I doubt it's what Narses intended when he told me to spend my own income ...'

'In penitence, yes, Mistress.'

Theodora stared at the man beside her. She had not brought him with her as a penitent might bring a religious adviser, but although they were united in faith, he was still a priest, and a fervent one at that. John of Tella opened his mouth to speak and then stopped himself, turning his face away, looking at the wall where the artist was working out his design.

Theodora reached out an open palm, offering permission, 'Say it.'

The priest kept his dark eyes trained on the wall, he rubbed his forehead and as he did so, Theodora noticed flecks of grey in the hair at his temples, grey she had not seen before, age she had not noticed in this man, born within a year of her husband. 'Narses is far over the water, Mistress, it's not now, nor has it ever been, his role to advise on the Augusta's spiritual well-being.'

'You wouldn't have him judge me?'

John looked at her then and Theodora was taken aback by the anger on his face: 'I wouldn't have him persuade you that guilt can be assuaged with gold.'

There was silence until Theodora said quietly, 'I'm not sure I do feel guilt.'

'Or shame?' And now his hooded eyes were staring into hers.

Theodora looked away, the gaze too close. 'No. Nor shame either.'

John rose and bowed, ready to leave. 'In that case, it doesn't matter how much you pay, or what's depicted in the mosaic, but I'm sure our Eastern Church would be cheered by your support.'

The mosaic artist received his larger commission.

As much as the Augusta's caravan of litters, sedan chairs, carts and carriages carrying gold and cloth and food, and slowly divesting itself of a stock of alms, was a symbol of the power of the state, and as much as Justinian and Narses counted on it being so, the time away from the Palace was also a rest for Theodora. She who had worked since she was five years old spent long days simply playing with the babies, more time with Comito than usual, and found she was happy to do so, the sisters laughing in a way they had not done since they were girls. In each new town Theodora met with local dignitaries and with local performers, encouraging both to speak with her priest, a safe way to assure them of her religious support.

After a month of travelling Theodora took three days for herself in a small monastery. She went to the room the priests gave her, tiny and sparse by Palace standards, palatial compared to the shadow of a rock in which she'd spent her desert years.

Asking only for fresh water to be brought morning and evening, she began to study herself closely as her mentor had taught.

Theodora slept, dreamed, woke and slept again. Her dreams were of purple and power. The power she enjoyed and the power that scared her; scared to use it, tempted to use it, tempted to abuse it. When awake she studied her more recent actions, as Empress, as wife, as lover. In prayer and then in trance, she gave time to the desires she rarely had time to express, let alone to take seriously; the desire to dance, to laugh drunkenly with Sophia, to stay awake all night and sleep all morning if she wanted to, with no one calling her to a meeting or procession, correcting her on protocol. She weighed her previous freedoms against her current privilege. She listened late at night for the owl and was sorry she heard it only in her dreams. She remembered her father, his life ripped from him by the claws of his own bear, the bear he loved. She thought about her mother who had buried two husbands and two children before her own death, Anastasia and a little stepbrother Theodora had never really known, and in thinking about Hypatia was surprised to find a compassion she had not noticed before. On the last night alone, Theodora prepared to sit awake as she had done in the desert. She prayed to the emerald Virgin which travelled with her always, and then sat, silent and waiting. An hour before dawn she finally heard the owl in reality, not dream, and nodded to herself. She would have stayed longer if she had not heard it, would have been happy to wait, but the owl had always been an alarm for her, it was time to go.

Theodora stood and stretched back into her body. There was plenty to do – the religious schism to negotiate, fractious priests to placate. Belisarius would no doubt return triumphant from Carthage in time; if she took charge of the Triumph on his return, she could ensure he was praised and yet kept in his place at the same time. All that, and she missed Justinian, wanted his intelligence and his conversation and his body. She stretched again and heard a last owl screech as the sun finally back-lit the tip of the trees in the monastery's orchard. Theodora acknowledged the morning and, as her mentor had taught her, gave up her last insight to the new light – she missed Anthemius too.

She walked back to the encampment where her entourage were just waking and as she did so she realised there was another secret, an understanding darker than her desire for Anthemius. She had to do something about Pasara. Comito was right, there was no point persuading Justinian to cling to the purple if that purple was to go to Pasara's brat. Perhaps there were some things she could just make happen. It was time to go home.

Twenty-Two

The Augusta's homecoming was welcomed with public ceremony and personal fanfare. Justinian was on the dock to greet her, as were several priests, the small group of her household staff who had been left behind with Mariam, and Narses, standing beside his master, ready to bow to his mistress but keener still to see Armeneus after the long drought of the past weeks. The Empress's ships sailed into harbour, and Theodora's spirit was caught again, as always, by the sight. Her City, the seven hills, the landscaped terraces holding the villas of the rich, their wide balconies and perfect sea views, places marked by half-arcs of walls that spread north and east from the Palace, counting the ages of the City like rings in tree trunks. Hidden away at the base of the hills was the distant chaos of tenement housing where she had grown up, barely hinted at from the sea, leaving the full panorama of Constantinople as enticing as it had been for any of the seafaring refugees and fortune-seekers who had poured in since Constantine remade it in his own name. Even in her pleasure at coming home, the sight of Hagia Sophia's building works reminded her of the losses, and she held the little Sophia tighter. Then the City rushed closer, the ship was tied in, there was a precarious lean landward as women ran to the shoreside deck, waving to their husbands and their older children. The Empress's name was called and Theodora handed the baby to Comito, walked out of the crowd on the deck, head and neck fully weighted with all the ceremonial jewellery she had taken with her. She stepped carefully on to land. The Empress Theodora lowered herself steadily, elegantly in the perfect bow she reserved for her husband and the waiting crowd cheered.

That evening there was a feast, a dozen courses of the kitchen's finest dishes with well-matched drink to celebrate the travellers' return, City flavours and Palace wines welcome in their mouths after the simpler tastes of the Bithynian monasteries. That night Justinian was also welcome in Theodora's bed, in her body. In the morning, lying alone, her husband gone to his office before first light, she listened to the waking Palace and the constant murmur of the City beyond the walls, then she bathed and dressed and told Armeneus she wanted to visit the building sites, see the progress made in her absence. She did not mention Anthemius. When she was ready to leave the Palace complex she found Justinian waiting for her at the path to the Chalke.

'You're coming with me?'

'I've missed you.'

'Don't you have work to do?'

'This is also my work.'

Theodora smiled. 'Inspecting the building work or accompanying me?'

'Both. And we have a lot to catch up on.'

'We can do two things at the same time.'

'We can.'

They toured the building sites together. The newly completed Baths were the perfect combination of cool marble and elegant lighting, with beautifully moulded oil lamps carefully recessed both to protect them from the humidity and to give the most subtle illumination.

Theodora picked up one lamp, studying the assembly of half-naked charioteers on the relief. 'Have you seen these?'

Justinian took it from her, peered at the scene and then handed it back, shaking his head. 'Narses suggested a Greek artist.'

'Obviously.'

They laughed and moved on, the lamp-maker in question following behind with the other designers, pleased his provocative image had not caused any greater interest, and relieved he'd allowed Narses to persuade him not to use the more explicit lamps in the Baths. The lamps that now graced Narses' private rooms.

The water had yet to run through the piping, the heating mechanisms still to be tested, but it was clear that, no matter how fine the new Senate buildings, the new Baths would be, once again, where the City's real business was conducted. The August couple applauded the builders, praised the site supervisor for bringing the project in on budget, and then moved on to the Hagia Sophia site.

The great foundations had been completed in Theodora's absence and Isodore stood at the edge of what would be the southern entrance, arguing with his foreman over the exact date the cranes would arrive for the next phase of construction. Justinian and Theodora moved quickly on, not wanting to halt proceedings with the formalities their presence demanded. Back in front of the Chalke they spoke to several recently engaged mosaic artists who were preparing to decorate the last sections of the formal entrance as soon as they were completed. Finally they headed on to the site of the Church of Sts Sergius and Bacchus, where Justinian promised

Theodora would be delighted with the building and with its architect.

They made their way slowly downhill, a street-sweeper ahead of them, a retinue all around, constantly stopped by alms-seekers or those who asked for the August's blessing. The gentle walk from Hagia Sophia to the smaller church site gave Justinian plenty of time to share the details of Belisarius' preparations for war against the Vandals in Carthage, to tell his wife about the fleet of ships they were readying for his command, the Roman treasure they hoped to bring back to its rightful home.

'Will Antonina go too? Neither she nor Belisarius are keen sailors.'

'I know, but the generals agree this is the best way to attack Gelimer, and Belisarius' men will follow him wherever he leads.'

'Then I wish him success.'

'But not too much success?'

'No, just enough.'

Theodora was easy with her husband, she knew they made a good team. Although the nickname was rarely whispered these days, if Theodora-from-the-Brothel could be their ruler's guide and adviser, then the poor and the non-conformist faithful, the refugees and the outsiders who also made up Rome, trusted she might speak for them. Theodora knew this, and Justinian knew it, and they walked on, well aware of the image they presented.

They were also aware of the man they were about to meet. Both husband and wife felt the tension rise. Theodora's colour became a little warmer, Justinian's hand held hers more tightly, as they rounded the corner to the site of the church of Sts Sergius and Bacchus, Anthemius and Isodore's prototype for the new Hagia Sophia.

And then neither Theodora nor her husband thought of the people. They were thinking about the young architect – nothing like the idea of a mathematician, a worker in abstractions – charging towards them, fitter and leaner than ever, dirtier too, covered in fine dust from the stonecutters' workshops in the west of the City, out of breath from running to the building site when he'd only just been told the Emperor and Empress were coming to inspect his work. Anthemius flew at them, arms outstretched, hands ready to hold them back. The ceremonial guards accompanying the Imperial couple looked to each other wondering if they were finally meant to use the weapons they carried as part of their costume, and if so, how.

'No!' Anthemius was shouting. 'You can't look yet, not here.'

Theodora stopped, and Justinian held out a hand to the jittery guards as Anthemius threw himself into a hasty bow on the dusty ground; the road leading to the church was also part of the renovation work, and not yet finished.

'No?' Justinian enquired quietly, lightly.

Anthemius spoke from his knees: 'Master, the view is better from the other approach, they shouldn't have brought you this way. Please, if you will . . .' he hesitated, 'if you'll both close your eyes, I'll show you the proper vantage point, the best impression.'

Justinian, laughing, closed his eyes and held out his arm to be led. Theodora had no choice. Anthemius stood between them and took both their hands. Theodora felt his gritty palm in hers, and bit her tongue to keep from speaking. Anthemius walked them a hundred paces to the east, carefully guiding them, aware that no matter how ceremonial the guard, the swords they carried were very real.

'You can look now.'

They blinked and looked past the scaffolding that created the shell of the little church, the perfectly formed baby sister to their great church on the hill. When Justinian applauded the work and Theodora nodded, Anthemius again fell to his knees, kissed Theodora's foot and then looked up, utter joy in their appreciation of his work, of his paper plans made real, shining on his sun-darkened face.

'It was as if we'd never been lovers,' Theodora complained to Antonina.

They were seated in the long sunny room looking down to the shore and the lighthouse, the Bosphorus sparkling against the green backdrop of Chalcedon.

Antonina shifted her sleeping daughter against her shoulder. 'Did you want him to slaver all over you in front of the Emperor?'

'Of course not. I just . . .'

'Wanted him to give his attention to you, only you, with no interest in the August's opinion of his work, his art?'

'Yes.'

'Theodora, for an ex-whore, you really have very little understanding of men.'

'I hate to disillusion you, Antonina, but whoring has very little to do with understanding men.'

Her friend reached for another stuffed fig, felt the baby begin to wriggle herself awake and passed her quickly over to Mariam, the feeding and cleaning of children never her speciality. 'Then it's your loss. You can't expect to go away for six weeks and not have your lover—'

'Keep your voice down,' Theodora snarled, watching Mariam blush.

'Mariam doesn't mind what I say about you, she's the perfect servant, devoted and silent. Aren't you, dear?'

Mariam turned to Antonina, curtsied, and then carried on with her work, minding other women's babies.

'Don't be cruel,' Theodora said quietly, 'not all women are as hard as you and I.'

'Hard? You?' Antonina laughed. 'Empress, you may have lived a hard life – some time ago now – but if you were truly hard, the architect's behaviour wouldn't upset you in the slightest. He's young, he's proud of his work. Yes, you've enjoyed each other in bed, but your patronage, your husband's patronage, will do more for his life – his career, his reputation – than anything the two of you have shared.'

'He wasn't using me, Antonina.'

'Of course not. Any more than you used him, as a distraction, an enjoyment.'

'More than that.'

'Fine, it was lovely, but it's over, and it's safer that way. You're not me, Theodora, you don't get to have lovers and still trust that your husband believes the best of you.'

'Only because Belisarius chooses to disbelieve the evidence of his own eyes.'

Antonina grinned, eating another fig and licking the sticky residue from her fingers. 'Lucky me. And you were lucky to get away with having Anthemius as your lover, don't push it. If all he is now is your architect, then at least it shuts Pasara up for a bit.'

Theodora frowned. 'I certainly didn't miss her.'

'My family are Anicii, my aunt was Juliana of the Anicii, Germanus is the nephew of Justin, just as Justinian is ...' Antonina perfectly aped Pasara's elegant patrician voice, reverting to her own accent to add, 'You should get rid of the bitch.'

Theodora started to tell Antonina what she'd contemplated while away, the possibility of doing just that, and then bit back the words with a smiling sigh. Despite her casual demeanour, Antonina was easily as ambitious as Pasara, Theodora knew better than to trust her with this secret.

The Empress shook her head. 'Germanus is too important to upset his wife any more than necessary.'

'What if Germanus had a new wife? Obviously something would have to happen to the old one first . . .'

'Don't tempt me,' Theodora whispered, making light of Antonina's speaking her own dark impulse. 'Anyway, there are others more threatening, Amalasuntha for one. All we ever hear from Italy is how fully she supports Justinian's new Rome, how wise she is, how beautiful. If any wife is to be let go, I'm more likely to be dismissed. It would be a sensible union, the Emperor of Rome and the beautiful, refined Regent Queen of the Goths.'

Antonina lowered her voice and said, 'There are ways. It wouldn't be the first time. Amalasuntha, and Pasara—'

Theodora interrupted her, 'I know. It's not that easy.'

'Of course not, you're only Augusta, you have no power at all.'

Theodora sighed, stretched, looked around the room, searching for something to distract her old friend who was too close to catching her thoughts, thoughts she didn't want to acknowledge. Antonina followed her gaze, from the slaves stationed by the door to answer any call, to the children seated with Mariam and their maids, to the stunning view, the delicately inlaid table between them covered with figs, grapes, peeled and quartered pomegranates, tiny pastries laid out between the fruit, dripping with honey. She counted the four jugs of different wines, the cool fresh water, changed more often than it could ever be drunk so that it never tasted stale to Imperial lips, and leaned back against the perfectly soft, perfectly stitched upholstery of the couches they had been lying on for half the morning. Then their eyes met and Theodora burst out laughing.

'Yes, it's so damn hard being me,' she said, her arms wide, taking in the incongruities of her life.

'Not as hard as a month at sea with a bunch of soldiers who loathe sailing as much as Belisarius and I do.'

'You don't have to go.'

'Oh, I'm as bored as you are in the Palace, I like the roughness of the soldiers' camp.'

'And the roughness of the soldiers?'

'Some of them,' Antonina agreed, 'but I doubt I'll enjoy their company on the journey there, they're drunken bores at sea.'

'Don't let them drink – fill the wineskins with water. And don't tell them until you're well away at sea.'

'Perfect, sober bores.'

'They'll be kept busy enough on board, preparing for the assault,' said Theodora.

'They'll have to be, there's been no preparation here. I know it makes sense to go so soon: if the first assault goes well we could be in Carthage long before the Christmas festival. But it's a risk with men so unready.'

'Your husband believes they'll manage?'

'My husband believes in his own fortune, yes. And he's been right so far. Then you, Mistress, will organise his Triumph.'

'For a soldier?' Theodora asked. 'That'll be the first in a very long time.'

'Yes, but the Emperor's already writing him up as conqueror of all Africa, they've started the mosaic celebrating his victory. Belisarius will merely be fulfilling the prophecies of the Empire's civil servants.'

'The August is very sure of your husband's success.'

The two women smiled at each other, aware that Belisarius' ambition stung Theodora even as it delighted Antonina.

Theodora changed the subject: 'What about your godson? Now that he's joined Belisarius' ranks, will you demand a Triumph for him too?'

Antonina leaned closer to refill their wine glasses and whispered, 'Theodosius doesn't need a triumph, Augusta, he has me.'

Theodora turned sharply to her friend, taking the glass offered her as Antonina's smile confirmed she had begun another affair.

'You amaze me,' said Theodora, half impressed, half shocked.

'He's of age to go to war, Belisarius believes him one of our best, and – since just last week – I agree with him.' Antonina grinned. 'My godson will be journeying to war with us.'

The women toasted complication then, and passion, and Antonina's freedom to do what Theodora could not.

Then Antonina's daughter Joannina started crying again. Mariam lifted her and settled her on her lap where Ana's boy Anastasius was already comfortable. Joannina stopped her cries and the little boy, half a year older, reached out to her. The two children stared into each other's faces; matching small bodies, matching smiles.

Theodora watched her grandson with Antonina's daughter and spoke her friend's thoughts. 'Yes,' she said, 'they are a good match.'

Twenty-Three

Belisarius' Triumph took Theodora almost as long to organise as it took the triumphant general to sail home from Carthage with Gelimer, King of the Vandals, safely stowed in a spacious cabin, befitting his status. Contrary to many expectations – though not his own, or his Emperor's – Belisarius proved himself as capable on sea as on land. Just as the equinox heralded the beginning of the cooler months, he had led his troops into Carthage, where the Vandal kings had worn the purple for almost a century. Although the city was taken, Gelimer escaped capture, hiding for six months among the Berber tribesmen in the mountains of Numidia. When he was finally found and brought before Belisarius, Gelimer asked for three things.

'A lyre, a sponge and some bread.'

Belisarius' adviser and scribe Procopius noted each item, as the general asked his captive why he wanted them.

'I no longer have a kingdom, but I am a poet, and I need a lyre to accompany myself.'

'Of course.'

Belisarius waved a young soldier off to find a lyre.

'My eyes are tired, I am not used to mountain life, or life on the road. I'd like to wash my eyes.'

Belisarius nodded; another boy ran for sponges and water.

'As for the bread,' the deposed king went on, 'I've spent six months in these mountains . . .'

'The Berbers have been generous to you.'

'Yes, and you'll face a challenge if you intend to fight them off the land as well, they're a strong people.'

'But?' asked Belisarius.

'But they don't eat wheat, and whatever Rome may think, we Vandals are a civilised people.'

'And civilised people eat bread?'

'We do.'

That night, Belisarius and his men broke bread with Gelimer, captured King of the Vandals, and Antonina sent the story of the meal in her regular letter to Theodora. The next day war began again and in summer, nine months after leaving the City, Belisarius was recalled. It was over two years since Theodora had persuaded her husband to stay and fight for the purple through the noise and blood of the Nika riots. A Triumph welcomed the soldier home and Theodora ensured that this one showed the Emperor's strength, not the general's, no matter how good the younger man looked in his ceremonial armour.

Theodora, Comito and Antonina stood to one side of the Kathisma, with a clear view of the whole of the Hippodrome. Justinian took his usual place in the centre, chief officials and highest-ranking priests on either side of him. Belisarius and his men had marched down the Mese, through the main squares, past the Chalke where the Emperor's African success was now depicted in glorious gilt mosaic. The men began to assemble in the Hippodrome, marching into the arena in full regalia and lining up in ranks to face the August. They were there to present their trophy: Gelimer, King of the

Vandals, draped in purple and followed into the rapidly filling ground by cart after cart of gold, jewels and other spoils, many of them treasures the Vandals had taken during the sack of Rome a hundred years earlier, all of it now coming home, to the new Rome.

Standing proud among the heap of warm gold was the great menorah that Titus had originally confiscated from the Jews' Temple of Solomon in Jerusalem. Taken in the century of the Christ's death, it was saved from the Temple's destruction and brought to Rome only to be later captured by the Vandals. The menorah and other Hebrew treasures were known to bring bad luck to any who held them; bad luck evidenced by Gelimer's plight.

'We will return the pieces to Jerusalem,' Theodora had insisted.

Justinian was dubious. 'I know you count the Jewish weavers as your friends . . .'

'They were kind to me when I returned to Constantinople.'

'Yes, but Rome will not appreciate losing anything it once held so proudly – not now that it has been regained at cost.'

'It's not about what Rome appreciates,' she said. 'Those pieces have brought nothing but bad luck to whoever holds them. Look at Gelimer. Look at the Jews themselves. We can give them to a church in Jerusalem, but we're not keeping them here – our City has been broken enough.'

Justinian smiled at his wife's superstition, but he agreed: with things going this well, there was no need to tempt fate. The menorah was kept for the Hippodrome ceremony and would be sent back immediately afterwards.

Theodora had planned the spectacle meticulously, insisting Gelimer wear the purple when he was paraded through the City streets, expressly so that it could then be taken from him in public. The packed stadium watched as he was brought to the front, marched through the central arena crammed with fully armed soldiers standing to attention. At the point where Gelimer came level with the most senior of the military, in line with Belisarius, Germanus, Mundus and Sittas, all the generals shouted their allegiance to Rome and to the August as arranged. The soldiers took up the cry, and a full arena of spectators did the same, then the generals called again, the soldiers repeating, and the massed ranks of the watching public joined in, until the cries for Rome and Justinian and Justinian-the-great-Roman could be heard as far as the Wall of Constantine.

Eventually Justinian held up his hand for silence and spoke the words he and Narses had sweated over for the past week, the speech he had rehearsed a dozen times with his wife. The excellent acoustics of the venue required no raised voice from the Kathisma, but even so, the careful, measured tone he adopted meant the people had to make an effort to listen – just as Theodora wanted. The Emperor drew them in, speaking of justice, Christian Roman values and Roman Christian men and women. He spoke, too, of clemency where needed, passion where necessary. Raising his voice just a little, as he had been coached, he went on to talk of calculated risks, acting only when action was inevitable, when diplomacy and strategy had been tried to the utmost. Above all, Justinian spoke of the rule of law, Roman law, good law resulting in the common wealth of all. When he finished, the high-ranking Palace officials in the Kathisma and the soldiers and their generals in the arena waited as they had been instructed. They waited until the crowd began to applaud, until the people cheered and clapped, calling 'Justinian, August, Emperor, Rome!' Only then did the military and civil servants applaud, after the citizens' praise had been heard.

When there was silence again, Narses gave the signal. Gelimer, also rehearsed in his performance, took three paces forward. The crowd booed and jeered, the soldiers seemed to stand even more readily to attention. Belisarius stepped out and, at his signal, two of his lieutenants moved forward and pulled the purple from Gelimer's shoulders, stretching out the silk between them so the full effect was seen all around an arena perfectly lit by the mid-afternoon sun. The crowd whistled and stamped their approval, the purple robe was carefully draped into a neat skein of cloth and then the gilt-embroidered seam was passed forward and up to the Emperor, waiting in the Kathisma. The symbolism was lost on no one: the August reaching forward to take the purple, the young soldiers still holding it at ground level. The Emperor held the purple and by his grace it spread out and down to the military and the people, to Rome.

Gelimer, standing alone, chilled even in the afternoon sun, took in the image of himself as both the apex and the base of the picture, and sighed. He'd done this sort of thing often enough in Carthage, any good ruler knew the people were as much persuaded by a lowering of taxes as they were by scenes like this. He knew, too, that no matter how happy Justinian's soldiers were now, jeering as he lowered himself to the ground, prostrating himself before their Emperor, there would be grumbling in the barracks when pay day came and it turned out that Vandal gold was needed for the Empire instead of the men who'd worked to capture that hoard. His forehead on the ground, wearing only the thin robe they'd allowed him, his feet in sandals slightly too large, the better to make his gait hesitant and stumbling, Gelimer was relaxed and calm. In private negotiations over the past nights, Justinian had promised land in Galatia and a quiet retirement in return for information about the Berber tribes the Romans still hoped to subdue, along with Gelimer's agreement that he would fully play his part in today's proceedings. The Vandal king was almost the same age as Justinian and, since the death of his beloved brother on the battlefield, since the loss of his kingdom — and as he would be free to worship however he wished in Galatia, unlike Theodora's more careful faith in Constantinople — he was ready to retire. At Sittas' command he rose to one knee, offered allegiance to the Emperor and to Rome, and praised both Belisarius and his men. The crowd roared again, the soldiers were finally free to cheer without restraint, and Gelimer was led away, to an elegant room with expansive views and a table heavy with wine and good food. He was a king, after all; not for Gelimer the deep dark of the holding cells beneath the Palace.

As he went he smiled up at Justinian, and then across at Theodora, mouthing Solomon's words from Ecclesiastes, 'Vanity of vanities, all is vanity.'

Antonina laughed and called down to Belisarius who followed the deposed king through to the Palace, ready to join her for the private celebrations inside, 'He's finally learned he placed himself on a pedestal too high.'

Belisarius nodded in agreement, delighted with his work, with his army, and with his own standing.

Theodora and Justinian exchanged a look. Neither believed Gelimer had been referring to himself.

Making their way through to the celebrations in the inner Palace, Theodora asked her husband, 'Was it too much, do you think?'

'It was certainly too much for Gelimer,' Justinian said, 'but no, not for me. And if he meant the vanity of Rome, not his own, well, we have much to applaud. This is a good day, I don't mind comparison to Solomon.'

'Nor should you.'

'The people were happy.' He broke off to listen to the crowds leaving the Hippodrome and spilling out into the streets, faction catcalls replaced with united chants of Roman glory. He corrected himself, 'Are happy.'

'Yes, the people, who were screaming for our demise two years ago, from the same spot, now weep in your praise, forgetting the blood beneath their feet.'

'That's not entirely their fault. You put on a faultless show, they were swept along.'

'They were meant to be.'

They parted at the corridor that led to their rooms. Theodora wanted to wear different clothes for the Palace celebrations: the Imperial chlamys was too heavy anyway, but she also wanted to look her best. Comito had been preening herself for Sittas for days, and Antonina had rushed to Theodora's rooms as soon as she came back to the City, keen to share the delicious time she'd had with Theodosius while Belisarius was high in the mountains searching out the Vandal hideaway. While her women delighted in the glory of their men, Theodora had been coaching her husband in his speech, planning the perfect route for the Triumph, and working out how best to make sure Belisarius was honoured, yet keeping Justinian at the forefront of the public mind. She had done a good job and now she was ready to play. She and Justinian would re-enter the celebrations in the finest silks China could provide, but free of jewels and adornment. They would appear, even to their closest circle, as victorious yet pure, not revelling in Rome's success, but serving it. Those who worked in the Palace would understand and appreciate the symbolism. And those who worked for the Palace – Anthemius for example, who had also been invited to the party – might not understand the full significance of Theodora's simple gown, but would see it suited her perfectly, and that the lines of her neck and arms were as fine and elegant as those of Anthemius' own buildings. Even as she maintained a polite distance in their dealings, Theodora still wanted to make sure the young architect was aware of what he could not have; what she could not give him.

Long after Justinian had left the revellers to return to his office, Theodora was still in her favourite courtyard, seated on her own against a wall that held the sun's heat well into the night and was warmed now by hundreds of tiny iron braziers, each miniature fire providing warmth and the prettiest of light shows, flame-coloured stars flickering on the Palace walls behind. The children were in bed, their mothers had just left, Germanus and Sittas were arguing with Belisarius and Mundus about the best way to prepare their men for what would surely be war against the Goths within the next year, Antonina had used her husband's preoccupation as an opportunity to rush Theodosius off to an empty room, and even Narses and Armeneus had taken advantage of the lull to move to a quiet corner of the grounds, closer to the waterfront. Theodora stood up, ready to make her way to bed. This success in Africa simply meant Justinian and his staff had to work longer hours, aware of how much more there was now to do in Italy. She sent Mariam off to prepare her room and, with no one around to be shocked at the impropriety, took off her slippers, dropped her outer gown, hitched up the light silk robe she wore beneath, and tied it into a knot by her left thigh to leave her legs free, then began to climb the wall. There were few handholds but with effort, several broken nails, a grazed knee and a bruised elbow, she made it.

She had been wrong to think no one was there to see her.

Pasara, sitting on the other side of the wall, looked up as Theodora settled herself on the top, let out a cry that quickly turned into a barely disguised laugh.

'Mistress! Of course, once a circus girl . . .'

Theodora caught her breath and took a moment to calm herself, allowing her impulse to jump back down to be over-taken by Imperial calm.

'Pasara. What are you doing here, cousin? Hiding from your husband?'

'No, I'm waiting—'

'You'll wait a long time for Germanus to come to your bed tonight.'

Pasara stood, with a fixed smile and her eyebrows raised. 'You consider yourself an expert in the night-time habits of our men, do you, Mistress?'

Theodora would have taken it for the outright insult that it was, but as she spoke Pasara made an impeccable curtsy and lowered her eyes.

'Germanus is off with the other drunken soldiers,' Theodora answered, 'debating the best way to win Italy from the Goth hordes.'

Pasara smiled delicately now, standing again. 'I would not expect him to come to my bed when he has work to do. The women of my family are bred to put our own needs second to that of the Empire, we know our place.'

Theodora, stuck on top of the old wall, tried hard not to be stung by the words, but Pasara was right. Those women did know their place and she, quite plainly, did not. Pasara took the opportunity to rub it in even further.

'Of course you find all this ceremonial exhausting, Mistress. Having to stand around all day, being polite to the visiting dignitaries, speaking Latin so they feel more comfortable. It's not your first language, is it? You weren't raised to behave in this manner, it's no wonder you need to run wild occasionally.'

Ready to jump down and smack the woman across the face, but knowing that was exactly what Pasara was after, Theodora carefully crossed one leg over the other, adjusted the neckline of her dress so her breasts shone in the cloud-hazed moonlight, hitched the knotted skirt of her robe up just a little further, the better to show that her legs were still as shapely as they were strong, and lowered her voice even more, so Pasara had to come closer to hear her.

'You're very low down there, Pasara, I don't think you'll quite reach my foot, but you can blow me a kiss if you wish.'

'I beg your pardon?'

'Sorry, don't they teach Anicii girls to blow?'

Pasara stepped back and stared up at Theodora. 'Of course they do, Mistress, but unlike theatre tarts, they also teach us how to behave outside the bedroom. Anyone can learn the brothel skills to please a man. Anyone. It would appear, however, that it takes generations to breed the kind of woman who knows when to keep her mouth and her legs shut. Such a shame you and the Emperor have no children of your own, you might even have bred a girl with manners yourself, eventually.'

Theodora sized up the distance from wall to ground, reached her arms up and out for leverage, and dropped down without so much as dislodging the knot of her robe, landing just in front of Pasara. Any other time she would have been proud of her careful leap, now all she could think of was how much she wanted to hurt the woman in front of her. Her hand was up, ready to strike, ready to grab the hairpiece Pasara used to hide her thinning hair – a trick she'd learned from her old aunt, the equally balding, equally arrogant, Juliana Anicii. It was only Pasara's smile and the satisfied glint in her eyes that stilled Theodora's hand. The two women stood, a breath apart, and Theodora's fingers were claws, her brow furrowed, lips curled. She saw herself as everything Pasara believed her to be: an ill-bred brothel-tart backed into a corner, grasping for words. She was her father's bear – face red, teeth bared. Tendons bulging in her forearms as she stilled hands that were aching to attack, she brought herself back to Augusta, was herself again. Too late. The look in her opponent's face told her it was far too late.

Pasara turned and slowly, impressively slowly – Theodora had to give her that – walked from the courtyard and up into the Palace. She did not bow, she did not acknowledge the Augusta, she simply turned and left. Every quiet step was a barb. Theodora, knowing her words, and worse, her attitude, would be all over the building before morning, wanted to scream out her frustration but knew that would please Pasara even more. She sat on the seat Pasara had vacated, and leaned back, the cool marble mosaic welcome against the heat of her angry body. She closed her eyes, wishing to be anywhere but here, anywhere but held in by the walls and the noise and the etiquette required of a Palace celebration.

She was saved from the self-pity she despised by the sound of two men entering the courtyard, and opened her eyes to see them kneeling before her.

'Anthemius, I thought you'd left our party.'

'I found a friend, Mistress, I wanted to introduce you.'

While the men knelt to kiss her foot, Theodora quickly untied the robe, adjusted her hair, and let her skirt fall to the ground. The silk fell a little over Anthemius' wrist and he left it there for a second, before he caught it between his fingers and kissed the fabric as well. She stood, holding out her hand and raised him.

He looked at her, uncertain. 'If you would rather we made an appointment with Armeneus?'

'Of course not, it was just . . .' Theodora shook her head,

lifted her shoulders in a helpless shrug, trying to laugh away the anger that still held her, 'Pasara. She knows exactly how to rile me.'

'Then perhaps we can distract you, Augusta?'

The other man spoke from where he still knelt on the ground.

'Mistress, this is my friend, Peter Barsymes, we met when I was studying in Alexandria,' said Anthemius.

Happy to be diverted from her self-loathing, Theodora held out her hand and the man rose to stand. He was a good head taller and half again as broad as his friend. 'Barsymes — you're Syrian?'

'I was born in Syria, Mistress, but my father was a trader. My family travelled a great deal when I was a child. The Levant, Mesopotamia and Armenia have all been my home.'

'And where were you happiest?'

'As a youth, in Antioch.'

Theodora said to Anthemius, 'Good scheming, architect, you've found me a friend who praises my second-favourite city.' Turning to the Syrian, his pale blue eyes shining in the flickering lights, she asked, 'And which city do you prefer now?'

'Given what you've just said, Mistress, I should say Constantinople . . .'

'But?'

'But we happened to overhear your conversation with Pasara of the Anicii,' Anthemius interrupted.

'And I must admit,' Barsymes said, 'having travelled so much for my work . . .'

'Which is?' Theodora asked.

'Peter is both a financier and a trader, Mistress,' Anthemius explained, his eyes only on the Empress.

Barsymes continued, 'While I love Constantinople for its

opportunities, the centrality of its markets, I find the arrogance of some of the people here hard to take. Especially when that arrogance is founded merely on name or wealth, neither made by the current holder.'

Theodora laughed. 'Your father was an unsuccessful trader? He left you no wealth?'

'My father was very successful, but I've been more so myself, and achieved all I have on my own terms. I believe that was one of the reasons Anthemius wanted to introduce me to you, Augusta. He thought you might find my work interesting.'

Theodora turned her gaze to Anthemius now, approving, her voice quiet. 'My architect is very skilled in finding ways to please me.'

Theodora arranged for Peter Barsymes to meet her in the morning and then made her way to her rooms. She slept badly, and alone.

Twenty-Four

Peter Barsymes quickly became a good friend to Theodora, making a useful chaperon for her visits to Anthemius – his presence not only prevented any further gossip about her friendship with the architect, it also stopped any inappropriate behaviour. Left alone with Anthemius, Theodora knew her desire would mean a return to the physicality of their affair, but with Barsymes present, even if he did prefer to stand in the long corridor outside the draughtsman's brightly lit workroom, it was safe for the Empress and architect to study plans and draughts, hands always almost touching, never quite touching. With someone else so close, Theodora was more likely to remember both her status and the danger of that position, to confine herself to the pleasure of briefly-held looks and potential, rather than the recklessness of sex, a danger she no longer wished to give in to, and yet didn't want to lose entirely. She knew better than to pretend to herself that their relationship was over just because it was no longer physical, but as long as their contact was limited to hands on papers, hands on scale models, this was the best compromise possible. Peter Barsymes helped her make it.

As was to be expected given his Syrian birth, Barsymes was more inclined towards Theodora's religious leanings than Justinian's, but he understood and supported the August's desire for compromise, for a coming together. While there were plenty of well-read, well-bred people working in the Palace, most who found a safe place in the hierarchy congratulated themselves and stayed there; even soldiers like Belisarius and Sittas gravitated to Palace life when they were in the City. In Barsymes, Theodora found a man who brought the outside world back to her cloistered life. Well travelled, skilled in business and diplomacy, fluent in Greek, Latin, the shifting language of the Persians, as well as Syriac, he represented much she missed in the close confines of her Palace life. He also brought an ability to speak openly, something Theodora, still missing Sophia's too-ready mouth, prized in a friend.

'I can understand you find the Palace a confined arena, Mistress.'

'I have done.'

They were walking in the outer courtyards, each one opening into another, each one more sumptuously laid out, more intricately decorated than the last. They followed a route that brought them close to the wall beyond which were markets, shops, streets teeming with citizens and refugees, with old ladies and children, all committed to one faction or the other, all passionately espousing one type of faith or another.

'I'm not so sure now. I do find the Palace constricting, but ...' Theodora's voice drifted off and she stopped.

'Mistress?'

'You didn't know me before, Barsymes, before the riots, before my friend and so many others were killed.'

'Were you different?'

'I think so,' she said, carefully, deliberately, trying to under-stand herself as she spoke, 'I was just as Pasara thinks of me, one of them, one of the people. I felt I knew them and could advise on what was best for the City, I wanted what was best for them.'

'And since the riots?'

'I want to support the Emperor in governing well, I want to do what's best for Rome, but as for the people ...' she shook her head, 'I don't know if I'll ever forgive them.' She smiled, then said, 'Pasara might want to send me back. I don't think I'd want to go now.'

Barsymes leaned towards Theodora, his face impassive as ever, his tone conspiratorial. 'From what I hear, Augusta, Pasara has her own problems. They say she spends far too much time with the son, and Germanus finds it irritating, to say the least.'

'Good. Just now all our women seem to be obsessed with their babies or their husbands or their lovers—'

'Not all three?' Peter Barsymes interrupted.

'Rarely all three,' Theodora smiled. 'Even Antonina rests occasionally.'

'So you are grateful I can gossip like a woman?'

'I'm grateful, Syrian, that you scratch your beard.'

Barsymes looked at her, confused, and his hand went invol-untarily to his close-cut beard.

'The beard still marks you out as an outsider,' she explained; 'such an outsider that people forget they need to keep their mouths shut around you. And you can then share their stories with me.'

He nodded. 'Sharing is one thing, Mistress. I could also – if you would allow me – offer solutions?'

'Believe me, I'd exile Pasara if I could. For now, the only option is to hope Germanus' irritation turns to dislike.'

Barsymes frowned, then said, 'Then this is not the right time. Instead, I will tell you about the new silk routes I've been looking into.'

Theodora allowed him to change the subject. Pasara was too much of a barb to think on for long and the price of silk was always a matter of concern at court.

'The real goal would be to make silk here, in the City,' she said, 'but the Chinese have been both bribed and threatened, they'll never sell their secrets.'

He smiled.

'What is it?' she asked.

Barsymes shook his head. 'Nothing yet, but if I could find a way to bring silk production to the City, you would support it?'

'In every way possible.'

He bowed. 'I'll do my best.'

They turned back and walked towards the scaffolding for Theodora's new Petitioners' Hall on the edge of the women's quarters, heading through the kitchen and medicinal gardens where the late sunshine of the early spring evening warmed the beds of young herbs and flowers. The stronger light had only returned in the past weeks, and was now spinning gold from the gilt of the mosaic paths. Pasara had upset Theodora again, just this morning, when she lifted her son Justin from the children playing together and covered his ears as the other children squealed and giggled and rolled about. It was true they were playing close to the room where Narses was meeting with his generals, but that room was usually empty until the afternoon, Mariam and Ana had meant no wrong by taking them there to play, and the babies were happy.

'She'd rather have her son sobbing in her arms than

enjoying the company of my family's children,' said Theodora. 'There's long enough life for them to be unhappy, why not let them play now? All she cares about is place and propriety and ambition.'

'While you have no ambition at all for the children of your own line?' Barsymes asked.

Theodora laughed. 'That's different, my niece and grandson were born into the purple, it's their mission.'

'Of course' – he was smiling too – 'so why not get rid of the woman? If she's such a thorn to you.'

'Because it's not as easily done as those rumours of our dungeons and torture chambers might suggest.'

'Then they are just rumours?'

Theodora looked at Barsymes, and said, 'I couldn't possibly answer that,' and then laughed, and he laughed with her. She continued: 'The August values his cousin Germanus as a general, as an adviser, and Germanus' men love him. We need him, he's still married to Pasara, even if it's true they're not happy, she'll never leave him and he's too stolid to consider divorcing her. I'm stuck with the woman.'

Barsymes stopped, searching the herb beds for a particular flower he'd noticed earlier in the week. He jumped across a raised section just coming into new blossom, and from a fenced-off corner picked out a flower. He handed it to Theodora.

'Pretty.' Theodora held the stem he'd given her, the tight wad of small dark purple flowers fading to pale blue at their edges.

'The flowers are, yes,' Barsymes said, taking back the stem; 'pretty enough for a poison.'

'Like Pasara – a pretty poison?' Theodora shrugged and began to walk on. 'I didn't take you for such a poet, Peter. What's the flower?'

'Wolfsbane, lycoctonum. Those who live in the mountains

between northern Persia and the Chinese border use it on their arrows when hunting.'

'And are the border Chinese shooting at hunting traders who cross the silk route?' Theodora asked.

'Not usually, Augusta, they're good tradesmen, they prefer not to frighten us off.'

'Or perhaps they shoot at traders who veer from the agreed route, into territories where they're not welcome?'

Barsymes shrugged. 'I've done both in my time. No, these hunters use it to bring down deer, horses, whatever they need. Sometimes they use small doses to capture the horses to break and train them later, other times just enough to stun the creature, before cutting its throat. There's no point killing it with such a lethal dose that the meat becomes spoiled.'

'But our doctors use it for healing?'

'They do. Rome likes to think it knows everything, but these same plants grow across the world, and people have found uses for them wherever they have settled. The Chinese I trade with know them by different names and have uses for them we haven't even begun to consider.'

'So you've found a useful poison among our herbs. Should I have the gardeners remove it? Isn't the fence enough to keep the children safe?'

'It is, Mistress.'

'Then why show it to me?'

Barsymes smiled. 'I'm sure I could find other uses for it.'

The light was fading and Theodora turned to face her new friend, staring at him. He was no longer smiling.

'I don't think you should say any more now, about herbs or flowers or poetry,' she said.

'Or Pasara?'

'Or Pasara.'

'Of course not, Mistress.' Peter bowed in acquiescence.

They went inside; the spring sun was giving way to the damp of the night. Over wine and figs, dates stuffed with almonds, salted olives and honeyed pastries they turned their conversation to the other woman disturbing Theodora's sleep.

Narses had suggested that Barsymes would be the ideal person to travel to Italy with messages from the Emperor to the Goth Regent, Amalasuntha. While Belisarius and the other generals were readying themselves for a campaign in Italy later in the year, Justinian was still keen to keep channels of communication open, and the Regent Queen's recent eagerness to communicate with the August had done little to calm Theodora's fears. Theodora knew that many on both Roman and Goth sides believed a match between Amalasuntha and Justinian would be the perfect solution to all their problems. Barsymes was recognised for his knowledge of the fastest and safest routes across the Empire. Sending her new friend with the Emperor's messages would ensure they arrived safely; it also meant he could return with the more personal information she craved. All queens were spoken of as beautiful, all kings as powerful: Theodora wanted to know if Amalasuntha was beautiful in truth, and more, if she had any real interest in the Roman Emperor. No more was said about Pasara and, once Barsymes confirmed his willingness to travel as the Emperor's messenger, they dropped all talk of rivals and jealousies and returned to their favourite topic of discussion, the city of Antioch where they had both lived and loved in the past.

Later that week Justinian agreed to the proposal that Barsymes act as their messenger, but had one concern.

'I hope he'll confine himself to our work.'

'He's a businessman, a trader by birth,' Theodora said, 'it's unlikely he could limit himself to crossing the Golden Horn without finding something to profit himself.'

'Amalasuntha's more important than his purse. We've promised her Rome's support.'

'Barsymes understands protocol, he knows court manners better than anyone but Narses.'

'The Goths are very different,' said Justinian, then added, 'and so are the Syrians.'

'You Westerners never trust those of the East.'

'Nor they us.'

'There's too much of Rome spread out between you. Justinian, I'm sure you'd prefer Peter not to think of his purse as he works for us, but he's a dealer by nature, better we encourage him to use that knowledge on our behalf. Who knows what he'll find to benefit the Empire as he travels?'

Peter Barsymes left Constantinople that week, sealed messages for the Regent Queen Amalasuntha in his bags.

Twenty-Five

Less than five days after Barsymes' departure, Mariam brought news that Pasara was ill with nausea and vomiting. Theodora thought briefly of the dark blue flowers in the herb garden, of how her new friend had sounded when he told her of the plant, then thought no more of it. Barsymes had been well on his way before Pasara fell ill. He might be a highly successful merchant and skilled in social niceties, but it would take more than that to poison a woman in Constantinople while his ship was passing the coast of Greece.

Two days later, when Mariam told her Pasara was gravely ill, that the Palace physician had real fears for her life, Theodora decided she needed to speak with her herself. She stood before the closed door to Pasara's private rooms, in her wake any number of slaves and servants who had never before seen the Augusta in this wing of the Palace. They barely saw the Augusta from one week to the next in their daily duties, and it was a complete shock that she should walk in, with neither announcement nor entourage, asking after Pasara's health. The health of the woman everyone in the City, let alone the Palace, knew was her avowed enemy. Standing at the door, her hand out to still the slaves waiting to open it, Theodora took a moment to look at those around her.

The slaves would do as they were told. That was all they did. They didn't mind which room they were in or what was asked of them, no matter how often the command utterly contradicted what had been previously ordered. They carried out any task that was asked of them, and often did so with no need for asking at all. The Palace ran on the work of its slaves and Theodora noticed it now, for the first time in months. She reminded herself of her early weeks in the Palace when she used to thank every slave who opened a door for her, greet those who brought her food, acknowledge their presence constantly until Justinian pointed out that she was not only making them uncomfortable, but was wasting their time as they bowed and scraped to her, when the skill most highly valued in Palace slaves was that of invisibility in the August's presence.

The servants were another matter entirely. Many were from families who had worked since Constantine's time in the jumble of connected buildings that were the Palace. Often they had chosen to work here when they might have gone on to higher positions in non-Imperial households, and they understood their small gradations of status with more clarity than Theodora could hope to discern, even after a decade and more married to Justinian. It didn't matter to the slaves that Theodora was here now, waiting to visit Pasara. They would go back to their quarters at the end of the day, and the doings of the Augusta would be of no consequence in their all too brief free time. The servants, looking up nervously from the floor where they were prostrate, twisting heads and wrenching necks to eyeball each other, were quite different. Along with Pasara's shocked ladies, many of them were already planning what they would say to their counterparts in other Palace buildings. Those not from the City were lying on the ground composing letters home, detailing the appearance of the Empress in the rooms, her lightness of attitude, the quiet tone of voice, the way – basically – she did not conform at all to Pasara's usual impersonation of her.

Theodora raised her hand again, and the slave turned the handle, pulling back the door to the room where Pasara lay.

The first thing that hit her was the stink – a cacophony of vile smells in the over-heated room. Initially she caught what must be bile in Pasara's vomit; then a deeper but no less bitter tang of shit, recently cleaned away but lingering regardless; and blood. The overwhelming smell was of too much blood. Theodora waved the servants and one woman from the room. The woman was nurse to Pasara's baby; now Theodora held the boy herself. Shifting the baby to her hip, she quietly moved around the room. She opened a shutter just a little and was glad of the soft stream of fresh air. She turned back to Pasara's bed; the sickness was more clearly illuminated now. And Theodora, who had lain in an Egyptian desert mountain during her faithful conversion and seen her own death arrive, was a little shocked at what she saw.

Pasara spoke, a whisper of vowels: 'Give me the boy.'

Theodora stayed still, by the window. 'You have been awake all this time?'

Now the voice croaked from a dry throat, bloodied raw from retching. 'When everyone must fall on the ground at your coming, it is hard for you to arrive by stealth ... Mistress.'

As ever, Pasara took a moment too long to add the Augusta's address of Mistress, and Theodora found herself smiling despite her customary irritation.

'Give me my son,' Pasara asked again and this time her tone was softer.

Theodora brought the child to Pasara's bedside and looked down at the skeletal woman before her.

'Your disease may be infectious.'

Pasara blinked, slowly, and a sigh caught in her ravaged throat. 'This is no infection,' she said, 'and I will die anyway. The boy will be fine.'

She lifted her arms for him and Theodora saw the cuts from the physician's attempts to bleed the illness from Pasara's veins, red welts slicing her fine patrician skin.

Pasara nestled the child against her and the marked contrast of his healthy colour, his small and warm body, the fresh scent of him, was shocking.

Pasara looked up. 'The child has done no wrong, Mistress,' she said, and this time she did not hesitate with the title.

'No,' Theodora agreed.

'And if Germanus finds himself a new wife soon enough, my son may yet have a mother before he grows too old to need one.'

'Yes.'

'So you will allow him to stay in the Palace?'

Pasara's voice was hard, her tone imperious as ever, but the film of tears over her eyes showed she was pleading nonetheless.

Theodora stood and questioned herself. All the slights, real and imagined, from the Anicii family over the years, and from so many like them. The old men she had danced for – danced and given so much more, old men too full of the privilege Pasara exemplified, who breathed the rarefied air of entitlement from their first breath and all too often didn't notice they had done so until their last, if then. And too, the times Pasara might have made it easier for Theodora when she first came to the Palace, times when a friend would have been so useful, a woman who knew the protocol and appropriate behaviour as well as she knew the lines of the boy now sleepily nuzzling her sunken chest. She stepped back. She could feel her hands itching to grab the child away, to reach out and shake Pasara who even now was demanding birth rights for this boy, making demands of the Augusta.

Theodora took another step away and now Pasara really was begging.

'Please? Mistress? I am asking only for the child.'

Then hundreds of instances of anger and rejection slapped down Theodora's training in faith, in forgiveness, and while her heart moved to answer yes, to reassure the dying woman that her son would be safe, the hurts and losses pulled her lips together, a closed mouth admitting Pasara no hope.

The slaves opened the door silently and with perfect timing as they always did and Theodora left the room without looking back, ignoring prying servants and crying ladies, ignoring both Pasara's stricken, broken cry and her own desire to lash out. If she could not be good, she would at least be silent.

When Pasara died of her illness, after a final day of fever, shaking, vomiting and purging, the fever too high, her body too weak to fight it, the physicians kept a close watch on the Empress, in fear that the illness might have been contagious, that her generous sickbed visit might be her undoing. There was no return of the sickness, just Germanus bewildered at the sudden loss of a woman he had forgotten how to love and yet had not wanted to lose; left with an inconsolable son who had never learned to be held by another.

Within weeks there was news of another death. Justinian's messages had not made it to the Goth Queen after all. Amalasuntha was found strangled in her bath, the day before Barsymes' ship landed. His messenger, sent back to the City immediately, brought no explanation, but it was easy to imagine the Regent Queen murdered by her own people: infighting among the Goth aristocracy was legendary. It was also possible she had been killed because they'd heard

Barsymes was on his way; the Goth generals who were as eager for war as Belisarius may not have wanted their Regent making agreements with the Emperor, preferring a chance to fight for glory. Amalasuntha's long-distance friendship with Justinian had been a problem for some. A problem now solved.

Narses brought the news to Theodora, who covered her face with her hands, trying to hide both her initial shock and a much greater relief.

'Is it wicked that I'm not sorry?' she asked him.

'You didn't know the woman, there's no reason for you to mourn.'

'I knew Pasara ...' Theodora didn't need to explain how she felt at her husband's cousin's death.

'Yes, but she was vile. We might feel bad that we don't feel more sorrow for her, or for Germanus, but that's not the same as grief at her loss.'

They smiled, guilt and no-guilt together.

'Will Barsymes return soon?'

'Yes, Mistress,' said Narses, 'the messenger from Italy said he would conclude some business there first and then come back.'

Theodora laughed. 'I assured the Emperor he'd work well for us. I hope he doesn't prove me wrong.'

Narses looked out at the grounds, the sea wall, and the water beyond. 'He's working very well for us, Augusta. Certainly, as a trader, he knows the shipping lanes better than any. I suspect he'll be home sooner than we might expect.'

Theodora stared at Narses' back. 'So he might also have arrived in Italy sooner than expected, sooner than we were told?'

Narses turned to her. 'I believe that is a possibility, Augusta,' he said.

There was a moment of silence between them, longer.

Then Theodora shook her head, understanding. 'Oh. At least he'll be able to tell me if she was as beautiful as they said.'

'Perhaps best not to ask. Still,' Narses said, picking up his papers, 'I hear there's great disarray among the Goth leaders now, each blaming the other for this new turn of events.'

'Which should make it easier for our troops?'

'Yes, I imagine if anyone had planned such an event and considered the consequences, he would have hoped it might do just that.'

Narses bowed and headed for the door, the silent slave quickly opening it for him.

'I thought Barsymes was my friend,' said Theodora.

Narses turned back. 'He is, Mistress.'

'Working for – with me, I mean.'

'We're all friends in the Palace, Augusta,' Narses smiled. 'It's to be hoped we can now be friends across all Rome too. I'll be interested to hear any news he brings of Matasuntha.'

'Amalasuntha's daughter?'

'She's young, but Germanus will need another wife soon enough, and Matasuntha might well fill the gap left by Pasara's death.'

Even Theodora was surprised now. 'Matasuntha is already married to Witigis.'

'Unhappily, I believe. They say the Goth general's rough, not what she's used to. It could all work out very neatly.'

Narses left the room and the sounds of the Palace were muffled as the slave closed the door.

That night Theodora prayed to the emerald Virgin, surprised to find tears coming to her eyes, feeling sympathy for Pasara for the first time in her life, in her death. Then she prayed for herself, for the woman she was becoming, prayed because although she felt sorry for the two dead women, she felt no remorse. She went to bed tired. She was Empress, taking care of the business of Empire, there was nothing else to be done – or if there had been once, it was too late now.

When Barsymes returned from Italy a month later he was summoned to Theodora's rooms. He walked in smiling, expecting welcome and praise and was stunned to be greeted with anger when he rose from his bow.

'How dare you?'

'Mistress?'

'I thought you were working for me?'

'I was ... I did ... everything I did was for—'

Theodora held up her hand and Barsymes stopped, both of them aware he had almost said too much.

'I don't understand, Augusta?'

'I understand that Narses knew more about your exploits in Italy than I did.'

'Narses is ...' the trader paused, knowing that anything he said now might anger the Empress even further. 'Narses is very certain of what's best for the Palace, Mistress. And for the August. And for you.'

'Yes. He is also persuasive, I'm sure.'

'He's certainly that.'

Theodora turned away, looking out of the window and across the water, to where she knew the women of Metanoia would be praying at this time of day.

After a few moments she turned back and asked quietly, not quite looking at Barsymes, 'Was she beautiful?'

'She was. Her daughter Matasuntha is also quite lovely.'

Theodora nodded, wanting to ask how much of this had

been done for her, how much for the wider politics, yet aware that knowing would compromise her even more.

Barsymes spoke up: 'We can trust, Mistress, that Narses always has the best interests of the August and the Empire in his plans.'

'That's true,' Theodora answered.

'So there's no need to feel—'

'I don't,' Theodora interrupted him, annoyed at his presumption, 'I won't. I'm relieved the beautiful queen is no longer a concern. I found my faith under Severus, who also taught me that guilt is a luxury. I will not indulge it, it won't change a thing.'

Barsymes was impressed. 'They trained you fiercely in the desert, Mistress.'

'They did,' she agreed. 'Now, these monks you're sending into China, will they bring back our silk?'

Barsymes talked Theodora through his new idea: that a team of monks might be able to pass into the hidden interior of the land, in a way his own dealers and traders had not. The last two traders he had sent were exposed as spies, tortured, and put to death just a week's journey short of the border, the news of their capture sent back with a nervous Chinese messenger. The monks he had now recruited professed to be willing to die for their faith. Barsymes was not sure they were also willing to die for silk, but he had persuaded them that the revenue from silk production would support their mission and so they had agreed to go, further into the Chinese interior than any had tried before.

'Will they succeed?' Theodora asked.

Barsymes shrugged. 'They're young, and strong, and they have zeal on their side. It makes them much more likely to succeed than the hope of mere wealth.'

'And if they're not successful in converting the Chinese?'

'The promise of an income from silk at home will encourage them anyway.'

'You have it all worked out.'

'I hope so, Mistress.'

'Good.' Theodora nodded to the door slaves, the sign for Barsymes to leave. He bowed to do so and as he reached to kiss her foot she stood up, pressing the full force of her small weight down hard on his fingers, twisting to grind them into the sharp edges of the tiled floor.

'You work for me, trader. Not for Narses, the Palace, or even Rome. Do you understand?'

His teeth clenched against the pain, and more, against the anger he could not show, Barsymes nodded.

'Good.' Theodora bent down apparently to push her weight more heavily on to her foot, but also to get closer to Barsymes, to whisper to him without her servants hearing, 'I wonder, the loss in the Palace, while you were away, was that also your work?'

'It . . . was,' Barsymes confirmed.

Theodora stood up and smiled, lifting her foot. 'I'll look forward to what else you can achieve Syrian. For the state.'

He nodded and backed out of the room. 'Of course, Augusta.'

Theodora shook her head as the door was closed behind him, her hands over her mouth. She was smiling, and shocked at herself. Shocked that she didn't feel worse, that her overwhelming emotion was relief, and joy in that relief. She had an accomplice, someone on her side.

Twenty-Six

Following his triumph over the Vandals, Belisarius was made Consul and soon after, Sittas was made patrician. Both were given honours to acknowledge their achievements, but more, everyone knew, to encourage them to do what was expected of them in the months and years to come. War against the Goths in Italy was part of Justinian's grand plan to reunite all Rome, and a newly promoted Belisarius was never Theodora's favourite Palace guest; the sooner he was on his way to Italy and away from the adoring young men of the factions, the happier she would be.

Meanwhile the schism between the faithful dragged on even more painfully than before. Theodora's mentor Severus had arrived in the City early in the year, making the journey expressly at her request. He'd shown himself amenable to reconciliation even though his strongest supporters in the Levant and North Africa were not, but two weeks after his arrival the news came that the Patriarch Timothy, Severus' religious ally, had died.

Theodora sat for seven nights in vigil with Severus, praying for her mentor, for the Church, and for Rome.

When she was finally done praying she went to Justinian's rooms.

'You're very thin,' he said, holding her narrow wrists, seeing the dark rings under her eyes. 'You've been fasting too long. Severus can't approve of you making yourself ill?'

'He doesn't.' Theodora smiled and accepted her husband's offer of a seat beside him, and the glass of watered wine he held out to her. 'Nor does Jacob who has been praying with us.'

'Jacob Baradaeus is here? I hadn't heard he was in the City.'

'He left this morning, you know he prefers to remain unnoticed.'

'Or hidden.'

'Jacob has less reason than you or I to trust the Palace's handling of religious affairs,' Theodora said. 'I've assured him and Severus that I will not stop working for Timothy's beliefs, it will be a way for me to honour his memory.'

'I thought you'd think so.'

She shook her head, tears threatening again. 'This loss feels so real, more even than when Hypatia died. He and Severus were both new fathers for me.'

'I know.'

'I hope it's not an omen, losing him.'

'I hope so too.'

Justinian kissed his wife and held her. He looked at the mound of papers on his desk, at the scribes waiting for his attention. Ignoring them, he pulled Theodora even closer to him, then walked her back to her own rooms, where he and Mariam laid her down on her bed.

He turned to one of the maids, who was terrified to see the Emperor at such close quarters: 'Fetch some food for your mistress. Something light, and make sure she has plenty of water.' Turning to Mariam he added, 'Tell Armeneus – tell him from me – that she is to hear no petitions, do no Palace work, for a few more days. She needs rest, and peace.'

Justinian returned to his office where a river of papers awaited him, spilling from his desk to the floor – letters from religious all over Rome, messages from rival wings of Goth aristocracy, too much Empire to care for.

If Timothy's death was not an omen, it certainly heralded worse; before Easter the Patriarch of Constantinople also died. Theodora's favoured priest Anthimus prepared to take his place and she arranged for him to meet with Severus.

'How was your meeting?' she asked Severus.

The old man shrugged and answered quietly in Syriac.

'I'm sorry teacher, I don't understand,' said Theodora.

He raised his eyebrows and smiled, speaking now in heavily accented Greek, showing his stained teeth. 'You've done well to find a moderate Patriarch, he and I can speak together, that's good. But there are hardliners on both his side and mine: we cannot force them to join hands.'

'Your followers would do anything you told them.'

Severus spoke again in Syriac, and this time Theodora understood his answer. 'Compromise, Empress, is for politics, not faith.'

When Anthimus was appointed Patriarch, Theodora sent messages to Macedonia to look into the attitude of Pope Agapetus, asking if there was a chance that he too might welcome a more moderate approach to bring both sides together. Macedonia's reply from Rome was disappointing, and certain:

The man is an arrogant idiot, which you'll find out soon enough yourself. My sources tell me he's preparing to travel to Constantinople. The Goth king is sending him to ask that you halt Belisarius' march towards Rome; so you may have some bargaining power, but I doubt it. The friends I've made among his priests tell me he has no understanding of negotiation.

Macedonia was right, when Agapetus arrived in the City, he not only refused to meet Anthimus, but deposed him as Patriarch of Constantinople and installed his own candidate as Patriarch instead.

Narses caught up with Theodora as she headed back to her rooms having just received, with Justinian, a lengthy lecture from Agapetus.

'The Italian Pope isn't as generous as we might have hoped.'

Theodora didn't mention she'd had prior warning about Agapetus. Narses might know that Macedonia was working for her in Rome, but she wasn't going to tell him if he didn't.

'Horrid little man. Kissing the August and promising he'd give him all Italy if only we'd stop the young general, but barely acknowledging my presence at all.'

She sped on through corridors, fury powering her walk, servants and slaves ducking and bobbing as she swept past. Narses had to stride to keep up with her.

'Pope Agapetus is interested in maintaining power, Mistress.'

'We're all interested in that.'

'Of course, but there are less blatant ways than haranguing the Emperor on the best direction for the Church.'

Theodora's speed slowed a little. Narses leaned in closer.

'Go on,' she said.

'For a start, I suggest you get Severus back to Egypt, and soon. He's old and becoming more frail, the journey here can't have been easy . . .'

'Nor his grief over Timothy.'

'No. Another good reason for him to go back, his people will need him.'

'Even if I want him close to me?'

Narses smiled lightly. 'I've explained before . . .'

'It's not about what I want, yes, I know. And?'

'And it might be wise to move Anthimus from the City too.'

Theodora stopped. 'You want me to remove all my own priests, just because that arrogant Italian is here?'

'That arrogant Italian is the Pope, Augusta.'

'I'd rather we removed him.'

They had stopped by a doorway opening on to one of the smaller courtyards; a single fountain threw a soft spray against green and gold tiles.

Narses looked away from Theodora, speaking quietly: 'As I said, Mistress, it would be best for your own priests to be away and, if I may say, for you to be as respectful of Agapetus as your rank – and his – demands. Show him all the courtesy you possibly can.'

'Eunuch, I've known you to be tough on protocol, but not usually when dealing with such pompous fools.'

Narses smiled, and bowed. 'Protocol is simply about what looks best, don't you agree? What looks best, both in actuality and in recollection, especially when circumstances change and we think back to how people have, or have not, behaved.'

Theodora had Armeneus book Severus on a ship leaving for Alexandria in the morning, and sent Anthimus into hiding on her estate at Hieron in Bithynia. Her small palace there had recently been extended by Anthemius according to her own design, and if the architect wondered about the number of hidden rooms and secret courtyards she'd asked him to incorporate in the new wing, he was too busy working on Hagia

Sophia to complain; nor did he object when, having shown her around the renovations, she demanded he burn the only plans to the building.

A week after Severus set sail for Egypt, the Italian Pope was found dead in his Palace bedroom. He had prayed as usual before sleep, having lectured the August couple, again as usual, before prayer, and had, apparently, gone to bed pleased with his work. He did not wake. His death was viewed by the anti-Chalcedonians as divine retribution, and Theodora noted that Narses, though far more pragmatic in his own faith, had no quarrel with the suggestion of divine intervention.

The night of the Pope's death Theodora found a small posy of herb flowers left in her private room, tied with raw silk thread. She opened her mouth to call Armeneus, to ask who had been in her rooms – had Peter Barsymes visited? – and then thought better of it. She did, however, send a private message to Macedonia saying negotiation was no longer necessary. This time there was no soul-searching prayer to her emerald Virgin before she went to sleep.

The unexpected death of the Pope brought another flurry of messengers, talks and debates, halted for a day so that Theodora and Justinian could attend the consecration of the Church of Sts Sergius and Bacchus. The August couple were led into the little church by a long religious procession, statues held high above priests' heads, incense and chanting carrying their prayers up to the dome and beyond. The consecration took a full half-day, then the priests and dignitaries, the people and their rulers, trooped back into the Palace where a feast was laid out for them. Narses and Peter Barsymes were assigned to ensure that priests from either side did not start quarrelling, while Justinian and Theodora made the rounds, offering introductions where dialogue might be possible, and useful diversions where it was not. Barsymes made no mention of any flower-gathering, or visits to the Empress's rooms in the previous days, but before he left he knelt before Theodora and she saw, quite clearly, that the silk he wore at his throat was the same thread that had tied the posy. He nodded, she nodded back: neither needed to say more.

It was long into the evening before Theodora finally had a chance to speak to the architect alone, to praise his work on the church, and when she did it was obvious something had changed. His hands were scrubbed clean, and he was also far better dressed than when he had been coming regularly to her rooms to talk, to dream his designs, or reach across a desk simply to touch her hand.

'The church is a great success, Anthemius.'

'Mistress.'

He bowed, kissed her foot, and took the hand she offered him. As he raised her hand to kiss her fingertips as usual, she saw Mariam watching them from across the room, and Theodora knew immediately why his hands were clean.

She drew him closer. 'Your little church is a glorious model for Hagia Sophia. The poems praising St Sergius are a very good touch.'

'They praise the August and yourself as well.'

'Yes, but Sergius is loved by our troops just arrived in Italy with Belisarius. The army will be happy.'

'It's always wise to please the men who carry weapons.'

'Indeed.'

'You saw the carvings of your own and the Emperor's initials linked?'

'I did,' she answered, looking across to Mariam again, noting that she turned away even more hurriedly this time. 'And your initials, Anthemius – are they to be linked too?'

She looked at his sunburnt face, his fine arms, those too-clean hands, his open mouth. Unsure how to answer, she felt her smile twist just a little. She knew Narses was watching, which meant Justinian, somewhere behind her, was surely paying attention. Mariam certainly was.

Theodora leaned in so that Anthemius had to stoop to hear her and she whispered, 'It's a perfect rehearsal for the greater building. So wise to go from one to another, perfecting your skills as you go. But architect, I am not a try-out for Mariam ...' Anthemius tried to interrupt and she pulled him closer, digging her nails into his hand. Smiling even more softly, she continued, 'She's young, and good, and too much that is vile has already happened to her. I can look after myself, as can you, we know that. But I won't let you hurt her. You must not have her simply as an alternative to me, a way to get close to me.'

'I'm not ...' Anthemius managed to speak. 'Mistress, I love her.'

Theodora's gut turned, his words were a slap she hid with a broad smile. 'And you cleaned your hands for her, that's a good sign.'

'I'm sorry.'

'I have no claims on you, Anthemius. I'm a married woman, married Empress.'

'Yes.'

'Go to her, and be kind.'

He hurried across the room to Mariam, and Theodora was hurt and showing no hurt at all when she turned brightly to her husband and Narses a few moments later saying, 'Good, a marriage – that'll be some distraction from these interminable quarrelling priests.'

Justinian kissed his wife's hand where Anthemius had not, and soon after he went back with Narses to his office, to their military plans and the plotting of popes and priests. Theodora held her court alone.

The next weeks, while taken up with the constant debate between the faithful, and with both spies and soldiers reporting that the Italian campaign was about to begin, were also full of preparations for Mariam's marriage to Anthemius.

Thanks to the patronage of the Augusta herself, the blessing took place in Anthemius' new church. Mariam, old for marriage at twenty-one, was treated as any new wife would wish, and as few girls who had been forced into child prostitution actually were, law change or no. They knelt before the priest, the first blessing held within the octagonal of the lovely new pillars, watched by Isodore the mathematician who had calculated the impossible reality of the dome above them. They were married in the presence of the Emperor and the Empress, and the eunuchs Narses and Armeneus, the only men Mariam had felt safe with until Anthemius, and she was granted the status of a virgin bride – because the Augusta said so.

Afterwards Theodora gifted the happy couple their own rooms in a Palace building distant from her own, closer to the Chalke and the rapidly growing new Hagia Sophia. Easier for Anthemius, but a long walk for Mariam back to Theodora's rooms for her work with her mistress and the children. And still not quite far enough away for the moments when Theodora bit her palm to stop herself imagining her lover with the girl, came close to drawing blood to stop the jealousy, knowing it would hurt her far more to hate Mariam.

Twenty-Seven

Palace life was busier still as the year progressed. So far from the battle lines, Justinian and Narses were, nevertheless, up at all hours, awaiting the latest reports, the fastest messengers. In Illyricum, Mundus' soldiers began the invasion of Dalmatia, while Belisarius' troops sailed into Sicily, re-taking the island without a battle. Before there was time to celebrate, news came that Roman troops were mutinying in Carthage, the heat and Berber attacks too much for men still waiting for the wages they'd been promised long ago.

In her regular letter to Theodora, Antonina wrote:

> Belisarius travelled to Carthage to calm the men, leaving me here to calm Theodosius, the sacrifices I make for the Empire! Mistress, you must make Narses push the Treasury to pay the soldiers in Carthage, and soon – those with us in Sicily are aware we have a long haul ahead, they'll give up if they think we're here with no compensation for our pains – and I can't be expected to keep up the morale of every one of them, can I?

Theodora shared an edited version with Narses.

*

Just before the end of the year, word came that Barsymes' monks had been found, tortured and killed, their bodies dumped close to the border, a fine skein of silk tied around each man's stretched and broken neck. Barsymes organised another team, this time sending trade spies alongside the monks, hoping that a second expedition would achieve what the first could not. His work then took him to Ravenna for trade and a little light spying on Narses' behalf – this time with Theodora's full knowledge and using Macedonia's contacts to ease his negotiations with those who had taken over on Amalasuntha's death. In Constantinople, Justinian underlined his intentions for the Empire by declaring Greek the language of state – the Goths might speak Latin in the West, but the Emperor and his troops were forging the new Rome from the East. Belisarius sent word he was about to cross into mainland Italy and then the messenger came with the welcome news that he had taken Naples. Soon after, Goth soldiers turned against their own king, blaming him for the fall of the southern city. Theodahad was killed and the general Witigis proclaimed Goth king. In the north, Mundus was killed in battle and Antonina wrote that Belisarius had lost himself for a night in wine and tears for his old friend. War had truly begun.

The day after they received the news of Belisarius' success, Justinian sent notice for Theodora to dress in her finest ceremonial gowns. There was no explanation.

She dressed in the heavy robes, the embroidered slippers, waiting while Mariam helped her with the Imperial chlamys and the jewelled headdress, feeling anything but calm. Clearly her husband was about to make an announcement, and Theodora, who had once been a scared little girl begging alms from the crowd in the Hippodrome, believed he loved her enough not to ask her to dress up simply to get rid of her. But she had heard stories of women shamed in public, had seen it happen, knew that however strong a couple they were, he was still Emperor, and there were plenty who would welcome a divorce now. If Justinian were to marry one of the many useful Goth women, then marriage bonds might stop the western war, save the wages of all those troops.

Theodora walked into the grand chamber and, every part of her wanting to look into Justinian's eyes to see what he had planned before she heard it, bowed without meeting his gaze, as was appropriate, bowed as low as she could in the stiff robes. Justinian reached out his hand to raise her. Then he stood by her side and, Theodora following his lead, they turned in a smooth circle to the whole room. The chamber was full of councillors, senators and law-makers, representatives of the people and representatives of dominions and other lands: the Persian ambassador, the linguist-dealers who specialised in the Chinese silk trade, four wealthy merchants from the other side of the Black Sea – newly arrived in the City and noted already not only for their trading prowess, but also for their interest in the still-growing Hagia Sophia. There were representatives of every rank of their society, and each one took note as the Emperor introduced his wife.

'Theodora, our most pious consort, given us by God.'

Justinian spoke the words first in Greek, and then in Latin. And when the assembled company followed Narses' example and fell to their knees, he led her from the chamber.

They were back in Justinian's main office when Theodora finally spoke.

'Thank you.'

'You're welcome.' Justinian was smiling, waiting for the question.

'What was that for?' she said, her voice raised louder, her pitch higher than she had intended, a pitch Menander would no doubt have slapped her for.

Her husband laughed and, helping her off with the chlamys and the headdress, the robes and the embroidered gowns, he explained.

'I know it's been hard for you, these past months, years. You saved me, saved us, saved the purple during the Nika riots. And we might have hoped, since then, to have had a quiet time, time for each other. Instead it's been worse – greater struggles with the Church, more of my time taken strategising the war, the offensive against the Goths.'

'We're a partnership.'

'Yes, we are, we have been since Narses first brought you to me. We've known, felt – believed,' he shook his head, grappling for the right word, 'no, we have determined, that we were meant to work together, and we do so very well. Now, heading into a time of real battle in Italy, and as the spies tell us Khusro may yet be drawn into the war as well . . .'

'But the Endless Peace?' Theodora interrupted.

'Might end.'

'Oh.'

'And there's the loss of Timothy, you still grieve Sophia . . .'

'I have Comito's Sophia to think of now.'

'And to train, I see that.'

Theodora frowned. 'I didn't think I was so obvious.'

'Only to me.'

'Then also to Narses.'

'He knows more than either of us, I'm sure.'

Theodora nodded her agreement, aware that Justinian was also speaking about Anthemius, and that even in nodding her head she was acknowledging what neither of them would speak.

He went on: 'You're right to think of the succession, of the purple. I don't have time to do so, but it's good that one of us does, it's good that you do.'

Justinian held out his hand and Theodora, seeming younger now, smaller without the ceremonial robes, went to him. They sat together, looking out from his office, across the wall into the City.

'It's going to be hard,' Justinian said at last. 'We've lost Mundus, we may lose many of our soldiers, but I believe this is the right thing to do. One Rome, one Church, one people.'

'One language?' Theodora asked in Greek.

Justinian smiled, held up her hand to kiss it. 'Latin's fine for strategy, for law, for war,' he replied in Latin.

'We are at war.'

'For now. We'll be at peace too, and Greek is a better language for faith. Making it the language of state is just a gesture in some ways. People will always use the words that suit their purpose, but these public statements do make a difference. You're more than my wife; you are my partner, my consort. Even when you don't feel it, you have always been God's gift to me. Theou doron.'

It was a long speech for Justinian, longer than she had heard from him for years. Theodora walked to the door, ushered out the slaves, locked it behind them. She closed the shutters that let in the light and sound and smells of the City and the hills and sea beyond. She removed the cushions from the divan Justinian never sat on, a divan that was covered in papers and maps and folios and scrolls, some so terribly old she knew he would have to look away rather than watch her handle them, some so new the ink smelt fresh and slightly bitter. She laid out the cushions and spread her own purple cloak on the floor over them, Justinian shaking his head and grinning as she did so. She then slowly removed her clothes. First the heavily embroidered red slippers, then the chiming gold bracelets, each one engraved with her own monogram, the heavy earrings of beaten gold and the layered ropes of pearls around her neck. Each piece was taken off and carefully placed on the floor, a precious mosaic around the bed on her husband's office floor. She undid the silver and lapis brooch that held up the elegant draping of her tunic, the silk falling in a rush to the floor, the purples of her cloak and tunic clashing and chiming with the reds and greens of the finely knotted carpet, the deep blues of the cushions, with Theodora's dark hair, her green eyes, and her pale olive-toned skin now that she lay naked on the floor.

She was thirty-five, he fifty-three. They were August and Augusta and outside the room, beyond the shutters and the closed door, the great City and the labyrinthine, ever-expanding Palace kept on their constant pace. In the room, now, for this moment, they were the two people who had first astonished each other with their mutual pleasure in lust, in passion. They were Justinian who gained his skills early in life with a girl from his own village, and then perfected them forty years ago in the City with an older woman he had loved but could never marry. Justinian who believed both women had readied him for Theodora. He stroked her back, his hands sending goose bumps down her spine, across her lower belly. She was Theodora, star of the Hippodrome and plenty of bedrooms as well, child prostitute and theatre-whore, with too many images she wanted to forget. She kissed his lips, dark-ringed eyes, stubbled cheeks, full chin. Kissed his shoulders and arms and hands and flesh and the knock at the door and the City screams outside and the Palace tension inside were ignored in the pleasure of his mouth and her mouth, tasting the ink and parchment on his fingers, the rose oils on her back and arms, his fingers twining into the long coil of her dark hair, hers reaching up to stroke his curls, his finally, just this year, just-thinning curls. His body and her body, just bodies, just flesh, beating and rolling and sliding against the fine silk on the floor, in the room where the hardest decisions were made, in the Palace that was the office that ran half the world.

The Emperor and his pious consort slowly parted, breath returning to normal, hearts to a regular beat.

She leaned over him; his smile was relaxed, his dark eyes untroubled.

'I should do this more often, lock you in here and force you to pleasure me until you are calm,' she said.

Justinian sat up, pulling the purple over her shoulders, the room was cool now, her skin cool too. 'Forcing me to stain and rip this silk. That's exactly what those who speak against me want to hear, how profligate our rule has become, how debauched.'

'Those who believe us debauched have done so since you made me patrician. I'm not worried about them, we have the people on our side again, and they like it when you show them you're a man.'

'And all men want to bed Theodora?'

She looked away, wondering how many levels there were to his question, knowing that Anthemius remained unspoken between them. When she looked back Justinian was already eyeing the piles of papers she'd moved from the divan; she knew he was listening beyond the door to the impatient shuffling feet of any number of courtiers, that he was already present at the meetings he had to attend. She was sure he knew about Anthemius, sure too that his public declaration of her as consort, his private passion just now, and the work he had already moved on to, did not need the distraction of something that was firmly in the past.

She stood up, pulling her clothes back on. 'I'll go to my rooms.'

'Thank you.'

'Thank you.'

They kissed, not as the two people who had, moments earlier, been locked in the sweat and hunger of desire and demand, but as August and Augusta. She bowing to him, he blessing her in his response.

Twenty-Eight

After too long a wait, City spies finally returned with the news that Belisarius' troops were on their way to the city of Rome. The papal seat was vacant and Justinian sent for Vigilius, the papal nuncio to Constantinople. Relatively young to be papal nuncio, younger than the Empress by several years, Vigilius arrived breathless and hopeful, keen to support the Emperor he endorsed and keen, too, to hear of what he hoped might be a promotion, a rise in status and power he could only have dreamed of as a boy. He wasn't disappointed.

'We are sending you to Rome, Vigilius.'

'Yes, Master,' Vigilius answered, trying to keep the excitement out of his voice and hold his eager, round face in as solemn a mask as the occasion demanded. Excitement and fear – they were not sending him to a safe country palace.

'You'll be accompanied by your own retinue and our soldiers, of course. We have a letter for Belisarius that instructs him to make you Pope.'

Vigilius, who had begun to rise, fell back to his knees. All his plans, all his fear, all his hopes, in one simple command.

Justinian continued: 'The Augusta and I know you are with

us, our desire to make one Rome, one Church. We trust you'll be better placed to further our cause from Rome itself.'

Macedonia was waiting for Vigilius when he arrived in Italy and visited him in the rooms Belisarius had commandeered for him. She knelt for his blessing and he greeted her warmly, if carefully. He stood before a charming and good-looking woman, and again, just as in the presence of the Empress, he could feel his cheery round cheeks growing red with shyness. Very quickly those cheeks were red with rage.

'I have bad news,' Macedonia said.

'Yes?'

'The Goths have appointed Silverius as Pope.'

'But I have letters, and gold. The Emperor himself . . .'

'I know. And still, they have appointed Silverius.'

'He has St Peter's keys? He actually holds them?'

'He does.'

She looked at the man before her, ready to take up the keys of the highest office of faith, thwarted the moment he stepped on Italian soil, Goth soil. All that hope, all that desire, all that hidden, hungry ambition. He looked like a fifteen-year-old taken to his first brothel and told the whores were only for show.

Macedonia waited with Vigilius through the next weeks as furious letters came from the Palace demanding that Belisarius depose Silverius and replace him with Vigilius. But in early December Silverius showed his own military skill and ordered that the gates of Rome be opened to Belisarius and his soldiers. Belisarius, in turn, allowed Silverius to keep the papal throne.

With Belisarius finally in Rome, even if it was a Rome with a less amenable pontiff, Justinian and Narses agreed it was vital to build on that success. Vigilius was told to wait for now, and the consecration of the great Hagia Sophia was set for the days just after the Christmas festival.

The night before the consecration, Theodora and Justinian walked through one of the underground passages that took them directly from the outer offices of the Palace, beneath the wall and the Augustaion, into a screened-off section of the main entrance to the grand new church. Narses had wanted to come with them: like most of the City he was hungry to see the finished article. Anthemius had practically begged to show off his masterpiece, and Isodore walked off in exhausted exasperation when it became obvious that the Empress was not to be persuaded – she would view their great new church with her husband and no one else. The old Hagia Sophia had been Theodora's sanctuary as a child, its fall would always be linked to the riots, to Sophia's death; now it was the finest symbol of Justinian's regenerated Rome. The Christ's birthday feast was over, tomorrow they would attend the consecration of this great space. The thin, cold, winter light would filter through the finest alabaster windows, a thousand candles inside the building would bounce reflections from mosaics and gold and silver surfaces at every turn. There had been praying and feasting for days, and there would be plenty to come – priests and patricians, City gentry and half the Palace in attendance when the church itself became holy. The other half of the staff would stay behind to prepare the feast and celebrations. Tonight Theodora wanted to be only with her husband, looking on their achievement, their precious contribution to the City and its future.

Isodore might have stormed off, but Anthemius had not lost his theatrical touch. Every candle on every candelabra was lit and, as they walked into the warm, welcoming light, a single, bright, pure voice filled the space. A eunuch child, a boy who could not have been more than nine or ten, singing an old song Theodora knew from her childhood. Despite the nerves in his slightly trembling voice, she knew immediately he had been rehearsed by Comito: he had her sister's perfect phrasing, her intonation. It was a song Comito used to sing when soothing their little sister Anastasia, a song their grandmother had taught them, promising a better time, an easier life, in the next world, if not this. Justinian didn't know the song, but he did know his wife, and he also knew how terrified the child must be; he had once been that child, new to the Palace, to the August's presence, to the fuss and rigmarole of court. He waited until the boy came to a pause, then held up his hand. The child immediately fell to the floor.

Justinian leaned down, thanking the boy. 'It's hard to stand alone and you've done well. The Empress and I are grateful.'

'The Augusta looks sad,' the boy whispered as he knelt before his Emperor.

'We can be saddened, as well as pleased, by our memories.'

Having no coin for the boy, Justinian removed a gold ring and handed it to him. It was worth far more than anything the child had ever seen and the boy stared stupidly at what was being offered until the Emperor himself took the child's fingers and curled them around the ring. 'You may go now,' he told him.

The boy leaped up then, ran past Theodora, returned at double pace to prostrate himself, scrabbled with the folds of her gown to find her foot so that he could kiss it, suddenly realised what he was doing, and worse, what it looked as if he was doing, blanched, and ran even faster from the great building.

In the slamming echo of the side door, the only door a eunuch would ever be permitted to use, Theodora burst out laughing. The absurdity of the situation, her situation, her position, the echo of the child's life with hers was too much. As was the foolish generosity of her husband – who had just realised he'd given away the only ring Theodora had ever had made for him, and was guiltily awaiting her reaction. She was sad and happy, moved and remembering, and she was with him.

'I'll have another made for you.'

'Perhaps the child will put it to better use than either of us could.'

'Yes, or offer it to his pimp for payment to make up for the work he didn't do while he was singing for us.'

'You think so?'

Theodora shook her head. 'Maybe not, maybe you really did just change his life.' She stopped then and turned, slowly, astonished by the sound of her own voice in the church, the way the dome magnified her words and yet held their clarity. 'This is remarkable.'

Justinian was beside her, quietly moved, but there was no doubting his pride in the accomplishment.

'What do you think?' she asked.

Justinian shook his head and when he could speak he said, 'There have been times when I despised Anthemius.'

Theodora caught her breath, nodded.

Justinian went on, 'I always knew it was just a matter of waiting it out, that he would finish this project and go on to another.'

'Young men's passions quickly change,' she offered quietly.

'For which I am grateful.'

They turned together, taking in the size and scale, the delicacy of the gold and silver, the two shades of light that reflected from them, the care in the mosaics, the extraordinary detail topped by the vast rounded reach of the dome, the splendid columns, and the light. Even with dark night outside, they stood in warm, sparkling, glittering light.

'You know some in the City are comparing me to Solomon?' Justinian asked.

'Again?' Theodora asked, grinning. 'Was Gelimer's comparison not enough?'

'They say this will rival his temple.'

'Ah. Yes. He's a fine comparison for a leader.'

Justinian smiled. 'And for a lawyer. Though his greatest wisdom may have been in what he didn't do, his ability to wait for matters to come to fruition in their own time.'

'Then this will be your monument.'

'It is ours.'

Theodora smiled and took her husband's hand, kissing the indentation where his gold ring had been. Tomorrow everything would be about ceremony; she would be up in the women's gallery, surveying all; he would be down here in the main body of the building, and the church made by her one-time lover would be full of incense and priests. What really mattered was that Justinian, who had just given away a lifetime's fortune to a eunuch child in a single gesture, was the one person who truly knew her.

The next day, nearing the end of the lengthy consecration service hosted by the almost six hundred religious who now staffed the new church, their numbers swollen to ten times that amount by guests and dignitaries and still more religious, Theodora remembered herself rejected, homeless in Apollonia. She stood in the gallery, while the dome appeared to float above them and winter light flooded in from the windows beneath it, and pictured herself almost twenty years earlier. Sleeping alone in the women's gallery of a church she had broken into for shelter, she had dreamed that night of standing on a green marble spot, in a glorious building, safe, warm, and home. And now she was doing exactly that, standing on the green marble Anthemius had found for her, marking the place of the Augusta. The building complete, her marriage safe, her role further confirmed. As she turned to lead her ladies from the church, to take the blessing of the consecration to the thousands more gathered outside, she shivered. This was a glorious dream come true, but not all her dreams were hopeful: she had also dreamed the Nika riots. At least now she had balance.

Two weeks later, when the January winds really began to bite, Macedonia accompanied Belisarius' messengers back to Constantinople. She brought more depressing news for Theodora.

'It's hard there, Mistress, much harder than you might imagine.'

'Justinian had hopes of a bloodless war,' Theodora said, and shook her head: 'almost bloodless.'

'Impossible hopes. The Goth troops outside the city have cut off the water supply, there's nothing coming through aqueducts, no drinking water, no baths. Women and children have been evacuated to towns between Naples and Rome.'

'Those are towns we still hold?' asked Theodora.

'Yes. But there are only five thousand Roman troops in the city, and it's not like here, where you were rebuilding even before the riots. The city is crumbling, shattered, tired. The old walls need reinforcement, and Goths are marshalling outside. A bloodless war is a dream, Mistress.'

At the end of January Justinian agreed to send troops from Greece, but the siege of Rome lasted a full year and a week, every one of those weeks bloody.

*

While the men were busy with war, Theodora was anxious not to let the religious tide slip completely. Macedonia was sent back to Rome with a letter to the new pope Silverius. The Empress intended to bring Anthimus out of hiding and wanted him made Patriarch of Constantinople again. Macedonia's message arrived before Silverius', sparing Theodora the frustration of having to be polite to the papal legate who carried the official response. Silverius had refused her request.

Less than a week later, Armeneus came to her rooms, his face solemn. Theodora frowned.

'More rudeness from the Roman priest?'

'No, Mistress . . .'

'What then?'

'Mistress, I'm sorry, Severus is dead.'

Theodora clenched her hands into fists to stop herself crying; there were too many people in the room, too many who believed that her support for the anti-Chalcedonians was dangerously strong.

'How long ago?'

'Three weeks.'

Theodora nodded. 'The news has travelled slowly from Egypt.'

'It's still winter, Augusta.'

'Yes, it is.'

Theodora knelt, forcing everyone else in the room to their knees, heads bowed. She knelt so they wouldn't look at her, and Armeneus, knowing her so well, knowing she needed him now far more than she needed protocol, went to his old friend and held her shaking hands, shaking body, helped her to stand and lean against him as she staggered from the room.

Severus, old already when Theodora first knew him, was dead. The man who had guided her conversion was gone. She held her emerald Virgin and prayed away her tears, aware that her grief was, as Severus would surely have said, selfish. There was far more at stake than her own sadness. The anti-Chalcedonians had lost strong leaders in Timothy and Severus, and union was even less likely. With each side decrying the other and suppression almost inevitable, she was glad Jacob Baradeus was off in Syria and Anthimus still safe in hiding. Safer, certainly, than her old friend John of Tella who died that same week, the messenger recounting how he had died in a prison cell, the Antioch authorities condemning him for preaching too loudly against the accepted Church.

Infuriated by Silverius, heartbroken over her losses, and with no spiritual mentor to counsel either patience or propriety, Theodora called for Peter Barsymes.

'It's all very well my praying that things will work out in the end, but our letters take too long to get to Italy. By the time the responses come back everything has moved on again and we've missed another chance for change.'

'Diplomacy takes time, Mistress, inside the Church even more so. You can hardly travel to Rome yourself.'

'I don't need to. The Emperor has Belisarius to do his bidding, it's time I gave Antonina a task of her own.'

Macedonia was briefly recalled to the City and gave Theodora the best advice on what she knew of Rome. Best, and most private. Then she was sent to Rome again, carrying letters, orders and a gift of good wine for Antonina. Just before Easter, Silverius was invited to a meeting with Belisarius.

Antonina's letter reported the event to Theodora:

Silverius was separated from his men as soon as he arrived, we sent them to speak with the military, he was brought to us. You'd have loved this, and you'll understand how very hard I had to work on Belisarius to achieve it – the Pope found me sitting high on a great chair, all dark wood and Italianate severity, with my glorious general lying at my feet. As you asked, I told Silverius we suspected he was in league with Witigis, and that opening the gates had just been a ruse to contain us in this vile city. I accused him of not being interested in the Church's welfare. He denied it all, as you'd expect. Then he appealed to Belisarius, who simply looked away as I'd told him to. He's a far better actor than you'd think, Augusta.

Theodora stopped reading, and frowned. She was sure she knew exactly how good an actor Belisarius was. She took up the letter again:

In all, Silverius gave a delightful show of horror, and fury – I do love the fury of an impotent priest. So, as you've probably heard by now, Silverius is made monk and sent off to Lycia, and your young man Vigilius is Pope after all. Oh yes, and your not-so-young lady Macedonia seems very friendly with him all of a sudden. And you think I'm a tart!

Theodora grinned, knowing both Macedonia's faith, and also how likely it was she would find Vigilius' bashful ambition attractive. She turned to the end of Antonina's letter.

We persuaded the troops and remaining Romans by explaining that as Silverius was approved by Witigis, he couldn't really be a valid pontiff. Belisarius was worried we'd gone too far, but I've placated him the way only I know best – I'll leave that to your imagination, my friend. So, that's the whole story, or at least a fuller one than you'll get from my husband's messengers. It's still not quite spring here and I can't wait to come home. You're lucky you never visited this city, Mistress, the whole damn place is a marshland and I predict the mosquitoes will be hell come summer. I pray we're out of here by then.

Twenty-Nine

Contrary to Antonina's hopes, troops were not out of Rome by summer, or even autumn, and it was only when reinforcements sailed in, five thousand men, that things began to go in Constantinople's favour. To the surprise of all those stationed in Italy, Narses himself followed, commanding an army nine thousand strong. After long and tedious negotiations with Belisarius, when Narses declared he finally understood the Empress's irritation with the younger man – and while the Goths laid siege to the Roman garrison of Milan – Narses returned to Constantinople and Belisarius marched on Ravenna. The Goths, furious with what they saw as the ineptitude of their own Witigis, proclaimed Belisarius their new king in his stead. Belisarius agreed in public, sending messages to reassure Justinian that it was a ruse to gain entry to the city – unlike Hypatius' identical message during the Nika riots, Belisarius' loyalty was believed. Finally, four years after the initial attack, while Constantinople celebrated its feast day, the gates of Ravenna were thrown open, Belisarius announced he was re-taking the city in Justinian's name, and the women of Ravenna spat on their men who had refused to fight.

*

This time, when Belisarius returned to Constantinople, with Witigis and his wife Matasuntha, and a haul of royal treasures, there was no grand Triumph. The war had been too protracted and costly, with too many reputations and liaisons damaged in the process. Now that Narses was less convinced of the golden general's infallibility, Belisarius had to content himself with his Italian conquest being celebrated as a victory for the Emperor, rather than himself. The treasures he brought back were displayed in the Great Hall, spoils of war for the Palace staff to view, but not for the City as a whole.

The low-key Triumph was quickly overshadowed by other news. Sittas, appointed Consul two years earlier, was killed in a rebel revolt in Armenia. Word first arrived that he had fallen in an ambush. When more details emerged it seemed he had been killed not by rebels, but by Artebanes, a fellow soldier with whom he was known to disagree on everything from tactics to theology. Narses instigated an inquiry but there were too many conflicting stories and no man prepared to swear that Artebanes was the culprit, though several voiced their suspicions. Artebanes continued his rise through the ranks while Comito was left widowed and Sophia fatherless.

'I want Sophia at home,' Comito said, 'I need her with me, she's my only link to Sittas.'

Comito had been happy to allow Theodora to keep Sophia with her much of the time, pleased to have her daughter groomed for succession, but she felt differently in her grief, wanted Sophia with her, wanted to see the father through his child.

'Yes,' Theodora agreed, 'she's a link to Sittas, but I'm giving her more than you or he could ever give her. If things work out as I hope, she'll need to know the court, the Palace. You can't keep Sophia to yourself to satisfy your grief.'

Comito stared at her sister. Since the religious problems and the war in Italy had kept Theodora so busy, they had spent less time together. She also suspected that Theodora had pulled away since her affair with Anthemius had ended, Comito could always see through Theodora's deceptions, and the purple might prove a prettier cloak, but it couldn't hide everything.

'Sophia's an eight-year-old girl,' Comito tried again, 'you don't know what she may become. And you have Ana's son to groom for succession.'

'Ana was a bastard. It doesn't matter how well she raises Anastasius, it will always come back to that. As for not knowing what Sophia will become, I remember what I knew at eight, and what you knew. I remember how much else I wanted. Of course you're mourning Sittas, but you've always been ambitious for yourself. Why deny your daughter's hopes in your grief?'

'Spending more time with her would not be denying her hopes, it would be denying yours.'

'Really?' Theodora's tone was cold. 'Go on.'

Comito stared at her sister, and then nodded, the permission to speak giving her a chance to finally say it all.

'You left us,' she said. 'Anastasia had only just died, Hypatia was sick with grief and you left us for Hecebolus, desperate for your own advance, leaving me with your own daughter. You've always been cold to Ana, you showed almost no interest in Hypatia, barely cried at her death. You're so proud with what you have achieved for the women over in Metanoia, for this great new church that you – and the architect – have made between you, and you say it's for everyone else. For the women, the Church, for Rome. But I know you, Theodora, I know it's as much for you. You've always done what you want and you're choosing to do the same now. All I ask for is my child in my own home now that her father is dead. I have nothing else.'

Theodora waited before she replied. She did not want to shout as her sister had just done, nor did she want to throw the power of her position behind her words, though she was sorely tempted to, and she knew Comito must be afraid of that. She smoothed her gown, drank a mouthful of the pomegranate juice Armeneus insisted was good for her aching knees and back. She looked through the window to the water. Eventually she was able to speak.

'I have been a bad mother. I know that. And yes, I left you, with Hypatia and Ana and Indaro to care for. But I paid for those sins, and I still pay. Every time I see you laughing with Indaro or Ana about some thing the three of you did when they were little girls, I pay. There are whole days when the absurdity of my life as Empress strikes me so forcefully I can barely contain my laughter. Or my tears. But I am here, in this role, and I've chosen to embrace my role as Justinian's consort. And I am sorry that your husband has died. I was delighted to help find you a good partner, delighted he was a good man.'

She went to her sister, who was sobbing now, and they sat together.

Theodora held Comito close. 'You saved me so many times when we were girls, took care of me when you couldn't save me. We've grown apart recently and I regret it. It's also true that I have bigger things to think about. I care about the religious question, deeply, I wish you did. I want to make a difference for those women who could have been either of us. And I want to make a difference for Sophia. So please, take her with you today. But I won't give her up to an ordinary life, nor do I believe it is in her interest – or the state's – to do so. Perhaps we should move you back into the Palace. You

265

were happy enough here before your marriage – maybe you could be again? Then there'll be no question of Sophia going home, she'll always be here. What do you think?'

Comito was calm now, and she nodded, knowing that Theodora's suggestion was a demand, not an offer, that it made sense to move back, especially now she was widowed, even if she did find the Palace more of a cage than a home.

Theodora gestured for Mariam to bring wine for her sister, and a maid was sent to fetch water and a cloth. She bathed Comito's eyes herself, poured her a drink, and when they were both quiet she walked her to the door.

They kissed and Theodora whispered to her sister, 'And please, don't ever speak to me like that again in public, it does neither of us any good.'

Her words were soft, but the tone showed they were meant and Comito bowed to her Empress before she left.

That same tone was used far more aggressively the following week when Armeneus came to her rooms. He had an odd smile on his face and Theodora was in no mood for games. She had been with Justinian earlier when he'd received terrible news; Khusro, the Persian king and co-signatory to the Endless Peace, had renewed fighting in the east. Khusro's men had invaded Antioch, evacuating its citizens and massacring any who fought back, removing the rest of the population to a new city near Dara, a near-copy of Antioch. It was a wholesale attack on a people and a place where Theodora had once been happy and in love.

'Khusro has broken the peace. He's attacked Antioch, a city I love dearly, as you well know. So if you have no good news, Armeneus, please leave me alone.'

'There is a visitor at the Chalke Gate, a young woman.'

'Give her to the deaconess who takes the girls to Metanoia.'

'That's not why she's here.'

Theodora rubbed her face. 'I've told them before, there's nothing I can do for the prostitutes who want to keep working: the Church condemns it, the state condemns it. I can give them penitent sanctuary or nothing. Find a way to get rid of her.'

'Mistress, she's not a whore. At least, not yet. It's Chrysomallo's daughter.'

'Chrysomallo and Hecebolus' daughter?'

'Yes, Mistress.'

'And she asked to see me?'

'She did.'

Theodora realised she'd been holding her breath and slowly breathed out, shaking her head. 'She has courage.'

'Or innocence, Mistress. Apparently she and her mother have been living in Cappadocia since Hecebolus kicked them out.'

'So why is she here?'

'Chrysomallo died.'

Theodora frowned but that was all. There had been a time when she'd wished all kinds of pain on Chrysomallo. No longer.

'She didn't try her father?' asked Theodora.

'She was sent away when she asked to see him in Berytus.'

Theodora nodded. 'They tell me he works for his father's dye company now. He wouldn't want to be reminded of the days when he thought he had a future.'

She thought of the man she had once loved, and of her friend Chrysomallo who'd been carrying his child when she told Theodora the truth of their affair.

She sighed. 'For years I wanted to punish them. I was delighted when Justinian made it harder for the colonial governors to skim tax extras for themselves. I knew that was how

Hecebolus raised funds for himself, and I was happy to hurt him. And now . . .' she shook her head again, 'it's all war. The Huns have invaded Thrace and Macedonia, we heard last week that Bulgars have crossed the Danube, and then we get this news from Antioch. My own scars seem small. Send her to me.'

The girl, when she came into the room, was nervous, but she had been well trained by her mother, who had also served under Menander. She crossed the room, a cloak pulled tightly around her, bowed to the Empress, kissed her foot, and remained kneeling until she was asked to stand. When she did, her cloak fell back, revealing a high and round belly. The girl was tall, as her mother had been, with the long limbs, high cheekbones and dark eyes of her father. Theodora saw Hecebolus in the girl and felt a sharp pang of nostalgia and loss.

'How far gone are you?'

'Six months.'

'Like mother, like daughter. So why isn't he with you, the father?'

'He's just a boy.'

Theodora smiled. 'And you are?'

'Twenty-one.'

'Ah, old.'

'Old for marriage, Mistress, and too old for him anyway. He's only sixteen, and bright, his family have high hopes for him, they've saved for years, they're planning to send him to a university. They want him to be a lawyer.'

'He doesn't know you're pregnant?' The girl shook her head and Theodora said, 'That's kind of you.'

The girl frowned. 'Or stupid.'

'Your mother was none too bright herself.'

'She said you'd say that.'

'Chrysomallo told you to come to me?'

'Before she died, she told me the whole story. I never knew my father, it was always the two of us.'

'She didn't find another man?'

'With a young daughter …' the girl shrugged, aware she was describing herself as well as her own mother, 'her life was hard. She tried to make it better for me.'

'Was she a whore?'

'Sometimes. We worked for families mostly, cooking, cleaning.'

'Chrysomallo learned to cook?'

'No,' the girl laughed, relaxing for the first time since she'd entered the room and Theodora could see Chrysomallo in her more clearly, 'my mother learned to clean. I can cook.'

'Is that why you're here, to ask for a job?'

'I'm here because I have nowhere else to go.'

Theodora gestured through the window, to the distant tower on the opposite shore, just visible now after a morning hidden in thick fog. 'If you give up the child they'll take you over at Metanoia.'

'I won't give up the child, and I would make a very bad nun.'

The girl smiled again and Theodora liked what she saw. 'Then we'll have to find you a husband. What's your name?'

The girl bit her lip and mumbled, 'Theodora. Sorry.'

Theodora laughed out loud then. 'Dear God, your mother had guts. Good. In that case, there's a young man, Saturninas, son of one of our senators. He's an arrogant little bastard, promised marriage to his cousin's daughter, tricked her into sleeping with him, now he wants to dump her. I've had her tedious mother here in tears, her father storming and threatening, but as they're among our best supporters, it pays to keep them happy. I found her a kinder young man, a young officer, but I've been looking for someone to show Saturninas the error of his ways. With the courage you've shown coming here, you might make a good match for him.'

'I'm not asking for a husband. A job would do.'

'A husband is a job, child, and his family are wealthy. Would you rather your baby grew up in the back kitchens of the Palace, trained to be a servant?'

'No.'

'He's neither ugly nor old, just too full of himself. With any luck marriage will bring him to his senses. I'll make sure he's good to you.'

'My mother said you'd be kind to me. She said—'

'Your mother,' Theodora interrupted her, 'fucked my lover, ruined my hopes – for a time – and broke my heart. Believe me, I'm not doing this for her.'

'Then why?'

Theodora looked directly at the girl. 'Because no one ever did it for me.'

Saturninas was brought before the Empress and forced to agree marriage to the young woman who was penniless, pregnant, and much more assertive than the girls he usually dealt with. The Empress threatened him with an unlimited time in her personal dungeons if he refused. No one was actually sure if these dungeons existed, but her threat made them sound real enough and Saturninas didn't want to risk it.

On the day of the marriage Theodora called for Armeneus: 'The gift Hecebolus sent for my marriage to Justinian, what happened to it?'

'The jewellery box you said I could keep, or sell, or get rid of however I wanted, Mistress?' Armeneus asked, grinning.

'That one.'

'I have it still.'

'Give it to the girl, she needs a dowry and if she finds she can't bear him she can always sell it.'

Armeneus bowed and turned away.

Theodora called him back. 'I've just told you to give away a valuable trinket that you were keeping for yourself, why are you smiling?'

'You and Chrysomallo were my friends, Mistress, long before all this.' The sweep of his arm took in the fine-knotted silk carpets, the lapis and amber mosaic fountain in the corner of the day room, the soft divans with softer cushions, the wealth and comfort, the privilege everywhere he looked. 'We were friends, the three of us.'

'You think I don't remember?'

'I think you rarely have cause to, and even when you do, it's not always appropriate to acknowledge those memories. So yes, I'm pleased you took care of Chrysomallo's daughter. It was kind.'

'And solved the problem of Saturninas.'

'That too. I'll go and find the jewellery box.'

'Tell Narses to give you its worth in gold, from my own account.'

Armeneus nodded his thanks. He did not say he had intended to do so anyway. He didn't need to, she knew him well.

Thirty

Theodora walked into her husband's office, sending the slaves, servants and clerics scrabbling to the floor as she threw herself down to bow to him. When she stood up it was clear she was ready to rant. Justinian held up a hand to silence her, then calmly added his signature and seal to a letter, nudged the cleric closest to stand and take the paper, and welcomed his wife into his office, telling everyone else they could leave, including the door slaves. He closed the doors behind them himself, and at last turned to his furious wife.

'What is it now? Khusro? Totila? Vigilius? The Persian king, the new Goth upstart and the Pope have all conspired against us? No? Belisarius, then? Germanus? Surely not Armeneus?' Justinian was smiling, teasing, 'But you like Armeneus.'

'The Cappadocian.'

'I see. You've disturbed the one time in my day when I have an uninterrupted opportunity to get through the ever-increasing mounds of paperwork, in order to complain about my treasurer – again.'

'You know I didn't want you to reinstate him.'

'We needed his help.'

'I don't trust him.'

'You don't trust Belisarius either.'

'With good cause. Either of them would take the purple from you, from us, in an instant.'

'And either of them might be successful in the role, but that these days Belisarius almost seems more driven by his passion for Antonina than for battle, and the Cappadocian is universally disliked. He raises taxes, and the people hate him – not me. We brought him back so that he could do the dirty work, while you and I stand in the Kathisma, applauded by a public who, right now, approve of us. Honestly? I think he's doing very well.'

'I'm happy for him to be the scapegoat. It's his arrogance I'm not happy about. And now he's demanding an income from Metanoia.'

'What would you like me to do about it?'

'I want you to believe me when I tell you he's dangerous.'

Justinian bit his lip. 'Theodora, you would have me believe Germanus hungers for the purple, that Belisarius will usurp me one day no matter what loyalty he professes, and that most of my senior staff are out to take my place. You might even be right, but I have to choose to trust some of them or I can't work with any of them.'

'What if I could prove the Cappadocian can't be trusted?'

Justinian sighed as her words were rounded off by the chimes from his water clock. It was time to meet with his military advisers: there were spies with reports from Totila's progress in Italy, others with word from inside the Persian border. 'Of course, if you can find any evidence against him, then he'll have to go. Again.'

The Emperor picked up an armful of scrolls, shrugged on a fine cloak with a heavy purple hem, and put his free arm around his wife, walking her to the door. He kissed her as the door was opened for them, and then walked off down the long corridor, smiling as he went. He was coming up to sixty, Theodora had recently turned forty-one, and she still had the same fire she had when they first took the purple almost fifteen years earlier. Her passion, often excessive, occasionally irritating, always heartfelt, might not have been the reason Narses and Timothy brought her to him twenty years ago, but it was one of the reasons he loved her. And her energy made him feel younger, for a while at least, until he faced his next meeting, his next room full of worried men.

That summer, for the first time in her married life, Antonina did not travel with her husband and his troops, who were heading for the Persian-held area of Mesopotamia. She stayed in Constantinople, ostensibly to take care of her daughter Joannina, but actually to safeguard her affair with Theodosius. Even Antonina realised that maintaining the secrecy of their relationship through a third campaign was too risky, and so she remained in the City, visiting Theodosius in camp when she could, and sending lengthy love letters the rest of the time. But she quickly became bored, eager for distraction, and John the Cappadocian was the perfect object for her excess energy. Theodora despised the man, both for his behaviour to her in the past and for the ambition she still saw in him, and Antonina was always happy to dispatch anyone who posed a threat to the long-term hopes she had for Belisarius. Between them, they decided to help Justinian see the truth of his treasurer.

The Cappadocian's daughter Euphemia was a sweet girl, ruled over by a father who held her on a too-tight rein and had therefore taught her none of the useful sophistries needed for life in the Palace. Antonina began visiting Euphemia at home when she knew her father would be away. She sent little gifts of jewellery and fine silks, telling her to keep them for her private use, saying that had her mother lived, a woman Antonina barely knew, she would have wanted her child to have only the best. Once the girl was won over, Antonina brought her to meet the Empress.

Theodora was surprised the child was so pretty, and horrified at her naivety. She poured Euphemia a second glass of barely watered wine, which the girl again downed in two big gulps, offered her the plate of rich pastries, dripping with honey and more sweet wine, and asked her to explain what she meant when she said her father had promised her a lovely room when they moved to the Palace.

'He said you have all the best rooms,' the girl said, nodding at Theodora, 'but when we move in, I can have them instead.'

The girl was slurring a little but, for all his faults, Theodora had to admit the Cappadocian had trained her well. She still sat elegantly, and despite moving on to her third glass of wine in less than an hour, not a curl was out of place, nor had a drop of honey fallen between greedy fingers and chattering mouth to spoil the lovely silk robe Antonina had insisted she wear on this momentous visit with the Empress.

'And did he say when he thought this move might happen?' she asked, smiling.

'No.' Euphemia shook her head, the tightly wound curls shaking with her as she leaned across the divan to whisper to Theodora, 'but it will be before I'm married. He wants the best husband for me.'

'I'm sure he does,' Antonina interrupted, 'and you'd want that too, of course. But I'm curious, why will you need to live in the Palace?'

Euphemia took the fourth glass of wine from Theodora and this time a small drop fell on to her gown. 'Oh no. Papa hates me to make a mess, please don't tell him, will you?'

Theodora saw real fear in the girl's face and promised she would give her a new robe to wear home – her father was away, he would never find out. It would be their little secret, especially if Euphemia kept this meeting a secret too.

'But I want to tell him I've met you and you're much prettier and nicer than he says.' Euphemia pouted, this time taking care of the drips as she finished her glass and held it out for more.

'Let's not tell him, this time,' Theodora said. 'If we're to prepare for the move to the Palace, it'll be better to keep it a secret, don't you think?'

'Of course,' Euphemia said solemnly.

'You were explaining why you'll be living in the Palace?' Antonina prodded.

'So Papa won't have to travel so far for his work.'

'His work as?' Theodora asked.

'I don't know, how does it go? There's a list, he has to rise through the ranks of course, they can't just appoint him Emperor right off – you'd know that.'

Euphemia was talking into her own chest now, half slumped on the divan.

Theodora nodded without replying. Anyone else would have fled the room at that point; even Antonina was wondering if she had gone too far, bringing the child to Theodora.

'Go on,' said Theodora.

'Something like ... Treasurer, Councillor, Consul, ah ... then something else, I can't remember ... another title, anyway, it ends up with Emperor. When they make him Emperor. And then I get to have this room, which is lovely, for me. Sorry, you'll have to move, won't you? But I will like it a lot. Yes. I will.'

Euphemia was asleep.

'What if she tells the Cappadocian she was here?' Antonina asked.

Theodora shook her head. 'She won't, she doesn't want to risk a beating.' She waved for a slave to pick the girl up. 'Give her some of Mariam's old clothes, take her home, then have these cleaned and returned to her,' she ordered.

The slave left with the slumped and lightly snoring girl, and Theodora sat in silence.

Eventually Antonina asked, 'Mistress?'

Theodora turned to her friend. 'Right. Let's get rid of the bastard.'

First Theodora shared what she had learned with Justinian and Narses.

Her husband shook his head. 'I can't dismiss my minister because his drunken daughter suggests he has ambition. This is just a frightened girl saying that her father wishes to better himself. He has no wife, no knowledge of how to raise a daughter, it may be simple boasting on his part.'

'Treasonous boasting, August,' Narses said quietly.

'Do you think it's true?' Justinian asked his Chief of Staff.

'I'd take a cohort of men and find out.'

Justinian stared at his two most trusted advisers, wife and eunuch; he bit his lip and finally spoke: 'Go ahead, but keep me informed.'

Antonina spoke again with Euphemia, telling her now was the time for the Cappadocian to begin his rise to the purple. She asked Euphemia to set up a meeting to discuss how they could help him. The meeting was duly arranged at Antonina and Belisarius' home by the sea, where it was easy for Narses to hide himself behind a screen, his men stationed close by in the grounds.

For a long hour Narses listened to Antonina lead the Cappadocian along, with stories of how she and Belisarius felt they were owed more by the Empire, how the Cappadocian himself must surely be feeling the same. Antonina was careful not to complain too vociferously about Justinian – it wouldn't do either her or Belisarius any good for Narses to think she meant what she said – but the Cappadocian had no such qualms. Narses waited until he heard the thin man express his treasonous ambition for the second time, and then called his men out of hiding.

They stepped forward into the room, and immediately the Cappadocian, clearly smarter than Antonia had imagined, called his own men out of hiding too. They came over the walls, up through the grounds and in through the open patio doors. The fight began immediately, no time wasted surveying opponents, considering action. The house was full of noise, shouts of surprise and anger and bloody pain. One of Narses' men had his leg broken by an iron bar snapped across his knee, another had his face gashed down both sides, the Cappadocian's men adept with a weapon in either hand. The sharp scrape of clashing knives, the yelps and groans at sliced flesh, crunching bone, brought Joannina and a dozen servants and slaves running into the room. Narses rounded on the Cappadocian, his own knife drawn, and the treasurer grabbed Joannina by the hair, pulling her to himself. Antonina screamed, Narses stepped back and called his men to stop.

'I'm leaving, with my men,' said the Cappadocian. 'We won't harm the girl if you let us go.'

Narses shook his head. 'Don't be stupid, you're adding kidnap to treason.'

Narses motioned his men to step back, put his own knife down, and began to walk towards the Cappadocian. The treasurer pulled Joannina closer, close enough for her to smell the mint leaves on his breath, and brought his knife right to her throat.

Narses continued, speaking slowly and carefully the whole time, 'You have a daughter of your own.'

The Cappadocian spat on the tiled floor, 'A daughter this bitch made drunk, took advantage of, fed lies.' He nodded towards Antonina, now white with shock and fear: 'Along with her mistress, the whore in the Palace.'

Narses was within a wide arm's reach of him now; the Cappadocian's knife tight against Joannina's throat. 'Whatever's been done, John, it's your own words that have condemned you today. Don't make the girl pay for her mother's faults,' she said.

Narses could have reached out and knocked the knife from the Cappadocian's hand, but his own words brought Antonina out of her fear into anger.

'My faults?' she shouted. 'My faults? Here's your thief, the bastard who dares to stand with a knife at my child's throat. My faults? Damn you, eunuch!'

Antonina lunged between Narses and the treasurer, grabbing her daughter, the Cappadocian's knife cut into the child's skin, and the sudden sight of red at the girl's throat startled everyone. Joannina screamed, the treasurer pushed back and away towards the only door that was clear of horrified staff and slaves, and Narses found his way blocked by the furious mother and her terrified daughter, hemmed in by his own men fighting the Cappadocian's men. In the mess he had created, John the Cappadocian sprinted away.

Two days later the bedraggled treasurer claimed sanctuary in the church of the Stondios Monastery, close to the Golden Gate, where he waited until Justinian imposed sentence. Despite Antonina's rage that her daughter had been dragged into the violence, Justinian still felt uneasy that the Cappadocian had been tricked into revealing his ambition.

'You and Antonina used his daughter, just as he used Joannina,' he said in response to Theodora's furious glare.

'We didn't have a knife at Euphemia's throat.'

'No, but none of you come out of it all that well, do you?'

Theodora shrugged. The Cappadocian had signed his own death warrant as far as she was concerned, but she knew Justinian was determined to be lenient in this case: he still had gratitude for the treasurer's financial acumen, as well as his willingness to be the government's scapegoat. The eventual sentence was exile to Cyzicus in the east, part of his estate to be held in trust for his daughter and the rest confiscated by the crown.

'Happy now?' Justinian asked Theodora when his ex-treasurer was finally led away to begin his exile.

Theodora shook her head. 'No. I don't believe that's the last we'll hear of him and I don't believe we're truly safe while men like him are alive.'

'We can't put all our foes to death.'

'It's my job to protect you, you're too trusting.'

'Perhaps I have more reason to be trusting than you do; more people have shown themselves trustworthy to me.'

'Long may it continue.'

'Amen to that.'

When they went to their own beds, Theodora knelt to her emerald Virgin and prayed that her husband was right to trust, and that she was right to give in to Justinian's leniency, allowing the Cappadocian to keep his head.

When the anti-Chalcedonian Bishop of Cyzicus was found murdered several months later, the local magistrate reported that the Cappadocian and the Bishop were known enemies, but lack of evidence meant all the city of Cyzicus could do was enforce an even greater exile on their unwelcome guest.

Theodora was glad to hear he had been sent further away and Justinian acknowledged there could be no rehabilitation for the Cappadocian now. It was time to appoint a new minister in his place; Peter Barsymes was delighted to accept the job.

Theodora and Antonina had no opportunity to revel in their triumph over the Cappadocian. Within weeks a message came that Belisarius had halted his campaign and was demanding that his wife join him immediately.

Theodora joined Narses and Justinian in the Emperor's office.

'It appears the general has stopped short of the Persian border because his stepson is concerned about his inheritance,' said Narses.

'Photius? I don't understand.'

Justinian growled under his breath, 'You didn't know Antonina was having an affair with her godson, or you didn't realise her own son by birth might find it disturbing?'

'None of us know the truth of these rumours.' Theodora stopped to glare at Narses, who had laughed at her words. 'None of us know the truth of any marriage.'

'True,' Justinian said, 'but your friend is well known for her interests.'

Theodora agreed. 'And your general is well known for his ambition – but that doesn't stop you promoting him. I'm sure this is simply a case of Photius' jealousy, given his own status.'

'As her first son?' Justinian asked.

'As the son of a too-early marriage, to a husband who was an irrelevance, yes,' Theodora answered. 'Photius should be grateful his mother's rise in fortune has benefited him.'

'His mother is having an affair with the adopted brother who's half his age. Of course he's concerned about his inheritance and of course he's jealous,' Narses said.

'I don't need the details,' Justinian interrupted them. 'What matters is that despite an urgent need to build on his gains in Persian Mesopotamia, Belisarius has refused to go on until Antonina joins him. And Photius has imprisoned Theodosius somewhere even my own spies can't tell me, rendering all three of them incapable of leading their own men. Our men. The one common factor – and I say that advisedly – is Antonina. Which means you will have to deal with the problem, Theodora. Unless you'd like me to?'

Theodora didn't need to be asked twice.

The next morning Antonina was sent to Belisarius' encampment to make peace with her husband and bring him back to the City, while Theodora's messengers demanded that Photius return to appear before the Empress.

When Photius refused to reveal where Theodosius was hidden, he found that the rumours of the Empress's dungeons were no exaggeration. He spent five days in a narrow cell, deep in the cellars of the Palace, with neither torch nor blanket, only revealing Theodosius' whereabouts when Theodora sent a servant to remind him that she could keep him there until he gave his answer. The damp seeped from the cold, heavy walls into his bones, the guard watching him had orders not to speak, the food ration was far less than he was used to as a soldier, and none of this pain was what he had hoped for when jealousy prompted him to reveal his mother's affair. Theodosius was returned to the City and Photius waited another two nights in his prison before Theodora set him free.

When Belisarius and Antonina returned to Constantinople, Belisarius making a point of keeping his wife under humiliatingly close watch, Theodora called them all to her rooms. She greeted Antonina warmly and ignored Belisarius entirely.

'My dear friend,' she began, taking Antonina's hand, 'who has given so much for Rome. Who has travelled, as no other woman has, with her soldier husband, to care for him, and has sadly been denied the respect due from the husband who should protect her.'

Belisarius began to protest that he had always loved Antonina, still did, even now, but Theodora spoke over him. 'I have a gift for my good friend. A pearl for you,' she said to Antonina. 'Perhaps it will warm you when your husband is next away.'

The Empress finally looked at Belisarius, giving him a very brief smile: 'Soon, I'm sure, General? In your never-ending service to my husband and to Rome?'

She clapped her hands and a gilt-embroidered curtain was drawn back to reveal Theodosius, dressed in white. Antonina ran to him, just remembering to kiss the young man as her godson and not her lover. It was only Belisarius' years of military training that enabled him to bow before the Empress before he stormed out of the room.

That afternoon Photius left the City for the Persian front and in the evening Theodora sat with Justinian going over the religious celebrations planned for the coming winter festivals of the Christ's birth and Epiphany.

Justinian was quieter than usual and eventually Theodora put her hand over his and said, 'You're still angry with me?'

'Your friend's behaviour took my general from the battlefield.'

'He did that himself.'

'Yes, but she distracted him, and in return you made her a gift of her lover.'

'It was a game, a show.'

'They aren't actors, Theodora, for you to play with.'

'I agree,' she answered, 'but Antonina loves the fuss, the secrets and the spying. And Belisarius clearly likes her that way, or he would have divorced her years ago. I reunited them.'

'In public, so the whole City must be full of it by now.'

'In public, so Antonina had no choice but to return to the campaign with her husband. Belisarius gets his wife to himself, she thinks she's won when actually she's leaving her lover behind, her son Photius is exposed for the anxious gold-hunter he is . . .'

'And my general goes back to the field.'

'Your general goes back, yes. Out of the City and away from the gaze of the people who love him just a little too much.'

'Leaving behind the confirmation that he is a cuckold.'

'That's right.'

Justinian shook his head and laughed. 'You astonish me.'

'I try.'

The easy night they spent together made it even more disturbing when Theodora woke before dawn, sweating and shaking, pulled from a deep sleep by fear. As she groped for the emerald Virgin in the dark of her room she could recall only one image from the dream that had so upset her. A huge pile of bodies, men and women, children, old people, all dead, thrown on top of each other. No care, no prayers, no grave. She fell asleep again holding the Virgin and praying the image was only a memory from the riots.

Thirty-One

In the week that the City finally felt the winds easing from the north, when the first pale green buds began to push from bare branches, illness was reported near the mouth of the Red Sea. Another half-moon and it was in Alexandria, with the same symptoms, the same inexplicable attacks – a father, son and daughter from one family dead within a week, mother and baby of the same family untouched, the grandmother left sleeping unconscious, yet well on waking. By the time the winds turned fully, carrying hot breezes from the south, winds that usually brought irritation or frustration or anger between lovers with their swirling heat, the death rate was rising in Alexandria and Justinian's ministers were on the alert. Belisarius led the fight against Khusro's incursions on the Persian border, Totila threatened real problems in Italy, but the immediate danger was very likely already in the City, carried in by sailors or merchants, traders or soldiers. These were early days yet, but every messenger that came from Africa or the Levant, every ship that attempted to dock in the City's harbours, was checked for illness among its crew. If there was so much as a sailor with a headache, the ship was sent away to find harbour elsewhere. Not, of course, that every sailor told the truth.

Constantinople's grand rebuilding programme had meant a fine statue of Justinian for the Augustaion, the stunning elegance of Theodora's newly beloved Hagia Sophia, the wide and welcoming porticos of the revamped Mese, sparkling fresh water for the Emperor's fine new cistern, but those who lived on the streets saw the new work in a very different way. For the maimed Hun or Herule mercenaries no longer needed by the military but too old or ill to travel home, for the refugees arriving from Italy and those now retreating from the Persian border, for the many who simply came to the City hoping to find a new life and found hard graft instead – the glorious new buildings were just walls to lean on as they begged. With the threat of illness in the streets, housewives quickly began to limit their market visits, traders cut back on deals, and even the kindest-hearted giver thought twice about offering alms to a beggar in the Forum of Constantine. It didn't take a doctor schooled in Alexandrian medicine to point out that stopping to chat with the afflicted might not be wise.

The homeless were the first to fall, slipping away to die, away from their fellows who knew only too well that poverty is a soft nest for illness. Next the sickness attacked the whores, friends of the traveller, the women who opened their arms, legs and mouths to sailors, many of the ships offloading infection as well as regular grain shipments from Egypt where the disease had fully taken hold.

Three weeks before Easter, the rope-maker whose stomach gripe had sparked the Nika riots left his country villa for a meeting in the City. He kissed his wife and promised to be as quick as possible: the meeting was important, he would not have to go through the centre of Constantinople, he would not have to meet or touch any illness. The ex-hangman had done well since quietly returning to the City six months after the rebellion. He gave up hanging, went back to rope-making full time, and found that it might be less precise, less thrilling, but he could learn to be happy with quiet. He kept on with the family business, took over when his brothers retired; his eldest son had just started to work with him, the younger two were still at school and with the benefit of their father's income might yet make it to the university. And this year his dear wife, with whom he was still in love, had just given them their longed-for baby girl, many years after they'd abandoned hope of another child.

But the City that had skipped his debt ten years earlier caught him now. There was a traffic jam of horses and carts along the Mesc. Four bars had closed their doors against illness at the same time and drunken customers were turfed into the street, kicking off an inevitable brawl between faction youths. The rope-maker was left with only narrow alleys to ride down. When they became too crowded, he was forced to tether his horse, hoping the child he gave a coin to would take care of it rather than steal it, and walk through the very streets he'd most hoped to avoid. The illness was carried on the air from the exertions of the fighting, cursing, bleeding young men; or it was in the wine his host insisted was safe and demanded he drink to close the deal; or it was in the sweat of the horse he rode out of town. However it came, by the time he made it back to his little villa where the clean country air felt safer to breathe, the rope-maker felt sure he had spent too long in town.

Two days later the physician was called. He arrived having covered himself from head to toe in rosemary water and heavy orange oil before he left his own home. He stood at the door of the rope-maker's bedroom, took a quick look at the man now trembling in convulsions on his sweated bed, babbling about the rebels he believed were at his door, and he shook his head.

'If he has no buboes . . .'

'He doesn't,' his wife answered hopefully.

The physician frowned. 'Then the disease is eating at his brain. He'll no doubt fall into a sleep and either wake well, or not at all. You should check the children and yourself for signs of the sickness, pray that anyone else afflicted might show lumps or boils . . .'

'Why?' The woman interrupted again, her panic granting courage where the physician's status might normally have kept her silent.

'The disease sometimes relapses when the buboes burst. Sometimes.' Seeing her fear he went on, 'There is a new treatment, using butter to soothe the burning skin.'

The doctor lifted his hands, and let them drop. It was the best of his advice. He hurried away.

The butter eased the heat of the sores when the first son became ill the next day, but a week later the rope-maker, his wife, and his three sons were all sick; within a fortnight they were dead. The two servants and the baby daughter did not die, but both servants fell into a coma, one waking almost three days later, one after four days. Both were hugely relieved to see that while they'd slept the hot, fat boils at groin and underarm and neck had burst, with once-weeping pus and blood now crusted on their clothes. All that remained was the raging thirst from days of no liquid. It was too late for the baby girl. The disease had passed her by, but the two-month-old could not survive three days without even water.

By Easter itself the illness had spread to Palace workers. Tribonian, the legal adviser who had been sacked and then quietly reinstated, watched his wife and son both die in pain, his wife raving in half-waking nightmares, his son happy and well one day, violently ill and dead the next. He made it to their joint funeral, but his grief was such that he was pleased when he woke the next morning and felt the swollen lumps beneath both arms. He sent a messenger to tell the Palace, dismissed his servants, and locked himself in to die, praying to the Pagan gods he had never rejected. A message came from a monastery in the east that the athlete of God, Mar the Solitary, had died too, ranting about sin and damning heretics to the last, his huge athlete's body apparently struck down by nothing more than the beginning of a headache and a single boil at his neck. Justinian and Narses sent away all the civil servants they could spare, anyone who wasn't absolutely needed in the Palace was dismissed, soldiers were recalled to barracks to replace local factional police and firemen, until they too began to drop, their rigorous training no defence against the constantly mutating weapons of the disease.

Continuing to work all hours, despite Theodora's pleas that he rest and save his health, Justinian managed to put through one last law, banning divorce on mutual consent. He was so sure of his own happy marriage that he wanted it made harder for others to divorce. Theodora's contribution was to prohibit the common practice of a man divorcing his wife yet keeping her full dowry. As the death toll rose ever more rapidly, among their enemies as well as at home, the Emperor's legal papers were finally put aside, his military maps, the strategies for Persian and Italian campaigns laid down, all concentration now on the enemy within.

Three weeks after Easter, Justinian noticed a swelling in his groin. Theodora insisted that only Narses be told initially, and then she called Anthemius to her rooms.

Keeping at a distance, in case she herself was already ill, in case he was, Theodora said, 'Your brother the physician, where is he?'

'At his home, Mistress, in Sykae.'

'Is he well?'

'They're outside the central city, and we had a message two days ago to say they were all healthy, for now.'

Theodora winced inwardly, as she did whenever Anthemius or Mariam spoke of themselves as a couple, but she continued, 'Send him to me.'

'You're ill?'

And now Anthemius did not look like a younger woman's husband, a new father with a family all his own, he looked very much like the Empress's lover.

'No,' she said, 'nor do I want you to suggest that anyone in the Palace is ill, you know better than that. Just send your brother to me. Now.'

Theodora dismissed him. She had far too much to worry about, not least the dire necessity of hiding Justinian's present condition – she did not also need to see Anthemius, his concern for her all too evident, his worker's hands reaching out. With the future suddenly uncertain, she had no time for the lost possibilities of her past.

Alexander of Tralles was a very different man to his younger brother. Serious, faithful and demanding, he stalked into the Emperor's bedroom, did not bow to the Empress, told the servants to leave the room and began a full body examination of the Emperor, with no regard for usual protocol. Justinian had buboes in both armpits, several at his neck, and the beginning of lumps in his groin. Confining his speech entirely to the medical condition of his patient, and not his elevated status, the doctor gave his diagnosis to Narses.

'The patient is an older gentleman, blatantly lacking both sleep and regular exercise. Even if he were in the peak of physical fitness there'd be no guarantee of his escaping death.

This disease has no set paths, no clear pattern, all we can do is try various known remedies and pray.'

Theodora, furious that he had so far ignored her, spoke up from her seat beside Justinian's bed: 'Physician, you've been asked here to heal your Emperor. Your response offers little hope that you'll give your best to this task.'

Alexander stared across the bed at the Augusta and Theodora felt sure he was appraising her as his brother's former lover as well as his Emperor's wife.

'Mistress, I've seen the progress of this disease as it killed my neighbour's entire family, yet left him unscathed. I've read accounts of those mown down and then waking from a week of sleep to perfect health, of bodies bursting with vile liquids and yet surviving, and of others, with no symptoms at all one morning, dead that night. What I know best is how little I know. I'll treat your husband's body as well as I can. I cannot promise cure, survival, or even full health if he does survive. Now that I've seen the nature of his illness, I'll send one of your servants to fetch the instruments and salves I may need as time goes on. Allowing protocol and status – anyone's status – to get in the way of my work will do him no good at all.'

Alexander opened the door to call a servant, rattled out instructions on washing the semi-conscious Justinian hourly with a solution of rosemary and camomile, on massaging with bergamot and orange oils, and then left to look through the Palace medicine stores, in too much of a hurry to bow as he went.

When the door was closed behind him, Theodora carefully covered her sleeping husband.

Eventually Narses spoke up. 'He doesn't quite have the charm of his little brother.'

'I don't think he approves of me,' said Theodora, smiling, grateful to Narses for making light of the situation.

'As he said,' Narses replied, 'his work is better served by a concentration on the illness, not the patient. I'm sure he can be encouraged to extend that courtesy to the patient's wife as well.'

Theodora would have been grateful for Narses' discretion had she had time to think, but there was no time, Justinian's condition quickly worsened. A fever burned for three days, the Emperor slipped in and out of consciousness, boils and pustules broke out all over his body, spreading up his belly and down his legs from the groin, across his chest from the armpits. When the buboes were at their worst, Alexander burst them, draining out the thick blood and stinking pus, trying always to draw off as little as possible of what he called 'good blood'. His was the new method from Egypt and one the Palace physicians disagreed with. Theodora chose to trust the brusque, disapproving man. Just as his brother's plans for the astonishing beauty of their great church had made possible an impossible dream, perhaps Alexander would also be proved right. The Hagia Sophia dome stayed in place above the prayers now being said hourly for the Emperor's health, but Justinian's body continued to deteriorate.

Justinian had not eaten for over a week, had barely taken water or wine for four days, his skin was now a mess of lanced boils and scars that refused to heal. On the increasingly rare occasions he woke from groaning sleep or rambling delirium long enough to form a sentence, it was more often than not to demand that Narses dispatch messengers to Belisarius with orders to take full advantage of this disease, the Persians must be sick too – now was the chance to move on them, and on Totila in the west as well. One evening he spent the whole night shivering so violently in his sleep that Theodora, sure he would crack his teeth, held his jaw steady until her own hands were so cramped that Narses had to massage the blood back into them. When the trembling subsided, and Justinian woke, it was simply to remind his wife that the cistern should be protected, no one knew how the contagion was spreading, the City's water supply was always a lifeline.

Alexander was treating Justinian when the Emperor spoke, heard him speak to Theodora more as a clerk than a wife.

Seeing a quick look of pity cross his face, Theodora said, 'My husband was married to Rome long before we met.'

The physician looked at her, frowning as he washed his hands in the orange-water he always carried with him. 'That would make you his mistress?'

'I'm no one's mistress, doctor, I am his Empress.'

He had seen that she didn't sleep, barely ate or drank herself, was continually either nursing or praying her husband back to health, while all Justinian spoke of was his work, his Empire, not a word of his love for her. Knowing he'd gone too far, and knowing too that Theodora spoke her own truth, Alexander of Tralles bowed to his Empress for the first time since entering the sickroom.

'It's likely the August's fever will worsen over the next few hours. I need to fetch more medicine, a poultice I've been preparing. I'll be as quick as I can. If he survives this evening, if we get him through the night, then he might fall into the heavy sleep. If that happens, and as long as we can force liquid into him without choking, he may wake and be well.'

'Or he may wake insane?'

'If he wakes. If he survives the height of his fever and makes it through to sleep, yes, then it's possible he may already have lost his reason.'

Theodora hated Alexander then, for speaking her fears so plainly. Not that Justinian would die, that had been a possibility since he noticed the first swelling, but the dragging, deeper fear that haunted her prayer, that this fine man with his bright, sharp mind, might lose his sanity. Losing his life was one thing. Theodora knew that for Justinian to lose his mind would be a living hell.

For the rest of the night, she sat beside her husband's bed, the emerald Virgin held tight in one hand, the other resting lightly on his arm, praying she might feel the hot clamminess recede. Alexander dozed on a divan near the window, Narses stood against the wall where he had stationed himself days ago, never moving, dismissing all other servants and slaves from the entire wing. Narses was posted on one side of the door, Armeneus on the other. If the worst should happen, death or insanity, he wanted to be the first to know, and to be sure he controlled who found out.

Several hours before dawn the door opened and Armeneus let in an old man dressed in ragged clothes and carrying a bunch of dusty herbs. Alexander woke and jumped up to prevent him reaching his patient, but was held back by Narses, who introduced the two men.

'Physician, this is the priest, Baradaeus; Jacob, this is Alexander of Tralles.'

Theodora came out of her prayer-trance to hear her friend the priest approve the physician's method of opening the August's boils, to see him nodding as he went through the long list of herbal tinctures they had forced down Justinian's parched throat. Jacob offered just one more, the ragged bunch of herbs he held in his hand, herbs he had brought all the way from Tarsus when the news first broke that sickness was in the City.

'How did you know he would need it?' Theodora asked as Jacob added hot water to the dry twigs and swirled them around in the cup.

'I didn't know the Emperor would, Mistress, I knew some-one would. There is always someone who needs healing.'

Alexander stepped back, reluctantly giving his patient over to this beggar of a priest who had such presence that he fully commanded the Empress's attention, and also her confidence. Across the darkened room, neither the doctor nor the eunuch were able to see what Theodora saw, that Jacob Baradaeus made no attempt to pour the liquid down the Emperor's swollen throat. He simply leaned in with the cup as an excuse to get close to the sweating, wheezing man, grey-skinned but for those parts of his body marked by vibrant sores. With no concern for his own health, Baradaeus first stroked the Emperor's face, and then, carefully wafting the fumes from the cup close to Justinian's clogged mouth and nose, he began a litany of prayer in Coptic, Greek, Aramaic, Syriac and Latin.

He was finished before the liquid lost its steam, and offered it to Theodora, 'Drink this. It will help you later, when you need your strength,' he told her.

Theodora took the cup and did as she was told without question, and Narses silently offered up his own prayer – the Emperor on the edge of death, the Empress drinking a cup of some unknown herb, both attended by a beggar-priest most of western Rome's faithful would happily run out of the City, let alone trust with the well-being of their rulers. Alexander's horrified face confirmed that if ever the Chief of Staff should have intervened, this was the moment. Narses did nothing and the four continued, each in their own way, to pray for the desperately ill man in the centre of the room.

Justinian did not die. His fever broke in the very early morn-ing, by which time Jacob had left as quietly as he'd arrived.

Theodora noticed a slight temperature change beneath the

hand she kept on her husband's arm. 'Alexander, come here,' she whispered.

Narses was beside her before the doctor stood up and Theodora shook her head. 'He's alive, and cooler, I think.'

Alexander pulled back the sheet, checked his patient's heart, his pulses. Justinian's fever had, indeed, broken. There were no new buboes and the burning red rash around the site of those that had burst or been lanced appeared a very little paler.

'This is a good start. You must try to make him drink. Now that he's in a deeper sleep, he can fully rest. His throat will still swallow if you help him. His body may begin to heal.'

Theodora didn't want to ask, but Narses had to. 'And his mind?'

The doctor shook his head, reaching for the thin pipe and funnel to pour liquid into his patient's gullet. 'We'll know when he wakes. It'll be several days yet, if then. You should all sleep, and then you should look outside the Palace. The August is not the only patient in Rome.'

Thirty-Two

Theodora did sleep, but in her husband's room, on the divan the doctor vacated. There was no point leaving; she had not contracted the disease when Justinian's symptoms were at their height, all the signs were that she now never would. She lay with the emerald Virgin held close, praying her gratitude for Justinian's life and what she hoped had been Jacob's healing. The last thing she heard, as she finally gave in to the sleep that had been dragging on her back for days, was the call of an owl over the City, the last call before dawn.

When she woke, half a day later, she was more exhausted than when she had fallen asleep.

As she sat up, the servants in the room made to bow and she brushed away the gesture. 'How is he?'

'He's slept, Mistress,' the most senior answered. Senior compared to the others but, like most of the skeleton staff now running the Palace, not used to being in the Emperor's bedchamber and certainly not used to speaking directly to the Empress.

'He took a little honeyed water again, using the pipe and funnel as the physician showed us.'

'So we're waiting?'

'Yes, Mistress.'

'And Narses?'

'He asked that you attend him as soon as you are ready.'

The servant was well aware that in normal circumstances the Empress would not appreciate being told to call on Narses. That the circumstances were far from normal was confirmed as Theodora simply nodded, picked up her cloak and, having checked Justinian's colour and temperature for herself, did as she was asked.

'You didn't sleep at all?' she asked Narses.

The eunuch shook his head. 'Mistress, we've been neglecting our people while we attended the Emperor.'

'You're his Chief of Staff, it's your duty to be beside him.'

'It's my duty to make sure the Palace runs smoothly. I should probably have paid more attention to what else was going on, not that I have any solutions ...'

Narses held up his hands and Theodora realised that the man she had seen as invincible for more than twenty years was both exhausted and unsure. She listened as he explained what he now knew. The world outside had continued while they had spent a week waiting to see if Justinian would live or die. The world outside had been dying in that time. The City cemeteries had been over-full for weeks and already the bodies shipped across the water for burial were starting to overflow from those cemeteries too. The lack of regular gravediggers and priests for the funeral rites, neither vocation granting immunity to disease, meant the bodies could not be buried fast enough, nor granted the dignity of full rites. Mass graves had been dug, but another solution was needed and soon.

'We've lost over a quarter of our resident staff to illness or death, and another quarter of the staff who live outside the Palace walls are reported dead anyway,' Narses said. 'People have taken to wearing tags around their necks, bearing their name and address, in case the disease takes them while they're in the street.'

'Why are they leaving home, if it's safer to stay inside?' asked Theodora.

'The sickness has gone on too long. Even a well-stocked house finds its cupboards close to empty after a fortnight.'

'Yes, yes, of course.' Theodora was annoyed with herself, too used to the endless supplies of the Palace. 'So the City's stocks must also be low?'

Narses nodded. 'We've had virtually no grain shipments in three weeks. The few ships that have come in haven't always been able to unload – often there aren't enough dock-workers to do the job. The army and police are sending men where they can, unloading grain and food, keeping the cisterns full and working, helping in the graveyards, but their numbers are as low as ours, and everyone's been waiting for news of the Emperor. Decisions need to be made.'

'Then I'll make them; with your assistance, of course.'

'Well, yes Mistress, or . . .'

'Or what?'

Narses took a deep breath before he spoke. 'Belisarius returned to the City two days ago. He called a council of generals first thing this morning.'

'Did you attend?'

Theodora's tone was light, but her manner was not.

'No, Mistress.'

'You weren't invited?'

'I was,' said Narses.

'But I wasn't.'

'Apparently not.'

'Even though the Emperor has publicly named me his consort?'

'I imagine Belisarius assumed you would want to stay with
the August,' he said.

'And what did this council of generals decide, in my
absence?'

'Mistress, there is a suggestion that you could, if you
choose,' Narses' speech was slow now, becoming a question,
'allow the generals to make decisions on the August's behalf?'

And now Theodora did not look like the worried wife of
a very sick man. She was wide awake and the heat in her face
and stomach were very like, and nothing like, the fever her
husband had been suffering.

'A suggestion?'

'Yes, Mistress.'

'Have they held only one meeting?'

'I believe so.'

'And when do they convene again?'

'Late this afternoon, I've been told.'

'Good. Then I can interrupt their meeting and tell them to
damn themselves?'

Narses smiled and rubbed his eyes. 'You could, Mistress, or
you could take a middle way and ask them to meet here in the
Palace. I can have a messenger inform them you mean to
attend?'

'No,' Theodora said. 'I think I'll just go along to their
meeting. It'll be useful for me to see what's going on in the
City, and good for the people to see I care enough to go
among them.'

'And it might also be useful for you to discover who
Belisarius has called to him, rather than those who would
come here simply because the Palace commands it?'

'Yes, it might.'

Narses remembered, years ago, when he was a much younger man, his lover Menander coming home from training his dancers, ranting about the little dark one, the dead bear-keeper's brat, Theodora. How infuriating, aggravating she was. How she might do so much, be so much, but time after time she allowed her passion to rule and instead of living up to her promise, became over-emotional, made mistakes, let herself down. And despite this, how all the other girls, even those prettier or more skilled, looked up to her. Menander always said Theodora was a leader, he had no idea what or where she would lead, and died long before she was even made patrician, but Narses knew his old lover was right. He too had always hoped Theodora would finally give in to it one day, give in to the constraints and the regime and the burden, as well as the glory, of true leadership. He smiled as he watched her realise that much as she wanted to stay by Justinian, much as she wanted to sleep, to collapse, now was the time to move.

'In that case,' Narses said, 'I believe you have enough time to wash and dress before the generals' meeting is scheduled.'

Theodora thought for a moment. 'I'd have to be carried most of the way if I wear the full Imperial robes. Better to travel on foot, yes? If we walk quickly it won't take long to get to Belisarius and Antonina's home.'

'We'll be walking among those who may be ill, Mistress.'

'Are you scared, Narses?' she asked, no taint of judgement in her tone.

'Not for myself, but if you are the only August able to rule right now, perhaps we ought to take more care of you.'

'It's too late,' Theodora said. 'We've both been this close to Justinian, all through his illness, and we're well. What's the point of the purple if not to take risks when necessary?'

'The purple does not grant freedom from disease.'

'No, but it insists I stand up to the demands of the role. And right now, the pressing need is to go out, see the City for myself, and find out what the hell Belisarius is up to.'

'Mistress.'

Narses bowed and Theodora made for the door. It was opened by terrified slaves, promoted due to the death of too many others, neither of whom had ever seen the Augusta up close before. One slave bumped into the other and the door-opening became a fumble, not the seamless, quiet elegance it should have been.

They were both on the floor in apology within a moment and Theodora leaned down to whisper, 'Nerves make us all screw up – the trick is to breathe deeply, and slowly, and to keep breathing, you understand?'

The slaves mumbled agreement into the tiled floor and she said, 'Good, now try again.'

This time the doors were opened perfectly, as if by unseen hands, and Theodora – as Empress – swept out, without a glance to either of the slaves. Behaving exactly as the purple required.

Theodora walked beside Narses, through streets deserted by all but the hardiest stallholders, the most needy shoppers, those rushing from their homes or sickbeds to purchase, at vastly inflated prices, what little medicine or food was available. The Empress and the Chief of Staff stopped briefly on one side of the Forum of Constantine, watching as a dozen young men from both factions presented themselves to Blue and Green leaders, ready to make up numbers replacing sick or dead firemen, police, gravediggers.

'A shame they can't put aside their differences on a daily basis,' Narses said.

'It's as much our doing as theirs. The Palace works the

factions, we always have. We like them against each other when useful, together when necessary.'

They walked on, and Theodora remembered it was Narses who had first forced her – trained in dance and whoring and little else – to become well-read in law, history and strategy, so that she could support her husband, equipping her now to face this meeting of her husband's counsellors. Few noticed them, those who were on the streets were too concerned with their own matters to pay attention to the tall shaven-headed older man and the small middle-aged woman beside him, a handful of servants following.

As they turned into the broad avenue where Antonina and Belisarius' new home had been built, a modest City house to complement the much larger villa where they had ambushed the Cappadocian, the clouds that had been threatening rain all day parted briefly, letting through a flash of sunlight, striking the Sea of Marmara beyond. Theodora stopped, calling the servants to her. One opened a cedarwood box and another carefully lifted out the Imperial chlamys, while a third smoothly unrolled a soft leather pouch to reveal a robe of deep purple silk, hemmed and picked out in gold stitching. With Narses' help, Theodora was fastened first into the robe, then the chlamys was secured into place with pins of warm red gold. From another box came five strings of pearls, each one finer than the last, and a pair of black pearl earrings. Finally Theodora put out her feet, one after the other, and the dusty street sandals were replaced by the densely embroidered red slippers she always wore in the Palace.

Belisarius' doorkeeper had spent all afternoon opening up to soldiers and generals, civil servants and high-ranking patricians, each one with his cloak pulled up to his eyes, his mouth covered, attended by as few servants as possible; many brought none at all, feeling it safer to move through the dangerous streets as quickly as they could, with no entourage to hold them up. The doorkeeper greeted each new entrant carefully, maintaining his distance, for his own protection as much as to assuage the guests' fears, and then led them through to the large open courtyard where Belisarius was holding his meeting, believing – as would any soldier – that fresh air was beneficial to all. The guests' servants, left to fend for themselves, chose not to gather as they usually would, sharing a meal and gossiping about their masters, but sat each apart from the other in a lower courtyard, their silent division a clearer indication of the state of the City than any physician's report.

Opening the door to the Empress and her retinue, the doorman, who believed all the guests were now accounted for, gasped at the sight that greeted him. Long a soldier and more recently working privately for Belisarius to supplement his pension, he immediately prostrated himself. He kissed the Empress's foot, though without actually bringing his lips to her slipper, and then, maintaining a half-bow while walking backwards, he led her through the villa into the courtyard that now housed twenty or more chiefs of the military and government, deep in worried discussion. Far more worried when they looked up and saw Theodora.

The men bowed, as did Antonina, hurriedly summoned by the doorman, and Belisarius politely vacated his seat at the head of the table to make way for the Empress. She took his place and looked around the men, noting each one, noting the looks on their faces.

'Go on gentleman, whatever you were discussing must surely be of interest to the August, yes?'

'Mistress . . .'

Belisarius began to speak, but was cut off by Theodora, still smiling, still speaking calmly. 'What I don't understand is why you chose to hold your meeting here and not in the Palace. And I gather this is not your first meeting. I'd understand if a first meeting was held here, in haste, of course. But a second? Without notifying the Palace? When did you think you'd alert us to your plans?'

This time Germanus tried to answer: 'Mistress, we felt it would be better—'

Theodora stopped him with a raised finger: 'To stay away from the Palace until your coup was complete?'

At that there was general consternation. Half the men at the table stood up to protest, and then, seeing that the Empress remained seated, hurriedly sat down again, so as not to tower over her. Theodora waited until there was silence again.

'Then what am I to think? You sneak into Belisarius' little City home to chat cosily among yourselves when you have the whole Palace available? When the entire structure for the Empire is based in the Emperor's offices? Or perhaps you are afraid to enter the Palace, so scared of contagion you'd prefer to make the big decisions here, in your ...' she looked at Antonina, 'back yard? Are you that frightened? I had thought you more brave, soldiers.'

There was no reply, but Theodora knew her words had hit home; she suspected that as many would be terrified of catching the Emperor's disease as might be plotting with Belisarius to take power from her.

'We didn't want to disturb you. Or the Emperor,' Belisarius finally said, Antonina's nudge encouraging him to add a mistimed 'Mistress' at the end of the sentence.

'Of course, that must be it,' Theodora said. 'You didn't want to disturb the August, which is why you sent your messengers to ask how he was eight times a day in the past week. You'll be pleased to know his fever has broken.'

At this everyone in the courtyard, from lowest slave to Belisarius, breathed prayers and blessings of relief, and although Theodora felt some of their prayers sounded more heartfelt than others, she chose not to dwell on that for now.

'The August needs rest, and nourishment, and – with the Christ's help – he will be healthy again. Until then, I'll assume this show of action indicates your willingness to stay in the City, when I know many of you might prefer to return to your safe country villas. Very good of you to put the work of the Empire before your own health.'

She nodded at a couple of the older senators who she was sure had every intention of hurrying from the City the moment the meeting was over, no doubt leaving Belisarius in charge. Theodora scanned the courtyard, picking out individuals as she went. John, the son of Vitalian who had travelled to Italy to support Belisarius and his troops. Bouzes the Thracian who had often been Belisarius' right-hand man in battle and was loyal enough to work for him in any capacity. Artebanes who had been under suspicion at the time of Sittas' death and whom Theodora had distrusted ever since.

She made sure each man knew she had seen and noted him, and then went on, 'So, it's business as usual, in unusual times. You'll all stay in the City – and I am August.'

Theodora looked around her, at the men whose fists were clenched in an effort not to exclaim their surprise or horror, and at the few who could look her straight in the eye, relieved and pleased at her words.

'As the August's named consort and the only one of us, along with Narses, able to visit and take his counsel, it's my duty to stand for him. I'm ready to work as hard as my husband, and

I'm delighted the dedication that sees you all here, so far from the Palace, so careful not to disturb our Emperor, means you too intend to work hard. To work with us.'

She stood then, forcing the men to their knees. 'Leaving your campaign must have been very difficult for a passionate soldier such as yourself, Belisarius.' She smiled and asked, 'Unless you had some other reason to bring these gentlemen together?'

'Mistress, the sickness attacks Khusro's men as brutally as it does ours. There is less danger to our border forces just now than there has been in some time.'

'So you've come home to be useful?'

'I have.'

Theodora frowned, she hadn't finished with him. 'Yet you didn't come straight to the Palace? You chose to meet here, generals and senators together, almost in secret?' She leaned down to stage-whisper to Belisarius, her words perfectly clear, 'Were you planning to depose my husband before he even awoke, General?'

The courtyard was silent. A gull screamed in the distance. Slowly, Belisarius stood up, Theodora straightened with him. When he spoke his tone was no less careful, and no less threatening, than hers.

'Mistress, now and always, I have only had Rome as my first thought.'

'A careful answer,' said Theodora.

'An honest one,' replied Belisarius, holding in his anger with difficulty. 'It's true some have been asking what might happen were the August not to return to full health.'

'Are you considering taking his place?'

Belisarius shook his head. 'No Mistress, that would be treason. We merely wanted, needed, to discuss how best we can support you through the August's recovery.'

Theodora stared at Belisarius and the courtyard held its breath, waiting for her outburst, but it didn't come. Instead she smiled and continued as if he had not spoken at all.

'Gentlemen, bring your emergency council to the Palace this evening. I'm sure you all have much to teach me. And – as Augusta,' the word was spoken lightly, softly, her stance and her face indicating the opposite, 'I'm keen to learn from the best. I'm also keen to make sure Rome comes first – not the ambition of any one man.'

She looked directly at Belisarius, turned on her heel and walked away.

As they left the house Theodora shrugged off her Imperial robes for the waiting servants, pulled on the dusty sandals and then sped through the streets, her hands shaking with rage, her words coming in bursts as she reined in her temper with great difficulty.

'I want you to set up an investigation,' she said to Narses.

'Mistress, there's so much to do—'

'I want to know,' Theodora spoke over him, charging on uphill, 'if they were planning to take over from the August and, if so, who they intended to suggest as Emperor.'

'The people will never believe Belisarius would plot against the Emperor.'

Theodora pointed at a couple huddled and sobbing over the body of their dead child. 'Look at them, Narses, the people are sick, dying. They need stability. The August gives us that, anything that takes that stability from them is treason.'

'Yes, Mistress, but—'

'With no trade, the markets practically closed, we've lost an enormous amount in revenue, in taxes. The people are fond of Belisarius, but I doubt that fondness would include leniency if he was found plotting to depose the August. Some might even appreciate the income from the confiscation of his wealth. War has made Belisarius a prosperous man.'

'I know.'

'Good, then you begin an investigation and we'll get on with running the state. And have Bouzes arrested,' she added, almost as an afterthought.

'Bouzes?'

'The people may like Belisarius, but no one cares for Bouzes; his own soldiers have always said he's too harsh. Have him put away. His men will be grateful, and the people will know we mean business.'

'Those who are alive to care.'

'Those who are alive to care are the only ones that matter.'

Theodora left Narses talking with guards at the Chalke Gate as she ran back into the Palace to check on Justinian. Only when she had assured herself that he was still sleeping, his colour better, his breathing easier, did she go on to her own rooms. She dismissed her servants and, making no sound, careful not to spread rumour even in the semi-deserted Palace, she screamed her fury, open-mouthed and silent.

Then she knelt at her private altar and, holding the emerald Virgin to her breast, she whispered, 'You will not take this. Not one of you will take this from us. From me.'

Thirty-Three

Theodora set herself up in Justinian's offices, leaving Armeneus in charge of the Palace household while she and Narses were preoccupied with state and City. The drastically reduced number of regular staff were happy to take their orders from the Augusta through Narses. The people and the vast majority of the household staff were told the August was recuperating: only Theodora, Narses and Alexander knew that Justinian was still critically ill, rarely awake for more than a few moments at a time, his breathing constantly laboured, his weight loss terrifying and, on the rare occasions he was fully awake, his speech far from sensible.

Theodora took Justinian's place, Rome went on as usual, and the Empress prayed beside her husband from the time she quit his office, late at night, until Armeneus bodily carried her to her own room, and left her to Mariam's care. She rarely slept more than four hours. Her first question on waking was always about Justinian's health, her first action to kneel and offer thanks that he had made it through another night. Then she washed quickly, dressed simply, and got to work. Theodora knew her every move would be scrutinised by those looking for an excuse to step in, she meant to give them no opportunity to find her lacking.

Each day she held a council with the chief advisers. Some had been at the meeting with Belisarius, others, like Peter Barsymes, were those she chose herself and then immediately promoted so they were able to work at the highest level. She brought Anthimus out of hiding and made him her personal spiritual adviser.

'Anyone who's more worried about the Church than the fact that half their family have died will feel safer, knowing I've brought a priest into the Palace.'

'A priest you've protected for years, who probably owes you his life?' Narses said, a smile already on his lips.

'That's right.'

'And if the Patriarch Menas and Pope Vigilius in Rome wonder why you didn't appoint one of them as your adviser?'

'Let them wonder. We have far more to worry about than the politicking of priests.'

Every morning Armeneus reported on household matters and went back to ensure the huge Palace machine ran as best it could on so few staff. Narses called in extra advisers as and when they were needed, as and when they were still alive. Macedonia's reports from Italy confirmed Belisarius' belief that Totila's army was badly affected by disease, and spies along the Persian border said the same. Minor insurrections in both directions had not entirely abated, but the borders were quieter than they had been in many years. Justinian still lay groaning in his sleep, often beating his face and brow with his bony fists whenever his attendants accidentally allowed his hands free, attacking the pain deep inside his head. Narses was busy running a state that was perilously close to starving, and Belisarius was still under investigation. Unlike Bouzes,

Belisarius was at least free to go about his business while the investigation continued and Theodora was relieved she did not have to make any major military decisions. She didn't trust Belisarius, but she couldn't fault his military knowledge. Antonina tried just once to speak to Theodora about the investigation, and stopped mid-sentence when the look from her old friend made the present distance between them quite plain.

Even if Theodora had been willing to discuss Belisarius' behaviour with Antonina, there were simply too many other things to get under control first. The spiralling death count, the senior clerics and civil servants who had died leaving vacant posts, the unrest among the state's generals – everything had been left to slide during the ten days of Justinian's crisis. It all needed attention at once, and the urgent need to bury the corpses took precedence. Initially the daily death toll in the City had been in the hundreds, but it had quickly climbed to thousands of deaths every day: some suggested as many as fifteen thousand in one awful night, the true toll impossible to judge while the bodies still lay heaped together. The City graveyards had long overflowed and the mass graves on the Asian side of the Bosphorus now filled more quickly than the gravediggers could work. All too often, when the graves were not ready, the dead were simply dropped from the boats commandeered to ferry them across, waves washing the corpses away, only for them to return as bloated death on the shifting current.

Theodora had sent her own immediate family to stay in the country, along with Mariam, Anthemius and their little son, and as many of the Palace staff and civil servants as could be spared. Her palace at Hieron was now full of those they would need when the sickness finally ended. It would have to end eventually, Theodora could not allow herself to believe it would not, and she wanted a healthy government when it did. Anthemius was called back to advise on the possibility of building more graveyards, still further out of the City.

It was late afternoon, the much warmer sun setting on a near-silent City. The markets and Mese were deserted except for those who had no choice but to try to find a scrap of meat or grain, and those others carting bodies with nowhere to bury them. Theodora and Anthemius met quietly, with only Armeneus in attendance, and she was pleased to see that Anthemius smiled with genuine pleasure when she reached out to raise him from his bow.

'You've been busy in the country?' she asked, feeling the calluses on his hands.

'Your palace at Hieron now has a walled summer courtyard, Mistress. The new planting will allow you to enjoy it next year, when you can rest, when all this is over.'

She smiled. 'I'll look forward to that. For now, we work.'

Anthemius shook his head when she suggested a huge new graveyard further outside the city walls. 'Even with both factions working together, there's no point building further out: all that does is create the extra problem of transporting bodies, finding gravediggers in the less-populated areas. It'd make more sense to bury the bodies in the City.'

'We've used all the space in the City.'

'We haven't used all the space inside the spaces in the City.'

Theodora shook her head. 'We have, that's the point—'

No,' he interrupted, 'there are still the towers, Mistress. The towers along the Theodosian Wall and those in the wall over in Sykae. We throw the bodies into the towers and then block them up.'

'Make a mausoleum of our own walls?'

'Better that than a graveyard of our streets.'

Theodora agreed. Narses promised soldiers for the job.

'Could we use Belisarius' men?' asked Theodora.

'We could, Mistress,' Narses replied.

'Good, then he can supervise them, under Anthemius' orders.'

'He probably won't appreciate that,' said Anthemius. 'The general's never had much respect for me, he doesn't have the August's interest in design or construction, and there's . . .'

He stopped then, there was no need to mention the rumours of their affair in front of the two people who knew it to be fact.

'Exactly.' Theodora smiled and a messenger was set to Hieron to tell Mariam not to expect her husband back for some time.

Over the next few days, the City was once again full of the sound of stone-cutting and sawing and men shouting over the dust as Belisarius' soldiers became builders under Anthemius' command. Theodora thought Justinian almost smiled once, as she sat with him, listening to the clatter of building work, and she whispered that all was well, failing to say the noise was of death rather than construction.

Anthemius supervised first the dismantling of the tower roofs on both sets of major walls. Soldiers quickly trained in stonemasonry blocked up the tower windows, and then, using a series of cranes, hoisted bodies on pallets into the towers. Isodore returned to the City to work with his partner and supervised the shifting of cranes from one tower to another as the dead filled the now-enclosed spaces. For all that it was dreadful work in many ways – the cloying stink of quickly rotting corpses had the workers wrapping their faces in rose-oil rags – Anthemius relished the task.

'You enjoyed that, didn't you?' she asked him when the first set of tower-graves was completed.

Anthemius nodded, rubbing sandy grit from his eyes. 'It's good work. Necessary, practical, but beautiful too. The simplicity of function, remaking one form for a more urgent use. I enjoy it. Or I will once I get the reek of rotting flesh from my skin.'

Even so, Theodora kept Anthemius in the Palace only as long as it took to train up a team of workmen and soldiers. Once they were working steadily under Belisarius' supervision, she sent him back to Hieron where his wife and child waited.

'I don't want to find myself enjoying your company too much, architect.'

'Nor I to miss my wife and child, Mistress,' he replied.

Anthemius left and Theodora returned to Justinian's side, his hands even smoother in illness, in contrast, than before.

Within a fortnight, the rising heat of early summer and the hot wind that whipped along the Golden Horn had sucked the stink of rotting bodies into every corner of the Palace, and the inhabitants of the City covered their mouths and noses with tightly knotted cloths to keep back the putrid stench that caused them to retch at the slightest crack in a door or a window.

'Your architect might be asked back to the City to experience this, Mistress,' said Armeneus, his voice muffled by several layers of rosemary-infused silk.

'He's not my architect and I will not call him back. Anthemius helped us keep the bodies from rotting in the streets and on the shores: this isn't an ideal solution but it's the only one we have. My concern now is my husband's health, the City, and Rome – in that order,' Theodora replied, in a tone of voice that assured him she had no intention of discussing the matter.

Despite her constant care for Justinian, Anthemius' presence had been more painful than she had expected and Theodora knew better than to allow any wound to fester in this climate.

In the weeks that followed, as Justinian slowly regained a little strength, Theodora found herself becoming comfortable in his place. With Belisarius still under investigation, military decisions were left to Narses. Peter Barsymes who, like Theodora and Narses had proved immune to the illness, became even more useful as an adviser on trade. Not only did he know all the routes, including the few that remained untouched by disease, he also knew the rare traders who were still working. He advised her which captains she could trust to make it to Egypt and back with a full hold, which street markets they could close against contagion and still allow the people to buy the minimum they needed to survive – not hard, given that only the minimum was available for purchase – and he helped her stockpile a remarkable array of silks.

'The Chinese have some of the best healers I've ever met, but even they haven't yet divined the secret of eternal life. So far they've been less affected than us, but only a little. They too are missing trade. Now's the time to buy.'

'Have you heard from the men you sent out?'

'Not recently, Mistress, but I have reason to believe they'll bring good news, eventually.'

'Go on.'

He shook his head. 'Not until I know more.'

'I could force you to speak.'

'You could.'

'What if you were to become ill and die without telling me?'

'Then you would lose your finest negotiator in trade, and even the Augusta can't force me to tell what I don't yet know.'

'You'd be surprised,' said Theodora. 'Bouzes has offered up all sorts of information we had no idea he knew.'

'Since you've been keeping him in your hidden torture chambers deep beneath the Palace?' Barsymes asked, his smile revealing that although he too had heard the rumours of his mistress's terrifying dungeons, he didn't fully believe them.

'Yes, since he's been chained against the sea wall, having seen no daylight for five weeks, standing always in a hand's depth of water so the flesh on his feet has begun to rot ...' Theodora shook her head. 'I have no idea where these stories come from.'

'Of your delight in torture?'

'That and the poisoning skills I picked up in Alexandria, the witchcraft I learned in Antioch ...'

'The sexual slavery in which you keep all your lovers?'

Theodora's head whipped round and Peter Barsymes saw the mask of Empress slam down on the face of the woman who had been joking until now.

'Sorry, too many years as a traveller, I always go too far ...'

Then Theodora smiled and he realised her game, shook his head and grinned. 'Of course Mistress, you do little to dispel these rumours. You could let Bouzes out, show the people he's been perfectly well kept.'

'I could, but Narses taught me long ago that while compassion and empathy are fine skills for the August, a little fear can be useful too.'

'So it's Bouzes who is afraid?'

'Yes. And we just can't shut him up on the matter of Belisarius' private funds.'

Far below the Empress's rooms, in a tiny cell off a dark corridor where no light entered, a man stood, chained to the wall. Stood where he had been chained for weeks, stood in sea water, his feet rotting on his body.

Thirty-Four

When Justinian woke fully it was not immediately clear that his mind was saved. Whatever had caused him to beat his head during the bouts of agony between long periods of unconsciousness might well have damaged his sense. Only Theodora, Narses and the Patriarch Anthimus were allowed near him for the first ten days, and even then, on Alexander's orders, there was to be no talk of state business.

'You can sit beside him, quietly, as a good wife should,' said Alexander, gaining a brutal glare from Theodora, and a hidden grin from Narses.

And so they sat, quiet hours at a time, the Empress and her Chief of Staff, hushing Justinian's concern, assuring him all was well, all would be well, and paying no attention to his slurred speech and the words that were missing, either from his sentences or his mind; ignoring, too, the constant tremor in both of his hands. Theodora kept the emerald Virgin close. Prayer was her only relief.

Armeneus found her, late one evening, standing in the Church of Hagia Sophia, the evening sun angled high through the windows at the base of the dome, the gold and glass mosaics spinning their soft amber light through the whole building. The candles were not yet lit and, but for a few priests muttering quietly among themselves, the great church was almost empty. Once inside, the shouts from the market beyond the square – each day more full, each day more lively – were muffled, and he spoke quietly as he approached.

'Mistress?'

Theodora turned and her face was bright with tears, eyes swollen and red. 'We may need to tell the Persian ambassador I'll be late for dinner,' she said. 'It's a shame Mariam is still at Hieron, she's always been better at applying the makeup mask that makes me look like an Empress.'

'You are Empress, Mistress, it doesn't matter how you look.'

'You know that's not true, and certainly not now, when I'm meeting men who would rather meet my husband, who are here purely to decide whether or not we return to full war.'

'I'll tell them you've been delayed. You know you enjoy it once you're in the room with them, you do it well.'

Theodora smiled. 'Your lover's lover gave me a rigorous training.'

'Narses says Menander would have been proud of what you've achieved these past months.'

'He does?' she asked.

'He didn't tell you?'

'He wouldn't, Narses has always been keen for me to know my place.'

'He's that hard?'

'You know he is. And I've thought about nothing but my place since Justinian began to recover. I have enjoyed some of the power while he's been ill, I've liked being able to make my own decisions.'

Armeneus peered at her. 'You're not crying because you have to share power again?'

'No,' she smiled, shaking her head, 'I'm crying because I'm relieved to find I'm not the woman some think I am. I've had no chance to question what I felt, other than my fear of losing Justinian, my worry that Belisarius and the others might push him out. These past few months everything else has been about the day to day, keeping it all going.'

'And now?'

'Now, yes, I feel some reluctance to hand over the full extent of this power, but my greater feeling is relief, gratitude that he's alive, that he'll recover.'

'He is your husband.'

'And there are many who've accused him of being less of a man because his choice was to share with me, accused me of being not enough of a woman to yield to him. In twenty-one years I've become used to our partnership and these past months by myself have been exhausting, but they've also been thrilling. Half a lifetime of hearing those stories about myself from those who call me all ambition, all power-hungry, sometimes I've wondered if they were right.'

Theodora stopped, taking in the surprise on her assistant's face. 'Even I experience self-doubt occasionally, Armeneus, it's just not very useful to show it in public. You and I watched Hecebolus become so preoccupied with his lack of power in the Pentapolis that he became a different man. We saw the Empress Euphemia's face turn from plain to plain ugly when she believed me her usurper. I know what power can do, and I know it often does so without the powerful noticing.'

Armeneus frowned. 'So you're crying because you're relieved you aren't the woman that those who dislike you believe you to be?'

'At least not entirely, yes.'

He shook his head. 'I'm sorry, Mistress, but while other men rate their balls higher than gold, I've always been grateful

I was made a eunuch. I could never have married a woman. I don't understand your thinking at all.'

Theodora nodded, rubbed her hands together, and turned to leave the gallery, speaking over her shoulder: 'And I'm sure there's a woman somewhere, unaware of her good fortune that she was saved having you as a husband.'

Theodora's stature was straight, her speech clearer; even with her red cheeks and swollen eyes she was now every step the Empress. The muttering priests below suddenly realised the Augusta was in the building and were immediately on their knees, just as she had intended.

It was another two weeks before Alexander allowed Justinian to sit up, a full month before he finally allowed Theodora to carefully, quietly, explain the true state of the nation to her husband.

The Emperor listened in silence as she talked.

'There are businesses shattered. Families broken too, and faith – there must be many who find their faith damaged. When things are back to normal we'll need their belief, in us as well as the Christ.'

She paused, sipped from a glass of wine, undiluted for the courage she needed to tell him the rest.

'And there's been a count, not a formal one, it's not been possible, we don't have the staff to do it, but from what we can tell, from the numbers we have … there are, perhaps, three hundred thousand dead.'

Justinian began to cry softly and Theodora felt she was punishing him even more by telling him the rest, but when his crying turned to agitation, to a mouthing and stuttering as he tried to ask what else had happened, she knew she had to say it all.

'We think three hundred thousand, and many more

exhausted from fighting disease, plenty of walking wounded in half-empty streets. All of Italy, other than Rome and Ravenna and a few of the port towns, is ruled by the Goths again. Totila has a new strategy of expelling landlords and freeing slaves, he's good to the peasant farmers and has the smallholders on his side. We have your spies to tell us so, and also Macedonia, who returned to the City this week: she says the people there are happy to be with the Goths.'

Then Theodora held the hands Justinian still fought to stop trembling, and promised life had begun again. 'We've started negotiating a new peace with Khusro, the Persians are as battered by disease as Rome. There are shops opening all along the Mese, one at a time yes, but they're open, we are trading. There aren't many stalls yet in the markets, and the goods on offer are sparse. Narses was complaining only yesterday about the lack of meat. But it's a start, it's a good start.'

The Emperor, exhausted, relaxed as she spoke and allowed Theodora to quiet his worries with careful words that neither fully believed.

As the dregs of summer gave way to the welcome cool of autumn, the stench from the towers finally began to recede, heavily pregnant women gave birth to perfect babies who had miraculously survived the deaths of their fathers and whole families of siblings, and the many who believed the illness was a punishment from God now considered that perhaps they had been spared for a reason. And if they had been saved for a reason, then surely the Emperor had too.

Justinian and Theodora walked through the corridors to the Chalke, heading across Augustaion to Hagia Sophia for a service of thanksgiving, both for the Emperor's life and for the new life, the saved life, of Rome. Later there would be speeches from the Kathisma, the Emperor using the Mandator to speak for him. Protocol certainly allowed it, and though his speech was improving, both Theodora and Narses advised against risking his voice, still hoarse from weeks without use. The people would be pleased to see their Emperor, whole and standing, able to walk to church and wave to them. That was plenty. No one needed to hear the Emperor's voice croak or – and Justinian knew this was Narses' real concern – watch him grope for the right word, his fine legal mind too often confusing leg for hand, paper for water, wine for chair. There seemed no reason for the confusion in his mind and Alexander had promised all would be well eventually.

'Master, you need to give yourself time, you have survived a brutal illness and, with the greatest possible respect, you are no longer a young man.'

'He's only sixty,' Theodora interrupted, glaring at Alexander and looking to Narses who, although already seventy, seemed not to have aged a day in years.

'Yes, Mistress,' said Alexander, 'I just meant . . .'

'The Emperor needs rest,' said Narses. 'We know, but Rome needs her Emperor.'

'And Rome . . . comes . . . first.' Justinian spoke, clearly but very slowly, underlining both physician and Chief of Staff's concerns.

After the speech from the Kathisma, the Emperor would stay to watch one race, and then rest until the evening when Theodora was hosting a celebration for all the Palace staff and servants, a gesture of thanks to those who had worked so hard during the time of disease. The inner courtyards were already set up with lights for the evening, braziers laid against the evening chill. Theodora gave one of the theatre troupes a list of routines she wanted them to perform. The set list contained several songs well known as accompanying pieces for the Empress in her Hippodrome heyday, all of them from the respectable end of her repertoire, but nonetheless, there was excitement among those readying the Palace, hoping that perhaps tonight, after all this time, they might finally see the Empress doing what she was famed for – playing Theodora, rather than acting Empress.

Theodora was shaking. Breathing with the control and calm Menander had taught all his girls didn't seem to work, and slapping herself all over lightly as she used to before entering the stage space only had her skin on fire with more goose bumps, her hands quivering, her breath coming in tighter, shorter bursts.

She turned to her husband, horrified. 'I don't think I can do it.'

Justinian reached out a trembling hand of his own, 'We walked to ... Hagia So ... Soph ... Sophia,' he finally completed the word, and his pleasure in doing so made the next phrase easier, as Theodora had known it would. Even in her agitated state, she knew better than to undermine him by helping, filling in the gaps.

'I stood alone and you waited ...' he shook his head, 'watched me, from the top. The up. The there ...' again Justinian struggled for the word and again Theodora waited, 'the gallery,' he sighed having found it and thanked her with a lopsided smile, 'then the Kath ... is ... ma. They ... applauded and I ... spun ... spoke.'

'Even though we'd all agreed it would be better for you not to.'

'I didn't get it ... wrong.'

'No, you didn't,' Theodora conceded.

'I did ... everything you and ... him ... him, eunuch ... Nar ... ses asked. I did it all this day. Now. Today. Now you ...'

'Yes.'

'Now you have to do, as you ... promised.'

Justinian was shaking even more with the effort of getting his words out in the right order, small beads of sweat on his brow.

'Yes, I have to do what I said I'd do, but please, take your seat? The whole point of this event is to encourage the people to believe all is well, not confirm the rumour of your imminent demise.'

Theodora called over the slaves who now waited close to Justinian at all times, ready to help him whenever needed, as unobtrusively as possible. As they walked their master to his seat, the crowd of Palace slaves, staff and civil servants assembled in the courtyard became quiet and bowed to the August. Theodora, her thoughts on Justinian, forgot her own stage fright and gave her concentration to her husband. Which made it all the more surprising when she watched him shake off the slaves on either side and move to his seat with ease and almost grace, his still hand carefully placed over the one that was trembling. Armeneus arrived to give Theodora her cue and caught her grinning at the sight before her.

'You're less nervous now, Mistress?'

'I was forced to think about something else and my nerves disappeared entirely, which I'm sure is exactly what Narses and the Emperor intended.'

'I don't know what you mean, Mistress.'

'Liar.' Theodora glared at him. 'Come on then, announce my entrance, the sooner this is over, the better.'

Mariam and Ana entered first, dressed as handmaidens of Leda. Even the lowliest of the Palace staff guessed what was coming: everyone knew this was the beginning of the scene for which the Empress was famed, the woman who had been Theodora-from-the-Brothel. Comito sang and the connoisseurs in the crowd praised her choice to sing with no backing; it was exactly right, her voice had matured well. Mariam and Ana reached into their robes and pulled out golden bags, slowly turning a full circle and spilling streams of silver-covered grain. Mariam played her part quietly, with the elegance she was now noted for. Ana surprised everyone by actually engaging with her audience, smiling at those she knew in the crowd, apparently enjoying her moment on stage, applauded by her laughing, loving husband. A bell chimed, Comito repeated the note, the younger women joined in harmony, and finally Theodora entered.

Dressed in an old man's robe, with an old man's beard and fat belly, she waddled to the centre of the circle and the crowd erupted in applause and laughter. This was not Theodora playing her notorious youthful role; instead she was playing the old actor who had been Zeus in their infamous sketch. And, just as Petrus of Galatia had once opened his robe to reveal the geese that famously pecked grain from Theodora's naked thighs, now the bearded Empress opened her cloak to reveal Ana's son Anastasius, Comito's Sophia, and Antonina's Joannina, all dressed as geese. The three children leapt out, hissing and squawking, they scrabbled about the mosaic paving, collecting the beads of solid silver grain, and gave them to the crowd, one perfect grain for every person, from Narses and Armeneus standing either side of the seated Justinian, down to the new team of slave boys who silently followed the Emperor, their only job to be ready for him, twenty-four hours a day.

Theodora plucked off her beard, and pulled the cloak tight around her. She applauded her fellow performers, giving a special smile to Ana. When each of the crowd had their silver grains, Narses called for silence, and the Empress spoke.

'The August thanks you for your strength through the illness, for your forbearance when we know every one of you must also have lost dear ones. We also give thanks for your courage to continue; working from the Palace, the heart of Rome, for the good of Rome.'

The staff applauded, Theodora bowed to them, and three big slaves then lifted each of the children high on their shoulders to wave to the crowd. Justinian stood and came forward to his wife. He waved and took her hand.

'Nice speech,' he said.

'You wrote it,' she answered, holding his hand tightly so that the people, still cheering, didn't see how it shook, beyond his control.

'Words, I mean ... speaking ... I ... dictated it.'

'Yes, you did. There've been plenty of rulers who could neither read nor write, Justinian, you'll do both again, and well.' Beside her, Theodora felt her husband lose his footing just a little, felt him falter. 'No, not yet, two more steps,' she said.

Justinian took a deep breath, and then turned, a broken smile on his tired, baggy-eyed face; with his better hand, he waved to his people. Then his wife led him inside.

Thirty-Five

Theodora sent away Justinian's chamber slaves, and began to undress her husband herself. She unpinned the two large brooches holding his outer robe in place and helped him shrug off the heavy silk, carefully laying it on the carved wooden chest so his servants could take it back to the robing room later. Free of the weight, Justinian sat down heavily on the bed, exhausted. His clothes were the finest available in Constantinople, the silk woven expressly for the Palace by the Jewish weavers who had housed Theodora when she first met Justinian, and dyed with the deepest purple Tyre had to offer. Leah, Esther's daughter who had yet to be born when Theodora lived with the family, was now famed for her skill in working precious stones into intricate embroidery, creating mosaics with gems and gold thread. Hers was a lauded craft, loved more by those who looked on the garments than the few who had to stand up under their weight. Theodora helped Justinian off with his slippers, also embroidered, jewel encrusted. She unpinned the sleeves hiding the deep pox scars on his arms, scars that rounded his back, his torso, and she saw, as if for the first time, the soft, hanging skin of his upper arms. She removed the gold chain belt from his waist, more of a waist now, she noticed, than before he was ill; her husband had never been fat, but she was small and to her he had always seemed a big man. She saw that his frame was still wide, still tall, but somehow hollow, the sickness had taken a great deal from him, and not just bodily. Justinian, strong in his hopes, sure in his ambitions for the Empire, the husband who had rarely seemed his full eighteen years older than her, appeared to have given in to age.

Naked, Justinian rolled over and into his bed, his eyes already closing. Before his sickness Theodora had never known Justinian to fall asleep before her or wake after; now half of his days seemed to be spent dozing. Alexander had warned it would take a long time for him to regain his full energy, if ever, but she hadn't understood such depletion could be possible, not until she saw it in the flesh, the lack of substance to his flesh.

She pulled the covers up to his shoulders, doused the lights closest to him and turned to leave the room.

'Don't go,' Justinian said, 'lay ... lie beside me.'

'You're exhausted, you need to sleep, I always disturb you when we sleep together.'

'I want to ... be distract ... disturbed – Theodora, I don't want to sleep. This c ... constant tiredness will turn to ... lethargy –' he took a deep breath, forced his tongue and lips around the words, 'if I'm not careful.'

'You? Lethargic?' Theodora laughed. 'Not you.'

'Take off your clothes ... get into bed ...'

Theodora looked at her husband in the half-light, she could see he was struggling to stay awake, but he wanted her there. She did as she was told.

'I don't want to feel like this,' he said as she stretched out alongside him, her dark skin against his pale, her smooth arm holding his trembling one. 'I hate ... that I can't do ... everything I want. I hate ... speaking ... like ... this.'

'It will come back, Alexander said it would. And you'll do everything you want, you just need time.'

'Yes, but he also ... told us I may never full ... fully recover.'

'You're alive, many are not.'

'I know ... I'm ... lucky. But I saw it ... Theodora, I saw ... my death.'

She nodded, she too had seen her own mortality, many years ago in the desert, knew how it felt to truly realise that her own flesh, her own spirit, were not invincible; to know, for certain, that death was corporeal, utterly real.

'And it is ... was ... frightening ... as the sages have said ... said it was. I was scared, lying there, unable to hear you much of the time, unable to see ... at all, scared of what was to come.'

'You're a good man, Justinian. Faithful. You don't need to fear death.'

'I didn't, I feared, I fear ... not living. Not living long ... enough. Our one ... Church, one ... Empire.'

'We've achieved a great deal.'

'Achieved and lost ... gained again. Lost. It's always been like that with l ... l ... with land, with borders. I should not have expected more.'

'You won't give up on Italy?'

'I'm from the west – how could ... could I give up on west ... western Rome? But we'll always spend time and gold and ... too many ... men holding borders. That's what land does. The Church though ...' he stopped to breathe, the effort of speaking so much was exhausting him. Theodora watched him frowning in the half-light: 'Seeing my ... my own death ... I'm no longer sure. About anything.'

Theodora held her husband tighter. 'Justinian, many men, many women, never learn that in their lifetime. Well done.'

In the pale light before full dawn, as sailors left port and whores went back to their beds, when the windows let in the cries of market sellers laying out their stalls, and the City air was delicious with the smell of baking bread, stronger for the first time in many months than the stink of the dead, Justinian turned over and slowly lifted his good hand to Theodora's face. His fingers passed over her lips, waiting for a moment to feel the sleeping kiss of her light breath, then down to her collarbone, his thumb tracing the line to her breasts. Theodora woke to feel his touch and kept her eyes closed, her breathing regular, waiting. Justinian moved his seeking hand to the slight concave of her upper stomach, the hungry dip between her ribs. Yesterday had been too big, too long, neither of them able to eat much, though the kitchens had provided the best that could be bought from a market half its usual size, the best that could be prepared by new staff unused to old ovens, replacing old staff in new graves. He was stroking now, smoothing her skin, her stomach rising, falling, quivering as she woke fully, to his hand, to his breath, to her husband.

Theodora reached up and Justinian turned, reaching out across her, with the flat palm of his trembling hand. Working to hold it as still as he could, he stroked the fine line crossing her lower belly. The scar she never mentioned, other than to dismiss the sickness during her year in the desert. Theodora rarely spoke of her conversion, she had told him simply that it was painful and wonderful and that Severus had taken care of her. Justinian had never asked for more, not even when she failed, month after month, to get pregnant when they were both so much younger. He had married Theodora because it

332

was wise, useful, and – surprising them both when it happened – because he loved her; he had not married her for children.

Theodora was concerned about succession. Justinian was not: he was concerned about creating, re-creating, the finest Rome he could build in his lifetime. And now he was worried that his best years were gone. Justinian knew he might have died, and had not. He knew he needed to make use of the life he had, work harder than before, even while he was so tired, so hungry to lie still, lie down beside his wife, his lover. She twisted beneath him and her hands were on his back, his shoulders, his thighs, pulling him into her, his trembling hands, his thin, muscle-wasted body an irrelevance. They were fucking as they always had. Fucking with the abandon and passion that had stunned Theodora the first time and now delighted Justinian and only slightly embarrassed the young slaves that stood outside, keeping the bedroom door. The slaves who had seen more than most, heard more than they had seen, and yet were still astonished that a couple like this, this August couple, at their age, could rut so passionately, so ferociously, so deliriously. And so loudly.

When they pulled apart, both sweating, both laughing, Theodora shook her head. 'Narses will kill me.'

'Prob . . . probably not.'

She smiled. 'He made me promise to go easy on you.'

'Hah!' Justinian laughed, 'The eunuch tells you . . . of all women, to spare me. It's jealousy.'

'No, it's care.'

'I know, but it's . . . funny . . . too.'

They laughed and kissed and Theodora called in the Emperor's chamber slaves, sending them for hot water and oils, fresh clothes. She washed Justinian herself, oiling his skin and refused to exert him again, even when he asked nicely. She did not want to cross Narses twice in one day.

When the slaves had dressed Justinian and he was ready to go to his office, he leaned down to the bed, clumsy in his reach, kissed Theodora again and thanked her.

'What for?'

'Reminding me I . . . I'm . . . a man.'

'Not just the Emperor?'

'The Emp . . . Emperor always knows he is a man – I do. No, for . . . reminding me I'm not just an . . . invalid. That I am still . . . here.'

She held his trembling hand, kissing each finger and said, 'You're easily reminded.'

'With you, yes.'

'I could help.'

'H . . . help?'

Theodora hesitated. Her husband had been fully in her care for weeks, had relied upon her for water and what little food he could keep down, to wash him and to clean him when sometimes, a dozen times daily, he soiled himself, dirtied the sheets, the bed, the clothes she had carefully dressed him in, dressed him so that more often than not the servants and chamber slaves saw only the August, when the man in the bed was anything but.

'Go . . . go on?' he asked.

'I could help you,' she spoke slowly, quietly.

'You could help me st . . . st . . . ,' he sighed and tried again, 'stop th . . . this?' he finally stuttered out, holding up the hand, shaking now more than trembling, moving his arm, his shoulder, his upper body with its ferocity. 'And . . . my . . . words?'

'With time, with the right exercises, I think I can. And if not stop, then control. Or hide, mask. If you can't be better, fully, I can help you ...' she stopped: even between them the words sounded too harsh.

'Seem ... better?'

'I could help you control your hand.'

'And my sp ... speech.'

'Yes, if you work at it.'

Justinian walked slowly back to his bed where Theodora lay, surprised that she seemed not to realise how painful it was for him to talk about this. And then, when he was closer, he saw she knew exactly how painful it was for him and still she had dared to speak, dared to hurt him to help.

He stood above the woman who was digging her finger-nails into her palms in an effort not to cry, not to show the pity she felt for her husband, the pity she knew he'd hate, and he nodded.

'It won't be easy,' she said.

'I ... expect not.'

'I'll try and find interesting texts for you to practise on.'

'Pr ... practise ripping up, with this?'

He held up the offending right hand, trembling more than ever. They both knew he understood, both appreciated his attempt at making a joke.

'I can ask Narses to set aside some time in your schedule,' Theodora asked hesitantly.

And Justinian replied, very slowly, very carefully, 'I will ... tell .. Narses.'

Theodora brought her hands together in supplication, in prayer and gratitude. 'Yes, Master.'

The Emperor covered his wife then, lifting pure cotton and softest silk over her back and shoulders, and she happily allowed him to do it. He gave the slaves instructions to let her sleep, the morning had barely begun, their mistress would rest for a few hours.

Justinian was at the door when she called to him. 'August?' she said, old tears just escaping in her voice, but a new thought there too, a new idea.

'Yes?'

It was morning and he was already tired.

'We still have to do something about Belisarius.'

'Yes.'

Theodora sat up. 'You're not going to say how wonderful and loyal he is?'

Justinian turned back to her. 'He is whole and ... younger than I. The people ... applaud health.' The deep breath he took before speaking again told its own story. 'I need no ... challengers now.'

The man holding Bouzes' head under water was impassive. He waited as the servant by his side counted, slow counts, carefully measured, up to fifty. He dragged Bouzes up from the bucket of water, allowed him not quite enough time to grab for air, suck breath through a mouth clogged with vomit and spittle, with blood too, from the slow but constant beating across the face he had endured before this water torture began. This time the count was to sixty. The bucket was filling with as much bile as water. Bouzes was pulled up, a new bucket filled.

The man asked his question again. Bouzes shook his head, unwilling or unable to answer and he was forced down on to a stool. The man asking questions spoke to him softly now, quietly, offered a towel to wipe his face. He asked after Bouzes' feet – five weeks in a cell that was ankle-deep in sea water had done its damage. Bouzes stuttered out an answer, it was not enough, did not satisfy and the questioner nodded to his accomplice. The pulpy rotten feet were lifted, one at a time, the flesh on the toes especially swollen and split, blood and pus spilling from the putrid flesh, with here and there a glimpse of startlingly white bone. The freshly filled bucket was brought closer and it was only when it came near him that Bouzes, partially blinded from all this time in the darkness of his cell, felt the heat of the boiling water. One foot was held into the water, then the other, the man asked his questions over the broken screams, the servant pushed the feet down, sitting on Bouzes' knees, sitting on his lap as if they were a pair, a couple. No one smiled at the incongruity of the image.

Bouzes passed out, and was laid down on the floor, on a clean blanket. The servant washed him as ordered, wiping away the piss and shit of fear, wiping away the blood, new and dried. He carefully wrapped Bouzes in a clean robe, warm and soft, and then the questioner brought him round with a strong herbal tincture, offering a salve for the feet, a rinse for his ripped lips, fresh water, water to drink not drown in. He spoke kindly and quietly and now Bouzes answered his questions. Every one, just as the questioner wanted him to, giving the story that was required. A scribe was brought, who wrote down the answers, then Bouzes signed the paper with a hand he willed still, showing a strength no one in the room had expected of him.

Theodora watched from her bench seat against the far wall, watched from the shadows. She rose, took the paper from Peter Barsymes' hand, and left. Bouzes was taken away to a warm and dry cell, and still his flesh continued to rot.

A day later, based on the full extent of Bouzes' information, Justinian signed the edict confiscating to the Empire a large part of Belisarius' private wealth. Theodora had been suggesting this for years; now it would be a useful income for the

337

plague-stricken Palace. Belisarius was removed from his post as adviser on military matters in the east, and his own retinue of soldiers, those committed specifically to him and not purely to Rome, were disbanded, doled out to other Roman armies where plague had lessened their number.

Antonina was in Theodora's rooms within hours of receiving the news.

'Why are you doing this?'

'I am protecting my husband, who protects Rome.'

'Belisarius is no threat to Justinian.'

Theodora stared at her friend. 'Don't be stupid Antonina, of course he is.'

'He could have taken the purple in Ravenna, Witigis offered it to him.'

'Yes, and he rightly refused. Now he can show us again what a good Roman he is by sharing his vast wealth with the City. You've managed to garner a good deal from your war travels, haven't you? He can help further by sharing his soldiers with those armies that desperately need them.'

'It will look like an attack on a good man.'

'I don't think so. I think, if you make a fuss, it will look as if the two of you who have so much – health, wealth, a full family where others are bereft – are out of touch with the people. I'm sure you'll find a way to make this work to your advantage, especially as your general will be sent to Italy now, not Persia which you so despise. We've taken his wealth, not yours, his men, not yours. Belisarius needs you far more now, Antonina. You should thank me.'

Theodora stood then, and there was no more to be said. Antonina bowed to kiss her mistress's foot, and left the room, inwardly screaming in frustration.

⚓

Armeneus watched her go. 'Oh dear.'

'She'll get over it. She has Belisarius where she wants him, he needs her now.'

'You really think they are that ambitious?'

Theodora nodded. 'I do.'

'So why have you stayed friends with her for this long?'

'She makes me laugh. And it's safer, keeping him at a distance, keeping her close. Antonina is never going to give up her young men, and because she likes having me as a confidante it's easier to discover her secrets, their secrets. Secrets are always useful.'

'She won't forgive you in a hurry.'

'I think she will, it's almost time to consider their daughter's betrothal. Joannina and Anastasius would make a good pairing, don't you think?'

Armeneus grinned. 'You have it all worked out, don't you?'

But Theodora wasn't smiling. 'I wish I did. I'm just making it up as we go along, hoping for the best. I was always a better improviser than an actress.'

Thirty-Six

Autumn became cooler, sharper, the Mese filled up with people and stalls, soldiers and even more beggars than before. Those who gave alms, those sharing some of their bread dole, did so more generously than they had seven or eight months earlier, all too aware that the blind beggar, his pockmarked arm outstretched, might have been any one of them. Eventually there was another summer, one with warm days and cool breezes at night and no stink of death. Justinian's speech improved, his trembling hand came more under his own control, his wife stopped insisting on twice-daily sessions of body and voice work, and the August and Augusta spent more time in their own offices, dealing with their own matters. Dealing with the same matter, differently – the Church.

The anti-Chalcedonians in the East were calling louder than ever for self-determination and Justinian went to work with advisers and priests from both sides, hoping to finally create a workable union of the faithful. It was clear the differences were not merely about the preference for chanting over song, language over litany; they were about government.

'Western Romans might be content under Western Goth kings,' Justinian said, 'though we would prefer them serving us,' he added to the nods and smiles of the civil servants and theologians at his table, 'but in the east it is all Rome can do to keep one people talking to another. They call for their own languages of state, their own rulers, and their own practice of the faith. If we can only bring the various branches of faith together, all Rome might yet be one, eternally.'

The men set to work.

Theodora meanwhile met with Jacob Baradaeus. The priest was keen to head back to his parishioners in Syria, in the Levant, and as far south as Egypt.

'If you preach to them, what will you say of us?' she asked.

'I'll tell them Rome understands their desires, but that Rome is cumbersome, it will take time. And that the state must stop its persecution of those who believe as we do if it would rather a union than another fight.'

'Syria is tired too, Jacob, and Egypt, the Levant. It's not only Constantinople that's grown old with disease.'

'No, Mistress,' he agreed, 'but it's only Rome that wishes to oversee every other part of the world. The rest would just get on with their lives. Rome wants us to get on within Rome.'

Some concessions were given, Theodora made them on behalf of her husband, and she was present when Baradaeus was quietly ordained Bishop of Edessa.

'Will he bring them to our beliefs?' Justinian asked his wife.

'Perhaps not,' answered Theodora, turning from the window where she'd been looking out to sea, watching Baradaeus' ship move slowly into the strong winds of the Bosphorus, 'but he may stop them agitating against us even more. Will your edict bring them together?'

Justinian looked at the mound of papers before him on his desk, at the notes and suggestions offered, forced on him some-times, by the priests and scholars he consulted. He lifted his hands uncertainly. 'I think they'd unite against even more distinct teachings. If I can get the Pope Vigilius and our patriarch Menas to agree, if I can write the damn thing well enough.'

It was winter, and very cold. Theodora pointed to the fireplace and the servant added more wood; she brought a warmed wool cloak to place around her husband's shoulders.

'Then while you exhaust yourself on this, I'll get on with the one union we can enforce.'

'You'd have me related to that woman yet?'

'And me related to that man?' Theodora laughed. 'Anastasius is a good boy, he's twelve, old enough to betroth. And Antonina and Belisarius' daughter – don't look like that,' she interrupted herself, seeing Justinian's raised eyebrow, 'you only have to look at Joannina to see she is Belisarius' girl, no matter where else his mother has been ... anyway, they like each other.'

'Too much, Narses thinks.'

'He's said so to me too. Is there anything that escapes the old eunuch?'

Justinian shook his head.

'Apparently they think they're in love,' Theodora went on, 'so we betroth them to each other now, and plan for marriage in a few years' time.

'You could marry them sooner.'

'We could, but Belisarius is returning to Italy soon, he'll want to witness his daughter's marriage. Knowing him, he probably plans to bring her the spoils of Naples for her dowry.'

'If he returns the whole of Italy to Rome, he can give her whatever he wants. Besides, she'll have to share her dowry with her husband,' he smiled.

The betrothal went ahead, both families standing by their children, whose hands were clasped and united in a lightly tied cloth of purple silk as they were blessed by several priests and toasted with good wine. A feast was to follow.

Although Belisarius was no longer the golden boy in the Palace, his men still loved him, and Justinian needed him to do well on this next campaign to Italy, even if, as Antonina hissed crossly to Theodora while they watched the blessing, 'He has to pay for all his own soldiers, and Chief of the Imperial Grooms is hardly a fitting title for someone entrusted with such an important task.'

Theodora smiled sweetly and ignored her friend's complaint, whispering, 'You know Antonina, if you really want me to support your husband, maybe you should start supporting him yourself. You are still screwing Theodosius, aren't you?'

Her friend had no reply, and mother and grandmother stood side by side, watching their offspring promise to become one.

As they walked the slow ceremonial route back to the Palace for the post-betrothal banquet, Theodora called Sophia to her: 'And shall we start planning your betrothal, little one?'

Sophia frowned. 'It depends.'

'On what?'

'Who you suggest for me. I'll take whoever you wish, obviously,' she added politely and seriously, her fair curls bobbing as she nodded in deference.

'Obviously,' repeated Theodora.

'But it would be nice if I approved of him too. I don't just want anyone Narses thinks is appropriate.'

'Narses is skilled in diplomacy, he would be a useful adviser on this matter.'

'The eunuch is not as kind to me as he is to you,' said Sophia.

Theodora smiled, knowing Narses had often berated the child for not bowing in the right place, smiling at the correct people. 'He wasn't always kind to me, Sophia, and he is a stickler for protocol.'

'In that case he should be more polite to the niece of the Empress.'

'Yes, he should,' Theodora said, knowing he never would. She waved to the people who were crowded around the edge of the Augustaion, and then with a gentle nudge encouraged Sophia to walk on towards the Chalke.

'I know you'll find me a husband at some point, and I'll be grateful for it, I'm sure you'll do your best for me ...' Theodora gasped out a laugh at the girl's audacity and Sophia finished her train of thought, 'but I can't say I'd like it until I know who you have in mind.'

Sophia fell back a little to allow Theodora to enter the huge doors before her, then caught up with her aunt. At only eleven she already reached Theodora's shoulder so it took little effort for her to look the Empress in the eye, and Sophia had no problem doing so. She had her mother's clear-minded ambition and a great deal of the passion Theodora had been forced to tone down as a child. It was the passion Theodora had adored in her friend Sophia, and even when the child's version bordered on rudeness – as it often did, no matter how Comito tried to rein her in – the Empress liked young Sophia's attitude. It was everything that had stood Theodora in good stead herself, but in a far more useful form – that of a Palace princess with a huge future ahead of her, rather than a child actress–whore, scavenging hope.

They passed into the main corridor leading to the central halls. 'Perhaps I should ask if you have anyone in mind?' said Theodora.

'The general Germanus has a son.'

'He does, yes, Justin.' Theodora's face gave nothing away but the girl could tell from her aunt's tone that her answer was not welcome.

'You don't like him?'

'I barely know the boy.'

'You didn't like his mother.'

'Who told you that?'

Sophia spoke more slowly now, picking her words carefully, 'Antonina told Joannina.'

'What, exactly?'

Theodora was seated now, servants hurrying to bring jugs of wine, wide silver platters loaded with bite-sized morsels of grilled meat and cheese, fruits stuffed with nuts and covered in honey, flatbreads to mop up the juices. Foods chosen for those who'd spent all morning in church and must be both tired and hungry.

Sophia arranged herself on the raised dais, carefully sitting by her aunt's feet, the better to be head-height with those who prostrated themselves before the Empress. She looked around the room, to where Antonina was proudly walking her newly betrothed daughter from one high-ranking woman to another, while Anastasius was seated much more quietly on a silk couch beside Ana.

'Joannina's mother,' began Sophia, speaking quietly, 'said Justin's mother . . .'

'Pasara?' Theodora asked.

'Yes. Joannina's mother said she had been very rude to you and we were all damn lucky that things had gone in my uncle Justinian's favour back then. She said Pasara deserved . . .'

Theodora held up a finger to silence the girl. 'That's plenty, thank you. Joannina's mother should know better than to share old gossip about a dead woman.'

'But she was mean to you.'

Sophia looked up and Theodora was startled again by the girl's eyes, their striking resemblance to her own, but set in Comito's open face, with Comito's fine fair hair. Sophia was turning into a beauty.

'It's true Pasara and I were not friends, and now she is dead,' said Theodora, 'so we pray for her as we do for all the dead.'

'Yes, but what about . . .'

Theodora watched her niece stop herself with some difficulty. 'Go on.'

'Should we pray for the old Emperor's wife too?'

'Euphemia?'

'Because Joannina's mother said she hated you and the work you'd done in the theatre.'

'Joannina's mother does like to gossip,' said Theodora, watching Antonina now, on Belisarius' arm, leading him from senator to statesman, working her husband around the room as she had been working her daughter only moments before. 'Yes, Sophia, we pray for them all.'

'Why?'

Theodora took a long sip of the cool, sweet wine the servant brought her and waved away the tray of food. 'Because they're dead. Because even if they're sorry for the things they did wrong in life or for wicked words spoken, it's too late for them to make amends. So we pray for them now because none of us know how long we have to live, how much time we'll have to make things right in our own lives. We pray for them in the hope that others will one day pray for us.'

'And do you forgive Euphemia?'

'Dear God no, she was an evil bitch,' Theodora laughed, 'but I pray.'

And Theodora did pray. She prayed with the rest of the City as Belisarius took his troops back to Italy, his lower rank irrelevant to the thousands who turned out on the streets and at the docks to wave him off. She prayed in uncertain remorse when Bouzes was finally well enough to be released from his captivity in the Palace; silent and hobbling, he left the City the next day and never spoke of Constantinople again. She prayed with Justinian that his latest attempt to heal the religious divide, his Three Chapters edict, would make a difference. Then, when it helped a little but not enough, she prayed with her husband that Pope Vigilius would support their attempts for union from Constantinople, rather than schism under Totila's Goths in Rome. She, and Justinian and the whole of the government prayed that the vastly expensive peace they were negotiating with the Persians would hold this time. The Persian ambassador and his retinue in return prayed with gratitude to their god of fire; the terms were very much in their favour and their treatment in the Roman court could not have been better. Theodora prayed too, for the priests and spies working for Peter Barsymes in China, from whom there had been no word in over a year. She prayed for Macedonia, now working alongside Barsymes, posing as the trader's wife; a respectable City housewife, listening to stories other house-wives told of their husbands' business; market-stall secrets relayed to Theodora to keep the Palace better informed of the world they ruled. She prayed, as she always did, for her men-tors Timothy and Severus, prayed in gratitude and an old grief that never quite left her.

Above all, and silently, sharing her entreaties with no one but the emerald Virgin and the owl that stayed awake with her through the night, Theodora prayed for health. She was forty-five years old, it was half her life ago, more, since she had collapsed in a desert mountain, haemorrhaging in fierce pain and woke weeks later in the care of Severus' people, told by his physician that she would probably never have another child, that the growth they had removed from her belly had been too big, too strong. Theodora had seen her grandmother die from the pain of the growth that took over her flesh, her insides. She watched as the old woman sank into her bones, the thing inside becoming bigger than her. For twenty-five years Theodora had waited, knowing that once the illness had been in her life, it was always likely to return.

It was a spring morning. Across Constantinople everyone was preparing for the City's feast, a day of prayer and processions and receptions to come. Theodora's rooms were full of the careful haste of her women; ceremonial gowns were removed from storage boxes, old threads pulled into place, small rips and tears hidden with new jewels or gold embroidery by Esther and Leah, Sophia assisting them. The craftswomen were training Sophia in their skills at Theodora's request. Mariam and Ana laid out Theodora's jewellery – the five-strand pearl necklaces, the emerald earrings, the jewelled brooches that held her robes in place.

In the privacy of her anteroom, Comito was arranging her sister's hair: 'You have no grey at all – how is that? Are you dyeing your hair without telling me?'

Theodora shook her head beneath the fine comb and smiled. 'It's one of the Imperial secrets, my sister, you'll never know.'

Comito laughed and with a careful twist, caught Theodora's hair up into an ivory pin, adding height and elegance to her little sister's little frame. She then shook out her own blond hair, threaded now with silver strands and, taking another ivory needle, pinned hers up in the same way.

The sisters stood in front of the mirror, smiling at each other. They were easier together now that Sophia was older, and it was this closeness, magnified in the mirror, that made Comito feel it was possible to reach out and put her hands around her sister's waist.

'You can't escape age entirely,' said Comito. 'I can't tell when you're fully dressed, but here, in this thin slip, even you seem to be gaining the belly of an older woman.'

Theodora laughed it off, told her sister not to be so rude to the Augusta, acknowledged she probably had been eating far too many of the sweet treats prepared for the Persian ambassador's delegation during the peace talks.

That night though, when Theodora had finally gone to bed after the long day celebrating Constantine and the City, she felt her lower belly, ran a hand over the small swelling, and she knew it had nothing to do with the honeyed cakes.

Now, six months later, with the Persians gone and Belisarius asking for reinforcements in Italy, with Comito in love again and preparing to marry for the second time, Theodora hid her swollen belly with swaddling and loose robes and bedroom excuses to Justinian about her exhaustion or his. There was too much to do: Anastasius was betrothed but not yet married, Sophia was still unpromised, both children must be woven into her plans for the succession, Comito wanted her sister by her side when she became a wife again and Theodora knew her main task was to support Justinian in his lifelong struggle to reunite the Church and the state. She was not prepared to succumb to her body, knowing only too well what her swelling belly might mean. She chose to believe it was purely age, only age, and to pray for time.

Thirty-Seven

Luckily there were plenty of distractions. Things were not going well for Belisarius in Italy, and much of Justinian's time was spent analysing messages that came to and from the military camp in old Rome.

Theodora's version of what was happening came from Antonina's letters.

They say Pope Vigilius is preparing to flee Rome now that he's give it over to the Goths. We've been asking for months for more help from the Palace, and still none comes, we expected Vitalian's damned son John to arrive weeks ago and yet even when he finally arrived, he seemed intent on taking as many of the smaller towns for himself and his own glory as he could. You can accuse my husband of many things, Mistress, but his personal success, at the expense of Rome, is not one of them.

Still, there's some hope. Belisarius tried a new tack the other day. He appealed to Totila's sense of elegance and refinery, which, given how Totila has been turfing our people off their land and giving it to their slaves, certainly needs some appealing to. You know how the Goths love to think themselves more civilised than Romans? I helped Belisarius write him a beautiful letter begging he preserve this city's 'immortal glory' (my phrase) and to take care that all this battling over one stretch of land does not turn it to 'sheep pasture' (mine again). We don't know if it will work, but we're hopeful.

The Christ knows why anyone chose to build a city here, surrounded by these vile marshes, give me our own seven hills and sea views any day. It looks now as if Totila will be in Rome to celebrate the Christ's birth and we'll be doing so in our damn tents. I trust when I next see you we will be done with Italy for good.

Antonina's private letters to Theodora were often useful to Justinian, and this one, once censored of the material about the young soldier Antonina was keen to entertain, was no less so. Orders were sent to an Imperial troop to capture Vigilius and bring him to Constantinople. The Pope was clearly too comfortable under Goth rule, and Roman law might be far better applied in Constantinople than in Rome.

While the siege of Rome dragged on, Theodora dealt privately with her own personal unrest. The stabbing pains had spread to her lower back, waking her more often, and she called her old theatre wardrobe mistress to attend her in the Palace. The woman had been adept at procuring abortions for the young girls in her care, and Theodora took the herbs the old woman offered on the basis of the half-stories she gave, scared to fully share either her fears or the extent of her pain with anyone else. Antonina was in Italy, Comito was newly married and newly in lust, Macedonia was a better spy than confidante – Theodora had no one to talk to about her fears. Until Sophia asked her.

'Are you in a lot of pain, Mistress?'

They were walking from the Palace, through the underground corridors to the great church.

Theodora checked her posture, took a breath before she spoke. 'Why do you ask?'

'You cried out last night, in your sleep.'

Theodora shook her head, annoyed with herself for allowing the child to get so close that she now slept in Mariam's old room, the door between the two often ajar.

'Perhaps you should stay closer to your mother, if I'm disturbing you?'

Sophia shook her head, well aware there was no substance to the threat. 'You like having me around, more than she does now, anyway.'

'You should be patient with your mother, she's in love.'

'She's almost fifty.'

'And fifty can't love?'

Sophia sneered, 'It doesn't need to be so public about it.'

Theodora smiled, it was true that since Comito's marriage she seemed to have lost some of her famous reserve.

'We were trained to show nothing but whatever was required of the dance or the piece we were working on. Menander was a formidable teacher; all these years later, it is hard to ignore his lessons. It's good your mother feels more free.'

'Menander was Narses' lover?'

'Yes.'

'They must have made a fierce pair.'

'I didn't know them as a pair, I only met Narses after Menander had died. But you can't tell, not really, not from the outside.'

352

'You can with my mother.'

'Only at the moment. Most couples don't show who they are to the world, they present a united front, work to make it look as if they are one.'

'Except when it's useful for you to support different sides?'

'As with the Church?' Theodora said. 'Yes. I didn't mean just the Emperor and myself, but of course it's been useful. Showing a united front also means we have some privacy, we are one – a unit – as August, but we are ourselves too. Only a partner can know your private self as well as the world thinks it knows your public self. It's important to keep something back, Sophia. The world would consume it all and still want more.'

'Which is why you cry only in your sleep?'

'Which is why I prefer to cry only when I can control it. Unfortunately I have no power over my sleep or my dreams.'

They were at the Hagia Sophia. The great carved wooden doors were held open for them, they swept into the church and up to the gallery in a procession of women, Theodora taking her usual place on the green marble, Sophia beside her. The whole sumptuous interior of the great church was swimming in pale afternoon light, with the dome apparently suspended above. No matter how often Theodora stood here, it never failed to move her, one of her own dreams that had become real, one of the good ones.

'I'll pray for your happiness, Mistress,' said Sophia.

Theodora looked at the girl beside her, very nearly a woman now, her whole life ahead; a huge life if Theodora managed to arrange her betrothal and marriage well enough. The girl was smart and thoughtful. Theodora couldn't remember the last person apart from Justinian or Armeneus who had asked about her well-being – most came to her begging for themselves.

'Thank you,' she said, 'and I will pray for yours.'

Theodora's fears for her health made her even more determined to take care of the succession. Germanus had mourned Pasara and then married the Goth princess Matasuntha. With a son now born from that marriage, Theodora was no longer content to allow Justinian his relaxed attitude to the succession.

'Germanus is going to keep breeding successors of Justin's line, there's nothing we can do about that,' she said.

'We've tried,' Justinian said, and reached an arm around his wife's waist.

'Not now,' she smiled, pushing his hand away, smiling to hide her fear of his feeling the swollen belly she hid beneath heavy gowns, 'we need to make a bigger leap.'

'What do you suggest?'

'We forge our own links back to the old Emperor Anastasius. Your sister's girl, Praejecta, there's talk of her marrying Artebanes.'

'Really? He's given up his wife?' Justinian asked the question lightly, well aware that Theodora loathed the practice of men summarily divorcing their wives.

'Artebanes' wife doesn't want to be given up. She's asked for my help. Even the new divorce ruling can't protect her.'

'Of course, she knows you'll do your best to help her, as do all our women.'

Theodora glared at her husband. 'It's not just the divorce question, it's also who Artebanes is.'

'Because you believe he killed Sittas?'

'Because everyone believes he killed Sittas.'

'Yes, and our law requires more than suspicion.'

Theodora held up her hand and her husband stopped. 'Law may try to run on truth, but politics thrives on rumour and supposition. And the rumours about Artebanes killing Sittas, even with no evidence, were rife.'

Justinian nodded. 'True.'

'More than that,' she went on, 'Narses agrees with me that Artebanes is too ambitious.'

'So you've been working this up, between you?'

'It's my job to work with Narses. Artebanes will be too close to the purple if he marries your sister's daughter.'

'And he cannot marry Praejecta if he is still married to his wife?'

'Correct. So we send him back to his wife's family and keep him at a safe distance from Praejecta.'

'I assume we don't plan to leave her alone for long?'

Theodora smiled. 'You know how young girls can be without a man.'

'I believe I do,' Justinian replied, smiling as he pictured the Theodora he had first met, fierce and opinionated and trying her hardest to control her passions.

'Pompeius had a son. John. He's good-looking, only a little older than Praejecta. I'm sure his mother will agree.'

'You think so? The last time her family had any dealings with the Palace was when we put her husband to death.'

Theodora shrugged, 'Nika was a hard time for us all.'

'And this way we can link my sister's family with the family of the old Emperor Anastasius, as well as the ties we already have through Ana and Paulus?'

'Yes.'

'Impressive.'

'I do my best.'

The Empress bowed then and turned away, a middle-aged woman with an uncertain future and a great deal of hidden pain, practically skipping off to make her arrangements. He watched her go, awed and grateful, as ever. And then he turned back to his papers, as ever.

Theodora lay on her bed. She had just sent away the servant who ran in, disturbed by her cries, telling her it was only a dream. It was no dream. The servant had left a light as instructed and Theodora reached her hand down the bed to feel the warm, sticky blood that was leaching from her. She was faint with both blood loss and the pain. It was worse than childbirth, worse than that she had experienced in the desert: this time it was pain so acute that there was no hope of falling unconscious and away from it, this was pain that held her, pinned to the bed, soaking in her own blood. A pain that ripped up and through her, with seemingly no central point. A pain that filled her belly, her gut, her torso, her back; her limbs and head becoming useless extremities as it surged through her core.

She lay there concentrating on her body, trying to clear her mind, trying to see her room through the tears that would not stop, muddying her vision. She began counting heartbeats as Menander had taught her, counting to one hundred and then again, slowing her racing heart with force of will. Seven times she did this until her heartbeat finally slowed; so too did some of the blood loss, and the pain receded to a point where she thought it might be possible to move away, lift herself up from the bed at least.

The first time she tried to sit up she fell back immediately. She counted another hundred heartbeats and tried again, rolling on to her side and sliding herself up, carefully, carefully. Tears and sweat poured down her face at the effort it took to bring herself upright. She pulled her night-cloak to herself, using it to soak up the blood that was still

356

coming away from her, no point in using the soaked bed sheets.

She had no idea how long she sat there, on the side of her own bed, whispering to herself, a mumble of prayers and incantations and orders, the kind of orders Menander would have barked at his girls when they were being lazy or crying at the pain his routines put them through.

Eventually the blood stopped. Theodora was able to stand. Dawn was breaking outside and she pulled the shutters back to let light into the room. When she turned back to see the bloody mess of the bed she bit her hand to stop herself crying out. It was impossible she could lose so much blood and still live, and here she was, living; the slow, soft pain in her belly and back assured her of that.

Quietly, carefully, Theodora went about clearing up the mess. She bundled the sheets together, ripped off her nightgown and threw it into the pile. She poured water over her body and washed away the blood on her stomach and thighs, now starting to stick, to cake. She wiped herself dry with a cloth that came away pink with sluiced blood and washed herself again. When she was clean, she pulled on an old, loved gown, one she could no longer wear in public because it was so out of fashion, but which gave her pleasure still, because it was so comfortable, had worn so soft.

She combed her hair, pulled it back, and opened her door, telling the servant to call Sophia to her.

By the time the girl arrived, the morning was well on its way. Theodora kissed her as she rose from her bow and pointed to the large bundle on her bed, bloody sheets and cloths now tied into an old woollen cloak.

'Do you know your way to the furnace rooms, Sophia?'
'I can ask,' she answered.

'No, I want you to go alone. I'll tell you where, and you are to take this pile, give it to the slave who tends the fires. Only to him. Tell him to throw it into the fire. If anyone asks what you are carrying, tell them your Mistress is throwing out her old gowns to have a new spring wardrobe, that she doesn't want anyone aping her style. They're as likely to believe that as not.'

Theodora gave Sophia directions to the underground furnaces and then had her door servant call a housemaid to bring new sheets. Theodora made up the bed herself, and if the slave wondered about the comings and goings, the absurdity of the Empress making her own bed, she did not comment. She had seen far stranger things in her time.

The Empress finally took herself back to her bed. When Armeneus called on her she told him she had a light cold and wanted to sleep it off. When Sophia came back to see if her aunt was all right, she told the servant to send her away, she was fine, there was nothing to say. Theodora fell asleep worrying about how much she still needed to take care of, wondering when the next episode would come, wondering if she would survive another.

That night Justinian came late to Theodora's rooms. He sent away her servants and climbed carefully into her bed.

She turned, half sleeping, 'Master?'

He whispered, 'Go back to sleep.'

Theodora groaned. Her fear that Justinian would know what was happening to her cut through the exhaustion and pain of the night before, and she sat up.

'You wouldn't be here if you didn't want to speak to me, what is it?'

'Nothing. Sleep.'

'What is it?'

Justinian pulled her close and kissed her on the forehead, 'Menas and Vigilius have agreed a reconciliation.'

She was fully awake now. 'Really?'

'The beginning of one. It's not as neat as I wanted, and we've had to push them, hard, but both sides look as if they will come together, for now.'

Theodora got out of bed to bring the light closer, every step hurt her and she forced herself to walk slowly, carefully. She looked at her husband, twenty years Emperor and twenty years before that working in the Palace. His hair was mostly grey now, and receding. His eyes were, as always, heavy from lack of sleep, his lower lip calloused where he bit it when worried, and he had been greatly worried in the past few months.

'An answer to our prayers.'

Justinian nodded. 'Yes, but it's also forced. And in the long run, I doubt it will stop the Egyptians or the Syrians or those in any of the Levant wanting their own faith, their own languages for prayer. It certainly won't stop the rebels calling for their own nations and leaders.'

Theodora shivered and climbed back into bed beside him, pulling the covers closer. It was spring and the nights were less cool, but she found she was cold now, much of the time, no matter how warm the sun or the fire.

'I support you,' she said.

'Yes, and that sometimes means you don't say everything you believe.'

She laughed. 'I wish you'd tell those who write so nastily about how I have you wrapped around my little finger.'

'Oh, you have that, of course, but I don't always have your real opinion.'

'You don't want it.'

'I do. Tell me.'

Theodora shrugged. 'I wish you would let it all go.'

'Rome?' Justinian's voice was low, quiet, he was shocked already, she could tell.

She went on, speaking into the darkened room, glad the light was low.

'I've lived in the Pentapolis, in the desert in Egypt and in Antioch, I prayed with the people there, believed with them. Those countries have never been truly Roman, no matter what the centre says, what the centre wants.' She took a deep breath and continued, 'I don't believe Rome can hold those lands for much longer. The East is fractured and divided and, more importantly, it wants to be that way. They want their separate nations in a way the West doesn't. Or doesn't yet. I don't believe we can hold them just by force of wanting.'

'That's what you want to tell me?' he was asking Theodora who by now had her face hidden in his chest.

She spoke into his breastbone, feeling the rhythm of Justinian's heavy heart against her mouth: 'No, it's not what I want to tell you, I want to say anything I can to support you, to help you continue in this work that drains you, exhausting and demanding still more of you, because you so firmly believe in the one Rome and the one Church. What I want to say ...' she looked up and was shocked to see they were both crying, 'what I want to say is stop. Give it all up. Come away with me to Bithynia and we can be quiet there and rest, let Germanus or Belisarius have it, let them try to make it work. I want to make you sleep for a week and wake refreshed and delighted to do so.'

'And yet you continue planning our succession, making betrothals and liaisons between our families?'

'Yes, because even while I wish peace and ease for you, and for myself ...'

'You know there are things we must try to achieve, however impossible,' he added the last phrase with a sigh.

'And I don't know how long we are here,' she said very quietly, 'how long I have.'

They were silent then. Justinian lay with one arm around her, holding her close, he took her hand, twisted the ring she wore, his ring. It was loose on her finger. He knew she had stayed in her bed all day, but had simply believed the servant who told him she wanted rest. He had seen that her belly was a little rounder and assumed when she pushed his hand away she was merely shy that age had finally caught up with her, that time had given her any woman's body instead of that of the Hippodrome star she once was. Now, looking at the lines pain had carved into her face, feeling her body beside his, he realised what was happening.

'I didn't see ...'

'You weren't supposed to. No one was. No one is.'

'This may not be what you think.'

'I saw it with my mother's mother, have seen it take too many others.'

'You might get better?' Justinian's tone betrayed a question.

'I don't think so.' Theodora was shaking her head. Looking up, she said, 'You could marry again, find a young wife, have children with her.'

'I won't,' Justinian's tone was certain. 'I won't. Have you spoken to Alexander?'

'No.'

'Why not?'

'He knows too much, knows too much of me.'

'Other physicians, then.'

'So they can speak of it to others, and then the whole world will know? Then I become the focus, not our work, your work.'

'You are my focus.'

'I shouldn't be, there's too much still to do. I'm not sure I can trust Antonina to fulfil Joannina's betrothal to Anastasius, and those two are very much in love. I need to make sure their union is solid.'

'And Sophia,' Justinian spoke quickly. 'Sophia needs you.'

'She does. I still have to arrange her marriage. Let's wait to see what news Belisarius sends from Rome, shall we?'

Justinian nodded, holding his wife lightly, holding her with all of himself. 'Let's wait.'

Thirty-Eight

The news from Italy came quickly. Totila and his forces had left Rome and left it undamaged, Belisarius entered the city with no fighting and he sent the keys of the old city back to the Palace in a gold-inlaid ebony box.

While Theodora was particularly pleased for Justinian, that his ambition of a united Rome appeared to have been realised, she was also aware that a triumphant Belisarius would soon return. Antonina had already arrived on the advance ship, singing her husband's praises wherever she went and, Theodora had been told, suggesting that perhaps she had been too hasty in agreeing to her daughter's betrothal to Anastasius.

Both mother and daughter were called to the Empress's rooms. Theodora sat in the wide gallery overlooking the Palace courtyards, all the windows and doors thrown open, letting in both light and heat, along with the view. Sophia sat close by the Empress as she always did now, carefully sewing an embroidered hem, her work easy and lovely.

A young man stood against one wall, charcoal and paper in hand, making fast, light sketches of Theodora's face, of her hands, the shape of her neck, her shoulders.

Theodora explained his presence: 'The church in Ravenna is nearly finished, apparently they need a recent likeness to complete the finer points of my face – these sketches are to be sent to them.'

Antonina bowed beautifully to her friend, her daughter did so with only a little less grace. 'I hope they do you justice, Mistress.'

'Unlikely,' Theodora replied, 'I'm not feeling my best, but you look very well.'

'I'm home, and delighted to be. Give me our own coastline any day.'

'So Joannina, are you pleased to have your mother home? Looking forward to your father's return?'

Joannina glared at her mother, who glared back and didn't even try to hide the sharp pinch she delivered to the back of her daughter's hand.

'Thank the Augusta for her interest and answer her question,' Antonina hissed.

Theodora smiled. 'You've grown used to living as a woman, Joannina, it's no surprise you find it a little difficult to live under your mother's rule again.'

'It's not that,' she said, sulking.

'Oh?' Theodora asked and Antonina swore under her breath.

'She doesn't want me to marry Anastasius.'

'I didn't—' Antonina tried to interrupt, but Theodora held up her hand.

Sophia's rhythmic stitching slowed a little as she listened more closely.

'Go on,' the Empress asked.

'She says,' and now Joannina smiled openly at her mother before turning her very pretty face to Theodora, 'that I can do better.'

Theodora looked at Antonina for explanation.

'Not quite, Mistress,' said her old friend. 'I said my daughter is still young, they were young when they were betrothed. It may be that there is someone better for both of them.'

Theodora turned to Joannina. 'And what do you want Joannina?'

'Anastasius and I are in love.'

Antonina shook her head and Theodora smiled. 'In love. Really?'

'And we would like to be married sooner rather than later.'

'I see,' said Theodora.

'That's not love, child, that's lust,' Antonina growled at her daughter and though she and Theodora were looking directly at one another, and though each knew the other understood more about lust than either of them would ever share with the girl, neither said so.

Theodora spoke directly to Joannina, 'I'll speak to Anastasius' mother. It's good to be in love when you're about to be married, less useful if you have to wait for any length of time. You'll need to be very careful.'

'Yes, Mistress.'

'Good. Joannina, go with Sophia. I would like to talk with your mother a little longer.'

The women waited until the girls had left the room, then accepted the drinks the servants brought for them. The heat pouring into the room through the open windows was fierce and the cold sherbet – originally made to the Persian ambassador's recipe twenty years earlier and now a staple in the Palace – was refreshing, though not to Antonina's taste.

'Wouldn't you prefer wine, Mistress?'

Theodora shook her head. 'I don't want to be any less than perfectly clear with you.'

'And wine will muddy your thoughts?'

'It will in the heat I have to endure so this artist can capture my ageing likeness. Are you nearly done?' she asked the young man.

'Almost, Mistress,' he answered in Italian-accented Latin.

Theodora shrugged, turned back to Antonina. 'I'm tired.'

'So I've heard.'

'From many?'

'From a few.'

'Let's keep it that way. We made an agreement,' Theodora went on, speaking carefully, 'our children are betrothed, and we're fortunate they believe themselves to be in love. Do you have someone else in mind for her?'

'No. I just don't feel there is any urgency for a marriage.'

'She's old enough to be a mother.'

'Yes, but she's also ten years younger than you were when you married. There's plenty of time,' Antonina stopped, peering at her friend, 'isn't there?'

Theodora shrugged, and smiled, gesturing for the door slave to open the door, Antonina's signal to leave.

Antonina bowed, kissed Theodora's foot, and left the room. Theodora stared after her, hating that she was powerless, not only over her own future, but the futures of those she loved.

Theodora continued to press Antonina to proceed with her daughter's marriage, Antonina continued to find reasons for waiting: Joanina was too young, Anastasius needed to complete his studies, take his military training. There was always an excuse and the days were passing too rapidly for Theodora.

The Empress managed to hide her illness for most of the year, but by the time the celebration of the Christ's birth gave way to that of his death and resurrection, her weight loss was obvious and her inability to stand for any length of time meant she was unable to fulfil her usual role in the Easter processions.

Narses decided it was time for the Palace to admit that the Empress was ill, but Theodora had no intention of making the news public.

'Mistress, they saw you couldn't stand for the ceremony in Hagia Sophia . . .'

'I'm no longer twenty-one, there's no disgrace in that.'

'Nor are you eighty-one, Mistress. Every other year you and the Emperor have made the full procession for the City's feast day, right up to the Chora Monastery.'

'And we will again this year.'

Narses shook his head. The woman before him seemed to have grown even thinner in the past day. This morning, before she had spent half an hour making herself up, her skin had been a sickly grey.

'And what if you don't make it? All I'm suggesting is we carry you.'

'On a byre, perhaps?'

'A sedan chair will do.'

'Putting me in a chair will make it all the more obvious, they'll have buried me before we even get to the Column of Marcian.'

'And if you try to walk and fail they'll think the same before you get through the Chalke.'

Narses sighed, he couldn't bear to see Theodora's decline, nor could he bear how hard she pushed herself to hide it.

'We can do it,' she went on, 'I'll just walk more slowly than usual. The Emperor has no concerns about the pace I can manage now.'

'The Emperor is older, the people expect him to walk a little slower.'

Theodora looked at the man in front of her, four years

367

older than Justinian. She raised an eyebrow and the tall, muscled, shaven-headed eunuch smiled.

'What can I say? We age better.'

Theodora laughed aloud even though to do so stabbed her
ribs and shook her frame. 'Half my life we've worked
together, and only now you let out your eunuch-bitch?'

Narses shook his head and he was serious again, the man
she had trusted and fought since coming to the Palace, 'The
Emperor looks his years.'

'Showing the hard work he's done for the Empire all this
time.'

Narses agreed, 'Yes Mistress, and the people understand
that.'

'Good, then tell the people I'm walking slowly for him.'

'I would rather tell the people ...'

'I will not have you tell them I am sick.'

'Mistress,' Narses knelt now, close to her, looking into her
yellowed eyes, 'I would rather they heard you were sick from
my office, where I can control what's said, than in trying –
and failing – to walk you confirm the rumour that you are
dying.'

Theodora sat silently for a long time and Narses feared that
perhaps even he had gone too far this time.

Then she looked up, ran a heavily veined hand over her
darkened face and nodded. 'Damn you, eunuch, why must
you always be right?'

He shook his head, too sorry to reply.

She took a deep breath and continued, 'I'll use the sedan
chair. Tell them I've hurt my knee, or my back, it's what they
expect of an old Hippodrome tart anyway.'

Narses bowed, ready to leave the room.

'But when we get to the Mese, on the return of the procession ...'

He turned back to hear what she was saying.

'I will walk. I'll save my energy and they can carry me about like an old relic if you insist, but that street is the spine of the City, I would like to walk down it.'

'Of course, Mistress.'

'I'll walk through the Chalke back into the Palace too. I entered those gates willingly, if frightened, meeting you for the first time . . .'

'Frightened and late.'

'Yes,' she smiled, remembering, 'and the Palace has been my magnificent prison ever since. I'd rather walk back in than be carried, it feels more like a choice.'

Narses was about to speak, to tell her that of course she had a choice, she was Empress, could command anything she wanted, and then stopped himself. He knew as well as she did that since her marriage to Justinian, since they assumed the throne together, their choices had become more and more limited, the role itself making decisions for them, until now he stood before a woman clearly dying, insisting he knew best how she should make her last journey into her own city, insisting that protocol come first.

'We'll make the Mese especially beautiful for you, Mistress.'

Theodora looked up. 'You'll knock down the statue of Juliana of the Anicii? About damn time.'

The Empress was laughing as he left the room, the eunuch general knew he was close to tears.

Thirty-Nine

The City's feast day celebrations were always a huge joy. Theodora had adored them as a girl, when she was part of the troupe entertaining the public in the Hippodrome before the real stars came on stage, the racing teams, their trainers, the fierce horses, drivers as crazy as they were brave, dealers and bookies at every entrance. The buzzing sense of pride and passion, and a certain anarchy too, rippling out from the centre of the City into the old Hagia Sophia, the Chalke, the Hippodrome, and up through the Mese, out into the Empire itself. An arterial flow of passion with a pulsing background beat of chanting monks, intoning priests, beggars' insistence, horses' hooves, and the ever-present call-and-response of the factions. It was the sound of her city and, sitting in her sedan chair, propelled by the energy all around her, Theodora drank it in.

The procession had been going for over five hours, stopping at every monastery and church and shrine on the way. The priests and deacons walked at the head, followed by Justinian, with Narses and Belisarius and other generals behind him, then Theodora in the chair, Sophia close by, and her women fanning out to the sides. They were halfway back down the Mese, just before the Column of Marcian, the sun close to setting now, the warm day picking up a little moisture from the air as well as the sea. The stallholders who'd earlier shut up shop to party had begun lighting fires in street braziers, evening meals being prepared on them already. Theodora inhaled the heady scent of flatbread, stuffed with fish, a few nuts and a little honey, a drop of oil, a dollop more of garum paste, a handful of spices, another of fresh herbs, and then toasted on a brazier, given out as feast day gifts by stallholders who usually haggled over every last crumb. She called her bearers to wait and Narses, who had been listening for Theodora's call for the whole of the march, stopped the procession with a precise signal and made his way to her sedan chair.

The bearers bent down, the half-curtained door was opened and Theodora stepped out. There was a palpable intake of breath as those standing closest saw their Empress properly for the first time in many months. Theodora had attended church services, had been seen in the women's gallery, wearing a tight shawl sometimes against the chill, or with her head veiled; neither were unusual, it had been a long and cold spring. But the woman who stood now, who quickly grasped Narses' arm, was thin to the point of emaciation, and her hands so grey there seemed to be no blood running in her. There had been rumours for a while, impossible to keep anything hidden for long in the City, and here she was, the wild child of the Hippodrome, the Emperor's mistress, whore and queen, Theodora-from-the-Brothel, standing hunched like an old lady, hanging on the eunuch for every step she took, her breathing slow and laboured. Plainly ill. Plainly dying. And then, astonishingly, extraordinarily, apparently starving.

She pushed Narses away, stood up straight, pulled her cloak

tighter to her body so it seemed to accentuate her even tinier waist while lifting her breasts. She raised her arms to shake her hair loose from the veil she'd been wearing, rubbing her cheeks at the same time and forcing some colour back into them, biting her lips to do the same.

Then, looking much more like herself, she walked, unaided to the closest stallholder, while calling to another fifteen paces away, 'Which of you makes the better dish? Your Empress is exhausted from all this ceremony and I've had my fill of watching you lot enjoy yourselves while I miss out. It's bad enough to sit in that great palace and catch the scent of food I can't eat in there, I will not sit in that damn chair and be carried past it. Nor will my people. Hey, Treasurer,' she called across to the man standing shocked alongside the Emperor, and the treasurer tentatively raised his hand, 'we'll eat here, I'll have a taste of both men's work, we all will. Make a note of how much is served and pay these stall-keepers tomorrow.'

The civil servants bowed, the keepers tending their braziers went to work, Theodora collapsed gratefully backward on to Narses and Mariam who were standing close, waiting for her, and was happy to be led back to the sedan chair. She sat, watching her husband and his men, as well as her ladies, enjoy the street food of her city.

'Some of your fine Palace-bred stomachs might give you trouble in the night,' she said. 'If so, it's no more than you deserve. This is your city, you should know its food.'

Theodora herself had less than a mouthful of each trader's offerings, assured them she was getting on in years and needed to keep her figure in better check. 'You know what they say about dancers – lean and lithe while young; broad and broken when old – it can't be helped, but I try my best.'

The traders and the many who'd gathered around the royal

and religious party, streaming forward from the long procession, applauded and cheered. The people laughed as more food was brought out from shops that had been closed all day and had now opened because the royal procession had stopped, or from stallholders hurrying to lock-ups to find the perfect mouthful to tempt the dieting Empress, also offering the dishes to the crowds of people. In the twilight, the wide Mese warmed by braziers and just-lit torches, Justinian thought Theodora looked as well as he'd seen her in months. From the back of the crowd someone began to sing; it was one of Comito's old songs, and the cry went up for the songbird herself.

Comito was having none of it at first, shaking her head, until Sophia turned to her mother and whispered, 'You might not sing for her again, not like this. Not in pleasure.'

When Comito looked up she knew her daughter was right. Theodora, who couldn't eat beyond a mouthful, who could barely drink without choking, actually looked happy. Her eyes were bright, her skin, tinted with the flames, seemed warm and alive, and she laughed in encouragement, clapping along with the chants of the crowd, clapping her bird-fine hands to 'Com-i-to! Com-i-to!'

The more senior members of the Palace staff, those who'd grown up behind its walls, born into civil servant families and progressing within them, looked on in surprise as Narses took charge. He ordered two market stalls to be brought over, laid them end to end, then he and Armeneus knelt, each on one knee, making steps of their thighs for Comito who, as if she had never stopped performing, never left the City's lead company, ascended their steps and took her place on the makeshift stage. She bowed low, impossibly impressive from that height and on those rickety stalls, first to the Emperor and then to the Empress and, with a smile for Sophia, began to sing. It was an old song, one she and Theodora and Anastasia had learned from their father, the man who had famously trained the last of the great bears, a song he and the other animal trainers used to sing, before the Emperor Anastasius outlawed animal fights. It was a song that probably dated back before Constantine, before the very reason for today's feast. And it was a song anyone who had been raised in the City knew, everyone who had ever been cared for by a grandmother, looked after by a neighbour's old aunt. To children, unaware of the meaning behind the words it was a lullaby; later in life young girls recognised in shock that it was also a love song, a song of desire, and old men had always enjoyed it as a drinking anthem. It was a song of the City and it had once been sung by both factions, in competition and in harmony. Tonight it was led by Comito, she of the golden voice, and was sung by everyone present and by those who had heard the rumours and were struggling to hurry up the Mese, to the place where they had heard Theodora-from-the-Brothel was about to perform once more.

Theodora did not perform. Comito sang just the one song and was helped down again. The priests took up their relics and the monks resumed chanting, Theodora was half sleeping long before they reached the end of the Mese, but managed to open her eyes just long enough as they processed past the Hippodrome, to look up and see, or imagine she saw, above the high bank of top seats, the owl engraved on the obelisk, the owl her father had told her to look out for, the owl that would guide her back to him if she was ever lost.

In the Augusta's rooms, Mariam undressed Theodora and laid her in her bed. She was dousing the lights when Theodora stirred.

The Empress hauled herself up in bed, every action an agony, she shook her head. 'Get me some wine, with warm water.'

'Mistress?' Mariam asked as she waved the servant off to fetch hot water.

'My stomach. Damn street food, and on a festival day at that. I should know better, never ate it in the old days, always kept to bar meals only.'

'But you said . . . ?'

'I said what the people wanted to hear and were happy to believe. But there were no fishing boats out today, that was yesterday's fish and no amount of herbs or spices or burning on an open fire can make it any fresher. Why do you think I barely ate a bite of each?'

'I thought . . . because you were ill. Are ill. That's why . . . ?'

'Yes, that too,' Theodora said, settling back against her pillows and accepting the cup of warm, watered wine from the servant, stirring in the honey she also offered. 'But I knew better than to eat all they were offering, you need a strong stomach for that stuff, and I've been far too long in the Palace to risk it.'

Mariam smiled and then she laughed. 'But the priests, and the monks, all the civil servants, the Palace staff, you encouraged them to eat!'

'I think, if you paid attention,' Theodora paused for a moment to cough, a cough that racked her body and made tears stream down her face, 'you'll remember I only encouraged the more annoying of the Palace staff to eat, the most pedantic of our civil servants. Belisarius must have the stomach of a dog anyway, after his years of service, all the generals will. But some of those very annoying priests? Especially the fat one who glared at me last week when I needed to sit in the gallery? And that man who assists in the Treasury, the one with the heavy brow who thinks he's too good for the rest of us?' Mariam named the man and Theodora laughed, mucus roiling through her breath as she did so. 'That's the one. I don't imagine his night will be any more comfortable than mine.'

'Poor man.'

'Good.'

Mariam helped Theodora back beneath her covers, soft silk and light wool to ease the cloth against her thin skin, her sharp bone.

'Will you ask the Emperor to come to me tonight?'

'He comes every night, Mistress.'

Mariam answered honestly. Justinian had not slept in his own bed for weeks, nor had he slept in Theodora's bed, too scared to hurt her by turning or moving near her.

'I know,' the Empress said, 'I know he sits here every night. But tell him I want him to sleep beside me. He can't hurt me now, and I need his warmth.'

'I will.'

Mariam sat beside her mistress, her foster-mother, and held the Empress's thin, fine hand, until the woman who had saved her from a life of sex slavery, who had only ever been kind to her, who had given her a future and a husband, slipped into the half-sleep in which she now spent much of her time. A semi-stupor brought on by the combination of the herbs Alexander provided and Theodora's own ability to will herself into a state where the pain was less bitter. Justinian had finally been able to persuade her that Alexander would be able to treat her better precisely because he knew her better, and the physician was the only person outside her immediate circle she had allowed to see how ill she really was. Menander had trained all his girls in total control of their bodies; the illness that was eating away at her had eroded much of that control, but with effort Theodora could still command her mind, if not her flesh or the bones that were now splintering from within. She knew this power would leave her soon, that her body, the body she had subdued and worked and controlled for so long, would take over, that the growths inside her would have their way and her mind and heart would have no say. For now, she still had some power, and chose to use it to sleep as much as possible. Theodora knew the time was coming when she would need every measure of energy she had, simply to open her eyes, to swallow the herbal draughts, to pray.

Mariam sang a little of Comito's lullaby and in Theodora's half-dream state the younger woman's singing sounded like the owl beyond her window. Theodora wanted it to sound like the owl beyond her window.

Forty

The Empress retired to her rooms, while outside spring became summer and the bright gold of the early morning sun turned the Sea of Marmara beyond her window an even richer green, the green of the emerald Virgin she now held constantly in her hand.

Business matters were brought to and from her room and for a few weeks the Empress tried to contribute to the City and the state as she always had. It soon became obvious she was too weak to continue.

Armeneus ushered out the last petitioner of the day, shaking his head at the grey of Theodora's face, lined still more deeply with exhaustion and pain.

'You have to stop this, Mistress.'

'These people come to me for help.'

'Yes, and they leave regretting it, sorry they bothered you when you're too ill to think straight.'

'That girl just now, begging me to release her from the marriage her family want for her, who else can she go to?'

'You sent her to Metanoia, she could go there herself,' he said.

'But they would have taken longer to give her a place without my consent, she needs help today. Those two old whores, they needed help today.'

'And you gave them each a gold ring. Don't you think they're going to spend it on wine tonight?'

'I don't care how they spend it, they asked for help now, I gave them help now.'

'Fine, but that's enough. You have Peter Barsymes and Macedonia waiting to see you, I'm telling them both to come back tomorrow.'

Theodora's face broke into a smile broad enough to cut through Armeneus' concern, even if she was now so thin it was the smile of a skull rather than his Mistress.

'Show them in.'

'But you're exhausted . . .'

'Damn you, eunuch, I'll send you back to Africa yet. Call them in.'

Peter Barsymes and Macedonia entered the room, and before they had even had a chance to bow, Theodora spoke: 'Well?'

Barsymes the trader, the dealer, the spy, the master of secrets, reached into the bag he was carrying and pulled out a fine skein of silk thread. Macedonia took it to her Mistress.

'You insisted on staying awake for this? For them to bring you some thread?' Armeneus was horrified.

Theodora was holding the silk, turning it over in her hands, trying not to cough, trying to draw breath through laughter that was half tears. 'Not some thread, Armeneus. Silk.'

'Yes, silk,' Armeneus said.

'Our silk.'

'Which you could buy any day you wanted.'

'Peter didn't buy this silk. They grew it, made it, here, in the City. This is our silk.'

And then Armeneus realised what his Mistress was holding.

*

Over a year earlier, Barsymes' men, bedraggled, exhausted, and half the number that had set out, returned to the City with a few moths in a bamboo rod. Looking at the men's drawn faces, no one asked what they had been through to steal the moths, nor would they have told. Barsymes paid their fee, far more to the trader-spies than the monks, and they parted, the spies to a new engagement under Macedonia's leadership, the monks to the peace of their monastery across the water, taking the moths with them. The precious moths were cared for, as were their eggs, becoming moths in turn themselves, and in time, they bred. In spring, while Theodora and the rest of the City celebrated Constantinople's feast day, the moths laid new eggs. The priests had paid highly for the instructions that brought the eggs from worms, to feeding, to cocoons that were taken and finally, finely, unravelled and re-spun, into silk. The silk Theodora was now holding. The first silk made in the City.

Two hours later the celebrations were still going on in Theodora's rooms and Armeneus was threatening to lift the Empress bodily out of her chair and take her to sleep in his own room if she didn't send them all away. The fact that the Emperor himself was part of the general carousing didn't help his case. Eventually the room was cleared, Mariam helped her Mistress to bed, and Theodora and Justinian both slept well that night, delighted with themselves, delighted with their achievement.

The next morning Theodora had her staff set up a loom in the corner of her room, and Esther came in to supervise Sophia's weaving of the precious thread. There was only a little thread so far, but it worked, and under Esther's careful eye, Sophia began to turn it into a fine silk.

'You'll make me a beautiful cloth,' Theodora said to

Sophia, 'then Esther's brother will colour it with the purple dye he keeps for the Palace, all the way from Tyre. I'll wear your work.'

Theodora was happy then, listening to the regular soft thud of Sophia's shuttle, to the rhythmic clicking of the small spindle Esther always carried, to the quiet murmurs between her women, Comito lying beside her on her bed and singing softly. Ana, who had never really known how to talk to Theodora, at least took solace in the fact that, now there were no words to be spoken, she was finally comfortable in the presence of her mother, of the Empress.

In that long room, the balcony doors thrown open to let in light and warmth, the women organised Sophia's marriage to Justinian's nephew Justin, decided which robes would be worn, sorted through Theodora's jewels so the young Sophia would be stunningly adorned, sewed her marriage gown and beaded her headdress with fine pearls taken from the necklace Theodora had given Sophia-the-half-size to wear at her own marriage to Justinian. Theodora had hoped to finalise arrangements for Anastasius and Joannina's marriage too, but Antonina continued to stall, and the Empress now knew her grandson would never marry the general's daughter.

'She's not doing anything I wouldn't do for my own family,' Theodora said, late one night when Justinian joined her.

'Antonina thinks the grandson of the Empress isn't good enough for her daughter?'

'She doesn't think ...' Theodora stopped to cough, each spasm racking her body further, so ferociously Justinian thought she might break her ribs with the effort. Eventually the coughing subsided and Theodora continued, 'She doesn't think the Empress's grandson from her bastard daughter is good enough for Joannina. I'm sure she's not the only one.

She'll find some wealthy senator's boy for the girl, she probably already has. Ana and Comito will have to take care of Anastasius.'

Justinian didn't contradict his wife, tell her she would be around to do the match-making herself; neither of them pretended she wasn't dying, they wanted only truth now.

He shook his head. 'It's a shame – Narses tells me those two are truly in love.'

'Narses does?' Theodora was smiling.

'What is it?'

'I just can't picture that tough old eunuch deigning to notice something as frivolous as young love.'

'He noticed you, brought you to me.'

'Yes, he did.'

The Emperor and the Empress held hands then, through the night as always, Theodora slipping in and out of consciousness and Justinian beside her for when she woke, hoping she would wake.

When she did wake, late in the morning, it was to beg Armeneus to make Alexander give her stronger medicine for her pain. She greedily sucked down the thick liquid he brought for her and began immediately, gratefully, to feel the drowsiness spilling through her body. She whispered to Armeneus that she wanted to speak to a priest, a specific priest. She wanted Thomas, the young man who had tested her penitence before she was deemed ready to marry Justinian.

'Mistress, he was preaching in Jerusalem, and then we heard Antioch, perhaps. That was some time ago. I don't know if we'll be able to find him . . .'

'Of course you will.' She was speaking slowly, quietly, all her effort on taking the painkilling medicine deep into her body. 'The Bishops will know, they keep records of every-thing, every appointment. They'll know.'

Armeneus nodded. 'I'll see to it.'

But she was already asleep and so he didn't need to explain he hadn't meant it would be hard to find Thomas, rather that it would be hard to bring him to the City in time, that it was obvious there was so little time.

When Theodora next woke, she sent for Esther and Leah to finish the silk cloth Sophia had been making. Told them to make sure it was dyed the deepest purple possible.

Another time she woke to sit up, bright and almost her old self, but for the cadaverous body she had become. She called for Narses, and for the first time in the twenty-seven years they had worked together, they talked openly of the time before they met. They talked about Menander, about the old days when the man who was her taskmaster had been his lover. She shared stories with Narses about her youth, her time in the Pentapolis, in the desert, stories she could never have told him before, when he might have used that infor-mation to force her agreement to this policy or that, and when Narses smiled and then roared a wicked, dirty laugh, she saw him fifty years younger, saw exactly what Menander must have seen in him.

She slept the rest of that day, and for several days after.

On the afternoon of the longest day, when the City outside was drowsy with midsummer heat, Theodora woke from what seemed to her an impossibly long sleep. She looked around at the people in her room: Justinian on one side, Comito on the other, at the foot of her bed, all kneeling, all praying, were Ana and Anastasius, Antonina and Joanina, Mariam and Macedonia. Sophia was standing behind them, her eyes closed in the prayer-trance Theodora had taught her. Most of the women's eyes were red from crying, and many of the men's too. Behind them were ranged any number of chief civil servants and the highest-ranking Palace staff, many kneeling, all of them praying. Narses and Armeneus stood against the far wall at either end of a long line of quietly intoning priests. She stared at them for a moment, the room went silent, each one waiting, and then Theodora opened her mouth to speak, her dry lips cracking as she did so, her voice hoarse from lack of use, but with a smile at their shocked faces.

'Not today ... I don't think.'

Justinian covered his face with his hands and let out a slow groan.

Theodora took his hand and whispered, 'I'm sorry, this is impossible for you. It won't be long, I promise, then you can move on, get on.'

Her husband stared at her, horrified and accepting, furious that she was preparing to leave him and telling him he could live on without her. Even more angry that he knew he had no choice.

'The priest is here,' said Justinian.

'There are many priests here,' Theodora said, 'more than I've seen in my room since the last time Sophia-the-half-size and I ...' she stopped herself and nodded across at Narses, 'there ... didn't say it. See how far I've come?'

Narses nodded back. 'The priest Thomas, Mistress,' he said, indicating the man beside him.

Theodora peered, her eyes cloudy from the infusions Alexander had given her. It was indeed Thomas – an older, stouter, greying version of the man who had insisted on hearing the depth of her truths more than half her life ago.

'You should all leave us,' Theodora said, 'I need to speak to this priest.'

Slowly the rooms emptied, Justinian leaving last, and eventually Theodora was left alone with Thomas.

He bowed and waited for her to speak, and after a while she did so, slowly. She talked of her fears, of her anger, the losses she had endured, and the pain she was suffering now. She told him about Palace plots and her involvement in them, she told him about intrigues she'd only ever guessed at, things Justinian and Narses planned between them that she regretted – and plenty she did not. She told him about Anthemius and her love for the man who was now her adopted daughter's husband. How she had never ceased to find him attractive and that she thought the barb of seeing him so happy with Mariam was more than enough of a punishment. She said she regretted she had not been able to do more to help Justinian bring the Church together, but that she was also pleased about her work with Jacob Baradeus, even though that work might have partly caused the failure of union.

She frowned. 'I am a living contradiction, Thomas. A dying one.'

'Few of us are as purely intentioned as we'd like.'

'And my work as one who allowed beatings and imprisonment, who knew of poisonings and political murders and did not stop them, even benefited from them?'

The priest opened and closed his mouth. There was no stock answer to her admission, and none he dared give his Empress.

'Exactly so,' she said. 'Still, I am proud of being my husband's consort, I can say that.' She was holding the emerald Virgin, turning it in her hand. 'This stone, it was stolen from a bishop in the Pentapolis.'

'You stole it?'

'Yes, Severus told me I could keep it.'

'Oh.'

'I think it's time to give it back to the Church.'

'Shall I have it returned to the Pentapolis for you?'

'No. That bishop is dead now, I hope, old bastard. Have them send it to Ravenna, there's an artist, working on the new church, he'll use it well.'

Theodora was sleeping again before Thomas blessed her, sleeping when Justinian came to lie beside her. She wrenched herself back from the half-comfort of sleep for a moment, to remind him of his promise to care for Sophia, to care for the future Theodora had planned for her, and then dropped gratefully back into the daze of Alexander's medicine, away from the pain that bloated and shrank her body in waves, threatening to split her skin as it shattered her bones.

For the next week she was tossed between sleep and pain, pain and sleep. She woke, close to dawn, her body burning.

'This is breaking me, please, make him help me, make Alexander help me,' she said to Justinian, crying.

Justinian knew what she was asking and shook his head. 'I can't, I'm not good enough to give you up. I want you to stay.'

'In this pain?' She was incredulous.

'Yes,' he was crying now too, 'I should be kinder, but I'm not. I can't let them help you leave me.'

'It's too hard,' Theodora said.

Justinian agreed, 'Yes it is.'

He kissed her, gently, and she kissed him back, fiercer, pulling him against her.

She screamed then, silently, her mouth wrenched open, a breath of pain, and her breath smelt sweetly foul.

'Please?'

And then, slowly, Justinian nodded. He lifted himself from the bed, kissed her lips, her eyelids, her brow. 'I won't be long,

Alexander is just outside, I'll call him, he'll make it better, make you better.'

'Thank you, sir.'

'I love you.'

Theodora sighed her love, her thanks; she had no breath to speak.

Justinian had taken less than a dozen steps towards the door when he knew. The room felt different, no longer on the blade edge of his beloved wife's pain. She was no longer hurting. He turned back. Her hands, for weeks clenched in agony, were already becoming loose, softening. Her brow was not creased, her eyes were open and clear, and the tears on her cheeks had not yet dried, but she was gone.

He bowed then, deep and low, at the foot of her bed, and kissed her foot, 'Theou doron.'

Narses sat with Justinian and Armeneus guarding the Empress's door as her women washed her body, Comito singing prayers softly under her breath, preparing to bury a second sister. The cleansing rituals done, Theodora was draped first in a thin, fine cloth, as was customary. The priest made the blessing over her body, and then she was wrapped in the purple silk Sophia had made for her, the City's silk for the City's Empress. As Theodora had predicted, it made the perfect burial shroud.

Her funeral was attended by dignitaries from the Persian royal family and by Goth, Vandal, Berber, Cathar, Hun, Slav and Herule leaders. A full Imperial procession of priests and bishops followed her body, Justinian at the head, her women behind, followed by the forty deaconesses of the Hagia Sophia and every penitent from Metanoia. Citizens and slaves alike lined the streets as the Empress was taken up to the Church of the Holy Apostles, where she was buried in the Imperial Mausoleum, the rest of the church still to be completed around her. She was laid to rest as the priests called 'Theodora', calling her to the Christ.

For a year, Justinian visited her sarcophagus every second day, then every week. The Church of the Holy Apostles was consecrated on the second anniversary of her death. It had grown its finished self around the figure of the Emperor, mourning his consort.

Forty-One

In Ravenna, a master mosaic artist placed a small piece in a section of a much larger work. He was high in the centre-piece of a new church, his back ached and he was tired, had been tired all day. Stephen's much younger wife was pregnant with their third child; he wondered if the pain he felt was connected to her. They already had two daughters, he would be happy to have a son, someone to take on his work. He would have been happy to finish the job and go home, but there was a great deal more to do, and this was his most important commission to date, one he had requested for him-self, so long ago. He would stay working until the light in this almost-complete church was fully gone.

Quietly, carefully, he cut another piece of the precious stone. It was not usual to add true gemstones to a mosaic, but his subject was no usual woman. The work was painstaking, he was careful to get the balance right. The image he was com-pleting came both from memory and from the sketches sent to him last year, charcoal drawings of a small, thin, tired woman in pain, nothing like his memory of her.

He placed one tiny piece of deep red smalti, half the size of his youngest daughter's fingernail, into the cement, and then another, checking colour and shape, moving it a hair's breadth to the right, then back again, thinking about his wife who hated that he spent his days staring into the face of the dead Empress. At fifty, Stephen was an old man compared to those friends of his youth who had died in battle and siege, from plague or the simple accidents that come to young men. He'd seen much in his life, in his own travels, but none of it compared to the sights he had seen in the City. The hills, the constant presence of shifting water; the light, above all. He remembered how the old men of his childhood spoke of Rome, recalling the glory days of their grandfathers' youth; now all faces looked East.

He returned to the precious stone. It had been brought to him a week ago, he was told it must be part of the mosaic. He made a prayer over the stone, its once-sharp edges smoothed by the years it had been held in the Augusta's hands, and then he cut into the emerald Virgin. He cut it in secret, and he placed it in secret too. It would not do to tempt the young artisans in his team, better they thought he was simply handling the finer pieces because he wanted to get her face just right. Hiding the real emerald and true pearls in amongst the marble and handmade molten pieces, as was requested when the gems arrived. Hidden in with the real blood too, where his apprentices' fingers had slipped, splitting skin and opening flesh on the thousands of razor-sharp shards of marble and glass that made up the whole. Stephen himself had fine long fingers, cross-hatched with the scars of his own apprenticeship. He carefully placed another piece of the deep green stone, and thought how well it looked, how much it suited her, warm against the cool marble of her skin. He would work for a little longer, his wife would wait, the image was growing under his hands, Theodora taking shape.